DARK SHADOWS

SIBEL HODGE

Dark Shadows

Sibel Hodge

"In a time of universal deceit, telling the truth is a revolutionary act."

~ George Orwell

BEFORE

"The greater the power, the more dangerous the abuse."
~ Edmund Burke

CHAPTER 1

VICKY

Vicky stepped into the entrance hall of lecture theatre block two, the pressure building in her head. Except it wasn't really pressure. It was a tinny sound, like white noise—buzzing and throbbing. The voices in her head were back, telling her to do it. *Walk up the stairs.*

A student jostled her, his backpack connecting with her shoulder, sending her staggering backwards for a second. He muttered a hurried apology, but Vicky didn't notice. Later, he'd wish he'd paid more attention. Later, he'd spend months wondering if he could've done something to prevent it.

Do it, Vicky. There's nothing to be afraid of anymore.

Vicky nodded to herself as she walked up the stairs between a swarm of more students bustling around her. The noise inside her own head drowned out the noise of their chatter.

She was climbing the mountain, something she'd always thought would be the scariest thing in the world. But she could do it. Everything seemed so easy now. One step up.

Another step. She felt as if she were floating above the ground—there, but not there—her footsteps light, determined. She had one goal. Get to the top. And then... and then... relief. That was what they'd told her.

'Hey, watch it!' a girl cried out as Vicky nudged her shoulder. But Vicky didn't hear her. Didn't see her. She was oblivious.

Oblivion. It'll be yours soon.

All Vicky could see was the mountain above her, looming in its brilliance. Its glory. And the funny thing was, even though she was on top of Everest, she wasn't even cold. The snow-capped peak glittered in the sunshine. Excitement swelled in her chest. It was exhilarating. Euphoria blossomed inside her. She'd finally kicked her fear of heights.

Nearly there, Vicky. You're doing the right thing.

She reached the top of the stairs. The summit!

She'd thought the air would be thin this high up, but it wasn't. She'd thought she'd need oxygen to breathe, but she didn't. She was invincible. An angel. She smiled to herself. An angel on top of a spectacular white cap of mountain.

Someone shouted in the distance. Maybe a Sherpa or her guide. Except she didn't remember a guide. Or a Sherpa. She didn't remember how she'd reached the top.

She looked over the metal stair rail. All she could see was white snow below her. White everywhere. So brilliant, it blinded her. She leaned against the cold metal. Cold mountain. Cold snow.

Jump, Vicky. Prove you can do it.

Carefully, she held on to the top of the rail and lifted one leg over. Then the other. She stood on the edge of a six-inch-wide ledge of concrete. But it wasn't concrete. It was a ridge. A ridge of ice at the pinnacle of Everest.

She lifted her arms high above her head. She knew she could fly, because she was an angel. She'd reach the bottom, and she'd be free.

She took an exhilarating breath. And dived into the abyss.

THREE MONTHS LATER...

DAY ONE
"Lightning makes no sound until it strikes." ~
Martin Luther King Jr

CHAPTER 2

DETECTIVE BECKY HARRIS

The alarm on my phone burst to life, invading a very nice dream I was having that involved me, Tom Hardy, and strawberry-scented massage oil. The sound was supposed to be one of those soothing-waterfall-type chimes that woke you up gradually, but it sounded more like a fog horn as it jerked me back to the land of the living.

Eyes still closed, I groaned and slid my hand from beneath the covers, reaching by touch for my phone to turn the thing off. That's when Tom Hardy recessed to the deepest parts of my mind and I woke up properly, realising it wasn't the alarm making a noise. I was just starting two weeks' annual leave, and I hadn't even set it. The doorbell was going at... I squinted at the phone's screen... at 07.11 a.m.

I thought about ignoring it, but I rarely had visitors, and definitely not so early in the morning. Whoever was ringing the bell—for the third time now—definitely wanted me to open up.

The room was stuffy and hot as I threw back the covers with a huff. No matter what time of year it was, I couldn't sleep unless I was rolled up into my bed clothes like an enchilada. My husband, Ian, had always complained about my duvet-hogging habits, because he'd always ended up with a thin slice of cover. Still, I didn't have to worry about that anymore. Since we'd split up, I could roll away to my heart's content.

Dressed in my faithful summer sleeping attire, a faded vest top and a pair of Ian's old boxers that he'd forgotten to take with him, I padded downstairs to see who my early-morning wake-up call was.

A tall shadow loomed behind the privacy glass at the front door. That shadow rang the bell, yet again.

I yanked open the door, expecting to find the postman with a package that needed signing for, but it was Chief Constable Derek Sutherby. I'd only actually met him a few times, including once when he presented me with a commendation for my work on a previous case. I was a detective sergeant in CID, still way too low on the food chain for him to be on my doorstep, dressed in his beautifully pressed uniform, at this time in the morning.

'Sir?' I frowned, rubbing one eyelid. For a horrified moment, I thought I must actually still be asleep and that somehow my Tom Hardy fantasy dream had morphed into a *really* bizarre dream—or nightmare—about Sutherby.

He gave a practiced smile that he used in front of the media, but I could tell something was not right about it.

My first thought: *Uh-oh. What have I done wrong now?*

'Good morning, Detective Harris. I'm sure I was the last person you were expecting to turn up out of the blue like this, but would you mind if I come inside?'

'Um... of course, sir.' I stepped back to let him in and did a quick mental rundown of all the cases I'd worked on lately, wondering which one was going to get me a bollocking so huge that it was delivered by the big, big boss and couldn't wait until I was back at work. 'Do you want a tea or coffee?'

'Are you having one?' He entered the hallway, wafting aftershave all over the place.

'Yes.' I shut the door. 'Follow me.' I went into the kitchen-diner at the back of the house and found my newly acquired cat, Pickle, sitting in the middle of the floor like a sentry, glaring at me as if I never fed her. After Ian had left, I'd thought a cat would keep me company. I'd visited the local animal shelter and found Pickle doing an impression of Puss in Boots from *Shrek*—all hard-done-by, innocent eyes. When I'd got her home, the cute doe-eyes lasted about a week before she decided *she* ruled the house.

'Morning, Ickle Pickle Wickle,' I said to Pickle, who was giving me her best 'you're a bad mother' stare before meowing nonstop until I opened the cupboard door to the cat food. 'Have a seat.'

Sutherby stood in the doorway, briefcase in hand, watching the cat as if he didn't want to enter for fear he'd get white hairs on his immaculate black clothes. 'Are you talking to me or the cat?'

I grinned, filled Pickle's empty bowl, then switched on the kettle. Sutherby sat while I rooted around for mugs, milk, and sugar.

'Tea or coffee?'

'Whatever you're having is fine.'

I opened the box of tea bags and discovered I only had one left, which was slightly better than the coffee selection, as that jar had only a crusty brown lump of dregs at the bottom. I stabbed it with a spoon, but it was too hard to break up, so I resorted to using the end of a knife. At least the milk wasn't off yet, but I definitely needed to go food shopping later. I'd just finished working on a lengthy case and had been neglecting my housekeeping for weeks.

He glanced around my kitchen as I leaned against the worktop, and we made small talk while I waited for the kettle to boil excruciatingly slowly. I wanted to ask him what he was doing at my house, but I also didn't want to know. Maybe it was better to delay the whole bollocking thing until I'd at least had my first cuppa of the day. And, depending on how bad it was, I could always slip a brandy in there when he'd gone.

Finally, drinks made, I deposited a mug of tea in front of him and sat down with my coffee, which had little brown blobs floating on top, stubbornly refusing to dissolve.

He took a sip. I took a sip.

Well, this is awkward.

'I'll get straight to the point, Becky. I know you're on annual leave, but this is something that can't wait, I'm afraid.'

Another inner groan. It was serious then. 'Have I done something wrong, sir?'

'On the contrary, I'm here because I've been following your career quite closely.'

'Riiight...' I dragged the word out, not knowing whether to be scared or flattered. I often broke the rules and went against my superior's orders, but on the plus side, I'd handled some unusual and high-profile investigations and got great results.

'Since you were commended on the Palmer case, I've been taking an interest in you. Even more so after the Brampton Hospital nightmare that you and DI Carter dealt with so professionally. And I need someone bold, with tenacity and discretion, who'll be able to blend in.'

'I'm sorry, sir, but I don't understand. Blend in with what?'

His lips flattened into a thin line. 'This is a little unorthodox, but I'm concerned about a potential situation at St Albans University. Recently, they've had three tragic incidents involving their students.' He paused for a beat. 'At the moment, there seems to be nothing to connect them, but I'm worried there could be something more sinister going on.'

My interest was already piqued. 'What kind of incidents?'

'Three months ago, a student called Vicky Aylott publicly committed suicide by jumping from the stairway of a building at the university in front of many other witnesses. Not long after that, a student called Ajay Banerjee set himself on fire in his bedroom and died in the blaze. He was sharing a house with four other students, all of whom were thankfully out at the time.' He took a sip of his tea and carried on. 'Then ten days ago, student Natalie Wheeler was driving in her car and ran over an elderly man walking across a zebra crossing. He died at the scene. It happened in broad daylight in front of witnesses, and afterwards, she drove back to her accommodation block at the university as if nothing had happened. She was arrested a little while later and said she had no memory of the event.' He put down his mug. 'These students had no history of mental health problems, none of them appeared to be depressed or suffering from stress, and none of them had a history of substance abuse. What each of them did was apparently completely out of character.' He sat back and watched me.

'Okay.' I took a minute to let that sink in. 'I vaguely remember hearing something about one suicide at the university, but I haven't heard about anything else. What's your specific interest in this, sir?' It wasn't like he got involved in day-to-day crimes. The brass were more interested in manipulating crime figures to wrap them up in a neat shiny bow to make him look good, not investigating potential crimes where there didn't seem to be any. I was betting two suicides and a hit-and-run wouldn't even make it onto his radar, so there had to be some kind of ulterior motive for his visit.

'It was my ex-wife, Anthea, who brought these incidents to my attention. She's an administrator at the university, and she's concerned that there could be some kind of hazing group at work or...' He shifted uncomfortably in his seat. 'Someone coercing these students into doing horrific things. And that it's going too far and people are ending up dead.'

'Presumably, these incidents have already been investigated?'

'Yes. Vicky's and Ajay's suicides fell under the coroner's officer's investigation. He spoke to their friends and family and can't find a specific reason pointing to why they'd take their own lives.'

'But that's not uncommon, is it? Sometimes you never know exactly what triggers it.' As a patrol officer, I'd attended plenty of suicides where the deceased's friends or family were never aware the person had been depressed or suicidal.

'Of course. But two suicides in a few weeks of each other seems fairly high. An inquest was opened and adjourned into both deaths, but the coroner's officer is recommending to the coroner that both are recorded as suicides. And there doesn't seem to be anything suspicious about them that the police can actively investigate. The post-mortems showed no drugs or medications in their system when they died. And they were both very healthy individuals.'

'Pretty horrible ways to kill yourself, though. Especially setting yourself on fire. You'd have to be in a very disturbed place to choose that method.'

'Yes. Both Ajay's and Vicky's friends were all spoken to by the coroner's officer, and none of them thought either student was having any significant problems. They did, however, mention that both of them had been having trouble sleeping. Both had nightmares, and Vicky had started sleepwalking.'

'Which could be down to stress or depression that they'd been hiding from their friends,' I said. 'Often the people closest to them are the last to know.'

'It's possible. But there's something else, too. Taken separately, they don't seem connected, but together... they all have one thing in common. According to their friends, both students seemed to become distant recently before their deaths. Their work started suffering. Both were acting strangely, and there were incidents of them disappearing for periods of time. When questioned about it by their friends, both Vicky and Ajay said they couldn't remember where they'd been or what they'd been doing. It's almost as if they were being secretive about what they'd been up to.'

'And Natalie? What's happening with her?'

'She's in a secure mental health facility. She had a breakdown after the accident. When she was first arrested, she said she couldn't remember anything about hitting the victim and driving away. Then she went to pieces and was declared unfit for interview. She's still being assessed by a forensic psychologist, but it looks like she's not going to be fit to stand trial. They suspect she's suffering from schizophrenia.' He took a sip of tea, wincing as he swallowed. 'Now she believes that she has a moth in her brain that told her to drive into the man.'

'How awful—for everyone involved. If she had no history of mental health problems, do they think the schizophrenia could've started suddenly then?'

'They believe so, yes. But I'm not convinced. Prior to this, she was a vibrant, happy girl. And recently, she also began disappearing or acting strangely for periods of time and had no recollection afterwards of where she'd been or what she'd done. The fact that all three students were exhibiting the same kind of odd behaviour before these incidents occurred seems suspicious to me and could indicate a cult's influence.'

I raised my eyebrows. 'A cult?'

'It's not as strange as it sounds. There have been many incidents in recent years of cults infiltrating universities in the UK. People tend to think of cults being an American problem, but experts think the UK actually has the same problem per capita as the States. I'm sure you've probably heard of some famous ones on the extreme spectrum—the Waco siege, the Manson murders, the Jonestown massacre, which resulted in mass murder-suicide of members of the Peoples Temple Cult at the behest of their leader. But many of them are tiny and based in small homes or meeting places. And it's the smaller ones that can actually be the most insidious and sinister, because they're very difficult to rumble. Often, the leaders or people recruiting members are very different from the crazy, bearded messiahs stereotypically associated with these groups. They're seemingly ordinary people—teachers, dentists, sports coaches, friends, students.'

'Seriously? I wasn't aware it was such a problem here. It's not something I've had much experience with, but I'm guessing most cults have political, religious, or financial agendas? So how does that fit with what's happened?'

'Often they do have those overtones, but there are multiple possible agendas and motivations at play. Some leaders want to acquire great wealth. Others want to take over the world. Some believe they're God. Some just like the control and power—the ability to bend people to their will. And others are just sick, twisted individuals who want to live out their evil fantasies.

'In 2016, in the UK, there was a group called the North Shields Death Cult, led by a violent psychopath who, on the surface, seemed to be a harmless, disabled man in a wheel-chair. But he managed to brainwash a group of women into luring a vulnerable man with mental health problems to his flat before stealing his bank card then torturing and murdering him.'

I took a sip of coffee that tasted stale.

'That's just one example of a cult coercing people to kill others, which could fit with what Natalie did. There are also many examples of suicide cults over the years—the Peoples Temple, the Solar Temple, Heaven's Gate, Adam House. The idea that a cult could be operating at the university is not as ludicrous as it sounds. Even way back in the 90s, cult activists were discovered to have infiltrated most of the ten halls at University College London. So it's entirely possible, and it would be a prime recruiting ground.'

I frowned. 'Were Ajay, Vicky, or Natalie particularly political or religious?'

'No. According to their friends and family, none of them were religious or outspoken in any political or social causes, although Ajay had dabbled in Buddhism before, but he wasn't practicing. But cults are dressed up as multiple organisations—self-help groups, social or community groups, and yes, religious groups. And the fact that people have actually joined one doesn't often occur to them, or their family and friends, until it's too late and they're in too deep.' He leaned his elbows on the table. 'But if there *is* some kind of cult operating in my county, then I want to know about it. And if they're influencing or coercing the students to commit suicide or kill or injure people, then we need to stop this before anyone else dies.'

When he put it like that, it didn't seem so far off the wall, but I didn't have a clue why he was coming to me when a) I was supposed to be on annual leave, and b) there had to be plenty of other officers of a higher rank who should be dealing with a potentially high-risk investigation into possible cults. And just as I was wondering all that, he hit me with the reason for his breakfast-time visit.

'I want *you* to go undercover and see if you can find any evidence that something sinister might be going on there. If we launch an official police investigation, it's likely any cult members, if they exist, could go to ground. This needs to be handled discreetly. Talk to the three students' friends and mingle with other students, because they're more likely to open up to someone they see as an equal rather than the police.'

I was swallowing a mouthful of coffee and almost choked. I put my hand over my mouth, coughed, and waited until I could breathe again. 'Me? I'm not a trained under-cover officer.'

'No, but you've got guts, and you know how to use your initiative. And you're more than a little unorthodox. You're also young enough to blend in as a slightly mature student.'

I didn't know whether or not to be offended by the

'slightly mature' reference. Since when did being thirty make a person *slightly* anything?

'I think you'd be perfect. And all the undercover officers we have are either unsuitable or tied up with longstanding investigations. You look at least four years younger than your age, and you'll easily be able to pass yourself off as a student who's taken a break to do some travelling before doing her degree. I know you're on annual leave, which is the perfect cover. Right now, no one's expecting you to be at work. I asked around, and your colleagues said you weren't going away anywhere.'

My jaw was still hanging open with surprise as I looked at him.

'I want you to report directly to me and only me. This is a strictly hush-hush investigation. If you find there's nothing untoward going on in the two weeks you're supposed to be on holiday, then it will put my mind at rest.'

I chewed my lip, thinking. It was a great opportunity. Being singled out for an undercover operation would be a huge challenge, and it would look great on my CV. Plus, it wasn't like I had anything planned for my time off. I'd been forced to take it due to all the hours I'd stacked up in over-time and untaken leave. To be honest, I'd been dreading filling the days until I could return to work.

'You'd be doing me a big favour, and I'd be eternally grateful.' He laced his fingers together on the table. 'And it goes without saying that this will look fantastic on your record for the next round of promotion recommendations.' His words dangled in the air between us.

But I didn't need any more time to think about it. I could already feel the excitement building at the thought of a new opportunity. I grinned. 'I'll do it, sir.'

He smiled back. 'Good.' He picked his briefcase up from the floor beside his chair and opened it. He pulled out several files, a laptop, and a mobile phone. 'Use this phone only to contact me. I've programmed a number into it already. I've also written down an email address and password. Use that for our emails. Everything you need to know about the previous cases are in these files and on the laptop. Take a read through this stuff today. I'll arrange everything with Anthea so that you're in the university's system. Tomorrow will be your first day as a new student.'

CHAPTER 3

DETECTIVE BECKY HARRIS

After Sutherby left, I curled up on the sofa with my breakfast, which consisted of a packet of Hobnobs that were just about to go out of date. Munching through them, I opened the files Sutherby had given me and read through them. Pickle sat on the arm of the sofa, eyeing the biscuits for stray crumbs as I perused the post-mortem reports for Ajay and Vicky, along with the statements from their friends and families, who all reiterated that their suicides had come out of the blue. They didn't seem to be suffering from any personal problems their loved ones knew about, apart from the trouble sleeping, instances of disappearing, and somewhat secretive behaviour.

I turned to Natalie's file, going through more statements from friends and family, her medical history, and the preliminary psychiatric evaluation. On the laptop, I watched a video of the initial police interview she'd given before being declared unfit to carry on. I studied the distraught and confused young woman as she told how she couldn't remember anything about the incident. She said she must not have seen the elderly man she'd hit and killed. She'd driven away, straight back to the university, where she'd been arrested a little while later. Witness statements said that the seventy-five-year-old victim had been on the pedestrian crossing when she'd driven straight into him at speed. They said it seemed as if she'd hit him on purpose, but she didn't know him, and her friends spoke about what a nice, kind girl she was.

None of the students had criminal records. Not even a hint of mental health problems in the past or drug abuse. Apart from attending the same uni and their recent strange behaviour, they apparently had little in common. Ajay Banerjee was studying medicine. He was a high achiever with excellent grades. He lived off-campus in a rental house with four other friends. Vicky was studying accounting and Finance. She lived in one of the on-campus student accommodation blocks. Natalie was doing a degree in English literature and lived in a different on-campus block to Vicky.

I reread the statements from their friends again, trying to build up a picture of what was going on in their lives recently. None of them appeared to know each other, and after going through their social media accounts—Instragram for Natalie, Facebook for Vicky, and Snapchat for Ajay— none of them had friends in common or appeared in each other's photos. There'd been no communications via phone or email found between the three. Ajay was gay and a member of the uni's LGBTQ club. Vicky and Natalie didn't appear to belong to any uni organisations or clubs. There was no mention of them being involved with any remotely cult-like organisations, or any specific groups that used hazing rituals. I doubted the LGBTQ club had an initiation ritual that included cremating themselves. And none of them were reported as being in a relationship.

I searched the internet for hazing and initiation ceremonies in the UK. The Greek system of fraternities in the US had had a lot of well-publicised incidents over the years, but they didn't operate in the UK. So I was shocked to find plenty of university staff interviews saying that the hazing culture in Britain was actually quite common. Excessive dares or dangerous rituals that had gone catastrophically wrong, mostly involving excessive consumption of alcohol, had resulted in several serious injuries and deaths recently. One student had drowned in a lake. One had fallen from a six-storey building. One had jumped from a stairway, which was similar to Vicky's death. One had been hit and killed by a vehicle when playing chicken on the motorway, and one had died because the level of alcohol he'd consumed had led to fluid filling his lungs and starving his brain of oxygen.

Purring, Pickle nudged my hand with her head, cat-speak for 'Stroke me'. I tickled her under her chin until she got bored and decided to push the half-eaten packet of biscuits onto the floor with a swipe of her paw.

'You little minx,' I said to her as she pounced on the crumbs spilling onto the carpet, trying to gobble them up.

I picked up the packet, and she stalked towards the door, tail haughtily raised in the air. Then she paused a moment to give me a glare for ruining all her fun before scarpering off.

I put the biscuits on the coffee table and then looked up information on cults and read through several articles. One expert defined a cult as a group or organisation which used any form of psychological coercion to recruit, brainwash, and influence people, so all their previous sets of values, whether it be social, intellectual, spiritual, or financial, were replaced with the cult's motivations and agendas. Often, though not always, the organisations hijacked religion or politics as a way to ensnare victims. Even seemingly innocuous groups could be poisonous traps, with some sects luring recruits with offers of therapy, self-help, and even things like yoga and meditation or smoking cessation strategies.

Often, they were set up and registered with the government as religious organisations or simple charities. According to the Cult Information Centre, a group defined as a cult formed an elitist, totalitarian society. Its leader was charismatic, dogmatic, messianic, and unaccountable. The cult believed the ends justified the means in order to solicit funds or recruit people. And its wealth didn't benefit its members or society as a whole. I snorted out loud. It actually sounded to me like they could well be describing any country's government.

I reached for my phone and called my friend and mentor Detective Inspector Warren Carter.

'Morning. What are you up to on your first day off?' he asked. 'You've certainly got nice weather for it. It's going to be a scorching week.'

'Yeah, I know, but I'm not going to be here, actually.' I hesitated for a moment. This undercover operation was a huge opportunity for me, and I was frothing with chatter that I wanted to share with him. We'd traded secrets in the past many times, and I trusted him implicitly. But I didn't want to let Sutherby down, and he'd told me to report only to him. Maybe I'd tell Warren when this was all over. 'I've decided to book a couple of weeks away on the spur of the moment, and I need someone to feed Pickle. Would you mind?'

'Of course I don't mind. You deserve a break after all the ups and downs with Ian. Going anywhere nice?'

'Spain. Got a last-minute cheap deal to Marbella.'

'Sounds great. I'm jealous.' He chuckled. 'I don't want to overstuff Pickle, so how much food does she have?'

I gave him feeding instructions then said, 'Thanks, mate. I really appreciate it.'

'No worries. You have a good time.'

I hung up and turned my attention back to the laptop. Was it really possible some kind of cult was operating on our doorstep? I was buzzing with energy, ready to find out.

DAY TWO

"A secret's worth depends on the people from whom it must be kept."
~ Carlos Ruiz

CHAPTER 4

DETECTIVE BECKY HARRIS

Student ID? Check. Timetable? Check. Welcome pack? Check. Key to my new on-campus accommodations? Check.

I exited the admin block after receiving everything from Sutherby's ex-wife, Anthea, and studied the map in my hand to make sure I was heading towards the right block for my new room. There were several accommodation buildings arranged on the edge of the campus around a car parking area. Mine had an en suite bathroom—thank God. I didn't fancy going back to sharing communal showers with other girls. I'd had enough of that when I lived in the police hostel after joining the force at eighteen, before I could afford my own place.

Anthea had helpfully arranged for me to stay in Vicky's old room, which meant I'd be able to cosy up to her neighbours and do some digging. I was supposed to be studying English literature, like Natalie had been. Again, I was glad they hadn't arranged for me to study medicine, like Ajay. The sciences had never been my strong point, and even though I'd been to many post-mortems, it wasn't my favourite pastime, and I had a strong feeling I'd puke if someone ever tried to get me to dissect a cadaver.

I lugged my suitcase up the stairs to the second floor of the block, the backpack on my shoulders weighing me down. The corridors were quiet, apart from a faint sound of music coming from one of the doors I passed. I found my room, unlocked it, and stepped inside.

It was painted a warm creamy beige and had a double bed, a desk along the wall beneath a window overlooking one of the car parks, and a small wardrobe in the corner. I poked my head in the en suite. Everything looked bright and fresh.

I'd never done the university thing. I'd joined the police after finishing my A-levels and fell in love with the job. After my probationary period, I was a patrol officer for a while and was then fast-tracked to detective constable before being promoted to DS. I had no idea about being a student, although I suspected there was a lot of alcohol involved with a side order of hard work. Still, I wasn't there to study or get drunk. I was there to ask questions.

I looked in the cupboard and drawers and under the bed then fiddled with skirting boards to see if any were loose and could be used as hiding places, hoping I'd find something interesting that Vicky had left behind—a hidden suicide note, perhaps, because she'd never left one. The place had been cleaned, though, and there was nothing.

Leaving my unpacking for later, I studied my timetable. I had a free period before a lecture at ten, so I headed down the corridor to the communal kitchen. A black girl with sleek, straight hair that fell past her shoulders sat at the large kitchen table in the centre of the room, feet up on one chair and a lollipop in her mouth as she read a textbook.

'Hi,' I said.

She glanced up quickly, pulling on the lollipop stick so it emerged from her mouth with a sucking sound. 'Hey.' She looked me up and down, sizing me up.

For a moment, I was plunged back into the nightmare world of junior school, where I'd been the fat, ugly kid who was bullied. I suddenly had a flashback of my mum cutting my hair into a bowl shape to try and control my mad waves that would never look as neat as the other perfectly groomed schoolgirls'. I'd cried for days after she did it, and for months afterwards, the other students had called me ugly and a lesbian, sometimes adding, 'You look like a boy!' I'd been one of the thousands of kids who were never going to be cool or trendy, and I never really fitted in. Kids could be utter bastards to each other.

'Who are you?' She stared at me, oozing a confidence that came from arrogance.

My first instinct was to ignore the obviously calculating look on her face as she worked out whether I was worth talking to or not. I could tell instantly that this girl thought she was superior to me. In my real life, I wouldn't care. But if Ajay, Natalie, or Vicky had fallen in with some kind of hazing group or cult or had been subjected to bullying or coercive behaviour, then I needed to act like a meek and mild version of myself. Bullies loved someone they could manipulate and terrify.

I did a good job of hovering in the doorway, plastering on my best hesitant smile. 'Um... I've just moved in to a room down the corridor.' I pointed back down the hallway unnecessarily. 'Number twenty-four.'

She pulled a lemon-sucking face. 'Vicky's old room? Good luck with that. Do you know what happened to her?'

Well, there was one good thing about people like Miss Arrogant. She apparently loved scaring the shit out of fresh meat, which meant more info for me.

'No.' I approached the table to sit down. She didn't move her feet from the nearest chair, so I took the one opposite her. 'What happened?'

She closed her textbook and slapped it down on the table. 'Vicky dive-bombed off the stairs in one of the lecture blocks.' She raised her eyebrows and treated me to a smirk, bearing all the hallmarks of a gossip who loved drama.

'What... you mean, she just jumped off?'

She rolled her eyes, as if inferring I was stupid. 'I said *dived*. Like, literally dived off the top, as if she was diving into a swimming pool. Bam! Right in front of everyone. It was gross.'

I did a mousey gasp. 'How awful. Did you see it?'

She waved the lollipop around in the air. 'No. I heard about it from someone who was there.'

I thought back to the witness statements I'd read. Lecture block one had been packed at the time, and many students had seen Vicky's body lying broken and twisted on the ground below. A few had been next to Vicky at the time, not realising what was going on until it was too late, when she'd climbed over the railings at the top of the stairs, stood on a small ledge, and then put her arms above her head and dived off, falling headfirst twenty metres to the concrete floor below.

'I'm Becky, by the way.' I lifted my hand instinctively to hold it out for her to shake, a habit I'd developed in my professional life. At the last minute, I realised I wasn't in that world anymore and turned it into a scratch at the back of my head.

The girl didn't tell me her name. Just looked at me as she put the lollipop back in her mouth and sucked on it.

'What's your name?' I asked.

'Shakia,' she said, her mouth full of Chupa Chups.

'Nice to meet you.'

She made a hmph sound, as if it wasn't reciprocated.

'Did you know Vicky well?'

'Not really. I'm studying economics and business. She was doing accounting,' she said, like that explained everything.

'But I guess you must've seen her in here a few times if she lived down the hall.' I glanced around the kitchen.

Shakia shrugged. 'Sometimes. We didn't hang out. Hope you make less noise than her. She woke me up a lot, having nightmares. Screaming, shouting. I had to bang on her door loads of times, and I need seven hours uninterrupted sleep at least. *And* I caught her sleepwalking a couple of times. One day, she was in here making pasta at two in the morning in, like, this...' She waved her lollipop casually in the air. 'This trance or something. It was seriously nuts. She didn't hear me. Couldn't even see me.'

'That must've been scary.'

She snorted. 'Hardly. Freaky, more like. At first, I thought she was messing around. But it was real. I waved my hand in front of her face a few times, and she didn't notice a thing. I got it on video. Do you want to see?' Her eyes lit up with all the excitement of a malicious bully.

'Okay.'

She delved into her bulky handbag on the table with her free hand and pulled out a mobile phone with a bejazzled case. She tapped a few buttons and practically shoved the screen in my face.

I watched the scene unfold as Vicky moved around the kitchen with a glazed look in her eyes, going through mechanical movements, grating cheese onto a plate, turning the hob off, draining spaghetti through a colander, and emptying it into a bowl. Shakia did a commentary on screen as she filmed, with lots of giggles in between: 'Oh, my God! What is she *doing*? She's seriously psycho... and now she's eating it like she's awake.'

Vicky did indeed look like she was in some kind of trance state. Her eyes were unfocused as she appeared to sleepwalk through eating a whole bowl of pasta as if no one else were in the room with her. In between bites, Vicky muttered to herself. She spoke so quietly, I couldn't hear the exact words, but it sounded like she was saying, 'Must do it. No, I don't want to.' Vicky's lips carried on moving, and I strained to hear more, but Shakia's voice over the top of it drowned out Vicky's words. In Vicky's file, there was no mention that the coroner's officer had ever spoken to Shakia to find out more about Vicky. Certainly, this video was never mentioned.

The clip finished abruptly as Vicky took her last bite.

'Then what happened?' I asked.

'I don't know. I got bored and left her there and went to bed. I had to get up early for an exam.'

'You left her in that state?' My tone ramped up from the previous shy-girl level to incredulous contempt. I mentally kicked myself. I couldn't blow my cover or alienate any potential witnesses on my first day.

But luckily, Shakia didn't seem to notice as she plopped her phone back in her bag. She shoved the lollipop in her mouth and said out of the corner of her lips, 'She wasn't my problem, was she?'

'Do you think she was high on something?' According to Vicky's friends, she wasn't into any kind of drugs. At the post-mortem, none were found in her system. But recent studies showed an epidemic of drugs on campuses. By far, the drug of choice was cannabis, but not the old-school stuff. The majority of cannabis being seized these days by police was super-high-potent skunk, which could cause nasty side effects, like paranoia and hallucinations. What if there was some kind of strong or dodgy batch of substance knocking around campus that accounted for Vicky's dazed state on Shakia's video?

Shakia snorted. 'Vicky was much too goody-goody to get high.'

'You said there was another time it happened?'

'Uh-huh. But that was *way* weirder.' Shakia stood and gathered her books together. 'That happened in the daytime. She was spaced out, just walking up and down the corridor here, like she was asleep, but her eyes were open. She was obviously crazy.' She put her fingertip near her temple and wound it in a circular motion. Clutching her books to her chest, she tossed her hair over her shoulder before leaving.

CHAPTER 5

DETECTIVE BECKY HARRIS

I sat there for a moment, mulling over what Shakia had told me, wondering what she'd meant about Vicky seeming to sleepwalk in the daytime. Usually, sleepwalking was a symptom of underlying stress, but was it even relevant to my investigation?

I glanced at my watch. Half an hour until the lecture. I opened the huge industrial fridge in the corner of the kitchen and peered inside. The shelves were labelled with people's names. Vicky's label had been left in situ, but where her name was written in black capitals, someone had crossed it out with red pen and written *FREAK*. No prizes for guessing who the likely culprit was.

The cupboards along three walls of the room also had name labels. I found Vicky's, but that label hadn't been tampered with. I opened the door, and the only thing inside was a half-empty packet of cornflakes.

It was time to go. I collected my backpack, which contained notepads, pens, and the laptop I'd been given by Sutherby. Map in hand, I found my way to lecture theatre block two and the class Natalie would've attended, if she'd still been at the uni and wasn't being held in a secure mental health hospital.

As soon as I walked into the theatre, I realised my mistake. I'd been hoping I could meet up with some of Natalie's friends, particularly Millie and Jess, who'd both said in their statements that they hung around as a threesome and were very close. But the place was huge, with seats tiered at an angle so everyone had a view of the front platform. It was already three-quarters full of students, and there was no way I could single out any of Natalie's friends in there.

I stood in the aisle, glancing around, as people milled past me. The male lecturer stood at a lectern and told everyone to take their seats. I debated whether to leave, but then I sat in the nearest seat and opened my laptop. It would look as if I were taking notes, but what I really wanted to do was more research on methods used by cults or radical groups to indoctrinate people, because I hadn't had time to go through everything I'd wanted to at home yesterday.

I opened the laptop and connected to the uni's free Wi-Fi while the lecturer spoke. I searched articles by experts and also victims who'd escaped cults, reading firsthand accounts of how the groups actually managed to get people to do things which historically included mass murder, suicide, sexual abuse, theft of money or possessions, and much more.

No matter what their size or motivation, Cults always operated the same way. They exerted control with what police in one example had called 'invisible handcuffs'. They used powerful mind-control techniques which many victims said caused them to dedicate their life to the group, giving them every last penny, resigning from their jobs, cutting off ties with family and friends, and doing things they'd never have dreamt of doing in their previous lives and that often went against their core beliefs. And once the leaders had established power, the victims had believed them so completely, been radicalised so drastically, it was as if the things they did whilst under control were happening of their own free will. The victims no longer had their own normal thought processes. They could no longer critically evaluate what was happening. They were literally brainwashed into becoming someone else.

There seemed to be no particular personality type that was more susceptible to mind-control techniques than another, either, which surprised the hell out of me. It could happen to anyone, and people could even be brainwashed within a matter of days. Despite popular misconception, victims didn't have to be needy, unhappy, vulnerable, or socially bereft with no friends or family. Often, the opposite was true, and the kind of person most likely to be ensnared into a cult was from an economically sound family background, had average-to-above-average intelligence and a good education, and was idealistic.

I glanced up and looked around the busy lecture theatre, taking in the hundreds of young adults, studying their differences in looks, clothing, even their postures and body language. Could everyone in this room really be susceptible to a cult?

I turned back to my laptop again and read about the psychological techniques cults used, including deception, peer pressure, abuse, sleep deprivation, replacement of relationships, financial commitment, isolation, controlled approval, fear, dependency, and guilt.

'Wow,' I said, shaking my head.

The girl sitting next to me glared in my direction for daring to make a noise. I mouthed a 'Sorry' at her and looked back at the laptop.

Recruiting members would often be done by advertising in magazines, newspapers, universities, social groups, and sports clubs—basically anywhere and everywhere. A lot of people said they'd been recruited by family or friends.

I read through more articles of people who'd managed to leave cults and talked about how hard it had been. They'd often experienced withdrawal symptoms like hallucinations, delusions, insomnia, amnesia, guilt, fear, emotional outbursts, and feelings of isolation and helplessness. That list sounded similar to some of the recent behaviour the three students had been exhibiting. But then those symptoms could be put down to hundreds of possible coming-of-age problems. So was there a cult in operation on campus, or were the three students' actions completely unrelated?

I sat back and stared at the screen, thinking that the ways cults indoctrinated and radicalised people were exactly the same as how terrorist groups, and even the military, operated—coercing people to kill others or commit suicide as a way to prove their loyalty to a specific cause or ideology.

I was so engrossed in what I was reading that I didn't notice people getting up and leaving until someone asked me to move out of the way. I closed the laptop, hooked my backpack over my shoulder, and followed the swarm of people out into the open air.

CHAPTER 6

TONI

I carefully surveyed my office in the five minutes I had before my next client. Lavender oil in the oil burner. Cosy lighting. Slats on the blinds tilted just so. Enough paper left in my notebook. I adjusted the angle of one armchair a fraction. Perfect.

I'd been an associate counsellor at St Albans University's Student Counselling Services for one month, working four days a week. It was everything I'd hoped it would be, and more. The job was a great opportunity to build on my experience and develop a portfolio of counselling hours to accrue towards my professional accreditation.

I checked my laptop screen one more time, practicing the client's name in my head. Marcelina Claybourn. The only thing I knew about her was that she was twenty years old and studying marketing and advertising. When I'd first started work with the counselling services, I'd thought it would be strange to have so few details about someone before their initial appointment, but in fact, it helped me avoid forming preconceived notions about them. In this office, we practiced a person-centred approach. The clients were encouraged to open up in their own time, so there were no pre-appointment questionnaires, no rigid formality.

I gave the room one last check, opened the door, and walked into the reception and waiting area. A girl with choppy blonde hair sat in one corner of the room, hands clenched into fists at her lap, staring into space as she chewed ferociously on her bottom lip.

'Marcelina?' I smiled at her.

Her head jerked upwards, cobalt-blue eyes rimmed with red looking warily at me. Her face was blotchy, the skin around her nose raw and flaking, as if she'd been wiping it repeatedly.

I stepped towards her. 'Hi, I'm Toni.'

She stood abruptly and picked up her big handbag from the floor with a trembling hand.

'If you'd like to follow me?' I didn't let up with my smile. She was obviously nervous, and I wanted to put her at ease as much as possible.

We stepped inside my office, and I closed the door.

'Have a seat, please.' I indicated one of the two armchairs arranged so they were slightly off the opposite position. I didn't want clients to feel like they were in an interview under direct sightline, under scrutiny. This was supposed to be a comfortable space. A safe place.

Marcelina hesitated for a moment and swallowed as I sat down. Her gaze skimmed my face.

'You look very young,' she said with a doubtful tone in a soft Scottish accent.

She was right. I was young. But I'd been to hell and back, and I was still standing. Not that I'd ever tell her that. Apart from three other people, no one knew what had happened to me, and they would never tell. But what I'd been through, what I'd survived, was what would hopefully make me good at my job.

I nodded my agreement at her. 'I always get told I look younger than I am. Not so great now, maybe, but when I'm older, it'll be a good thing.' I smiled again. 'Let me tell you a bit about myself, if that helps. I'm twenty-one. And I completed a degree in psychology and counselling, so don't worry, I'm fully qualified. I *was* doing psychology and criminology at first, but I switched the course early on because it was a better fit for what I've always wanted to do.'

She perched on the edge of the armchair, thighs pressed together, handbag on her lap clutched to her stomach in a classic defensive and protective pose.

I tried to put her more at ease by explaining what counselling was all about, how we could talk about anything, how I was there to support her and help find positive solutions to deal with any issues, and how it was confidential. 'So, what brings you here, Marcelina?'

Her gaze darted to the window behind the desk over my left shoulder. The slats on the blinds were tilted to allow in light but not so any nosy students could peer in, but she still seemed worried about being seen.

'Do you want me to close the blinds completely?'

'Yes.'

I obliged and sat back down, waiting for her to start.

She inhaled a deep breath, looked up at the ceiling, and blew out the breath in one long rush, looking at the carpet. 'I don't know where to... This is going to... going to sound really strange.'

'Just start wherever you feel comfortable. We don't even have to chat about what's bothering you right now. We can just... chat. About anything. I love your name, by the way.'

She mumbled a thanks.

'Going by your accent, I'm guessing you're originally from Scotland. Have you lived in this area for a while, or did you move down to St Albans for uni?'

'Just for uni.'

'That's nice. Is your family still in Scotland?' I was hoping to ease her into talking about whatever was bothering her with a few normal, everyday questions. Even when people took the first step to choose counselling, it could still take time for them to open up.

'I'm an only child. My parents are still up in Scotland, yes.'

'And how long have you been at this uni?'

'Two years.' Her worried gaze darted towards the blind, as if she wanted to rip it off and crawl through the window.

'Are you enjoying your course?'

'I was. But...' She fidgeted with her hands, looking down at her bitten fingernails.

I waited.

'Something is happening to me,' she said in a quiet voice.

'What's happening?'

'I don't know. I can't explain it.' She blinked rapidly. Beads of sweat broke out on her forehead.

'Okay... let's try to break it down a little. Do you mean something happening on the course? Or something with you personally?'

'I keep losing time. I... I think I'm sleepwalking, but it's in the daytime. I do things, and I can't remember what. I'm at some place, and I don't know how I got there. At night, I have bad dreams. Nightmares.' She shook her head. 'But it's the daytimes that are more scary, because I can't remember.'

I leaned forward. Not enough to invade her space but

enough to send a silent signal of comfort. That I was there for her, taking her seriously. 'Can you explain a little more for me? It's normal for people to sometimes forget how they got to places. We all go into autopilot mode at times. I've driven to places many times and zoned out completely, thinking about other things. And when I got to my destination, I have no clear memory of how I arrived. Is that the kind of thing you mean? Or is this something different?'

'No, this is different. Very different. It's...' Her face twisted into an anguished expression. Anxiety came off her in waves.

I waited for her to explain more in her own time. She didn't, so I prompted her. 'Can you give me an example of what's been going on? When one of these events happened, what's the last thing you remember, and where did you end up?'

She was silent for a moment as she flattened her lips into a tense line. Then she looked up at the ceiling. 'Last week, I was in my room. I'm in one of the university's accommodation blocks. The last thing I remember was... I was in the en suite bathroom, and I was doing my makeup. It was about nine o'clock in the morning. I had a couple of study periods, so I was going to work at my desk before my lecture started at eleven. Then the next thing I know, it's one in the afternoon, and I'm in Verulamium Park, sitting on the grass under a tree.' She swung her head in my direction, her eyes huge pools of confusion. 'I lost four hours! I don't know what happened. What I was doing.'

'Okay.' I nodded and scribbled a few notes in my client notebook that I'd later transfer to our computer database.

'Then another time, I found myself at the bottom of the accommodation block I live in. In the stairwell. I was just, like, sitting on the floor, and I don't know how I got there.'

'Can you think of any physical reason it might've been happening? Have you been feeling unwell at all?'

She shook her head. 'Not really, no. And I'm scared to see a doctor. What if they say I've got a brain tumour or something.'

'It's possible there could be some physical reason, but maybe it's hormonal. Or maybe you have a virus of some kind. It could be something simple that a doctor could discover from a blood test.' I paused. 'Or it could stem from something like stress or anxiety. That's very common with students. There can be a *lot* of pressure here.'

She shook her head. 'I wasn't stressed or anxious before this started happening.'

'Okay. Have you been feeling lonely at all? It's a big step coming to university. For most people, they're leaving home for the first time. Away from the usual family and friend support structure. It's a very brave step. A lot of people struggle with adjustment issues.'

'No. I'm not lonely. I have friends, and I don't mind my own company.'

'Did something happen to you before these periods of sleep problems and lost time? Has there been anything traumatic going on in your life?'

'No. But—' She broke off. 'It all sounds mad, doesn't it?'

'No, it doesn't. I'm sure we can get to the bottom of this for you.' I nodded encouragingly and broached the next question. 'I have to ask you this... Are you taking any medication or recreational drugs? Because if you are, this could be a side effect.'

'I'm not taking anything. And I hardly drink alcohol.' She wailed and put her head in her hands. 'I knew this was going to be useless. You don't understand.'

'I'm trying to. I'm just seeing if we can figure out together what's happening.'

She sat upright and flung her arms down by her sides. 'None of what you've suggested would account for the other things.'

'What other things?'

'I don't know how to explain.' Her face crumpled in on itself. She looked down at her lap and mumbled something so quietly that I didn't quite catch it, but I thought she said, 'I'm hearing voices.' Then she looked up at me, tears in her eyes. 'This was a bad idea. You can't help me. Maybe I *am* crazy.' She stood abruptly and hurried towards the door.

Before I was even on my feet, she'd yanked on the door handle and hurtled out into the waiting room. I called her name as I rushed past Janet behind the reception desk like a whirlwind, trying to catch up with Marcelina, who was running out of the building and into the open air of the campus.

By the time I got outside, she was sprinting past one of the medical faculty blocks. I hesitated for a moment. Should I follow her and make sure she was okay? Or should I respect her right to walk out of the session?

Of course I couldn't leave her. And she obviously wasn't okay. So I ran after her.

Dodging students sitting on the grass, taking in the unseasonably warm May day, I gave chase. As I rounded the medical block, she was nowhere in sight. I ground to a halt and looked about, trying to spot her in the crowd of students who'd just exited lecture theatre block two.

As I was giving up hope, I saw a flash of her blonde hair in the swarm, heading towards the university's entrance gates and the main road beyond. I jogged after her, calling her name.

Marcelina slipped through the gates. There was a pelican pedestrian crossing with traffic lights on the main road, but she didn't stop and press the button to halt the traffic whizzing by. In one second, she was there on the footpath, looking across the road to the other side, but by the time I got within a few metres of her, she'd taken a step off the kerb into the oncoming traffic.

'No!' I yelled.

But it was too late. A big black 4x4 slammed into Marcelina, sending her flying up into the air before she bounced on the tarmac like a rag doll.

CHAPTER 7

GLOVER

Glover stood on the opposite side of the road from Marcelina, slouched against the wall of the house, with his phone pressed to his ear. But he wasn't making a call. He'd been preparing. He'd been watching and waiting.

No one would notice him amongst the others looking on at the accident scene with horror, and there were no traffic cameras at the lights. He'd already checked before Marcelina started questioning things.

He wore jogging bottoms and a light sweatshirt with a hood that was pulled up. Sunglasses masked his eyes. He could be just another student out of the thousands in the area. What no one would know was that he'd filmed the whole thing with the high-definition pinhole camera in the messenger bag hanging from his right shoulder.

Some of the bystanders in the milling crowd were screaming; some had tears in their eyes. He surveyed the scene with satisfaction then watched the driver of the 4x4 get out of his vehicle, hands shaking, his mouth gaping open in shock.

Glover watched a young woman with long dark hair shouting for someone to call an ambulance while she kneeled on the tarmac beside Marcelina.

He pulled the phone away from his ear and dialled a number. This time, he really did make a call.

CHAPTER 8

DETECTIVE BECKY HARRIS

For the first time in a long time, my stomach grumbled with hunger. After Ian and I had split up on the first occasion, we'd been off and on again more times than I could remember, falling into yet another unhealthy pattern. But six weeks ago, he'd finally left for good. And now I was going through the process of sorting out the divorce paperwork, which had completely obliterated my appetite, an unheard-of occurrence for me. Since I hadn't had time to do a supermarket run before I arrived, I headed to the student union building, which, according to my welcome pack, had a food court, coffee shop, the Terrace Bar, a nightclub, a hairdressers, and even a bank.

I pulled open the double doors to the union and paused inside the entrance to look at the large notice boards lining one wall. I scanned the leaflets and flyers pinned to the first board. If there was some kind of radical group or cult operating here, then would they blatantly advertise for people to join?

I found ads asking for students to flat share, a leaflet for the student counselling service, and flyers for sponsored events to raise money for UNICEF, Great Ormond Street Hospital, and a local animal shelter. There were lots of items for sale and other leaflets that all seemed innocuous. I moved on to the next board and found much of the same. I didn't spot anything that looked particularly religious or fanatical, so I headed into the café next to the Terrace Bar.

The offerings were *far* better than in my school days of sloppy boiled cabbage and snotty tapioca pudding. I got a medium-sized pizza and an orange juice and then headed outside onto the terrace, where a large seating area was busy due to the unusually nice weather. As I stood, tray in hand, searching out an empty seat in amongst the picnic tables, a memory slammed into my head from my school canteen— being called 'Piggy' and 'Porker' by the bullies while trying to make myself as small and unnoticeable as possible under the weight of their jeers and stares. Thank God I wasn't a teenager again.

But no one noticed me scanning the crowd. The majority of them had their heads down, gazes trained firmly on their smartphones. On one table of eight, every single student was looking at a screen instead of interacting with the others.

Included in Sutherby's information had been photos of the students' friends, taken from their uni ID cards that he'd got from Anthea. I spotted Natalie's friends, Jess and Millie. Jess had white-blonde hair in a pixie cut. Millie had long hair in a vivid plum colour. They sat in a group with three guys, and there were two empty seats at the table.

I walked over, smiling. 'Hi, do you mind if I sit here?'

Millie and Jess looked up from their conversation.

'Course not.' Jess grinned. 'We need more girl power on this table. They're boring us about football.' She jerked her head at one of the boys in the group and rolled her eyes.

I smiled gratefully. 'Thanks.' I put my plate and juice on the table and leaned the tray on the ground against the table leg to make more room. 'I'm Becky, by the way.'

'I'm Jess.' She pointed to her chest. 'Millie, Shaun, Gaz, Tim.' She pointed round the table.

The three guys at the table gave me a distracted wave then went back to their conversation about a football game they'd seen. Millie and Jess looked at my pizza.

'You going to eat all that?' Millie laughed.

'That's nothing.' I laughed back. 'I could probably eat two.' Luckily for me, my metabolism had gone into overdrive after my teenage years. I wasn't stick thin, but I wasn't the fat kid anymore.

Jess pulled a face. 'That's so unfair. You're tiny. I can put on a couple of pounds just sniffing the same air as food.'

I picked up a piece of pizza and took a bite. It was amazing. I chewed, groaning in appreciation. 'Tastes horrible anyway,' I said to Jess. 'You're not missing anything.'

'Yeah, right.' She grinned.

I swallowed another mouthful while I quickly ran through in my head what I'd read about them in Sutherby's files. Both of them had given statements to the police. Jess and Millie hadn't seen Natalie drive into the elderly man at the pedestrian crossing, but Jess had been in the uni car park when Natalie arrived back in her Mini afterwards. Jess had noticed the broken windscreen, dented bonnet, smashed grill, and blood on Natalie's car and asked Natalie what had happened and if she was okay. Jess had said Natalie got out of the car and stared at the bonnet as if she were completely surprised it was in that state. Jess had asked if she'd hit an animal. Natalie had said she couldn't remember doing anything like that and had seemed completely 'out of it'.

The guys at the table got up to leave, said their goodbyes, and sauntered off.

'Were you in our lecture just now?' Jess asked me.

'Yep, that's right.'

'I thought so. Have you joined halfway through the term?' Millie asked. 'I haven't seen you before.'

I came out with the cover story I'd invented to hopefully elicit some kind of insightful information—mature student who'd been travelling Europe for a few years, blah, blah, blah. 'I missed the first couple of terms, but the uni sent me some of the coursework and lecture outlines, so I've been working from home until now. I had a car accident, you see. Well, *I* wasn't driving. I was cycling and got hit by a car. Broke my leg.' I pulled a pained face and rubbed at my shin for emphasis. 'I didn't want to be hobbling around campus on crutches with books and bags and things.' I took another bite of pizza and waited for them to take the bait.

'Ouch. Sounds painful. Luckily, I've never broken anything.' Millie tapped the wooden table. 'Touch wood.'

'Don't talk to me about car accidents.' Jess shuddered. 'There was a bad one here a while back.'

'Really?' I asked. 'What happened?'

Jess looked at Millie for a moment then said to me, 'One of our friends hit someone with her car and drove off.'

I did the fake-gasp thing again. I was getting good at it. I followed it up with a wide-eyed 'wow' look. 'Sorry to hear that. Are they both okay?'

Millie looked down at her fingertips still on the table and rubbed at an invisible spot. 'He died. He was an old guy.'

'That's awful. And how's your friend?'

'She's in a secure mental health place at the moment, getting treatment,' Jess said. 'I saw her after she did it. In her car. She parked up in the car park, and it was really weird. She was kind of spaced out and didn't seem to realise anything had happened.'

'Maybe she was in shock,' I said.

'I asked her what she'd done, 'cause I saw her car all dented with blood on it, and it was like she didn't even remember doing it.'

I frowned. 'Do you think she could've been trying to cover up the fact she'd hit someone by saying she didn't remember?' But I doubted that was true. If Natalie had wanted to try to cover it up, she would've hidden the car until it was fixed. Or at least cleaned the blood off the bonnet. Or said the car had been stolen. And how could she even think she'd have a chance at hiding what she'd done when there had been multiple witnesses on the street?

'No, it was like she seriously couldn't remember what had just happened. It was almost like she was sleepwalking. But she'd been a bit weird for a few weeks before that, hadn't she?' Jess said to Millie.

Millie's lips pressed together for a moment, her face etched with sadness. 'Yeah. And she thought someone was following her.'

'Around campus?'

'Yeah, and off campus, too, when she went into town. But she couldn't say who it was.'

That was news to me. None of the statements had mentioned that fact.

'And she was having bad dreams and stuff,' Millie said. 'Not sleeping. She kind of distanced herself from us, like she was annoyed with us or something. But we couldn't work out why she was pissed off. Every time we invited her out lately, she made excuses.'

'Oh.' I nodded sympathetically and thought back to what I'd read. People distancing themselves from existing friends was one of the ways cults isolated potential targets. 'Maybe she was hanging around with someone else. She might've joined a club or something and widened her circle of friends.'

Millie shook her head. 'No, I never saw her with anyone else. And she wasn't into any of the club activities stuff.'

'We think she was seeing this guy, though, and didn't want to tell us about him,' Jess said.

'Who was he?' I asked. Again, that was news to me. Natalie's parents said she wasn't involved with anyone, and neither Jess or Millie's statements had mentioned a relationship.

Jess glanced around the busy eating area before leaning in closer. 'We think it was one of the professors.' She raised her eyebrows.

'Which one?' I asked.

'We saw her chatting to him a couple of times, and it definitely looked like there was something going on with them. And one time, it looked like they were having a bit of an argument,' Jess said.

'Yeah, he's gross, though. And old,' Millie said.

'So who was he?' I asked again.

Jess's gaze darted to an oversized watch on her wrist. 'Oh! We need to go finish off that essay before three!' She jumped up and grabbed Millie's arm. 'We're coming down to the Terrace Bar tonight if you fancy joining us.'

'Thanks, that would be great. I don't really know anyone else yet.' And I needed to get an answer to my question, but it would look too suspicious to ask again before they left.

'Yeah, that's what I figured. It's horrible when you're new.

Let's exchange numbers.' Jess pulled her phone from her large handbag.

I told her my number and put hers in my phone.

'Great. Be down here at six.' Jess hoisted her bag over her shoulder and tugged Millie away.

'See ya!' Millie cried.

I took a swallow of orange juice as I watched them go, mulling over what they'd said. I wondered how the coroner's officer could've completely overlooked a possible boyfriend and the video Shakia had shown me. Was that because they just hadn't asked the right questions? Often, witnesses didn't volunteer certain information because they didn't know they held an important piece of a puzzle that linked to another piece. But there were definitely pieces missing here. And I intended to find them.

CHAPTER 9

TONI

'Call an ambulance,' I yelled into the crowd as I kneeled beside Marcelina.

She lay on her back, one leg bent beneath her, the other outstretched. Her head was twisted towards her right shoulder, with blood pooling out from a wound on her forehead.

'Can you hear me?' I leaned over her, watching her chest to see if I could detect a rise and fall. She was breathing, but it was shallow. 'Marcelina?' I ignored the crowd gathering around the road and took her wrist, feeling for a pulse. It was faint but still there. My head whipped up, searching the faces of the onlookers. 'Did anyone call an ambulance?'

'Yeah, I did,' someone called back.

I took Marcelina's bloody hand in mine and stroked it, staring down at her with tears in my eyes. 'It's okay. They're coming. You just hang on. Hang on, okay? You'll be fine.'

Marcelina's eyelids fluttered half open. Someone in the crowd sobbed loudly. The driver of the 4x4 shouted something about not seeing her. Marcelina's lips moved, but I couldn't hear her over the noise.

I leaned in closer. 'The ambulance will be here soon. Don't worry, you'll be in good hands.'

Marcelina blinked rapidly. 'They... they made me.' Her voice came out in a hoarse whisper.

'Who did?'

'Watching me... in the... shadows. He's there. Shadow... man.' Her eyes rolled up into their sockets, and her lids closed again.

'Stay with me, Marcelina. Don't go to sleep. Can you hear me? I'm right here.'

I stroked her hand until the ambulance arrived, but she didn't regain consciousness. I stepped away, my heart racing, adrenaline flowing, as a paramedic placed his equipment bag next to her and kneeled in the space I'd just vacated. I told him her name and age so they'd be able to access her medical records. I picked up Marcelina's big handbag lying in the road a metre from her body, wanting to take it for safe-keeping. The paramedic shouted instructions to another crew member, who wheeled a stretcher out from the back of the ambulance.

A police car arrived as Marcelina was being fitted with a neck brace. A young female officer got out of the patrol car, along with an older male colleague, and they made their way through the crowd.

'We're taking her to Watford General,' the paramedic called out to the female officer as Marcelina was carefully placed on the stretcher and loaded into the ambulance.

I took deep breaths, trying to calm myself. Some of the crowd dispersed around me, the nightmare scene over for them. They'd talk about it for a while to their friends and family then forget about it as they went on with their everyday lives. For me, it was just the beginning.

CHAPTER 10

I had fifteen minutes to kill before the LGBTQ club started their daily coffee meet in one of the function rooms in the student union building. Ajay had lived in a rental house a couple of miles from the campus with several people he'd met in that group. They'd given statements to the coroner's officer and described themselves as close friends of his. I was hoping they'd be able to give me more insight into his life and whether setting himself and the shared house on fire was a desperate act of someone mentally suffering or something else entirely.

I pushed my now-empty plate away and glanced through my welcome pack until I found a list of uni clubs for students to join. There were hundreds. Many were cultural or religious, covering various ethnic groups—the Arab Society, the Catholic Society, the Pagan Society, the Canadian Society, and every country or religion from *A* to *B*. Then there were a multitude of fitness groups like the Cycling Club, Dance Society, Rowing Club, and various self-defence disciplines. Self-help groups galore—art therapy, dance therapy, yoga, meditation, mindfulness... The list was endless.

The Book Club, Innovation and Tech Society, Law Club, Creative Writing Society, Economics Club. Music societies with different genres, including the Ukelele Society. Every interest was catered for—even obscure ones like a Game of Thrones Club, Peaky Blinders Appreciation Society, a Starbucks Society, a Nintendo Society, and the Boozy Bus Society. It seemed there was a group for everything one could possibly think of. Even with a whole team of officers to check them all out, it would take months to find and talk to every member. Jess and Millie didn't think Natalie had joined any clubs or societies. Vicky didn't appear to have belonged to any, either. And Ajay seemed to have been involved with only one. But if they'd been recruited into some club with hazing rituals that had gone wrong or if a cult was involved, would their friends even know, when cults operated in such a secretive way?

From the material Sutherby had given me, no sudden cash withdrawals had been made from Vicky's, Natalie's, or Ajay's bank accounts. No suspicious payments had gone to any organisation. In fact, both Vicky and Ajay had recently paid some money *into* their bank accounts. The month before she jumped from the stairway, Vicky had deposited two and a half grand. And Ajay had paid in three grand a few weeks before the fire. Just over two thousand pounds in cash had been found in Natalie's room under her mattress after she was arrested. All three of them had student loans and were pretty frugal with their money, so where had the cash come from?

As I thought of how cults cleverly recruited members, I watched an attractive guy walking around the outside picnic tables, chatting to people and handing out flyers before winding his way in my direction. Recruiters often gathered information about potential new members by pretending to have similar interests or values to create an initial bond. Or they made innocent invitations to go for coffee, dinner, free talks, or seminars, using a topic that the potential victim was interested in. If students *were* being recruited here, then the organisation would want to entice them with a nice-looking person, someone friendly, caring, and fun, before they got their claws into them.

The guy got closer to me, bouncing with energy, and I watched him interacting with the other students, laughing, smiling, and joking around with them.

'Hi.' I waved at him. 'I'll take one.'

'Hi.' He grinned, revealing perfect white teeth. He was mixed-race, wearing shorts and a red T-shirt that showed off amazingly ripped muscles. His greenish-hazel eyes were accentuated by the cinnamon colour of his skin. He was gorgeous, in fact.

He headed over, handed me a flyer, and sat down in the seat Millie had vacated.

I glanced down at the page. It was a timetable for fitness classes.

'This is the active student classes for this term,' he said. 'We've got volleyball, Zumba, hip-hop dance, badminton, yoga...' He ticked off the different activities on his fingers. 'Football, roller-skating. And loads more. Check it out.' He pointed to the flyer. 'It's all about having fun, keeping active, and making new friends. And it's all totally free. Just find something you want to do and turn up at the venue with your student ID card. There's stuff going on every day.' He gushed with enthusiasm.

'Thanks. Will do.'

'No problem. Hope to see you at something soon.' His

phone rang in his pocket then. He answered, his face morphing from a warm smile to worried frown. 'What? Now?' he asked before he hung up. 'Sorry, gotta go,' he said to me before jogging away.

When he'd disappeared, I read through the leaflet, wondering if this was something that might help me. Still, I doubted classes organised by the university, with vast groups of students expecting the same thing when they arrived, would be suspicious—apart from pickleball and maybe futsal, whatever the hell they even were. Overall, the offerings appeared to be pretty standard sports. Or were they a breeding ground for something more sinister? I didn't have enough time to spend on possibilities, though. I had to concentrate on what I knew for certain and go from there.

I folded up the leaflet and tucked it into my backpack. It was time for a coffee.

CHAPTER 11

DETECTIVE BECKY HARRIS

The meeting rooms in the union were past the food court and shops. There was a note on the closed door of number nine announcing 'LGBTQ SOCIETY. Coffee Hour Every Day 12.30 p.m. to 1.30 p.m.!'

Inside, I found ten people. Six were slouched on beanbag chairs in the corner of the room, but they weren't watching the film playing on a flat-screen TV in front of them. They were all typing on their phones. A group of two guys and two girls chatted by a coffee urn set up on a table along one wall. I recognised them from the photos I'd studied as Ajay's housemates—Toby, Jaxon, Phoebe, and Ivy.

Toby was lanky, with long hair pulled off his face with a black zigzag hair band. He turned my way. 'Looks like we have a new arrival!'

'Hi.' I waved, doing my practiced awkward smile.

'Hi. I'm Toby.' He gave me a welcoming smile as he walked towards me with his palm held up in a greeting. The three others with him watched on with interest.

'Becky.'

'First time? I haven't seen you here before.'

I nodded. 'Yeah, I'm an LGBTQ virgin.' I laughed.

Phoebe, who had a Mohican haircut and a lip ring, laughed, too. 'Ooh, I like your humour already. I'm Phoebe.'

'Welcome to the LGBTQ Society.' Toby swung around to the others. 'This is Jaxon.' He pointed to a black guy with short dreadlocks. 'And Ivy.' His finger swung around to a girl with auburn hair and lots of freckles.

'Thanks. Nice to meet you all.'

'Want a coffee?' Toby asked.

'Yeah, sure.' I stepped towards the group as Toby grabbed a paper cup from the table. 'How do you take it?'

'White, no sugar, thanks.'

'Toby runs the group,' Phoebe said. 'It's a friendly place to come and chat with each other or just hang out.'

'Yeah, and we also have workshops, film screenings, club nights, and other social events,' Jaxon added.

'Sounds great.' I took the proffered coffee from Toby's hand. 'It was a friend of mine who recommended I join. Well, not really a friend. We got chatting one day, and he told me about this place. Ajay. Do you know him?' I glanced at each one in turn, feeling awful for bringing it up to his friends, but I had a job to do.

Four pairs of sad eyes looked back at me.

'You haven't heard?' Ivy asked.

'Heard what?'

She rested her hand on my arm. 'Sorry to tell you this but... he died.'

I gasped. 'Oh, my God, that's awful.'

'Yeah.' Toby nodded solemnly. 'He... um... killed himself.'

'Wow.' I stared down at the ground and shook my head.

'I'm so sorry. I didn't know.' I looked up again, the sympathy I felt for them completely genuine.

'It was a massive shock.' Phoebe ran a hand over one shaved side of her head. 'You'd never have known he was feeling that bad. I mean, he was pretty quiet when he first joined, but he came out of his shell a lot with us, didn't he?' She looked around the group.

Jaxon nodded. 'Yeah. He was a genuinely nice guy. He'd do anything for anyone.'

'So you all knew him really well?'

They nodded.

'When we started uni, we all lived on campus at first,' Ivy said with a slight lisp. 'But this club is a really close-knit group, and you can make some really good friends here. We all decided to move in together. And it was there that... well...' Tears glistened in her eyes, and she couldn't continue.

'He set fire to his room,' Toby said quietly. 'With himself in it.'

'That's tragic,' I said, eyes wide, thinking of the dreadful photos of Ajay's body, parts of it burnt down to just the skeleton.

'All of us were out at the time. In town,' Jaxon said. 'Ajay was supposed to meet up with us for lunch, but he didn't show. When we got back to the house, we saw the fire engines and stuff. He'd...' He scrunched up his face with horror, eyes glistening. 'He'd poured petrol on himself and in his room and set himself on fire. The doors all locked from the inside.'

'That's awful.' I didn't need to fake the sadness on my face. It was a truly terrible way to die. 'I'm really sorry to hear that.'

An awkward silence descended over us then. I left it a respectful few moments before launching into the story I'd prepared to hopefully get them to talk more about it. 'I know how you must be feeling. I had a friend who killed herself when we were at school. It was horrible. I never even knew what she was going through. She must've been hiding her depression really well, because I never guessed what she'd do.'

'Exactly.' Phoebe nodded vigorously. 'It was the same with Ajay. We had no idea he'd do anything so... tragic. It just came completely out of the blue. But I know what you mean; we all feel really guilty. Like, could we have done more to stop it?' She fiddled with her lip ring.

'Although... he *was* acting a bit odd before it happened,' Jaxon added. 'But you kind of don't pick up on things until afterwards, you know?'

I nodded knowingly. I was turning out to be a pretty good liar. 'I agree. Afterwards, I noticed signs—little things that had happened with her, or things that she'd said—that just never clicked at the time. Then the guilt poured in. Like, if maybe I'd suggested she got some help...' I trailed off, hoping they'd pick up from there.

'That's right,' Phoebe dived in. 'It started a few weeks before he did it. He kind of distanced himself from us a bit. He didn't want to hang out as much. Kept disappearing places and not telling us where he was going. Then one night, when he did come out with us, we were in the Terrace Bar, and this guy bumped into Ajay as he walked past and spilled his drink over him. Usually, Ajay was the most chilled-out guy you'd ever meet. Really sweet, you know? But Ajay went *mental* and—'

'It was *so* out of character,' Ivy butted in. 'Ajay stormed across the room to where the guy was and started punching him!'

'Me and Jaxon and a few others had to pull him off,' Toby said. 'It was like he was in a daze or something.'

'Like he was possessed.' Phoebe leaned forward and raised her eyebrows. 'He went crazy.'

'We drove him back to the house, and he was like a zombie,' Jaxon said. 'Really not with it. Wouldn't speak. And the next morning, he didn't remember doing it.'

The incident was never reported to the police or the university, so the only details I had about what happened were contained in the statements these four students had made to the coroner's officer. What they'd just told me only reiterated those facts. I'd briefly wondered if the student Ajay had punched had wanted to get back at Ajay. Maybe the fire was a malicious prank that had gone wrong, but after reading through everything, it seemed exactly as it was—a tragic suicide.

Ajay had bought the petrol from a local garage two days before he'd struck that match to start the fire. There was CCTV evidence to prove it, which clearly showed Ajay turning up on the forecourt on foot with a plastic petrol canister, filling it with petrol from the pump, and paying for it. The footage even contained audio, and Ajay had made a comment to the man serving at the till that his car had run out of petrol, but Ajay didn't own a car. He'd smiled, seeming chatty and amiable. Not in the least as if he planned to use it on himself. And besides, the coroner's officer had uncovered that the student Ajay had punched was visiting his parents in Yorkshire at the time the house caught fire. And there was no evidence whatsoever suggesting someone else was at the scene.

'Was Ajay drunk when he hit the guy?' I asked. 'I mean, we all do stupid things when we're pissed.'

'No, he'd only had one bottle of Corona. It was totally weird and really out of character,' Ivy said.

'Could he have been on anything else?' I asked. 'Some kind of drug?'

'Nope.' Toby gave an emphatic shake of his head.

'Absolutely not,' Phoebe said. 'Ajay would never do drugs.'

'Definitely not,' Jaxon said. 'We lived together. We hung out with each other all the time. We would've known about it if he was taking something. I mean, yeah, I'm sure you could get stuff on campus if you really wanted to look for it, but that's not our scene.'

I took a sip of coffee and nodded.

'But it wasn't just that...' Phoebe said. 'Another time, we were all supposed to be going shopping together, and we were getting ready and stuff, and Ajay was in his bedroom. When it was time to leave, we called up to him, and there was no answer.'

'Yeah. That's right,' Ivy said. 'We went to the shopping centre without him, and then we found him there a couple of hours later, sitting in Costa on his own, just kind of watching people out of the window with this blank look on his face. He didn't even recognise us when we walked up to him. When we tried to talk to him, he walked off.'

'Was it some kind of sleepwalking episode maybe?' I frowned, thinking about Shakia's video of Vicky and what Jess and Millie had told me about Natalie. Their spaced-out behaviour sounded similar.

Toby shrugged. 'He was awake.'

'Yeah, but that's a good point.' Jaxon tilted his head at

me. 'My schoolmate's little sister used to sleepwalk. I stayed over at his house a few times, and she completely scared the crap out of me one night. We were asleep in bed in the early hours of the morning. I heard the door open, and she was just standing there. With the lights on behind her, eyes wide open, staring at me. It was really creepy.' He raised his hands and waggled them in the air. 'I asked her what she was doing, and she didn't answer. Then she just went back to bed. Next morning, she didn't remember a thing.'

'He can't have been sleepwalking. He'd already been up for hours,' Phoebe said. 'And in the bar when he smacked that guy, he was with us already, and he'd been awake all night.'

'Maybe Ajay was worried about what he'd done to that other student,' I suggested. 'You know, worried he might be chucked out of uni for it or something. Maybe that's why he took his own life. Sometimes stress can start out as something small and snowball.'

Ivy scrunched up her face. 'He felt guilty about it, sure. He even apologised to the guy he hit the next day. What was his name? Billy, yeah, that was it. But Billy wasn't going to press charges or anything. Ajay didn't even get a warning about it, because no one reported it. It couldn't have been that that made him do it.'

'No, he had to be going through something far worse to set himself on fire,' Phoebe said sadly. 'And we all missed the signs.'

'Was he in a relationship with someone?' I asked. 'Or maybe involved in some other groups or clubs? Maybe there was someone else he spoke to about how he was feeling.' Even though the witness statements said Ajay hadn't been in a relationship with anyone, I had to double-check, considering what else had been missed so far.

'No,' Toby said. 'Ajay said he didn't have time for a relationship. He was studying medicine. He had a full workload. And he never told us about any other groups he belonged to or other friends.'

Ivy nodded in agreement. 'Which was a bit strange, because he *did* seem to be distancing himself a bit from us, didn't he?' She looked at the rest of them. 'He kept disappearing from the house at odd times and being secretive about where he was going.'

'Yeah,' Phoebe said. 'When we asked him about it, he just kind of looked at us blankly and didn't really answer us.'

'Anyway, maybe we shouldn't be talking about this at your first meeting,' Toby said. 'Don't want to put you off the club with all this tragic news.'

'No, it's okay. He was obviously really important to you all. One thing I found helped me when my friend died was talking about it. You have to let the grief out. It's nice that you all knew him and can lean on each other.' I wasn't ready for them to stop talking yet.

'Uh-huh,' Jaxon said. 'That's true, actually. And this is a really supportive group. Everyone loved Ajay.'

'I agree.' Phoebe fiddled with her lip ring again. 'Most of us here know what it's like to repress our thoughts and feelings. I didn't come out to my family until just before I came to uni. All those years of keeping things inside.' She did a mock shiver. 'It's not healthy, is it?'

I took another sip of coffee, which had gone cold. 'I only met Ajay a couple of times, but he seemed like a really nice guy.' I pretended to think about what they'd told me, then said, 'My friend... before she killed herself, she was having really bad nightmares, too. They say dreams are your subconscious trying to tell you something, don't they? She told me about some she was having, but I didn't really pay attention at the time.'

'Ajay was having nightmares, as well,' Toby said. 'I had to wake him up a couple of times. He thought someone was trying to kill him. Thrashing around the bed and screaming, he was.' His gaze drifted towards the clock on the wall. 'Oops, it's about time to wrap up now.'

I downed my coffee and put the cup in the bin at the end of the table.

'Gotta rush.' Jaxon grabbed his backpack from a chair. 'I always forget the time when I'm in here. Nice to meet you, Becky.' He launched forward and gave me a hug. 'Hope to see you again.'

I hugged him back, and he shouted goodbye to the students on their phones then darted out of the door.

'I'm gonna be late to my lecture.' Phoebe pulled a cheeky gurning face. 'Hopefully, we'll see you here tomorrow.'

'Absolutely,' I said. 'I'm meeting some other people in the Terrace Bar tonight if you fancy coming down, too. Millie and Jess, do you guys know them?'

'No,' Phoebe said.

The others shook their heads.

'We can't tonight, though,' Phoebe said. 'We've got a friend's birthday dinner to go to. Maybe we can hook up tomorrow night in the bar?'

'Yeah, sure.'

'Cool. Let's swap numbers.' Phoebe got her phone out of her pocket.

We exchanged phone numbers, and then Phoebe cried,

'Group hug!' and threw herself at all of us, squishing us together in a circle.

Phoebe and Ivy left, and I helped Toby pack up the empty coffee cups and put the milk in a small fridge in the corner of the room.

I stacked chairs against the wall, thinking about the deposits into Ajay's and Vicky's accounts and the cash stashed under Natalie's bed. 'You don't know where I can earn some extra cash, do you? Student loans are a bitch.'

'They are indeed.' He piled one plastic chair on top of another, stood up, and tilted his head as if thinking about it. 'Actually... no, I don't. Sorry. None of us have tried to look for any part-time work.' Toby surveyed the room, making sure it was tidy for whichever group would meet there next. He found a stray coffee cup on the floor next to the beanbags and picked it up.

'So Ajay didn't have a job? That couldn't have been where he was wandering off to?'

'He didn't have time to get a job. Medicine's a full-on course.' He deposited the cup in the bin.

'It must've been really high pressured... Was he having any trouble with the work?'

'No. He was one of those super-brainy people. His parents were Indian, and he spoke fluent Hindi, English, French, and Spanish. You hear about people having photo-graphic memories, but I thought it was a load of crap. Until I met Ajay. He really did have a gift for remembering things. Studying came easy to him. Not like me, which is why I need to love you and leave you. I've got to finish off an essay I've been struggling with.' He walked to the door and opened it.

'No problem.' I followed him out into the corridor, unease creeping through me. The stories of the three students' recent behaviour were troubling me. They were strange and similar, but even though I'd found no tangible connection between them yet, my instinct was telling me something was wrong here. I didn't know what. But I could feel it.

CHAPTER 12

TONI

The female police officer walked towards me, talking into her radio, while her male colleague headed over to the driver of the 4x4, who leaned against the bonnet of his vehicle, his face pale with shock.

'I'm PC Chowdhury. Are you okay? Are you injured?' She looked at the front of my white shirt.

I glanced down and noticed Marcelina's blood smeared on the sleeve. 'No, it's not my blood. I'm just...' I looked in the direction of the ambulance heading off into the distance, its siren dissipating into the air. 'I tried to help her.'

'Did you see what happened?'

'Oh, God. I knew her.' I took a deep breath. 'Well, I didn't really *know* her. But I know who she is. She's a student here.' I tilted my head towards the university's entrance. 'Marcelina Claybourn.'

'How do you spell that?'

I told PC Chowdhury, who wrote it down in her notebook. 'And your name?'

I told her, and she wrote that down, too. 'Did you see the accident?'

'Yes, I did. I'm an associate counsellor at the university. Marcelina came to see me today. It was...' I tucked a stray tendril of hair behind my ear with a shaky hand.

Get a grip, Toni. Breathe.

I took a steadying breath in for five counts, held it, then breathed out for five. 'It was her first appointment, but it didn't go very well. She left after just a few minutes. She was upset, agitated. I went after her to make sure she was okay. I wanted to give her my card so she had my number if she wanted to talk. And by the time I caught up with her, she... she'd rushed into the road in front of that 4x4.' I pointed at the vehicle, even though there was no need. It was obvious what had hit Marcelina from the blood smeared on the dented bonnet. The driver sat in the rear seat of the police car now while the male police officer crouched in front of him, talking and holding a breathalyser in his hand. 'She was upset. If I'd done something differently, she wouldn't have been running away.'

'Did Marcelina know you were following her?'

'She must've done. I was calling her name. I should've backed off.'

She gave me a placatory smile. 'It's not your fault. You couldn't have known this would happen.' She glanced towards the 4x4. 'Did it seem like the driver was going too fast?'

I shrugged. 'I don't think so, no.'

'Was he driving erratically?'

'No. I don't think he had time to react. She just stepped out in front of him, like she didn't see him.' My gaze flicked over to the blood on the tarmac. 'I need to get back to the office so I can get my car keys and drive to the hospital. I want to be there for her. Her family are in Scotland.'

'Sure. I just need your contact details first. A traffic officer will need to come and take a full statement from you soon.'

I gave her my details and walked towards the university's entrance gates, passing a group of students leaning against them.

'Hey, do you know if she's going to be okay?' asked a young mixed-raced guy wearing a red T-shirt and a horrified expression. He had his arm round a black girl with long braids, comforting her as she cried.

'I'm afraid I don't know any more than you at the moment.' I hurried off, retracing my steps back to the counselling services block, concentrating hard on getting my wobbly legs to work.

Breathless, I stepped into the reception and found Janet talking to Phil, the head of Student Counselling Services and my supervisor. She must've told him about Marcelina's abrupt departure and me chasing after her, and the conversation stopped as I headed towards them, both looking at me.

'Is everything all right?' Phil's eyebrows furrowed with concern.

'Not really, no.' I relayed what had happened in one long stream. 'We'll need to contact Marcelina's parents and let them know what's happened. And I need to go to the hospital and be with her. I'll get my car keys and then—'

'Okay. Slow down and take a breath,' Phil said.

'You don't understand. It'll take a while for her family to get here from Scotland, and she shouldn't be on her own.' I didn't have time to think of myself. I needed to go and make sure she was all right. My role in the terrible scene hit me at full impact. If I hadn't chased after Marcelina, maybe she wouldn't have run out into the road.

If I'd said something different to her at the session... if I'd chosen my words more carefully, maybe she'd still be in my office, talking to me, instead of unconscious and battered and possibly fighting for her life. 'The accident was my fault.'

'I *do* understand,' Phil said calmly. 'And it wasn't your fault. It was an accident.'

'Yes, but she was upset. If I hadn't gone after her, she wouldn't have run out into the road.'

'You were trying to help her,' Phil said. 'I would've been concerned if you'd just let an upset client rush off *without* trying to make sure they were okay. But you didn't make her run into the path of an oncoming vehicle.'

I blinked away the tears threatening to form.

'And besides, I'm not sure you're in any fit state to drive. Sit down for a moment.' He led me to one of the plastic chairs used for waiting clients.

'I don't have time,' I muttered.

'Please, just sit.'

I sat next to him, putting Marcelina's black bag on the floor.

'What's the first rule of counselling?' His voice was steady and soothing.

'You're going to give me a supervision session now?' I asked, my jaw dropping open.

He smiled softly. 'Tell me.'

'Self-care.'

'That's right. You're no good to any client if you don't take care of yourself first. You've witnessed a traumatic event, and you need to take a moment for you. To process it. To calm your system down. Your adrenal glands will be working at full whack right now.'

'I'll make you a cup of tea.' Janet disappeared into the small kitchen area behind her desk.

'And another rule of counselling is that you're not responsible for other people's actions.'

'But my job is to help people. I failed her.'

'If Marcelina wasn't ready to talk to you, then you have to accept that. You went after her to make sure she was okay. You didn't force her to run in the direction of the main road.'

'She was trying to get away from me. I should've just stopped. Maybe if I hadn't—'

'Exactly. *Maybe.* We can all run through hundreds of "maybe" scenarios. What you're feeling is guilt, which is normal, but *you* didn't cause her any harm. It happened, and you can't change that. What you need to be wary of is compassion fatigue. We talked about it before in your supervision sessions, remember? You feel too deeply for your clients.'

I looked up at the ceiling, fighting to stay calm and professional when my stomach was churning with fear for Marcelina's condition. I nodded. He was right. I knew that. But the problem with me was that I was an empath. I felt people's pain and emotions deeply. I knew I needed to stop the negative guilty thoughts, but I wasn't ready to just yet. I sat there, feeling awful about the whole thing, trying to slow my racing mind.

'I'll handle speaking to Marcelina's parents, so you don't need to worry about that,' he said. 'We'll also email out our standard offer of the department's services to all students, in case anyone affected by the incident wants to talk about it. When you're feeling a bit calmer, what I would suggest is that you type up some brief notes of the session you had before the accident. You might not remember everything right now because you've had a shock, but that's okay; you can add to it later.'

I glanced at him. 'So you *do* think it's my fault.'

'No, I don't. But you still need to protect yourself.' He said it sympathetically, and yes, he was right again. Basically, he was telling me to cover my arse.

'I *need* to be with Marcelina. I'm supposed to be here to support her, and I let her down. Badly.' I had to apologise to her, if nothing else.

'I understand that, of course. Just type up a summary of the session first, and when you're finished, you'll be in a better state to drive to the hospital. You won't be able to see her right now anyway. They'll be working on her.'

I opened my mouth to argue that we were just wasting time, but he was still my supervisor, and I had to do what he asked. So I nodded and walked into my office.

I put Marcelina's bag on the edge of my desk, sat in front of my laptop, and brought up Marcelina's scant file. It contained only the details I'd known before she arrived.

Janet brought in a cup of tea and put it on my desk with a kind smile. 'It's got two sugars in it.'

I gave her a half smile of thanks but ignored the cup. It was very kind of her, but hot, sweet tea for shock wasn't going to help.

I typed in a brief summary of the session: Marcelina had reported trouble sleeping and nightmares. She'd thought she was sleepwalking. She'd said she wasn't on any medication or using recreational drugs. She was—

I stopped abruptly as I remembered that she'd mentioned hearing voices. Had Marcelina really said that, or had I misheard? I couldn't be certain, so I didn't include it. But what I'd *definitely* heard her say, as she lay bleeding and broken on the ground, were the words 'watching me' and 'shadow man'.

I frowned at the screen, wondering whether to add that into the report. What did that mean? Was she referring to the shadows of the crowd around her as she was disorientated? Was she confused from the head injury she'd suffered? I couldn't be sure, so I didn't put it in.

But being an empath meant I didn't just listen to people's words. I heard their tone, read body language—those subtle movements, expressions on their faces, their eyes. I read their silence, too, and could hear what people didn't say. And what I *was* absolutely sure of was that Marcelina had been scared. Terrified, in fact. And I knew better than most people what real fear looked like.

CHAPTER 13

DETECTIVE BECKY HARRIS

I watched Toby's retreating back and wondered what to do next. I needed some basic supplies, and there was a small supermarket in the union building—the place was like a village. I wandered around the food court then stopped outside a cookie kiosk with an amazing selection that I salivated over before heading to the Co-op to buy a few bits and pieces.

I still had more investigation files to go through, so I made my way back to my accommodation and went into the communal kitchen with my shopping bags. I put away milk, juice, and butter in the fridge on Vicky's shelf. It didn't feel right to scrub off what was left of her name, so I didn't touch the label. I opened Vicky's cupboard and chucked her left-behind cereal in a large plastic bin by the door. After putting away a box of Alpen, a loaf of bread, a jar of peanut butter, and a box of tea bags, I set myself up at the kitchen table and opened the laptop.

As I scoffed down a sandwich, I logged in to the new email account Sutherby had set up for me and sent a quick message to his equally anonymous address he'd given me, updating him on what had happened so far, which wasn't exactly a lot. Then I turned my attention to reading through the statements of the parents of Ajay, Natalie, and Vicky again. None of them had any inkling that their kids had fallen in with a wrong crowd or had been struggling with any particular issues.

None of them thought their kids had any mental health issues. Ajay's parents described him as very intelligent, conscientious, caring, and hard-working. Natalie's dad was dead, but her mum described her as a fun-loving, happy person who enjoyed life and had been looking forward to the whole university experience. Vicky was described as being shy, with only a few close friends, because she felt more comfortable in small groups. Her parents said she was serious and studious.

I thought about the video of Vicky seemingly sleepwalking. Ajay's and Natalie's friends had described the same thing. Was it possible they'd sleepwalked into their tragedies? I knew sleepwalking could be triggered by anxiety and stress, as well as medication and recreational drug use, but was it possible to sleepwalk in the daytime when these tragic incidents had occurred? I turned to the internet again and discovered that in extreme cases, the person affected could carry out complex activities, like driving a car. Most episodes lasted less than ten minutes but could be longer. After waking, the person usually had no memory of the episode or what they'd done, or their memory would be patchy.

It fitted in with Vicky's, Ajay's, and Natalie's described behaviour, apart from one thing. Sleepwalking episodes tended to occur in the first few hours after falling asleep.

They only happened in the daytime if someone was napping or sleeping beforehand.

I double-checked the coroner's officer's reports I'd read before. Prior to Vicky jumping off the stairway, she'd been in the uni's gym for an hour. Other students had seen her working out on the treadmill and rowing machine and in the locker room after, so she couldn't have been asleep before leaving there and the five minutes it took to walk to the lecture theatre block. And it seemed odd that she would go to the gym before she was about to kill herself. Ajay had been awake at home the morning before he took his life. Jaxon, Phoebe, Ivy, and Toby all said they had breakfast together before they'd left him to go into town. It was possible he'd fallen asleep in the thirty minutes after they'd left and before the first signs of the fire took hold of the house, but I thought it was doubtful. And Natalie had been in lectures for two hours before driving into town, where she'd run over the elderly male. Sleepwalking didn't fit.

I'd been working for hours without a single person coming into the kitchen, until finally a short girl with glasses appeared. I recognised her as Vicky's best friend, Tara, who lived in the room opposite what had been Vicky's—the room I was now in. But she wasn't just Vicky's friend; she was a witness. Tara had been in the lecture theatre block when Vicky plunged to her death.

I hastily shut the laptop and glanced up at her. 'Hi.' I waved.

'Oh, hi.' Tara walked in. 'Have you just arrived?'

'Yep. I'm Becky. I just moved into room twenty-four.'

Her face paled, her shoulders tensing. 'Oh, right. Yeah,' she said with hesitance before opening her cupboard door and pulling out a can of tuna and a loaf of bread.

'Sorry, did I say something wrong?'

'No.' She bent over into the fridge and retrieved mayonnaise and butter from one of the shelves. 'It's just...' She stood up and turned around, tears shining in her eyes. 'That was Vicky's room.'

'Yes. I'm sorry about that. I heard about what happened earlier. From Shakia.'

Tara's top lip curled up. 'Shakia's a total bitch. Thinks she's better than everyone else.' She put the mayo and butter on the worktop next to the tuna and bread.

'I know how you probably feel. One of my friends in secondary school killed herself, too. It was a huge shock.' I stood and walked towards the kettle. 'Have you got time for a cup of tea? I was just going to make one.'

'Sure. I was just about to make a sandwich and take it back to my room, but why not? I could do with a break. I've been stuck in there all afternoon, studying.' She sat at the table. 'Just use any of the cups.' She pointed towards a cupboard with the label 'Crockery' on it. 'We wash up as we go. Well, some of us do. Shakia usually leaves her dirty crap piled up for someone else to do.'

I filled the kettle and switched it on. 'Do you take sugar? I didn't get any from the shop.'

'No, thanks.' She paused for a moment then said, 'How come you're starting halfway through the year?'

I repeated my story. Car accident. Broken leg. Coursework at home.

'You're all right now, though?' She looked at my legs as I deposited two mugs on the table and sat opposite her.

'Yeah. It's still a bit sore, but...' I shrugged, took a sip of tea, and watched her pick up the mug with trembling hands, still visibly upset about Vicky. 'It must've been horrible for you, seeing what you did. Have you spoken to anyone—student counselling or someone else? I found, after what happened to my friend, that it was actually good to chat to people.'

She drew in a deep breath through her nose. 'I don't know. Sometimes you just have to get on with things, don't you? Talking won't bring her back.'

'You were close?'

'She was my best mate here. We hit it off straightaway. We had a lot in common. Neither of us came here to get involved with the whole crazy partying, social life scene. We just wanted to learn.' She glanced down at her tea. 'It sounds lame, doesn't it? Like we were both geeky.'

'It doesn't sound lame at all. Everyone's probably here to get something different out of the experience. And learning's supposed to be the main one, right?' I swallowed another mouthful of tea. 'Can I ask what happened?' Although I'd read the witness statements several times now, I didn't like getting information secondhand and still wanted to hear it directly from her. Finding the truth was all about asking the right questions, and a witness's answers could very well change depending on how good the interviewer was at their job—whether they had preconceived opinions or kept an open mind, whether the witness felt comfortable enough with them to have a truly open discussion. One thing Warren Carter had taught me was to never believe anything until I'd confirmed it myself.

She glanced up sharply, as if trying to work out if I was just being nosy, a gossipy bitch, or if I was genuine.

I gave her an encouraging smile. 'That's okay if you don't want to. No pressure.'

She pursed her lips together, looking down at her mug. 'I

still miss her. I don't know why she did it. I feel... actually quite guilty about it. Like I should've seen something or done something.'

'I know. I felt exactly the same when my friend died. I think it's quite normal to feel like that. But I learned eventually that it wasn't my fault. It's not yours, either.'

'Doesn't feel like that right now.'

I nodded. 'I know. It's like you micro-analyse everything. I kept thinking if I'd really paid attention when she did this or said that, maybe I could've worked out what she was planning to do and stop her.'

Her eyes lit up with recognition. 'That's *exactly* how it is.'

'Shakia told me Vicky was having nightmares and sleepwalking. Do you think she was stressed about her coursework? Or worried about anything in particular?'

'Don't listen to Shakia. She's full of crap.' She brought her feet up to the edge of the chair and wrapped her arms around her shins before resting her chin on her knees. 'But that is right. Vicky never mentioned being stressed or worried about anything, and we told each other everything. At least, I thought we did. That's why it's such a shock. She wasn't depressed. She didn't have any problems that she told me about. But the last month or so, she was acting a bit weird.'

'In what way?'

'She'd disappear for hours at a time. Miss lectures. When I asked her where she'd been, she was really vague. She fobbed me off by saying she couldn't remember where she'd been. I mean, if she had other friends she wanted to hang out with, that was absolutely fine with me. I'd rather she was just honest with me, but it was like...' She glanced down at the floor.

'Like what?'

Her head tilted from side to side, as if weighing up how to describe it. 'I don't know. It was kind of like she believed herself that she didn't remember. Or maybe she was just good at lying. I don't know. Anyway, she'd been a bit distant for a few weeks before it happened, as if she was cutting herself off from me. I tried to ask her if I'd upset her somehow. I wanted her to tell me if I had. But she just said no.'

'Do you think she was taking some kind of drug? That might account for how she'd been acting.'

She looked up at me. 'No. She wasn't into that kind of thing. She didn't even hardly drink.'

'Was she in a relationship with anyone? Maybe someone broke her heart, and that's why she took her life.'

'No, she wasn't. At least, not that she told me anyway. But I did see her going into the medical block a couple of times after hours, which seemed a bit strange, because it was late at night when it should've been shut up.' She planted her feet back on the floor, leaning her elbows on the table.

I raised an eyebrow. Was that a possible connection? Ajay had been a medical student.

'The first time was about nine o'clock one night,' she said. 'I just saw her as she went into the Watling Centre. Haven't got a clue who she was seeing as most of the lights were off, and I would've thought everyone would've gone home. The next time was a bit later in the evening a week or so after. There was only one light on in the building in a top office.'

'Maybe she was seeing a counsellor or doctor there. If she'd been feeling depressed, maybe she went to talk to someone about it.'

'No. Student Counselling Services is in another building. And I doubt it was to see a doctor. We don't have GPs on site.'

So who had Vicky been seeing late at night? I thought back to Jess and Millie telling me that they'd seen Natalie with an older guy on campus who they thought she was involved with and who was most likely a tutor. Coincidence? Or not? 'Maybe Vicky was in a relationship with one of the tutors or professors here. It wouldn't be the first time a student had a relationship with a peer. Maybe she didn't want to tell you.'

'Maybe, but I think she would've told me. I wouldn't have judged her.'

'Did you ask Vicky about seeing her?'

She glanced down at her mug, tears forming in her eyes again. 'Yeah. She denied it was her. She said I must've mistaken her for someone else. But I was certain it *was* her.' She sniffed and blinked for a few moments, taking time to compose herself again. 'It's actually good to chat to someone who understands. I didn't want to go to student counselling about how I was feeling.'

I nodded sympathetically, feeling a stab of guilt that I was lying to all these people, but if it prevented another death, that was all that mattered.

'That day... the day she... you know... I was supposed to meet her in the café for lunch after she'd been to the gym. But I spotted her before I got to the union. She was going into the lecture theatre building, so I went in after her. I called out to her before she went inside, but she probably didn't hear me. I followed her in, trying to catch up with her. One of the lectures had just finished, though, and people were piling down the stairs. So I waited at the bottom for them to get down instead of trying to push my way up through them.

'I lost her for a bit in the crowd, but then I saw her at the top of the stairs, in front of the railings. She kind of... She had this strange look on her face. Like she wasn't really there. Like she was miles away. In some kind of trance. But she had this weird smile on her face. I watched her from the bottom of the stairs as she climbed over the railings up the top. It was like it happened really quick but at the same time in slow motion.' Tara shook her head then rubbed at her face. 'That doesn't even make sense.' She laughed harshly.

'It does to me.'

'I didn't know what she was doing. It took a while for my mind to process it, because climbing over the railings isn't something you see every day. And by the time I did, she'd just...' Tara blinked a few times, and a lone tear slid down her cheek. 'Vicky put her arms above her head in the air, like she was diving into a pool, and just launched herself off.'

'I'm really sorry. It was horrible that you actually saw it all.' I put my hand on her forearm and gave it a gentle squeeze.

'Thanks.' Her voice cracked.

'She was lucky to have such a good friend. Do you have other friends that knew her who you could talk to, as well?'

She shook her head. 'Not really. We hung out with other people sometimes, but it was mostly just me and her together really.' She tilted her head, a frown pinching her eyebrows. 'Do you know what I really can't get my head around? She was scared of heights. She even hated some of the lecture halls because of how they're tiered up high. She told me she couldn't even stand on a ladder without crapping herself. It's strange that she... that she made herself do it like that. If I was going to kill myself, I'd do something painless like take tablets and fall asleep.'

I thought about that. Could a person suddenly overcome a fear just as they were about to end everything? 'Did you know Natalie Wheeler?'

She scrunched up her face, thinking. 'No.'

'What about Ajay Banerjee?'

She frowned. 'He's the student who killed himself, too?'

I nodded.

'He set himself on fire in his house-share, didn't he? That's a horrible way to do it.' She shuddered.

'Do you think Vicky knew him?'

She shook her head. 'No. I don't think so. I'm sure she would've mentioned him to me if she had.' She blinked and wiped at her moist eyes. She sniffed and sat upright. 'Anyway, I'm sorry for blabbing on. Let's change the subject.'

'You don't need to apologise to me. If you need to talk, you know where to find me.'

'Thanks.'

I swallowed the dregs of my tea. 'I've been looking at some of the clubs and societies to join. Can you recommend any? Maybe you or Vicky went to some?'

Tara went to the worktop and started making her sandwich. 'I've done some of the fitness classes on the active student programme. Me and Vicky went to the Buddhist Meditation Society once, but we never ended up going back. That's it, though.'

That clanged an alarm bell in my head. Ajay had dabbled in Buddhism before. Had he also gone to the society's meetings? I opened my welcome pack next to my laptop and flipped through to the Buddhist Meditation Society's info. They had an hour's guided meditation twice a day at

7.00 a.m. and 4.30 p.m. It was getting on for 5.30 p.m., so I'd missed both of them. There was no evidence so far that Vicky had joined some kind of cult or spent any significant amount of time with anyone other than Tara, but it could fit the religious element of a cult dressed up as a self-awareness or self-improvement group.

'Thanks for the suggestion. Maybe I'll go and check it out tomorrow morning.' I closed the welcome pack. 'You don't know where I could earn a bit of extra cash, do you? It would be nice to get a bit of beer money while I'm here.'

'Sorry, no,' she said over her shoulder, pressing two slices of bread together as tuna oozed out the middle. 'Vicky and I never bothered looking for anything like that. Got too much on with the coursework.'

I wondered again where the money the three students had in their possession had come from as I took both mugs to the sink and washed them up before returning them to the crockery cupboard.

Shakia sauntered into the kitchen then. 'Well, well, well, the two little nub nubs are getting very cosy together.' She looked down her nose at both of us.

Tara rolled her eyes at me and ignored Shakia.

I didn't have a clue what 'nub nub' meant, but from Shakia's tone and body language, it was clearly meant to be derogatory.

Tara picked up her sandwich and said to me, 'I've got more studying to do, but it was nice to chat to you.'

'Was it something I said?' Shakia smirked and reached into her cupboard to pull out a can of black-eyed beans.

Tara ignored her and walked out of the door.

'Yeah, bye.' Shakia did a sarcastic wave at Tara.

I fought the urge to call her out on her rudeness and said

a quick 'See you later' to Shakia before catching up with Tara along the corridor. 'What's a nub nub?' I asked.

'It means a newcomer or someone lame or inadequate.' She glared in the direction of the kitchen. 'She's *so* rude.'

'Sticks and stones, and all that. Listen, I'm heading to the Terrace Bar soon with some people I just met. Jess and Millie. Do you know them?'

Tara shook her head as we carried on walking.

'Do you want to come? I'll buy you a beer. It might cheer you up.' I stopped outside my room.

She glanced at the door to what was once Vicky's room, her face clouding over again. 'Thanks, but I'm not in the mood. See you later.'

CHAPTER 14

TONI

The parking situation at the hospital was ridiculous because I arrived during visiting hours. I drove around for twenty minutes before someone finally left and I could grab their space. Phil had offered to drive me there, but I'd declined, asking instead that he take over my remaining clients for the afternoon so I didn't leave anyone in the lurch. Plus, I was worried the office may well be even busier than usual if any of the students had witnessed the accident or knew Marcelina and needed to talk things through. And besides, it was my responsibility. My fault. No matter what Phil said.

The Accident and Emergency waiting area was packed with people. I stood in the queue for the reception and tapped my foot as the line shuffled forward excruciatingly slowly. When I finally got to the front, I asked a harassed-looking woman in a uniform where Marcelina had been taken.

'Are you a relative?'

'No.' I explained I was a representative of the university and that Marcelina had no family in the area at the moment.

She tapped Marcelina's name into a computer then studied the screen for a few moments. 'She's waiting to have some scans done. Take a seat in the waiting room, and I'll get someone to come and talk to you when they're free.'

'Thanks.' I stepped away and looked at the waiting area, where there was no hope of getting a seat. Instead, I leaned against the glass window and looked outside, into the ambulance bay, where some paramedics were bringing in another patient.

I fidgeted from one foot to the other for a long time until my phone rang.

I pulled it out of my bag and answered, 'Hi, Mum,' before making my way out of the building into the fresh air, where it was quieter.

'Hi. How's everything going? Are you still working, or have you got time for a chat?'

I didn't want to worry her, so I didn't tell her what had happened. My mum also knew all too well about guilt. My dad had died in combat before I was born, so it had always been just the two of us, and we were really close. For years, she'd blamed herself and Mitchell, a member of his SAS team, for what had happened to Dad. Guilt strike one.

When I'd been kidnapped by some brutal men, that had taken her personal guilt to a whole new level because she'd blamed herself again. But it was Mitchell she'd turned to in order to find me. Mitchell had rescued me. And in the aftermath, she'd barely wanted to let me out of her sight. It was only now, years after that horrific event, that she felt comfortable enough to let me go without being scared to death something would happen to me again.

When I'd taken the associate counsellor job forty miles away from where we lived, she'd finally realised I had to fly the nest and start my own life without her looking over my shoulder. She'd also worked through her guilt and anger over Mitchell, and the enemy had become the saviour. He'd saved me, but he was also a lifeline to her, too. They'd both been through trauma no one should ever have to suffer, and together, they were healing each other. One thing I was certain of was that if it hadn't been for Mitchell, I'd be dead. He'd been best friends with my dad, and they'd served together in the Regiment, risking their lives together, and even though Dad hadn't returned from his tour of duty but Mitchell had, I loved him to bits. Mitchell had become the father I'd never had—an unofficial godfather—and I was ecstatic that he and Mum were now in a relationship. They both deserved happiness. And the last thing I wanted to do was spoil things for them with my own problems, so I just said, 'Yeah, everything's fine. I'm learning a lot. The whole team is really supportive. And I've got quite a few clients already.'

'And how's the flat? The security intercom on the front doors and your alarm are still working, aren't they?'

I smiled. 'Yes, Mum.' Bless her, she couldn't help herself.

'Because if they're not, you need to report it straightaway.'

'Don't worry, I will do. How's Mitchell?'

'Oh, he's fine, love. He's doing the garden. He's planting some flowers in the borders. You know he can't keep still.' She laughed.

They were living together now. Mitchell had sold his own property the year before, and they'd bought a new house as a couple. Since then, he'd thrown himself into decorating and sprucing up the garden, hoping to put their own signature on the place. I smiled as I thought of the solidly built ex-elite special forces soldier on his hands and knees, planting daisies in the garden.

'He says hi, by the way,' Mum said.

'Say hi back.'

'Maybe you can come up for the weekend? It's supposed to be a scorcher. We could do a BBQ.'

'Yeah, um... maybe.' I glanced through the glass doors into A&E. I couldn't go off and have fun until I knew Marcelina would be okay. 'Can I call you later?'

'Yeah, of course. Love you.'

'Love you, too.' I hung up and stepped back into the waiting room.

The air was muggy with a strong stench of stale sweat. My throat was dry, and I had the beginnings of a headache behind my right temple, most likely an effect of the adrenaline that had long since worn off. There was a vending machine in the corridor, so I bought a bottle of water and drank thirstily. I'd just deposited the empty bottle in a bin when I heard my name being called from behind.

I swung around and saw a female doctor in a white coat striding down the corridor. 'I'm Toni,' I told her.

She stopped in front of me. 'Hello, I'm Dr Fellows. I'm treating Marcelina Claybourn.'

'How is she?'

'You're with the university?'

'Yes.' I showed her my uni ID card and explained again how Marcelina had no family here yet and that I was her counsellor. I tried to sound professional and assured, but I could hear the slight tremor in my voice.

'Did you leave her next-of-kin details with reception?'

'Yes. My boss was going to inform her parents of what's happened.'

'Okay, good. Well, her minor injuries consist of a broken leg and quite a bit of bruising. But she also suffered a head injury. She's unconscious, and we think there's some swelling in her brain. We're just waiting for her to have some scans before we'll be able to ascertain more.'

'When I saw her earlier, she mentioned some episodes where she'd had what sounded like blackouts. She described it as lost time.' I gave her the examples Marcelina had told me. I didn't feel as if I was breaking patient confidentiality, because it might be pertinent to her treatment.

'Thanks for letting me know. I'll add that to her notes.'

'Can I just go and see her quickly?'

Dr Fellows pursed her lips, hesitating for a moment, then said, 'I don't see why not. But just for a few minutes.' She guided the way along a corridor. 'It looks like she—' Dr Fellows was interrupted by her name being called from behind.

We both turned around.

'Appendicitis, suspected rupture,' a paramedic called out, striding alongside a trolley. A boy on it was howling and doubled over in pain.

Dr Fellows pointed further along the corridor and said to me, 'Marcelina's in trauma room one. Up there.' She diverted her attention to the child and paramedic and told them to use trauma room three, before disappearing with them into a private room to our right.

As I walked up the corridor, I found an open bay of beds, some with patients fully clothed and conscious on them, some with curtains around them. Trauma room one was a private room on the opposite side.

An alarm sounded from somewhere. Raised voices with shouts of 'We need a resus trolley!' rang out. Nurses appeared from one room and hurried to where the shouts for assistance were coming from.

I paused outside Marcelina's room. The door was open, but curtains had been pulled around the bed area so I couldn't see her. I entered the room as a male doctor in a white coat stepped out from behind the curtain.

'Dr Fellows said it was okay for me to see her for a minute,' I said. 'Are you treating Marcelina, as well?'

'I'm Dr Lahey, consultant neurosurgeon.' He moved away from the bed, sliding his hands into the pockets of his white lab coat with a grave expression on his face.

'How's she doing?'

'It's too early to say, I'm afraid. We're monitoring her carefully. Are you a relative?'

By now, I almost wished I had it tattooed on my forehead. 'No, I'm her student counsellor at St Albans University.'

'Right.' He nodded. 'Well, she's in good hands. We're going to do everything we can for her. Don't stay too long, okay?' He slipped out of the room.

I moved towards the curtain and pulled it aside. Marcelina lay on her left side, a blanket covering her body. A gauze pad was taped to the wound on her forehead, just above her hairline. She had a small cut about one centimetre long on the back of her neck, oozing fresh blood that was dotted on the pillow, some cuts on her face, and a lot of swelling and abrasions on her arms and hands. Her skin was pale, her short blonde hair making her look even more deathly white. The ventilator and various other machines she was hooked up to emitted steady beeping sounds with numbers flashing on a screen.

I walked around to the right side of the bed so I could

face her. Her right arm was outside the blanket; an IV drip connected to her vein with a cannula. I gently took hold of her hand. It felt cold and weightless in mine. She looked like a broken bird.

'Marcelina? Can you hear me?'

She didn't respond. I fought the tears threatening to form and swallowed the lump in my throat as I carried on talking to her. Hopefully, she could hear me somewhere in there. Hopefully, she'd know there was someone who cared about her and that she wasn't alone.

A little while later, Dr Fellows came in the room and pulled the curtain back. She looked at Marcelina then looked at me with a concerned frown furrowing her brow. 'What's going on?'

'I'm sorry?'

'She's supposed to be on her back. Did you move her?' Her voice was sharp, the frown deepening as she carefully turned Marcelina so she was lying on her back. 'All her tubes will be compromised if she's on her side, plus, it's not a good position for her to be in with her injuries.' Dr Fellows checked the monitors attached to the tubes. Pressed a button on one of the machines. 'Everything seems okay. But...' She looked back at me, the frown now morphed into a suspicious glare. 'I doubt she could've turned over on her own. She's heavily sedated.'

My eyes widened. 'All I did was hold her hand. She was like this when I came in.'

Her eyes narrowed, as if she didn't believe me.

'Maybe the other doctor moved her,' I said.

'Which doctor?'

'The one who was in here when I arrived. Dr Lahey.'

She picked up the chart hanging off the end of Marcelina's bed and flicked through some pages, shaking her head. Looking puzzled, she muttered to herself about consultants not bothering to record their visits. I glanced at the chart as she wrote down that Dr Lahey had attended.

Then she said, 'She's going for her scans in a minute, so you'll need to leave now.'

I let myself out of the room, sending up a silent prayer that whatever happened next for Marcelina would be good news.

CHAPTER 15

DETECTIVE BECKY HARRIS

B efore I headed to the bar, all I had time for was a quick change of clothes and a hair-taming routine that lasted longer than I usually subjected myself to. No matter what I did, my crazy waves had a mind of their own.

I undid my ponytail and tousled my hair with lots of product until it resembled something slightly better than a nest of rats' tails. The waves had gone straggly, and my split ends needed a serious trim, but I never could stand wasting time in a hair salon.

When packing to come here, I'd been stressing about what to wear. Most of my clothes were either work suits or casual stuff. In the end, I'd decided to be as generic as possible, so I dressed in a vest top, skinny cut-off jeans, and a pair of flip-flops, before slapping on a bit of lipstick, which was the usual extent of my makeup repertoire.

It was hot and humid as I stepped outside the accommodation block and walked to the union. There were plenty of students around, and I said hi to a few as I walked past. So far, everyone except Shakia had been really friendly. What she'd done, filming Vicky in the kitchen, was bullying. I wouldn't put it past her to have shown the video to many other people, either. Had Vicky found out and been embarrassed and upset to the point of killing herself because of it? That was possible. Sometimes it was the smaller things that triggered people to finally snap.

The terrace where I'd sat earlier for lunch was heaving with students. Most of the tables were full, and people sat on the grassy area nearby, nursing drinks. Laughter and chatter rang out as I approached the picnic tables, looking for Jess and Millie. A few people caught my eye and either smiled, looked away, or checked me out. I spotted the guy who'd given me the active-student classes flyer earlier sitting cross-legged in a cluster of people, looking fit and sexy. He saw me watching, waved, and grinned at me. I grinned back and felt a fleeting feeling of excitement as a hot flush crept up my neck. I hadn't been on a date with anyone since I'd split up with Ian. Just the thought of it scared the crap out of me. But now I was here, having very naughty reactions to a student. God, I must be bloody hormonal. Or it was the hot weather. Even though I was only about ten years older than these people, I felt a lifetime older. I'd seen too much horror in my career.

I found Jess and Millie at one of the tables and walked over.

'Oh, hey, you came. Cool,' Jess said. 'The band's really good, but they don't start till nine.'

'Great. I'm going to the bar. Anyone want a top-up?' I pointed to their glasses.

'Vodka and Diet Coke for me, please.' Millie wiggled her glass in the air.

'Bottle of Kopparberg, thanks. Any flavour,' Jess said.

'Be right back.' I headed past the crowded tables to the

inside bar area, which was more or less empty. A guy in his early twenties with tattooed arms stood behind the bar, serving a couple of girls. He sauntered over when he'd finished.

'Hi, what can I get you?'

I gave him the girls' orders and got a lime and soda for myself. I had to keep a clear head, so there would be little or no alcohol for me. As he was sorting out my drinks, I asked him if he knew of any work going behind the bar or anywhere else that paid cash in hand, but he just shrugged and said no as he put the drinks on the bar in front of me.

I handed over some money and was pleasantly surprised to get a decent amount of change. Subsidised drinks, a student's dream.

I headed back outside and sat down at the table. Jess and Millie were talking about the lecture I'd been in earlier.

'What do you think, Becky?' Millie asked.

'About what?' I asked.

'Thomas Hardy. "The Darkling Thrush". Creating sadness through imagery.'

'Uh...' I trailed off, searching around in my brain for something studenty to say and coming up empty. I wasn't a big reader in my real life. I didn't have time for it. When I wasn't at work, I was sleeping, especially after my promotion to DS and the big cases I'd handled recently. Probably the last time I'd read a book was on my honeymoon with Ian, and that had been *Bridget Jones's Diary*, hardly on a par with the required reading for an English literature course.

'Me and Millie are having an argument about the second stanza. What do you think of it?' Jess rolled her eyes in a good-natured way. '"The Century's corpse outleant, His crypt the cloudy canopy, The wind his death-lament".'

I tilted my head, wondering what to say. 'I think I preferred "We will destroy Gotham. And then, when it is done and Gotham is ashes… then you have my permission to die".'

Jess and Millie gave me a confused frown.

I grinned. 'It's from the film *The Dark Knight Rises*. Tom Hardy.'

'Ha ha.' Jess pointed the neck of her cider bottle at me with a grin. 'Funny.' She raised it in the air. 'Here's to Thomas *and* Tom Hardy.'

Millie chinked her glass against Jess's bottle, and I did the same.

Jess leaned over the table and whispered to Millie, 'Oh my God, don't look now, but Curtis is over there.'

Millie ran her hands through her hair to make sure it looked perfect then licked her lips. 'Where?'

Jess angled her head to the left.

Millie tried to do a surreptitious glance over, but it looked obvious to me. 'He's so peng,' she whispered back.

I didn't even have a clue what that meant, but by the look on her face, it was obviously good. I glanced over at who they were looking at. It was the mixed-race guy I'd been admiring before, now deep in earnest conversation with a group of friends.

'Why don't we go to the HIIT class tomorrow?' Millie said. 'He's always there.'

'What time's it on?' Jess asked.

'Eleven.'

'Can't. Got a lecture, remember?' Jess said.

Millie pouted. 'Yawn. He could HIIT me up any day.' She cackled drunkenly, and I wondered how long they'd been there before I arrived. Still, it worked in my favour. Drunk people had loose tongues.

Curtis looked over and caught us watching.

'Oh, shite, he saw us.' Millie giggled, and we all looked away.

'Why don't you go and talk to him?' I asked.

She shook her head. 'No way. I'm too embarrassed.'

The angst of teenage love. I remembered it well. But the angst wasn't just reserved for youngsters. After my on-off marriage with Ian had hit the rocks for the final time, I'd been feeling really down. Opposing thoughts knocked around in my brain, either worrying I'd never meet anyone else again, or worrying that I would and it would end with a repeat disaster. I shook my thoughts away. This investigation was helping to keep my mind firmly off Ian and my new single status, and I wanted it to stay that way, thank you very much.

I tried to work out how to get Natalie back into the conversation. Since they'd mentioned seeing her with someone who was a professor or tutor, I said, 'Curtis is a bit too young for me. I've actually got a thing for older guys.'

'Urgh!' Millie groaned. 'How old?'

I shrugged and laughed. 'This might sound weird, but I've got a thing for grey hair. Maybe I've got a bit of a tutor fantasy going on.'

Jess looked at me like I was mad. 'I think Natalie did, too.'

'Oh, yeah, you said you thought she was seeing someone older, didn't you?' I said casually then took a sip of my drink. I swallowed then waited.

'He *was* a tutor,' Jess whispered. 'When I asked her who it was I'd seen her with, she said he was called Professor... what was it?' She waved her hand in the air as she thought.

'Cain! That was it, I think. Professor Cain.' She raised her eyebrows and wiggled them suggestively. 'She swore nothing was going on between them, though, but she looked all embarrassed about us spotting her with him.'

'Do you know what subject he teaches?' I asked.

They both shrugged.

Tutors and students having relationships happened all the time, the whole world over. But if Natalie was secretly seeing someone, what other secrets had she kept from her friends? I noted the name in my head and then turned the conversation in a new direction. 'Before I got here, I was reading about some weird cults and societies that have hazing rituals in unis. They don't have anything like that here, do they?'

Millie's lips parted with surprise. 'Not that I know of. You mean like initiation ceremonies and all that? That's more like from America, isn't it? Sororities and fraternities and stuff?'

'You mean a cult like that Waco thingy?' Jess asked me.

'Yeah,' I said. 'Apparently, there are quite a few in the UK. And they like preying on students.'

'Seriously?' Jess shuddered. 'I thought that was just an American thing, too. Sounds freaky.'

'So you don't know anyone who's been approached by someone dodgy here then?' I asked.

They both shook their heads.

'Phew. That's a relief.' I put a hand to my chest. 'I'm thinking of trying the Buddhist Meditation Society tomorrow. But I was a bit worried I was going to get brainwashed!' I laughed, making light of it.

They laughed back.

'We've only tried the active student classes,' Millie said.

'They're just like going to a regular sports club class, though. No whackos there, thankfully.' Millie took a swig of vodka.

'Yeah, and we only go because Curtis goes to loads of them and helps organise them.' Jess snorted. 'I couldn't walk for a week after the circuit training class.'

I thought back to the statements about Natalie that said she didn't belong to any clubs, but I wondered if she'd been to the fitness classes, too. It hadn't been mentioned, so I said as casually as possible, 'Do you usually go to the classes in a group? Or is it just you two?'

'Just me and Millie,' Jess said. 'Natalie was never into the whole exercise thing, so she never used to come with us.'

I glanced around. The place was getting busier. The band inside the bar area were doing a sound check.

I approached the subject of Jess or Millie knowing where I could earn a bit of extra cash, but neither did.

Millie downed the rest of her drink. 'Right. My round. Same again?' She jumped to her feet and then swayed, gripping the edge of the table. 'Oops.' She giggled.

'I'm not going to have to carry you home like Natalie, am I?' Jess said to her.

Millie giggled. 'It's uni. We're supposed to be permanently drunk. What you having, Becky?'

I could hardly ask for a non-alcoholic drink while I was supposed to be blending in. Besides, the measures were small, and one shot wasn't going to affect me. 'Vodka, lime, and soda, please.'

Millie took my glass and weaved through the tables towards the bar.

'Was Natalie a big drinker then?' I asked.

'She liked to have fun. She'd get drunk but not wasted. Although one night we were here, and she was really out of it. We were inside.' Jess pointed towards the bar. 'We'd only had a couple of drinks, and Millie and me got chatting to a couple of people. Then, next thing we knew, Natalie had disappeared. We went to look for her when she didn't come back and found her slumped on the floor outside of her accommodation block's front door in a right daze. We asked her what had happened, and she didn't have a clue. She didn't seem drunk. She wasn't slurring her words or anything. She was just really kind of... I don't know, in a trance almost. Didn't know where she'd been. We thought she'd just drunk too much on an empty stomach.'

'It happens,' I said. But that was starting to sound suspiciously familiar about all three students... that they'd been found by friends, dazed and disorientated, in a trance-like state, doing things and saying things they appeared to have no memory of. 'Do you think someone could've spiked her drink?'

'I doubt it. She always drank bottles of beer, and we're not stupid about leaving our drinks around. But it was strange, because one minute she was fine, and the next, she'd just disappeared and was all weird.'

Millie stumbled back, and we chatted and drank. Chatted and drank. I brought up Natalie into the conversation whenever I could angle it in there, but I learned nothing more. The band started, and it was too loud to talk anymore, so they watched them while I kept an eye on the crowd in case Tara had changed her mind, but she didn't appear.

As the band took a break, Curtis came over to our table and rested his hands on the wooden top.

'Hi, ladies.' He smiled warmly at us.

Millie glanced up at him with a dazed grin on her face. 'Hi, Curtis!' She slapped a hand gently on his forearm. She was quite drunk and obviously throwing off her inhibitions. 'What'da'ya think of the band?' she slurred.

'Yeah, they're smart.' He glanced down at her hand, his lips quirking up into what looked like an embarrassed smile. He obviously knew the effect he had on women but seemed quietly flattered by it rather than arrogant. 'Can I entice you to the HIIT class tomorrow?'

'Yes!' Millie said instantly.

'Sounds too painful for me,' I said.

He laughed.

'We can't. We've got a lecture.' Jess rolled her eyes at Millie, most likely because she'd already told her that earlier.

Millie pouted. 'Boring.'

Curtis shrugged. 'No problem. Maybe see you at circuit training then?'

Millie put her forefinger in the air. 'Yeah. I *love* circuit training.'

'Cool.' He tapped the table, his friendly demeanour turning serious, the smile sliding off his face. 'Did you hear about the car accident outside the uni earlier?'

I sat up straighter. *Another* car accident? 'What happened?'

'Marcelina was crossing the road and got hit by a car. That's what was happening when I had to leave suddenly earlier,' he said to me. 'They took her to hospital.'

Millie gasped. 'Oh, no. That's bad. Who's Marcelina?'

'She's a student here. She lives in my block.'

'Don't know her,' Jess said. 'But that's horrible.'

Millie shook her head. 'I hope she's going to be okay.'

'Yeah, me, too.' Curtis rubbed the back of his neck as he looked down at the ground.

'That's awful,' I said, wondering if it was something else suspicious I should look into.

A pained frown morphed across Curtis's forehead. 'Yeah, she was just lying on the ground, unconscious. Me and some of her friends tried to go and see her, but they wouldn't let us in to visit yet. She's in a coma.'

'Do you know who hit her?' I asked.

'Some old guy in an SUV. He was proper shaken up. Police came and everything.' He sighed. 'Anyway, maybe I'll catch you later.' He turned and walked towards his friends, Millie ogling after his retreating back, tight T-shirt rippling over obviously well-toned muscles.

I got up. 'Sorry, I need to go, too. It was lovely to catch up, though. Thanks again for the invite.'

'Yeah. No worries. See you tomorrow at the lecture.' Jess waved.

'Laters,' Millie said then hiccupped, slapping a hand over her face.

As the band started up again, I walked away from the terrace until I was far enough away to be able to hear properly. I sat down on a bench in front of the Watling Centre medical block—the place Tara had seen Vicky disappear into late at night—and called the one and only number programmed into the burner phone.

'Hi, sir,' I said quietly to Sutherby, even though no one was around.

'Evening. I got your email. Thanks for that.'

'I don't have much more for you right now, but I just heard something about an RTA outside the uni earlier. Do you know about it? I was wondering if it might be related somehow.'

'I haven't heard anything. I'll check it out and get back to you soonest.'

'Thanks, sir.' I hung up and stared at the front of the Watling Centre. All the lights were off, apart from one in a top-floor window.

Why had Vicky been going there out of hours? I was chewing on my lip, trying to work out if it was relevant, when someone exited the front door. He wore jeans and a hoodie with the hood pulled up, which was weird, considering it was about twenty-seven degrees and humid out. I got a glimpse of his face before he tucked his head down, hands stuffed in his pockets, and walked along the path away from me.

It was hard to put an age on him, but he was probably anywhere between thirty and forty. He could've been either a mature student or a member of the teaching staff. His long nose tapered to a blunt end, and he had defined cheekbones and a squarish chin. His physique beneath his clothes looked well-built. I couldn't see his eyes properly in the low sodium lighting of the pathway, and his hair was hidden by the hood. But Hoodie Guy had sparked my interest. He moved like a panther, with an air of the hunter about him. I'd studied hours of CCTV footage from crimes, watching suspects and offenders. Police officers learned to read body language well, and I thought I was pretty good at it. That guy had been furtive, with a definite element of something suspicious about him.

I thought about Natalie possibly having a secret relationship with Professor Cain. Could that be why Vicky was visiting the Watling Centre late at night, too, because she was also seeing a member of the teaching staff and trying to keep it quiet? Meeting him in his office after everyone else had gone home. While it wasn't illegal for a tutor or professor to have a consensual relationship or sex with a student who was over eighteen and there would be a code of practice in place here to protect the welfare of both parties, it could still be risky. The obvious inequality of power at play could make the student very vulnerable, which meant a fine line between mutual consent and sexual harassment. How easy would it be for a student to reject a tutor? Would their grades suffer because of it? And I was betting any member of staff who did make a play for their students didn't do it as a one-off. There would most likely be repeat scenarios with newer, younger students. Was it possible there was a sexual predator on the staff here?

I got up and walked away, still full of questions and with little evidence to answer them.

CHAPTER 16

TONI

I let myself into my small rented apartment. It had come fully furnished, but I'd bought some things to put my own stamp on it and turn it into my cosy sanctuary—colourful throws on the worn sofa, prints of positive, uplifting quotes and hangings on the walls, plants, candles and incense burners, and my huge collection of research books that now filled a brand-new bookcase in the lounge. The main reason I'd taken it in the first place was the good security system—a video intercom, an alarm, and steel doors with heavy-duty locks. I still wasn't leaving anything to chance, though. After the kidnapping, I'd learned Krav Maga self-defence. Plus, Mitchell had taught me some of his SAS techniques. Still, nothing would ever be enough to stop Mum worrying about me.

I kicked off my shoes before heading straight to the kitchen area in the corner of the open-plan living space, where I put Marcelina's bag and my own handbag on the worktop.

I'd waited around until Marcelina's scans had been completed and Dr Fellows gave me an update. It didn't look good. Marcelina had widespread swelling on her brain and was in a coma. But no tumour or brain abnormality had been discovered that could've caused Marcelina to black out. She'd been moved to the critical care unit, where she could be monitored carefully before they decided whether to operate to relieve the pressure.

I grabbed a bottle of beer from the fridge and took a long swig, staring through the kitchen window to the car park below. For the first time since I could remember, I felt lonely. I'd always been the geeky loner girl at school, burying my head in a book or research rather than hitting the pubs, getting drunk, or hanging out with friends. I always felt more comfortable in small groups, and I'd had one close friend throughout high school, who was now working back in my hometown in Buckinghamshire. We texted and phoned regularly, but I hadn't made any new friends here yet.

Mum had always called me studious, conscientious, and ahead of my years. Other students thought I was weird. They'd called me a boring nerd, along with many other ruder versions throughout my life, but I didn't care. Yes, I was serious. Yes, I was focused and had goals. But trivial stuff just wasn't in my makeup. I couldn't worry about things like what I looked like, what I wore, or who a current celebrity was sleeping with, when there were far too many important injustices and atrocities going on in the world. Like a lot of empaths, I was an introvert who needed alone time. I didn't just feel people's pain and energy; I absorbed it, and that could be overwhelming sometimes. Other people's suffering stripped away a little piece of my soul, and the pieces stacked up, so I needed time by myself to reset my energy levels. But now I truly did feel on my own, and I didn't like it.

'Snap out of it, Toni,' I said. 'You're just upset.' I took another swig of beer and turned away from the window.

I thought about making a sandwich but knew I couldn't eat anything with the guilt still lying heavy in my stomach. I kept seeing the point of impact when Marcelina's body hurtled through the air and bounced on the ground. I knew I should practice what I preached about guilt in all the counselling sessions I did with clients, but I still felt at least partially responsible for what had happened to Marcelina.

All my life, I'd wanted to help people, to help them heal themselves. I'd been working towards this goal for years, and the main area of counselling I wanted to get into was helping young victims of crime. But I'd failed Marcelina with drastic consequences. She'd taken the first step by asking for help, and I'd let her down. She hadn't felt comfortable enough to talk things through so she could've left my office feeling calmer, instead of highly distressed. Maybe I didn't know how to say the right things to clients. Maybe I wasn't cut out to do this job at all. A tsunami of self-doubt and fears of incompetence hit me at full pelt.

I sat on the sofa, legs curled beside me, going over again in my head everything Marcelina had said in the session, trying to work out how I could've done things differently. Her words echoed in my ears.

I keep losing time. I think I'm sleepwalking, but it's in the daytime. I do things, and I can't remember what. I'm at some place, and I don't know how I got there.

It sounded like she was having blackouts of some kind, but why? Was she just stressed or suffering from anxiety? Was substance abuse of some kind causing her symptoms? She'd said no, so was there more to it? And what about the 'shadow man' reference? Someone watching her. Was that her way of trying to tell me she had some kind of stalker following her? She'd been scared. I'd felt it emanating from her. Scared of what? Or who? Had someone assaulted her? Perhaps her symptoms were trauma-related. A recent survey I'd read had said that almost two-thirds of students and graduates had experienced sexual violence at UK universities, but only one in ten reported it to the police or university staff. I wondered if she'd stepped in front of the car on purpose. Had she been feeling suicidal because of something that had happened to her? Because I'd handled things wrong, she'd never had the chance to tell me so I could try to help her.

I shuddered at the thought and took another swig of beer. Phil would tell me to let it go, but I couldn't. I was the one who'd got Marcelina in the situation she was in now. I owed it to her to find out. She'd need help more than ever when she woke up.

I glanced at Marcelina's handbag, my mind in overdrive. I got off the sofa and stood at the worktop, staring at it. If I looked inside, it would be an invasion of privacy, completely unethical, and an abuse of trust, but that didn't deter me. If someone out there *had* hurt her or threatened her somehow, I wanted to find out who.

I slipped a hand inside the bag, unzipped the compartments, and pulled everything out onto the worktop. A pencil case. A laptop. Mobile phone. A course textbook. Two notebooks. Hairbrush. Purse. Packet of Smarties. A set of keys. A half-drunk bottle of iced tea.

The outer casing of the laptop was cracked, and as I opened the lid, I saw the screen was smashed. No doubt when her bag had fallen from Marcelina's hand in the accident, it had bounced against the tarmac. I switched the laptop on, but nothing happened. I tried a couple of times, but it was completely dead, so I put it to one side and picked up her phone.

I pressed the Home button to wake it up, but it was protected with touch ID. Only Marcelina could open it with her fingerprint. I set it on top of the laptop and looked through her purse. There were some coins in the zip compartment and one hundred pounds in notes in the wallet side, along with a photo of Marcelina and a couple who looked as if they must've been her parents. A few receipts for food from the coffee shop in the student union building were stuffed at the back.

I picked up one of the notebooks and flicked through. It was a third full of coursework-related stuff, so I turned my attention to the second one, which turned out to be a journal.

The entries started six months ago and were just a few paragraphs at a time about ordinary, everyday student life.

16/9/18

Met Precious, Hazel, and Curtis for lunch in the union. He's so nice, but I don't think he's interested in me, and I'm too embarrassed to ask him out for a drink... or more! Ha! I'm eating too much junk food here. I've put on weight. Need to do some fitness classes. And no, not just because Curtis is always going. I really DO need to go on a diet.

20/9/18

Invited to a birthday party at the bar tomorrow night, but I'm so late on my essay I might miss it to study. Boring! Anyway, I went to Boot Camp class today. Hard work, but it was worth it to see Curtis in a tank top and shorts. Heee! Not that he'd like me looking a sweaty mess. Must get over this crush. Everyone likes him. I won't stand a chance.

24/10/18

Absolutely loving the course and uni life. Can't be bothered to join any clubs, but I've been keeping up the fitness classes. I can see real muscles now. I think it's actually addictive. Got an A for my latest essay. I rock! Maybe a slice of banoffee pie today to celebrate.

I read through lots of mundane excerpts of her life over the next few months and was about to give up when I came to the more recent entries.

30/3/19

Went to see PK today. Been thinking about it for a while, and I can earn some extra money, so I thought why not? Can't say anything about it. Shhh. It seems okay. Nothing too demanding. And it helps, so it's win-win, really. I'm doing something good.

7/4/19

Been feeling a bit weird lately. Can't seem to concentrate, and I'm having horrible dreams. Really scary stuff. Last night there was a slasher clown after me. Nothing seems that interesting anymore. Maybe I'm coming down with something.

. . .

10/4/19

Today was really strange. I sat in a lecture and couldn't remember anything about it afterwards. I'm having trouble concentrating. Precious asked me to go for a drink tonight, but I don't think I will. Just feel like... like... I'm going crazy.

15/4/19

It's been happening more. I keep losing time and forgetting things. Nightmares are getting worse. It must just be a virus. Or something. I had a talk with PK, and everything seems okay.

19/4/19

Right, this is REALLY strange. I keep hearing voices. It's like they're in my head but not. Like it's my voice but not. I'm really scared now because you know what that means, don't you? Rachel's sister in high school... she had schizophrenia. Everything's okay in my head—he said so—so it could be I'm turning crazy, couldn't it? But I don't want to find out. I do, but I really don't. I keep telling myself it's nothing. It's got to be nothing, right?

21/4/19

I think someone's following me. I haven't seen anyone yet. It's just like there's this shadow... you know that feeling, when you think someone's watching you? The hairs go up on the back of your neck and you just feel really uneasy. But when I look around, I can't see anyone. I'm imagining it, aren't I? Like I'm imagining the voices and the blackouts? It's not real. None of it can be real.

· · ·

30/4/19

Practice run. Just do it. I tried to stop it. It doesn't feel right. Is this to do with PK? The more I think about it, the more I know it all happened after I started this. But who do I go to to find out? He says no problem. Who can I ask? Who will help me? Am I right or wrong? I don't know. I'm SO confused. But I need to talk to some-one. I really do. Things are getting worse.

That was the last entry, dated one week ago. I stared at the pages, unease gnawing at my stomach. Was Marcelina suffering from some kind of mental illness? Was she really being watched? What was supposed to be a practice run? Who was PK, and what had she been doing with him to earn money? Had he hurt her somehow?

Something definitely wasn't right in her life, but what she'd written was pretty vague. I needed to talk to her friends and see if they could shed any light on what Marcelina had been going through.

I glanced at the clock. It was gone 10.00 p.m. Too late to go tapping up any of her fellow students. That would have to wait. There was one thing I could do, though.

I delved into my bag, retrieved my mobile, and dialled Mitchell's number. I swallowed the last of my beer and paced the tiny kitchen as it rang four times.

'Hi,' he answered. 'Is everything okay?' That was always the first thing he asked me these days. Every single time. *Is everything okay?* After what had happened with the kidnapping, maybe it wasn't surprising. But with my mum being so overprotective, too, sometimes it felt like I was suffocating.

'Yeah, everything's fine, thanks.'

'Were you trying to get hold of your mum? She's out with her work mates for a drink.'

'No. It's you I need to talk to.'

There was a pause on the line, like his antennae was on high alert. 'What's up? Has something happened?'

'Yes and no. Nothing's happened to me. I'm fine.' I told him about Marcelina's visit to the counselling session, the accident, and the journal entries. Yes, I was breaking client confidentiality big-time, but I knew it wouldn't go any further. Mitchell knew all too well about keeping classified information quiet.

'Poor girl,' he said.

'I want to help her, and that means getting the bigger picture. I think someone might've hurt her somehow. Or maybe she'd been threatened or stalked.'

'She could just be suffering from mental health issues. You said she mentioned voices. Maybe she *is* schizophrenic. Or maybe she's got something physically wrong with her if she's blacking out.'

'She could, but I think there's more to it than that. What she wrote... it's quite sinister.'

'I understand you feel bad about the accident, but it wasn't your fault. And if she does have mental health issues, then that's something the medical staff will help her with when she wakes up. She's in the best place.'

'I know, I know, I just...' I rubbed a hand over my forehead. 'She said something else, after she'd been hit by the car. She said a shadow man was watching her.'

'Shadow Man?'

'Yeah.'

'Sounds off the wall. She could've been confused. You said she had a head injury.'

'I don't want to write her off as mentally unstable. She seemed genuinely terrified of something or someone. And those journal entries are a bit disturbing. I'm worried that there could be some guy here who's hurt her.' I told him about the recent sexual assault survey. 'The memory loss she's been having could be some kind of post-traumatic amnesia.'

After another pause on the end of the line, he spoke again, his voice filled with worry. 'You know what happened the last time you started investigating something disturbing.'

A memory flashed into my head. A locked cell. Blood. My screams. Goose bumps crawled over my skin. I took a deep breath and concentrated on a vibrantly coloured hamsa print on the wall to block it out. 'I think she might need someone's help.'

'So what are you asking me to do?'

'Lee could do some digging,' I said, referring to his friend who'd been in the SAS with him. When Lee left the military, he'd set up his own private cyber security and intelligence company, and he was considered one of the best in the business. He could hack his way into anything, and he'd been instrumental in finding out who had taken me and where I was being held when I was kidnapped. 'I want to get hold of Marcelina's medical records and see if there were any substance abuse issues, or if she was on any medication. Whether there *was* a history of mental illness. Also if she'd ever reported an assault to the police or anything like that.'

He hesitated. 'Are you sure you want to get involved?'

'I feel like I owe her something. Come on, just a quick look. That's all. If there's nothing obvious, then I'll leave it to the doctors at the hospital.'

He sighed. 'And if I say no? That your mum and I don't

want you to get dragged into someone else's problems again?'

'Then I'd say I'll do it without your help.'

'Yeah, that's what I was afraid of.' He blew out a breath. 'Okay, I'll speak to Lee and get him to see what he can find. But promise me, if there's nothing obvious, you'll leave it alone.'

'Promise.'

'Yeah, right.' He snorted, not believing me.

'Thanks, Mitchell.'

'Is there anything else you need?'

'No, I'm good.'

'Made any friends yet?'

'I've got friends.'

'Books don't count as friends, I'm afraid. Any boyfriends?'

'Don't have time for boyfriends.'

Although I'd had relationships with guys, they'd always been casual on my part, because I wasn't good at small talk. I didn't have time for meaningless chatter. I felt things on a deep level, and so I wanted to connect on all levels with someone—spiritually and emotionally, not just physically. I hadn't found anyone with the whole package yet, and I couldn't even be bothered to look. It had to be something real or nothing at all.

'You don't have time for boyfriends because you're so busy with your inactive social life with no friends? It's not—' Mitchell stopped abruptly.

I knew what he was going to say. *It's not normal. It's not healthy.*

I got in there first with a chuckle. 'Because you're *so* normal, right?'

After leaving the SAS, Mitchell had set up his own private military company and made enough money to be more than comfortable for the rest of his life. After he'd wound the company up, instead of getting a regular hobby, he now caught paedophiles online, where he posed as different kids in chat rooms until he had enough evidence to pass onto the police to arrest the people trying to groom them. Catching child abusers had become his obsession after a VIP paedophile ring killed his son many years before.

'I'm normal,' he said. 'I'm with your mum now, and things are great. The episodes of PTSD are getting better. My life's moving on. Finally.'

'And I'm really happy for you both. But my life is great, too, so don't worry. Look, I'll let you go. Get back to your daisies or something.' I laughed.

'Oh, your mum told you about redoing the garden, did she? Anyway, they're not daisies. They're pansies.'

I laughed. 'Love you.'

'Love you, too.'

I hung up, stripped off the shirt that had smudges of Marcelina's dried blood on it, stuffed it in the kitchen bin, and headed towards the shower.

As I scrubbed and soaped and rinsed, trying to wash away the horror of the day, I repeated mindful positive affirmations to myself.

You're not a failure.

You didn't let her down.

It wasn't your fault.

By the time I'd finished, I almost believed myself. But not quite.

CHAPTER 17

DETECTIVE BECKY HARRIS

I grabbed a pint glass from the empty communal kitchen, filled it with water, and headed back to my room. Yawning, I picked up my laptop and notebook from the desk and sat on the bed. I made myself comfortable against the headboard, opened the laptop, and pulled up the uni's internal intranet site to search for information on Professor Cain.

I found his staff profile and studied his photo. He looked to be in his mid-fifties, with gunmetal-grey hair cut neat and short. He was good-looking in a Richard Gere kind of way. Malcolm Cain had graduated from the University of Sheffield twenty years earlier and had gained further PhDs. He'd taught cadaveric anatomy for St Albans University's Faculty of Medicine for fifteen years to both undergraduate and postgraduate students.

I scribbled those details in my notebook and then made a list of everything I'd found out about the three students. When I finished, I stared at it, chewing on the end of a biro. So far, I'd found no evidence of bullying, hazing, or a possible cult in operation. But all three of them did have things in common. They'd distanced themselves from their friends shortly before the tragedies occurred, but they hadn't isolated themselves completely, and when they'd disappeared, they were actually on their own and later found in trance-like states. They also all had what seemed like memory loss. Had the students been lying about their actions and whereabouts to cover for a cult? Or had they genuinely been in a fugue state? Had they been brainwashed? That was still a possibility.

I considered again whether they could all have had their food or drinks spiked with something like ketamine or Rohypnol, which could account for memory losses, but Jess and Millie had said Natalie was careful not to leave her drinks unattended. Her standard blood test after the car accident hadn't been positive for drink or drugs. One of Natalie's weird episodes had occurred after she'd been drinking, so it could've been simply alcohol on an empty stomach, but that didn't account for the other times she'd been acting oddly. Ajay and Vicky hadn't had any drugs in their system when they'd killed themselves, either. Ajay punching his fellow student had occurred after only one drink. Even if there was some new and strange drug knocking around campus, it was also highly unlikely all three of them had had their food and drink tampered with at different times at different locations. Based on all that, I had to discount the possibility of drugs.

Then there was the money they'd all had shortly before they'd died. Plus, Ajay had a connection with the medical block because of his course, and Vicky had been seen going into the Watling Centre after hours. Natalie was possibly in a relationship with Professor Cain, who was on the medical staff. Had someone really been following Natalie like she'd told her friends? And if so, who and why?

It was just gone midnight by the time Sutherby called me back.

'I didn't wake you up, did I?' he asked.

'No. I was just going over everything I learned today.' I filled him in.

'Sounds like you've done a lot of work already. I'm impressed.'

Even though he wasn't in the room with me, I still sat up a little straighter, pleased with the praise. 'It could be that Vicky was possibly having an affair with Professor Cain and sneaking into the medical block at night to see him, but then he ended things, and maybe she was upset about it. Love does strange things to people. Especially young, impressionable girls, but there's no indication she was unduly worried or stressed about anything in particular. And why take her life like that? Dive off the stairway when she was scared of heights? Even if Natalie was also seeing Cain, I can't see any reason why he'd be responsible for her hitting and killing a pedestrian. It's also highly unlikely that the same professor would've been having an affair with Ajay, too, and Ajay's only possible connection to Cain is that he was studying medicine. The faculty's huge here, though, and there are several people who teach the same subject, so Ajay might not even have known Cain well at all. Nothing really fits together yet, but I've discounted the drug and sleepwalking angles, and I believe something strange *was* going on with all three of them.'

'I'll do some background checks on Professor Cain and see if anything pertinent comes up. But all members of staff would have had criminal records checks to be working there, so I don't think there'll be much to find. Anthea certainly didn't mention to me any allegations of sexual harassment or misconduct against any tutors.'

'Great, thanks.'

'So there's no obvious sign of any sinister societies or cults?'

'Not yet, but it would take weeks—maybe months—to try and infiltrate all the clubs here. Vicky did go to a Buddhist meditation group before, and Ajay had been interested in it in the past, so I'm going to try that tomorrow.'

'Somehow I can't see you sitting still long enough for that.'

'No. Me, neither.' I took a gulp of water and set the glass on the floor beside my bed.

'Well, I looked into the RTA outside the university earlier. A student called Marcelina Claybourn ran out into the road and was hit by a vehicle belonging to a Greek national who's here visiting a relative. She's suffered a traumatic brain injury and is in Watford General Hospital's critical care unit at the moment. The driver wasn't under the influence of anything at the time. He said she came out of nowhere and he didn't have time to stop. Several witnesses interviewed at the scene confirm that. It looks like it's unrelated to what you're looking at, but I'll email over the witness statements we've taken so far and the traffic officers' preliminary reports anyway.'

'So the driver has absolutely no connection to the university or Marcelina?'

'None. Okay, that's it for now, then. Get some sleep.'

I hung up and got ready for bed. It felt weird being away

from home. Weird but kind of liberating. I could reinvent myself as anyone here, where no one knew me. Were Vicky, Natalie, and Ajay even who *they* appeared to be on the surface?

DAY THREE

"The general population doesn't know what's happening, and it doesn't even know that it doesn't know."
~ Noam Chomsky

CHAPTER 18

DETECTIVE BECKY HARRIS

The alarm on my phone went off at 6.15 a.m. I groaned and turned over, dislodging the notebook that had been on my chest when I'd fallen asleep and sending it flying onto the floor. Even though the window had been open all night, it was one of those British spring days where the humidity takes the pleasure out of *finally* getting some decent weather, and the air was still muggy and stale, like an electric storm was on its way.

I went into the en suite, hoping to wake myself up with a cool shower, but the water blasted out boiling hot, even on the cold setting. I shrieked and turned off the tap as my skin scalded, then adjusted the lever on the shower to hot in case the plumbing connection had been fitted the wrong way around. Nope, that didn't work, either. Hot gave me a temperature equivalent to a nuclear blast as steam filled the air.

I quickly soaped up, braced myself again, and turned it to a trickle on the cold setting for as long as I could stand, just to get the suds off while I gritted my teeth. I grabbed a towel I'd brought with me from home off a hook on the wall and dried off. I was just rubbing down my arms when I noticed the now steamed-up mirror above the sink. There were two words written in the condensation.

Help me!

Cue *Twilight Zone* music and pumping heart rate. My first thought was someone had got into my room while I'd been in the shower to scare me, so I checked the door, but it was still locked, and my keys were in it, just as I'd left it the night before. No one had been inside. That left the only possible explanation. Someone had written it on the mirror with their fingertip prior to my arrival here, and the steam had adhered to the grease and sweat, highlighting the word in relief.

So the question wasn't how. It was *who* had written it? And it wasn't too much of a stretch to imagine it had been Vicky, the previous occupant. The room had obviously been cleaned before I'd arrived, but it was very possible the cleaner had missed out the mirror, not even noticing what was written on it because it would've been all but invisible without any condensation. I hadn't noticed it while doing my hair in front of it the night before.

What did it mean? Was it the ramblings of some kind of disturbed mind? Or something more sinister?

I didn't have time to think about that, though. I was going to be late for the Buddhist's Society's 7.00 a.m. meditation if I didn't get my arse into gear.

I dressed in a pair of jersey shorts and vest top, grabbed my bag, and headed out into the already-sweltering air. A few students jogged past me in running gear as I walked to the union. Outside on the terrace, a cleaner was picking up plastic cups and remnants of food wrappers. I fanned my face as I walked. Even now I couldn't seem to cool down.

I found room three and opened the door. Eight students already sat cross-legged on mats in front of the... I didn't know what to call him... Guru? Zen master?

'Hi,' Mr Guru said. He was slim built with long hair tied back in a ponytail. 'Welcome to this morning's guided meditation. This is your first time, right?'

'Yeah.' I smiled around the room at the other students, hoping to be noticeable in case anyone remotely cult-like wanted to approach me later. And no doubt I was very noticeable with my sweaty forehead and lobster face.

Mr Guru put his hands together in a prayer position. 'Lovely to see you here. I'm Dave.' That threw me for a moment. I was expecting him to be called something new-agey, like Arlo or Leaf.

'I'm Becky.' I gave a little wave around the room and spotted Curtis. He grinned at me, and my temperature spiked again.

'Grab a mat, and we'll start in a few minutes.' Dave nodded towards a stack of soft mats in the corner of the room.

I took one, positioned it in a gap in the middle of the room, then sat down in a cross-legged position. Or I attempted to. Ouch. I wasn't sure my hip flexors could take that for a whole hour. I lifted one butt cheek, then the other, trying to get comfortable.

'Have you done any kind of meditation before?' Dave asked me.

'No.'

'No worries. I'm glad you're curious. With our practice, we're able to tame the mind, release any tension or stress, and help to build patience, compassion, and generosity, or just simply live mindfully in the present moment.'

'Sounds good,' I said, but his 'tame the mind' phrase had jarred with me.

'You don't have to sit like that if it's too uncomfortable. You can find any kind of position that feels good. Lean back against one of the walls, or even lie down, if you prefer.'

'I'll move over so then you can stretch out,' a girl to my right with dreadlocks said. She shifted the position of her mat and sat down in a perfectly straight-backed lotus position.

'Thanks.' I smiled my appreciation then lay on my back, surreptitiously checking out the other students. They seemed a complete mixture.

Dave glanced at the clock on the wall. 'Today we're going to do a meditation for letting go of anxiety. Okay, let's begin. Gently close your eyes. Relax the muscles in your body. Breathe in as deeply as you can through your nose. Hold the breath. Now push all the air out through your mouth. Breathe in deeply again. Hold. Let go of the air. Experience the chest rising and falling and the rhythm of your breath.

'On the inhale, repeat in your head the word "calm", On the exhale, repeat "relax". Feel your mind calming and relaxing. Let go of any critical thoughts or tension. Become aware of how you feel. Give yourself permission to let go.'

The sound of deep breathing filled the room.

'Now direct your awareness to your body, starting at your toes. Get in touch with any sensation you might feel and let it be. Move slowly on to your calves, your knees. Breathing. Calming. Work your awareness up to your thighs. Move up to your pelvis, your spine, where we can naturally hold a lot of tension...'

I woke up to someone shaking my shoulder. I opened my

eyes, and Dave was kneeling beside me. Everyone else had left.

I sat bolt upright. 'Oh! What happened? I usually have trouble trying to relax.' I rubbed at my face, trying to wake up.

He observed me, head tilted to one side. 'Yes, you seem like you have a lot of energy bursting to get out.'

'How embarrassing. Sorry, you weren't boring me or anything.'

'You must've needed the rest. You need to listen to your body.' He stood up lithely and picked up his mat. I bet he did yoga, too. 'Did you enjoy it?'

'I did, actually.' Weirdly, I hadn't been expecting to. I felt energised. Like I'd had an extra night's sleep. But was it possible that people could be hypnotised through a guided meditation? That I'd been subjected to some kind of subliminal messaging? I remembered listening to Dave's voice and the sound of the others, but then... nothing. 'Is there any difference between meditation and hypnosis?' I eyed him carefully as he rolled his mat up.

'Absolutely. The biggest difference is that meditation is induced purely by yourself. You have full self-awareness throughout. Whereas hypnosis is induced by another person, and if you're under hypnosis, you'd be in a state of trance or unconscious. But even with hypnosis, the person hypnotised would still be in control. They'd be able to wake themselves up.'

'But I was unconscious just then.'

He smiled. 'No. You were just asleep.'

'Right.' I stood up and yawned.

'Thank you for showing up on the mat today. If you fancy doing yoga, I teach the active student yoga classes.'

Sherlock Holmes had nothing on me. 'Great. I might do that.'

He turned around and put his mat on top of the pile in the corner. 'Cool. Have a peaceful and happy day,' he said before leaving the room.

I put my mat on top of his and went out into the corridor. No one was waiting to ambush me into cult recruitment. No one was lurking around to convert me to Buddhism or a radical splinter group. No one was there at all.

CHAPTER 19

TONI

I'd tossed and turned most of the night, unable to settle. Whenever I almost drifted off, a sickening image of Marcelina's head cracking on the pavement reared its way into my brain, the sound reverberating through my skull.

I rang the hospital at just gone 7.00 a.m., and Marcelina's condition had worsened to what they called a 'vegetative state', due to widespread damage to her brain. I felt sick as I got off the phone, wondering if her parents had arrived at the hospital yet. What a terrible thing to hear about their daughter.

I hadn't eaten since the previous lunchtime, but I still couldn't face the thought of food. Instead, I forced down a glass of orange juice to keep up my energy levels before I headed to the university.

My car was the first one outside the Student Counselling Services block as I parked up. I unlocked the main door then locked it again behind me. We didn't officially open until 9.00 a.m., and I didn't want to be disturbed. I walked down the corridor, past reception, and into my office. I slid the key in the lock and went to turn it, but the door was already unlocked.

I frowned as I pushed open the door, certain I'd locked it when I left yesterday. Client confidentiality was of utmost importance. The database for inputting our client records wasn't connected to the internet, so it couldn't be hacked, which was something that had been put in place about six months before I'd arrived, after an ex-student had got into the uni's system and leaked confidential information about other students online as a revenge vendetta. But we also had written patient notes, which we kept in filing cabinets, that we took during sessions or shortly afterwards so we had a backup.

I glanced around the room. Everything seemed normal. Had I just forgotten to lock the door in the midst of everything after I'd rushed through typing Marcelina's notes into the system before leaving?

I sat at my desk and turned on the laptop. I entered my password and looked at the screen. It all looked okay. Maybe it was nothing. Maybe I was overreacting. But I had a sixth sense that something wasn't right.

I went to the filing cabinet in the corner of the room and opened the drawer. I'd slowly built up a client base in the last month since I'd started, but there were only two Cs. Claybourn, Marcelina and Cotton, Jake. And that was the weird thing. After I wrote Marcelina's paper notes, I'd filed the page in a buff client folder alphabetically. Jake Cotton's file should've been behind Marcelina Claybourn's, but it wasn't. It was in front.

A cold prickle danced its way over my scalp. Again, it was possible I'd misfiled it yesterday in the panic of the moment when I was rushing to get to the hospital. Possible, but not likely. I was fastidious about a lot of things. It was one of my quirks. I liked order. Neatness. And I'd never misfiled anything before.

I pulled out Marcelina's file and heard footsteps and voices outside my office. I took a quick look inside the folder as they got louder. Just the one A4 page of handwritten notes. Exactly as I'd left it yesterday.

A knock sounded on my door before it swung open, and Phil poked his head around. 'Oh, good, you're here. How are you feeling today?'

I forced a smile and put the file back in the drawer. 'Better, thanks.'

'Glad to hear that.' His smile was more genuine than mine as he stepped inside and closed the door behind him. 'How did you get on at the hospital?'

I told him about Marcelina's injuries. 'What happened when you spoke to her parents?'

'They were going to drive down straightaway. They probably arrived late last night.'

'I hope so.'

'We should schedule a supervision session for later this afternoon so we can chat properly about things. I've got some time after three.'

'Yes, of course.' I leaned over my desk and called up my online diary. 'I'm free at four.'

'Lovely. In the meantime, I've got a police officer in reception who wants to take a statement about the accident. You're free until nine, aren't you?'

I nodded. 'I was just going to catch up on some admin.'

'Okay. I'll tell him to come in.' He turned and reached for the door handle.

'Phil... before you go, did anyone come into my office last night after I'd left?'

He twisted around towards me. 'Yes, Janet came in to make sure your oil burner was off. I asked her to because I thought you might've forgotten in the heat of things.'

'Right. Thanks.'

He hesitated. 'Is something wrong?'

I didn't want to get Janet in trouble in case she'd forgotten to lock up afterwards, so I smiled again and said no. I'd have to ask her about it. Either she had forgotten, or it was possible someone had been inside my office and looked at Marcelina's notes. But why would anyone be interested in them? Or had Phil been checking them to make sure I'd covered myself and the department? 'Did you have a look at the paper notes I wrote for Marcelina?'

'No. I did read the computerised ones on the system yesterday after you left. They're fine.'

'Okay. Thanks.'

Phil stepped outside, and a male police officer in uniform came in, introducing himself as Sergeant Wilcox with the Road Policing Unit.

We sat on the armchairs, and he asked me about the accident, wanting me to run through it in detail as he wrote down my statement.

After I'd finished telling him that Marcelina had had a brief appointment, that she'd left suddenly, upset, that I'd gone after her, and that she'd stepped out in front of the car, I asked, 'It *was* an accident, wasn't it?'

He looked up at me from the paperwork balanced on a clipboard on his knee, pen in hand. 'What do you mean?'

I thought about the strange things in her journal, the weird comments Marcelina had made about the shadow man and hearing voices, and the blackouts. I didn't know *what* I even meant myself, so it would sound ridiculous to him, and anyway, I couldn't tell him what Marcelina had confided in me because it was protected by client confidentiality. And then I wondered again... had she stepped out in front of that car on purpose?

'She didn't look to see if any vehicles were coming,' I said. 'She was just running away, and when she got to the road, she just stepped out in front of one.'

'Are you saying she was suicidal?'

'No, I'm not saying that at all.'

'Why did she come to see you?'

'I can't tell you that. It's confidential. But she didn't mention suicidal thoughts.' I thought about handing over Marcelina's journal, but what would that prove? The police wouldn't be interested in pursuing it because what she'd written was all too vague. It would most likely get filed in a drawer somewhere because none of it related to her accident.

'So you weren't concerned for her safety?' he asked.

'I was concerned she was upset, which is why I went after her. But there was nothing that led me to believe she'd be at risk.'

He looked down at the statement again, rereading some of what he'd written, then looked back up at me. 'So what are you saying?'

I opened my mouth and closed it. I had no idea what I was suggesting, just that something about this wasn't right. Eventually, I said, 'I'm not suggesting anything.' Then I had another thought. 'The driver who hit her, who was he? Did he know her?'

'I can't tell you who he is, I'm afraid. But what I can say is that he's a Greek national who was in the UK visiting a sick relative. He's got nothing to do with the university, and he said he'd never seen her before until she stepped out in front of him. From other witness statements, it seems Marcelina was just distracted. From what you've said, she was obviously upset. It looks like the driver didn't have time to stop. Accidents happen. Unfortunately more often than I'd like. A momentary lapse of judgement, switching off or being distracted for a few minutes, that's all it takes to have serious consequences.'

I nodded, looking like I agreed with him, but my gaze drifted back towards the filing cabinet as unease rippled through me.

CHAPTER 20

DETECTIVE BECKY HARRIS

My stomach twisted with hunger. I hadn't eaten since lunchtime the day before, and it was way past my fuelling-up time. I thought about the packet of cereal back at my accommodation, but I wanted to be as visible as possible. If there *was* a dodgy element of people here, they needed to notice me.

I sauntered down the hall to the food court, but most of the vendors didn't open until 10.00 a.m. I wandered past a table tennis table and a loungey seating area, saying hi to everyone I passed. A few people smiled and returned the greeting; others blanked me as if I were a weirdo for being too friendly. Good old British reserve.

A queue straggled out the door of the coffee shop, which was called Beanz and Thingz. A few years back, it would've been students surviving on tuna pasta and banana sandwiches for weeks at a time. Judging by the amount of people in the bar last night and here, it looked like they were spending their cash on booze and food. That was the trouble with student loans—it didn't feel like they were spending their own money. These young people were away from home for the first time, probably budgeting for the first time, until they were left with a huge debt to pay off at the end of it.

I joined the line of customers and eyed the large display counter of goodies, trying to decide between an avocado fudge brownie, a vanilla cupcake, and a flapjack. It all looked amazing. Maybe both, or a—

'Hi,' someone said from behind me, interrupting my conundrum.

I looked around and came face-to-face with a grinning Curtis.

'Hi.' I stared into his amazing hazel-green eyes. And then the flush was back. Oh, God, what was wrong with me?

He stared back, his gaze locked onto mine, studying me with a cheeky grin. 'So, you enjoyed the meditation then, huh?' He chuckled.

'I wasn't snoring or dribbling, was I?'

'Maybe just a little snore every now and then.' He put his forefinger and thumb about an inch apart.

'Do you go every day?'

'Most days.'

'And you haven't had any weird kind of effects?'

He lifted an eyebrow, an amused smile on his face. 'Weird, like how?'

'Like someone using suggestive thoughts to make you do something you didn't want to do?'

He frowned with confusion. 'I think that would be pretty impossible in meditation. You're in complete control of it.' He studied me carefully, his gaze searching mine, as if he could see right through me. 'What are you here for?'

'What?' I half laughed. There was no way he could know who I was, could he?

'I saw you looking at the display. What are you getting?'

'Oh! Uh...' I looked back at the goodies on offer. 'I haven't decided yet. You?'

'Overnight oats with chia seeds and cinnamon. Maybe a topping of blueberries. I can definitely recommend it.'

'Sounds yum.' It didn't. It sounded yuck. I'd always hated oats. My mum had forced me to eat porridge when I was a kid, and it was always either lumpy and dry or a sloppy, watered-down consistency, but hey, undercover work was all about adaption and improvisation. I'd force the gloopy frogspawn down if I had to. As the queue shuffled forwards, I asked, 'How's your friend? Marcelina?'

'Worse.' He pulled a solemn face. 'Still in a coma, and it's not looking good.'

'Oh, dear. I'm really sorry to hear that.'

He sighed and was silent for a moment. 'What course are you studying?'

'English lit. You? It's got to be some kind of sports programme, I bet.'

'Physiotherapy.'

I raised my eyebrows. 'Wow. Do you like the course?'

'Yeah, it's great. Hard, but good.'

'Do you have Professor Cain as a tutor?' I doubted it, since he taught cadaver dissection, which wouldn't be included in Curtis's physiotherapy course, but I wanted to find out if he knew Cain.

'No. Never heard of him.'

The line shuffled forwards as we made small talk.

The barista took my order for overnight slop and a large latte, and then I asked Curtis if he wanted to join me to eat, which he did. Lucky me.

We wandered outside to the picnic tables. A few people said hi to Curtis as we passed.

'You're a popular guy.' I sat down.

He shrugged. 'Just friendly, I guess.' He tucked into his bowl and swallowed a mouthful. 'It's my second year, so I know a lot of people now. But it's hard when you first get here and don't know anyone, so I try to take an interest in new people. Say hi, ask them how they're doing. Get them involved in stuff so they can meet other people and make friends.'

Yes, but what kind of stuff? I thought as I stared down at my bowl.

He threw his head back and laughed at the expression on my face. 'Just try it. I guarantee you'll like it.'

I scooped up a spoonful and ate slowly. 'Actually, it's all right.'

He gave me a knowing look. 'Told you.'

'That's nice of you, to look out for people. I was worried there was going to be a lot of bitchy people here. I got... um...' I did my best embarrassed, awkward face. 'There was a lot of bullying at my high school. It's actually one of the reasons I took a few years out before coming to uni. I couldn't face it again.'

His eyebrows furrowed with concern. 'That's horrible. I was pretty lucky. We had a zero tolerance for bullying at my school, but I've met a lot of people who had bad experiences. I can honestly say, though, I haven't come across any kind of bullying here with any of the people I've met. I mean, yeah, there are nasty people everywhere, and here's no exception. But not full-on bullying.'

I smiled. 'That's good to hear.' I took another bite of oats. 'I was actually thinking of going to another uni, but then I heard about a student who'd died there in some kind of hazing prank gone wrong.'

'Really? What happened?'

'They were playing chicken on the motorway after a drinking challenge. Got hit by a car.'

He let out a slow whistle. 'That's bad.'

'I know. I hope there's nothing like that here.'

He took a bite of oats and chewed thoughtfully. 'We've had a few suicides here, but nothing like hazing. The rugby club gets up to a few pranks. Although that's kind of standard for rugby clubs and usually involves a lot of alcohol. But I haven't heard of anything specific going on here.'

'That's good to know.' I paused for a moment then said, 'And I also heard about some cult in London who recruited students for some kind of dodgy stuff.' I stared at him, watching for some kind of giveaway that he knew exactly what I was talking about.

He raised his eyebrows. 'Seriously? I didn't know there were any cults here. Thought it was an American thing.'

'Yeah. I was shocked, too.'

'Hmmm.' He shrugged. 'You learn something every day.'

His body language seemed casual, as if he was genuinely unaware of such things. He didn't seem nervous or worried I'd struck a chord. My words seemed to have no significant impact on him at all.

We made small talk while we ate, but I didn't learn anything else of interest as we finished our breakfast, so I stood up to leave. I wanted to go to the scene of Vicky's and Ajay's deaths and Natalie's car accident to experience it first-hand and see if there was anything else the coroner's officer might've missed.

I said goodbye to Curtis and went in search of lecture block one, where Vicky had dived off the railings. It was nearly 9.00 a.m., and the campus had filled up with students out and about, heading to classes.

I entered the door to the two-storey building and glanced around the entrance hallway. Unfortunately, there were no CCTV cameras inside that I could've checked. The only ones in the uni were just inside the front gates and at the admin block. Directly in front of me were the stairs. I followed the flow of bodies upwards, got to the top, and leaned against the metal railings on the gallery landing, looking down to where I'd just been. I shuddered as I studied the small ledge on the other side of the railings—just wide enough for a small pair of feet to stand on before launching off. I imagined Vicky standing in the same spot, looking down to the unforgiving tiled floor below, wondering what kind of despair had been going through her mind.

'Are you lost?' a voice asked.

I turned to my right and saw a young guy with glasses and curly hair. 'No, I'm good, thanks.'

'Do you need any help? I mean, you weren't thinking of...' His gaze darted to the railings with a horrified look.

'Oh, God, no!' I smiled back.

'Phew!' He pressed a hand to his chest. 'Only someone else did it a while back.'

'I heard about that. It must've been terrible.'

He glanced down at his feet, a sombre expression clouding his face. 'Yeah, it was. I was just coming up the stairs when she went over. I had to give a statement to the coroner people.'

'I'm sorry.'

'I didn't know her. But... well, it's not the kind of thing I ever want to see again. That's why I asked if you were okay.'

'That was really sweet of you.' I glanced over the railings.

'So she definitely jumped then. She didn't... just fall? It wasn't an accident?' The witnesses who'd spoken to the coroner's officer had all said she'd dived, and I doubted someone could've accidentally fallen over the railings because they were about a metre high. Still, I wanted to make absolutely sure. If this guy was a witness, his statement should've been amongst the ones I'd read.

'Yeah. She definitely did it herself. I saw her climb over the railing.' He sighed.

'I'm Becky, by the way.'

'I'm Fred.'

Aha. Fred Parsons. I *had* read the statement he'd given about Vicky's death.

He glanced at his watch. 'As long as you're really okay, I need to get to my lecture.'

'Yeah, sure. Thanks for your concern, Fred.' I turned back to the railings and wondered again why someone who was scared of heights would choose that way to die.

CHAPTER 21

DETECTIVE BECKY HARRIS

I stood on the path next to the same zebra crossing where Natalie had run over the elderly man. Although it was a busy main thoroughfare, there were no cameras in the nearby vicinity.

I glanced up and down, getting a view from both sides. Traffic flowed steadily past. There was a park a hundred metres further down, so the crossing was used regularly by parents, kids, and dog walkers, hence the amount of witnesses who'd seen the accident that day.

I watched one young mum on the opposite side wait at the crossing for the traffic in both directions to stop before she walked across the black-and-white lines towards me, hand in hand with her little boy.

I turned my head to the right and looked along the road. Natalie's vehicle had approached from the south at an approximate speed of fifty-five miles per hour, way over the thirty-mile-per-hour limit. The seventy-five-year-old victim had walked slowly, his age, arthritis, and osteoporosis taking its toll. Natalie's vehicle had struck him when he was about two metres from the end of the crossing, and she'd ploughed straight into him. He'd bounced off her bonnet and fallen to the ground, hitting his head against the kerb and shattering several bones. The injuries had resulted in his death at the scene. She'd driven away, seemingly calmly, leaving a lost life in her wake as she headed back to the university like nothing had happened.

I walked further down, to where Natalie had approached from, and looked up at the crossing. It was a straight road with no blind spots. Witnesses had described how her head was facing forwards, in the direction of travel. She wasn't on the phone, fiddling with the stereo system, or eating or drinking. Surely she must've known he was there. They said it was almost like she'd driven straight at him with purpose. Was it simply a misjudgement in timing? Her foot hitting the accelerator in error? A split-second distraction? Those things happened with traffic accidents every day. Was it shock that caused her memory loss about the incident afterwards? Some kind of traumatic amnesia? Was her memory loss of the event real or staged? Perhaps some kind of schizophrenic episode had caused hallucinations at the time. It was a mystery.

I sighed with frustration. I'd hoped I might've spotted something pertinent that the traffic officers had missed, but I still had no clue what was going on, so I drove to the third scene.

Ajay's rental house that he'd shared with Jaxon, Toby, Ivy, and Phoebe was a five-bedroomed place on the edge of a residential street about two miles from the university. Most of the surrounding properties had been converted to flats or were rented out to students because of their size. The ground floor of the house on the opposite corner of the road had been converted to a newsagent's shop.

I parked outside the property, behind a builder's van, and pulled out the photos taken by the scene of crime officers after the fire. I perused through the ones of the house. The roof had partially collapsed on the right-hand side where the joists had caught fire. The PVC double-glazed window in what had been Ajay's bedroom was melted and charred, the glass broken. A small window next to it was also melted and charred. Soot marks licked up the outside of the brickwork. Apart from that, the exterior looked pretty much intact, but some of the internal upper floor and the stairs had been left in a bad state.

I put away the photos and got out of the car, looking at the house. The renovation and repairs were already in full swing, and as I approached, a builder exited the house, wearing a hard hat and carrying the remains of doorway architraving that was blistered and burnt. He dumped it in a half-filled skip on the road in front of his van.

I greeted him, pulled my warrant card out of my pocket, and showed it to him. 'I'm DS Harris. I need to have a look around inside.'

He wiped his hands together to get rid of some residual soot. 'Oh, right. I thought the police were finished with their examination. We have been working in here for a few weeks now.'

'That's okay. I just want to see where it happened. What's your name, sir?'

'Jakub. I work for the company employed by the owner's insurance company.'

'Is it safe to go in?'

'Yeah, no problem. But you'll need a hard hat.' He strode to his van, opened the back doors, and came back with a protective hat for me. 'We have taken the stairs out. They were wooden, so they were too damaged. There is a ladder to get to the second floor.'

I put on the hat and followed him inside. 'Did the insurance company tell you what happened?'

'Yeah. Horrible, isn't it? My oldest daughter wants to go to university. I don't think she should go. It is not worth it if this is what happens. Too much pressure on young people to succeed now. They think a high-powered job and money is the only thing important.' He snorted. 'And they all come out with too many of them overqualified because the government say they *must* do higher education or apprenticeship until they are eighteen years old. So they end up working in a coffee shop or supermarket with their degrees because there are not enough jobs.' He clicked his teeth with his tongue. 'They should be teaching them to be happy instead. We cannot all be Einstein.'

'I couldn't agree more,' I said, wondering again if it could simply have been the pressure or the stress of uni life that had forced Vicky and Ajay to do what they'd done. None of their friends thought so. But were they just really good at hiding things? And what about Natalie? I couldn't see how she fitted into things at all. But the coincidences were stacking up too much for my liking. There were more odd similarities between the three students than differences. I'd relied on my gut instinct in previous cases, and it had been right every time. And my gut told me that something sinister was happening here, even if I didn't have a clue what.

He pointed to the heavy-duty ladder reaching the second storey. 'The ceiling joists and floor have been replaced, so it's safe to walk up there, but just no stairs yet. Do you need me to be around, or can I get back to work?'

'No, you carry on. Thanks.' I climbed the ladder as he disappeared back outside.

Upstairs was a small square hallway with five doorways leading off to four bedrooms and a bathroom. The bedroom downstairs at the back of the house had been Phoebe's room. The doors were all gone because they'd been too damaged to salvage. The floorboards on the hall floor were new, but the smell of freshly sawn wood wasn't enough to cancel out the lingering smell of smoke.

I stood in Ajay's doorway and took in the room. The plaster had been removed from the walls, and it had been stripped back to the brick. The ceiling had been newly plastered, and more new floorboards had been laid in this room, as well. New wiring hung out of electric socket holes, ready for fixing. Apart from the smell, all traces of the fire had been removed.

Tears pricked at my eyes. Self-immolation must've been one of the worst possible ways to go.

I walked to the newly fitted window and looked outside, scanning the street before my gaze settled on the newsagent's shop. I checked the front of the building, searching for what I'd hoped might help me. The UK had the highest number of CCTV cameras per person in the world. Big Brother was definitely watching us. But while we seemed to be one of the most-surveilled countries, there'd been no correspondingly big drop in crime figures.

There were no local-authority-owned cameras in the street, and there was nothing obvious on the shop. It was possible they had a hidden one that could've caught someone who'd visited Ajay and incited him to do what he'd done. The coroner's officer had never enquired at the shop because all the evidence suggested suicide. Ajay had probably hidden the petrol in his room for two days before dousing himself in it and lighting the match. No suicide note had been found, but it was possible he'd left one that had been destroyed in the blaze. It was all too much speculation with no proof so far.

I wandered around the rest of the property, but nothing relevant jumped out at me, so I headed across the newsagent. A middle-aged woman stood behind the till, serving a young mum with a baby in a pram.

When she'd finished, I introduced myself and told her I was investigating the fire at the property across the street and was interested in whether they had CCTV.

'Yes. Because we had a burglary a few years ago, which we reported to you, but no one ever gets caught.' She narrowed her eyes at me, her voice sharp. 'By the time the police come, it's too late! They're gone! So we got cameras then.'

'I'm sorry about that,' I said. And I was. It was tragic how constant budget cuts in policing meant that the public were less protected every single year. 'Where's the camera? I couldn't see one up outside.'

'That's because it's tiny. New, modern high-definition stuff. It's hidden under the fascia board.'

'Do you record footage, or is it just real-time monitoring?'

She said it was recorded and stored, and I asked if I could look at the footage from the day of the fire. She looked as if she were about to say no, which would mean wasting time getting a warrant to seize it. But she just shrugged. 'Come with me. It's out the back.'

I followed her through some double doors into a storage area with boxes of produce stacked up. At the far end was another door that led to a small office. A closed laptop sat on a desk filled with piles of paperwork. She opened the laptop lid and clicked on the icon for her surveillance cameras. Then she scrolled down to a folder with the relevant date on it and clicked it open. Several video boxes appeared that showed footage for the external camera and the internal ones.

'This is the one you want that covers outside.' She pointed to one of the video boxes and left me to it.

I sat at the desk and clicked to play the video. The camera was positioned pointing downwards at a slight diagonal angle, so it had a view of the shop's entrance, plus the path in front of Ajay's house and part of the road.

I skipped to the footage of around the time Ajay's friends had said they'd left to go shopping in town, which was half an hour before the fire was reported by neighbours. And there they were—Jaxon, Toby, Phoebe, and Ivy exited the path and walked down the street, their backs to the camera, before disappearing from the frame. I sat back and tapped my foot, watching a few cars driving up and down the road. Some parked outside the newsagent and disappeared from camera view as they went inside to purchase something before driving off again a short time later.

Nothing much happened for fifteen minutes. Then another car arrived from the northern end of the street and parked just before the shop, but no one got out of the vehicle. I had a good angle of the silver Peugeot 206, including the registration number, but I couldn't see the driver clearly through the windscreen, just a shadowy shape. Whoever it was sat there for another few minutes. I zoomed in on the windscreen to get a better glimpse of the car's occupant, but his head was angled to his right, like he was watching Ajay's house. All I could see was the side of his head. He stayed like that for a few moments before turning back to face the windscreen, giving me a good shot of his face. I leaned closer to the screen, my back stiffening, eyes narrowing. It looked like the guy in the hoodie I'd seen exiting the medical block the night before.

I paused the footage and studied it carefully. He had a very distinctive long nose that tapered to a blunt point, squarish jaw, and prominent cheekbones. It was *definitely* the same guy.

'What the hell?' I stared at him frozen on the screen, chewing on my lip.

What was he doing outside Ajay's? And if he was watching Ajay, was he the same person Natalie had thought was following her, too?

I snapped a close-up photo of him on my mobile phone, before zooming out and taking a photo of the vehicle and registration number. Then I restarted the video, watching as he looked sideways at Ajay's house again. He stayed like that for another twelve minutes before anything else happened.

The first sign that something was wrong was when an elderly man walking his dog just outside the shop jumped almost out of his skin. He stopped abruptly, his gaze searching the street before turning towards Ajay's house. His dog barked and tugged on its lead, trying to pull the man away, obviously frightened. A neighbour next to the newsagent came out of his front door and looked towards Ajay's house. There was no audio to accompany the footage, but this must've been when Ajay's bedroom window exploded from the heat, the first external sign that the fire had taken hold.

I glanced at the stationary Peugeot. Hoodie Guy was still

in situ, his face in side profile, still watching Ajay's house. By now, the man with the dog had taken his phone from his pocket and was making a call. He would be Jerry McClusky then, the first person to ring the fire brigade. As the upper floor of Ajay's house was out of camera view, I couldn't see the flames pouring out of the front window, but from the reports and the damage, I knew that was what had happened.

About ten minutes later, a fire engine appeared in the frame from the southern end of the street. Before it had time to park, Hoodie Guy had started his vehicle and driven away, disappearing from view.

I watched the fire personnel leaping from the vehicle and gathering equipment and water hoses from the rig. But by the time they'd forced their way inside, it was already too late for Ajay. A lump formed in my throat as I tried not to think how agonisingly painful the burns must have been before he succumbed to the smoke inhalation that killed him.

A crowd of onlookers had formed in the street, watching the macabre scene unfold. An ambulance arrived and parked behind the fire engine, but the paramedics had to wait until the fire was contained and the property declared safe before they could enter. And besides, there would've been nothing they could've done.

I watched the aftermath for a while, until the paramedics brought Ajay's body out on a stretcher. They loaded him into the back of the ambulance and drove away. Then I paused the footage.

Hoodie Guy had sat there for about fifteen minutes before Ajay's window exploded and anyone realised what was going on inside. What was he doing there? He hadn't been making a call, having a smoke, meeting a friend, or going to the newsagent. He was waiting for something to happen inside Ajay's house. It couldn't have been coincidence that he was there, watching, at the same time Ajay took his own life. But after seeing him twice now in the circumstances I had, my gut wasn't just slightly suspicious; it was screaming at me.

CHAPTER 22

TONI

I had back-to-back clients until 11.00 a.m., helping them cope with everything from loneliness and anxiety to eating disorders and homesickness. After the last one had left, I went out to reception and asked Janet if she'd been doing any admin on Marcelina's paper file—a subtle way of asking her if she'd been in my cabinet and misfiled it. But she said no. She'd just checked the oil burner was off, as requested, and locked up again afterwards. Which meant someone *must* have been in there for the express purpose of reading Marcelina's file.

I wondered what the hell was going on as I stepped back into my office, trying to decide whether to tell Phil I suspected someone had been in here looking at confidential information. I was in two minds about it, because I had no real proof.

I quickly entered my handwritten session notes from the earlier clients into the database and then called Watford General Hospital to see if there was any improvement in Marcelina's condition, but there was no change.

I'd just put the office phone down when my mobile beeped. I had a message on Cipher, the end-to-end encrypted app Mitchell's friend and cyber expert, Lee, had designed. Mitchell had downloaded it onto my phone so we could send texts, photos, and documents and make calls, but it was highly secure. There were two words from Mitchell...

Call me.

I rang him back using the same app.

'How's it going?' he asked.

'Okay, thanks. But I think someone came into my office.' I told him about the misfiled notes, the door being unlocked. 'Which seems highly suspicious. Marcelina thought she was being watched. What if someone had followed her here yesterday and wanted to find out what she was saying to me?'

'It does sound strange, I'll admit. But I just got some stuff from Lee concerning Marcelina, and I can't see anything out of the ordinary. I can send copies through Cipher, but I'll give you a quick summary. Before Marcelina came to St Albans to study, she was registered with her local GP back in Scotland. Those records show no mental health issues, nor any mental health conditions in her family. There are no substance abuse issues, either. The only medication she was prescribed in the past three years was the contraceptive pill. When she came down to St Albans, she registered with a Doctor Elaine Ford.'

'I know her practice. A lot of the students use that surgery because it's local.'

'Well, again, there was nothing going on. She's had two appointments in the last year. Both were for the contraceptive pill.'

I swivelled in my chair. 'Okay.'

'Lee also got into Watford General's database. They did a blood test for alcohol and standard drugs when she was admitted, but she tested negative. She's also never reported a crime anywhere in the UK.'

'But that doesn't mean something didn't happen to her. I know she was scared. If she was being stalked or harassed, maybe there's some kind of text or call or email evidence on her phone, which I can't unlock without her fingerprint. I'll go to see her later if they let me visit and sort that out. I've also got her laptop, but it was damaged in the accident, so I can't turn it on, but maybe Lee can check it for me. He might still be able to get something off the hard drive. I want to find out if there are any references on her phone or laptop to this PK person in her journal.'

'Lee also took a quick look at her finances. She's got a student loan, and the usual payments going out of her account for her uni accommodation, food, and sundry items. But nothing relating to PK or anything that he paid her for.'

'Which means if that was the case, he probably gave her cash,' I said. 'But what for, though?'

'Your guess is as good as mine. But so far, there's nothing that seems sinister.'

'Apart from the journal entries.'

'Which could be the ramblings of a mixed-up girl. I think you need to just put this down to a terrible accident and let it go.'

'It could be. But I don't think so. I think she was in trouble. And I'm going to find out why.'

'I think you should stop this.' His voice was laced with concern. 'It's not your responsibility, and you get too obsessed with things.'

'You're exactly the same. If someone came to you needing help, you'd drop everything to do it. Look at what happened with Maya. With me.' I wasn't the only person Mitchell had rescued. When powerful and dangerous people killed his friend Jamie and threatened Jamie's fiancée, Maya, he'd risked his life to help save her, using his special skill set. 'So maybe I'm just like you, too. And I can't just walk away from this.'

He groaned down the line, probably trying to think of a suitable retort but failing, because it was true. 'Just don't tell your mum what you're up to. She'd be panicking again that something might happen to you, and she'd bloody kill me for being involved.'

'I won't. No need to worry on that score.'

'All right. Let me know when you've got the phone unlocked. If you can't do it, I'm sure Lee will be able to. And, Toni... don't do anything stupid.'

'I won't.' I hung up then called student admin to find out exactly where Marcelina was living. They gave me the room number for one of the on-campus blocks, so I picked up Marcelina's handbag and headed over there.

The only areas where a university ID card was necessary to gain building access were the accommodation blocks and the library. I swiped my card through the entry system to housing block B, walked past a couple of bikes chained to the bottom stairwell railings, and paused for a moment, remembering Marcelina telling me that was where she'd ended up one day, spaced out, with no recollection of getting there.

I headed up the stairs. Each floor had twenty rooms with en suite facilities and a communal kitchen at the end. Marcelina's room was on the second floor. I found number thirty-one and hesitated outside her door. Music drifted from the open kitchen doorway at the end of the hall.

I glanced up and down the corridor. No one was around. And anyway, I had a perfectly good reason to be there. I was returning Marcelina's bag to a safe place, even if it was minus her phone, laptop, and journal.

I unlocked the door with Marcelina's keys, stepped inside her room, and shut it behind me. I took a look around.

There was a double bed positioned underneath the window, the covers unmade in a rumpled heap. Along one wall, a small desk with drawers had textbooks and notes scattered on top. A bin in the corner overflowed with scrunched-up food wrappers, a banana skin, and an empty bottle of water. The wardrobe's doors were open, some clothes piled up on the bottom of it, some still on hangers. I glanced in the en suite shower room. A mixture of toiletries were arranged haphazardly on a single shelf above the sink.

The place was a mess. A smell of stale air with an undertone of rotten food filled the room. I walked towards the window and opened it a little, taking a look into the student car park below and the identical accommodation block opposite. Could PK be another student? Had someone been watching her in her room from the next block? Marcelina didn't have voiles or net curtains, just a plain pair of lightweight material ones. If they were open, someone from across the way could've easily seen inside. But that didn't explain the voices she'd said she was hearing or the other symptoms—the blackouts, sleep problems, and nightmares. Did she have an undetected physical problem causing the blackouts, or the start of some mental health problem, like the schizophrenia she was worried about? Extreme stress could've also caused strange behaviour, and if someone had assaulted her or was stalking or watching her, that could've created just the right amount of stress.

I turned away from the window and glanced around, unsure what I was expecting to find. I thought again of someone coming into my office to look through Marcelina's notes. If they'd come in here, too, it would be impossible to tell if this was the state she'd left it in. And if they had, what were they looking for? Something that connected her to this PK?

I sat at her desk and placed her handbag on the floor. I flicked through the textbooks and some novels, before turning my attention to her notebooks. There was nothing like the journal I'd found in her handbag. All of these were outlines for coursework or notes she'd taken in lectures.

I opened the drawers, rifling through. I found nothing weird and no drugs. I looked under the mattress then checked through her wardrobe, looking for any loose areas she could hide something behind, in clothes pockets, shoes, and bags. I found nothing until I got to a battered old shoebox and looked inside. There was a hairdryer and a plastic purse in the shape of a cat's head. Inside the purse was a roll of fifty-pound notes. I pulled it out and counted just over two thousand pounds. Was this money from PK?

I put it back as I'd found it and shut the lid, sighing. What was I even doing? I was seriously crossing a professional line. If someone found me in her room, going through her stuff, at the very least, I'd be disciplined, most likely sacked, but that wasn't going to stop me. I was risking my career before it even got started, but if Marcelina was in danger for some reason, I had to do everything I could to help her—because I'd been in danger once, too, and I couldn't just abandon Marcelina if she was in trouble.

I went into the en suite and lifted the toilet cistern. No drugs there, either. Back in the bedroom, I studied the floor. It was carpeted, with no sign that any part of it had been lifted to hide some kind of stash. The skirting boards were all intact. There was nothing else there to find.

CHAPTER 23

DETECTIVE BECKY HARRIS

I called Sutherby on my Bluetooth system as I drove back from the newsagent to the university, but he didn't pick up, so I left a message. I was just pulling through the uni's gates when my phone rang, but it wasn't the chief getting back to me. It was Warren.

'Hola,' he said. 'Just checking up on you. Seeing if you got to Marbella safely.'

'Buenos días.' I smiled. He'd been worried about me recently. Worried I'd been sinking into the same kind of depression about my split with Ian that had consumed him after his wife's death. But they weren't the same things at all. He'd lost the love of his life, his soul mate. Ian and I had never really been right for each other. And even though I'd been down, I wasn't depressed. I just needed to keep busy. It was a blip in my life. A big, sad, expensive blip, but still a blip. And I loved Warren for worrying about me.

'Yeah, everything's good, thanks.' I pulled up in a parking bay outside my accommodation block then switched off the engine. 'I'm just checking out the shops. Then I'll probably head to the pool for a bit of sun and sangria.' I winced inwardly as I said it, hating lying to him.

'Sounds nice. What's the temperature there?'

'About twenty-six degrees. What's it like there?'

'Actually, it's hotter here. We're still having a heat wave.'

'Lucky you. How's everything going?'

'Good. Fine. The usual.' There was still an undercurrent of sadness in his voice, even though he was finally moving on with his life and getting to grips with the grief that had floored him.

'And how's Mrs Pickle Pants?'

'God, that poor cat. No wonder she doesn't come back when you call her. She doesn't even know what her real name is anymore.'

'She loves my little nicknames.'

He snorted. 'She's fine, anyway. Eating like a pig, as usual.'

'Thanks again for feeding her. I really appreciate it.'

'What are friends for? Anyway, I'd better let you go and have fun then. Have a sangria for me.'

'I'll have a whole jug for you.'

He chuckled. 'You do that.'

I hung up and exited the car, heading towards my room. I'd just got inside the entrance hall when my phone beeped with a text. It was from Sutherby, telling me he'd sent through the information regarding Marcelina Claybourn's RTA outside the university gates.

I took the stairs two at a time and bounded down the corridor to my room. I doubted it had anything to do with what I was looking into, but I wanted to be thorough. An investigation was as much about discounting possibilities, however unlikely.

When I checked the laptop, I found Sutherby had sent witness statements, the traffic officer's preliminary report, and photographs of the scene. Unfortunately, the area wasn't covered by CCTV.

I opened the statements first and read through, starting with the driver, whose name was Darius Christakos. He was a Greek national who'd arrived in the UK two weeks before to visit his mum who'd moved to the UK ten years ago and was in hospital due to a stroke. Ironically, he'd just come back from visiting her at Watford General Hospital when he hit Marcelina and sent her straight to the same place. He owned a restaurant in Santorini, and the last time he'd been in the UK was two years previously, so I doubted he knew Marcelina. He certainly didn't appear to have any ties to the university. He'd said...

She came out of nowhere. One minute, I was driving along, and then I just saw a blur in my side vision, and my hire car hit her. I didn't have time to stop or react.

Five other witnesses so far confirmed the same thing. It was tragic, but I didn't think it could be related to anything going on here.

I clicked on the last attachment in the email, which was information that I'd asked for on Professor Cain, but it didn't raise any particular alarm bells. Cain didn't appear to have any suspicious associations or radical political or social ideas. No dubious financial transactions. No complaints or allegations against him from students or staff. He seemed like Mr Average.

I dialled Sutherby as I sat on the bed, jigging my knee up and down, waiting for him to pick up.

'Hi, Becky. I take it you got the email I sent.'

'Yes, sir. The accident's terrible, but I don't think it could be related to anything sinister.'

'I agree. And I've just got hold of another statement from a witness who the traffic officers visited at the university earlier this morning, and she says the same thing as the others. She's a student counsellor there who said Marcelina had just left a counselling session with her in an agitated, upset state. She went after Marcelina to try and see if she was okay, but Marcelina rushed off. By the time she'd got close to her, Marcelina had walked into the road.'

I thought about that in relation to my enquiries. The coroner's officer had investigated Ajay's and Vicky's mental health status, and the counselling services on site were one of their first ports of call. Neither had visited them for any help, so there was no connection there. Similarly, there was no indication of Natalie having mental health problems prior to the accident until the new subsequent suspicion of schizophrenia.

I rubbed at my forehead. 'Why did Marcelina see the counsellor? Do we know?'

'They wouldn't tell us. Client confidentiality. Besides, I think in light of the fact that it doesn't seem related, there's no point in you pursuing it further.'

'I have found some other things that are suspicious, though.' I told him about seeing Hoodie Guy coming out of the Watling Centre the night before and outside Ajay's house. 'I'm going to email a copy of the footage I downloaded at the newsagent. The camera was hidden really well, and unless you studied hard, you wouldn't notice it was there. I need to know who he is and who the vehicle is registered to. It's weird because it was like he was waiting outside Ajay's house for it to happen, but the only way he could've known was if he or someone else had put Ajay up to it or had some other involvement in it. That unknown man could be the key linking things together.'

'I've also done general background checks on all members of staff, and there's nothing obvious that raises any red flags. No complaints or allegations against anyone.'

'Okay. I think we need to also check out a physiotherapy student called Curtis. He's in his second year. Natalie knew him, he's very popular, and he seems to be popping up everywhere. He'd make an ideal recruiter for a cult.'

'Will do.'

'Oh, and there's something else.' I told him about the strange *Help me!* message written on the mirror. 'Not sure if it means anything significant, though.'

'Vicky could've written it when she was drunk. Or maybe it was a cry for help that no one noticed.'

'Maybe. I'll keep on digging from my end.'

I hung up, picked up my laptop and phone, and went into the communal kitchen. There were a couple of guys in there I hadn't seen yet, making a sandwich. I introduced myself, made chitchat, then casually asked them the same kinds of questions I'd asked everyone else. I learned nothing new or helpful. When they left for lectures, I logged on to the internet and dug a little deeper into Professor Cain, but nothing jumped out at me. I had no proof Cain was involved in anything untoward, even if he had possibly been having an affair with Natalie or Vicky. I wasn't getting anywhere. I was just going off on tangents. The suspicious guy with the hoodie was who I needed to concentrate on.

CHAPTER 24

DETECTIVE BECKY HARRIS

I logged on to the uni's intranet and looked in the student chat rooms, seeing if any threads or usernames popped up that seemed as if they were enticing people to join groups or participate in anything weird or suspicious. I went through posts relating to coursework, stress, depression, anxiety, relationship problems, and all manner of uni life. If there was some kind of brainwashing going on by a sinister group who wanted to manipulate people into doing the most awful things to themselves or others for some twisted and sick reason, I was betting Hoodie Guy was the leader. But after spending over two hours trawling, I found no online bullying, nothing about strange hazing rituals, and no possible cult-like behaviour.

I snapped my laptop shut. I was brain-dead, and it was coffee hour for the LGBTQ Society. Time to ask more questions.

I found Toby, Jaxon, Ivy, and Phoebe sitting on the bean-bags in the corner of the meeting room, eating lunch with their food perched on their laps, chatting away. Another guy sat at a table in the corner, staring down at his phone, his fingertip tapping frantically at the screen as if sending a message.

'Oh, hey!' Phoebe grinned at me, beckoning me forward. 'Come and join us.'

The others all greeted me. I grabbed a coffee from the urn and walked towards them.

'That's Ned, by the way.' Toby pointed to the guy at the table. 'Ned, Becky.'

Ned glanced up and gave me a distracted smile before his gaze glued back on his phone.

'He's chatting to a new guy he's met on Grindr.' Ivy nodded in Ned's direction. 'We haven't been able to get any conversation out of him, either, so don't take it personally.' She rolled her eyes as she perched on the edge of her bean-bag, managing to look elegant. I eyed an empty beanbag and then decided to sit on the floor next to Jaxon. No doubt I'd end up spilling coffee all over myself if I sat on it. I felt way too old for beanbag lounging.

'How're you settling in?' Ivy asked.

'Yeah, so far so good.' I took my phone out of my pocket. 'Only thing is... some guy pranged my car in the car park and drove off. I managed to take a photo of him before he left, but stupidly, I didn't catch the registration number.' I swiped through to the close-up photo of Hoodie Guy behind the windscreen that I'd snapped from the CCTV footage and held the phone in front of me. 'Do any of you know who he is?'

Toby peered at the screen. 'Nope, never seen him before.' He passed it on to Phoebe.

'No, sorry.' She shook her head. 'What a bummer, though.'

Jaxon and Ivy didn't recognise him, either, which meant

they couldn't have ever seen him watching the house or hanging around with Ajay.

'Bad luck—and only on your second day here, too.' Toby grimaced before expertly stuffing noodles into his mouth with chopsticks.

'I know.' I put away my phone and pulled a suitably pissed-off face. My stomach rumbled. The overnight oats hadn't filled me up as much as I'd thought they would, and I looked at Toby's food longingly. 'And I've got a problem with the shower in my room. Comes out scalding hot.'

'Don't worry; it's not just your room,' Phoebe said. 'There's some weird problem with the water system in the accommodation blocks here.'

'Oh, okay. Well, there's also a bitchy girl in my block. So I was actually thinking that maybe it would be better to live off campus. But I wouldn't know where to start looking. I found a room available in a shared house a few miles away, but I didn't know if it was in a dodgy area or not since I'm not familiar with this town yet.' I named the road where they'd had their previous rental, before it went up in smoke.

'That's where we were living.' Phoebe put down her unfinished sandwich on her lap, tears in her eyes.

I felt like a shit, bringing it all back up again, but it was the only way I could think of to get them talking about it. I reached out and touched her forearm. 'I'm so sorry. I didn't know.'

'It's not your fault.' Jaxon rubbed the back of his neck. 'It was a great place to live until... well.' He shrugged helplessly.

'There was never any trouble there,' Ivy said.

'No gangs or dodgy people hanging around?' I asked.

'Nothing like that,' Ivy said.

I couldn't really ask anything more in depth without

seeming suspicious, so I finished my coffee and told them I was going to check out the HIIT class. 'It was recommended by a guy called Curtis, who's a physio student.' I waited to see if his name rang a bell. No one batted an eyelid, though. 'Have any of you been to the active student classes? I'm a bit out of shape at the moment, so I don't want to make a complete idiot out of myself if they're really hard.' I laughed.

Jaxon snorted. 'We're not really into all that boot camp stuff.'

'Oh, speak for yourself.' Toby wiggled his eyebrows up and down. 'There's bound to be some pretty fit guys in there. Maybe I'll give it a go one day.'

I left them to it and walked past the food court, trying to ignore the amazing smells. I didn't have time for lunch yet. Instead I had two choices. One, go to the HIIT class and see if Curtis tried to hijack my brain for cult-like purposes, or see if he recognised the photo of Hoodie Guy. But if Curtis was involved in this, either with Hoodie Guy or alone, then I didn't want to tip him off just yet. I still very much doubted that any fitness classes were where a possible cult would recruit members. And I wasn't even convinced there actually *was* a cult at work. That left my second choice: go to the lecture that Natalie's friends, Millie and Jess, were supposed to be at and see if they recognised Hoodie Guy.

I still had twenty minutes before the lecture started, so I walked out of the union, followed the path towards the Watling Centre, and went inside. It was set up like a clinic environment, with a reception desk, a seating area off to the left, complete with six people waiting, and medical-related posters adorning the walls.

The receptionist looked up from her laptop and offered me a welcoming smile. 'Hi, do you have an appointment?'

'Appointment?' I glanced around at the people in the waiting area. An elderly couple sat in the far corner of the room, holding hands. A middle-aged man sat opposite them, reading a paperback. 'I thought this block was for medical lectures or practical classes.'

'No, that's the next block along.' She pointed to her right. 'This is the research clinic run by the university.'

'Oh. Right. What kind of research do you do here?'

'Gosh, a *lot*. Are you a medical student wanting to help out with the research, or are you thinking about participating in a study?'

'Maybe participating. But I don't have anything wrong with me.'

'Some of the studies involve patients who actually have a particular disease. But there are many clinics where we also need healthy study groups to participate. Let me get you some more information about all the clinics that might be suitable.' She went to a low-level long table behind her desk with a huge array of brochures fanned out on top. She picked up several and handed them to me.

I flicked through one. There were glossy photos of equipment and smiling doctors and patients. 'Do you get paid for being in these studies?'

'Yes.'

'And who funds them?'

'It depends. The university funds some. For others, we get research grants from the private sector.'

'Are the appointments during the daytimes?'

'Yes, all of the clinics run between normal office hours. Nine to five.'

'No one does any clinics or treatment outside that?'

'Not usually, no, but we're flexible with appointments, so

I'm sure you'd be able to slot a time in between your lectures.'

'Does Professor Cain have any clinics here?'

'No. He's purely teaching faculty.'

'Right. I'll have a look through these then and come back.' I wiggled the brochures in the air. 'Oh, before I go, I was wondering... someone hit my car parked in the accommodation block earlier, but he drove off. I've been asking everyone if they know who he is.' I pulled out my phone and showed her the photo of Hoodie Guy.

She peered at it then shook her head. 'No, sorry, I don't have a clue.' She handed it back.

'Thanks for your help.' I made my way outside and stuffed the brochures in my backpack, deep in thought. Tara had seen Vicky going into the Watling Centre late at night, after patient hours, exactly the same as with Hoodie Guy. Millie and Jess had said they thought Natalie was having an affair with Professor Cain, who was involved in medicine. Ajay was a medical student who could've been participating in a study here as a student for extra credit or as a patient. A tingle of excitement ran through me. This place was the first solid link I had tying them together, along with the unaccountable money they'd had. Money that they could've got from all being involved in some kind of research study.

I hurried to the lecture theatre and spotted Jess and Millie outside. Jess leaned against the wall of the building with a cigarette on the go. Millie sat on the grass, her face pale.

'Hi,' I said.

'Urgh.' Millie grimaced. 'How come you're so cheery? My head's still not right from last night. I just want to go back to bed.'

'Oooh, nasty,' I said.

'I'm not surprised, the amount you drunk.' Jess snorted and took a drag on her cigarette.

'So you didn't make it to any fitness classes earlier then, to catch up with Curtis?' I asked.

'No. But hands off him. I saw him first,' Millie grumbled, but it wasn't in a bitchy way.

'Not like she hasn't tried, though.' Jess laughed. 'She's been trying to get him to notice her properly for months, but he's too into his fitness. Maybe he's gay.'

'It would be a big waste to the female population if he was,' Millie said then pointed behind me. 'I'd rather have Curtis than *him* any day.'

I turned to see who she was pointing at. A tall man in his early fifties with thick sandy hair, a neatly clipped goatee, and red-framed glasses was carrying a briefcase as he strode along the pathway in his pinstriped suit. 'That's the guy we think Natalie was shagging. Professor Cain.'

I frowned. No, it wasn't. I'd seen Cain's photo, and this was someone completely different. 'Are you sure that's his name?'

Jess shrugged. 'I think so.'

I watched him until he disappeared from view behind another building, then I pulled out my phone and showed them the photo of Hoodie Guy, giving them the same spiel about him hitting my car. But neither of them appeared to recognise him.

Jess stubbed out her cigarette in the metal ashtray outside the building. 'Come on.' She dragged Millie to her feet. 'We'll be late for the lecture. You coming, Becky?'

'Actually, I've just remembered I need to do something urgent,' I said. 'I'll have to miss this one.'

'Lucky you.' Millie rubbed her forehead. 'Wish I could skip it, too.'

'If you catch up with us in the bar later, you can copy my notes,' Jess said.

'Thanks.'

I jogged away, hoping to find out where the man with the goatee had gone, but I was out of luck. He'd vanished.

CHAPTER 25

FARZARD

Farzad Nuri walked the mile and a half into town from his house. The sun bore down on him, but he couldn't feel it. He didn't notice the sweat pooling between his shoulder blades and dripping down his back beneath his T-shirt. He didn't notice the sound of traffic whizzing along the main road beside him, people's conversations as they walked by, and the child crying in the distance.

All he could hear were the thoughts in his head. His voice, but not his voice. He was heading towards the beach. When he got there, he could relax. Kick off his shoes. Feel the sand between his toes. Maybe take a swim. He hadn't been to the beach in a long time. He was from the town of Luton, but his parents used to take him to the coastal resort of Dawlish every year for summer holidays. He'd always loved it.

Shadows passed by him, peripheral shapes shifting. *Shapeshifters.* He smiled to himself. *What is a shapeshifter?*

I'm walking along the path to the beach. When I get there, it will all be perfect. But there's something I need to do first.

Walking. One foot in front of the other. Nearly there. *I'm in a vortex.*

Yes, but what kind of vortex?

A mass of air or water spinning around me? Or a dangerous situation I can't escape from?

No, there's no danger here. Just do it, Farzad.

Faces loomed in front of him, but he couldn't see them properly. His eyes were fixed on a distant goal.

A voice asked someone if they wanted milk with their coffee. They couldn't be talking to him. He was on a mission. He was going to the beach. He didn't know these people. So it must've been *the* voices. The ones that wanted him to do things.

Flashes of white light pulsed in his brain. And then there was screaming. Piercing noise. Someone shouting for the police. Others yelling at someone to get away.

The images on the edge of his vision swam into focus. There was blood. A knife in his hand. *A knife? In my hand?*

He stood over a man lying on the ground.

'What the...?' He twirled around, looking at the crowd keeping their distance. They looked scared of him.

Farzad stared down at the man. His eyes were closed. Blood oozed from a wound in his stomach. Farzad blinked rapidly, his mind drifting back to the present. 'What happened?' He kneeled next to the man, looked up at the crowd, and yelled, 'Someone call an ambulance!'

The crowd lurched backwards with a collective gasp as Farzad staggered to his feet, knife still in his fist, waving it at the crowd, trying to get them to listen to him. 'He needs help!'

Farzad looked at his hand with horror, his mouth wide

open with incomprehension. He opened his palm, letting the knife fall to the ground.

Run, Farzad! the voice said. *Turn around and run to the end of the road. Keep running, and I'll find you. Go now!*

He didn't look back at the man or the crowd. He just obeyed and started running.

CHAPTER 26

DETECTIVE BECKY HARRIS

I headed back to my room to do some research on who Mr Pinstripe Suit was and find out more about the Watling Centre. I sat down at my desk and opened the brochure the receptionist had given me. I paged through it until I spotted a photo of the same man sitting behind a desk. Within the first few lines I discovered his name was Professor Klein, *not* Cain. Jess and Millie had got it wrong. He was a neuroscientist research fellow at the university and ran some of the Biomedical Sciences and Engineering Department's research clinics. His bio was sparse. All it said was:

Professor Brian Klein has spearheaded developments in technology for medical diagnosis and use in the management of disease and human emotion prediction.

I flicked the page and found out he was specifically involved in a study for the Memory Research Group, which focused on using behavioural measures and brain imaging to understand memory and emotional function in both healthy populations and those affected as a result of

Alzheimer's, epilepsy, stroke, and dementia. My pulse quickened as I read, sure I was finally on to something solid.

We use a number of different methods, including diagnostic tests, which could include functional magnetic resonance imaging and CT scans, along with behavioural experiments and wearable smart technology that transmits information wirelessly to our data systems. We need volunteers of all ages for our research in both healthy and clinical populations.

St Albans University's Biomedical Sciences and Engineering Department is home to some of the world's finest minds in the field. The aim of our unique research in biomedicine science is to incorporate both biomolecular studies on disease mechanism and the invention of innovative medical technology for managing disease and treating illness and injury. It is our mission to extend life, ease pain, combat disease, and enhance a healthy state.

My heart pounded against my ribs with excitement. What did all that have in common? Memory and brain studies.

I sucked in a breath as I stared at the pages before opening up an internet tab to search for more on Klein.

But there wasn't much else to find. All I discovered about him was an article from 1999 that said he'd studied medicine at Johns Hopkins University in the States and then taken various postgraduate programmes in neuroscience and biomedical science. Afterwards, he'd worked for a neuroscience company called Lapika in the USA. There was no mention of him afterwards, which seemed very strange. Neither did he appear to have any social media accounts.

I frowned at the screen for a moment then searched the internet for a contact number for Lapika. I called them, asked to speak to their human resources department, and then gave them a spiel that I was trying to get a reference for Professor Brian Klein, saying he'd applied to be a research fellow and giving them the name of a fake university.

'He doesn't sound familiar to me,' the cheery woman on the other end of the phone said. 'When was he employed here?'

'I'm not sure.'

'Ah, okay. Can you just hold for one moment, please?'

I listened to some annoying music until she came back on the line.

'Yes, I can confirm that Brian Klein was employed here as a neuroscientist from 1989 until 1999.'

'Can you tell me anything else? What his role entailed? Where he worked afterwards? What his personnel record was like?'

'I'm afraid not. There's no mention here that we gave references to any future employers, and our full records don't go back that far. We destroy them after fifteen years.'

'Is there anyone else I can talk to who might know more?'

'Um... possibly. If you'd like to hold for a moment.'

More music. Until I was put through to someone who announced their name as Chad Cooper.

'You're asking about a reference for Brian Klein?' Chad asked.

'That's right.' I went through the spiel again.

'I'm not going to be much help as we didn't actually work together. But I believe when he left here, he went back to England for a position.'

'Can you tell me any specifics about what he did for your company?'

'Unfortunately not. Even if I could remember, which I can't, specific projects are confidential. Sorry, I don't think I can be of more help.'

I ended the call and looked up what a neuroscientist actually did. In a nutshell, they focused on the brain and nervous system, and its impact on behaviour and cognitive functions—how people think and the health issues that affect the brain.

A pain twinged between my shoulder blades. I rubbed at it, my muscles aching from all the sitting around. I stood up, rolled my arms in a circle, and stretched my neck and back, wondering why there was only one mention of Klein on the web, which wasn't even recent.

I grabbed my phone and called Sutherby. He'd done a check on Curtis, who had no previous criminal record and no known associations to cults or particular suspicious groups. He'd also checked out the Peugeot that Hoodie Guy had been in outside Ajay's house, and it had come back to a registered owner called Paul Clark at 124 Lower Claydon Street in North London.

'Right,' I said. 'So who is he?'

'That's the interesting thing. Satellite mapping has that street name listed, but it only goes up to a hundred and twenty-two. I spoke to the Metropolitan Police, and they confirmed it doesn't exist. If the address doesn't exist, then he probably doesn't, either. There are no Paul Clarks on the voter's register within a one-mile radius of that street.'

'That *is* interesting. So it's got to be a fake name and address, and the only reason for trying to cover his tracks is because he's dodgy. He's got to be involved in whatever's going on here if he was waiting outside Ajay's house and visiting the Watling Centre. What about getting Technical

Services to do some facial recognition against our databases?'

'That's in hand.'

'Can we get a CCTV and ANPR check done of the area surrounding Ajay's house to see if he pops up anywhere in that vehicle after he left there?'

'I'll look into that for you.'

'Great. And I've found something, too.' I told Sutherby about the mix-up with the professor's name and Klein's scant bio. 'We need to check out Professor Klein. He's involved in some kind of memory research here, and there's a definite link between the Watling Centre and Natalie and Vicky. Possibly Ajay, too. Maybe they were involved in some kind of research programme for the cash incentive, which would explain the money they all had that no one can account for them receiving.'

'What kind of research are we talking about?'

I told him what I'd discovered in the brochure. 'A memory study could explain why Vicky, Ajay, and Natalie were all found wandering at certain times in trance-like states with no idea of what they'd been doing or where they'd been. Natalie thought she was being followed, and Hoodie Guy *was* watching Ajay's house before the fire. So what if—'

'If what? Someone was messing around with their heads? A professor has been brainwashing them? Sounds pretty far-fetched.'

'Yes, it does, but is it any more far-fetched than a cult brainwashing them? And you know as well as I do, sir, that a job title doesn't exclude you from committing a crime— judges, politicians, world leaders, bankers, teachers, coppers. Anyone's capable of it. Maybe what's been happening to these students isn't intentional. Maybe it's some kind of side effect of whatever tests or studies Klein's doing at the Watling Centre. Maybe he's trying some new method of hypnosis. Sir, I really think I'm on to something. And the more I've looked around here, the less possibility there is of some kind of cult or society recruiting and influencing those three students. So what if it's something else entirely? We could also get the covert technical surveillance unit to hack into Klein's patient records and see if Ajay, Natalie, and Vicky *were* in any of his research programmes. And we should look into his phone and financial data.'

He was silent for a while then sighed loudly, as if he didn't buy it. 'Let me see what I can dig up on Professor Klein first before we think about those possibilities.'

'Good, because I haven't managed to find much at all.'

I heard a phone ringing in the background.

'That's my work mobile,' Sutherby said. 'The ACC is trying to get hold of me. We'll speak soon, okay?' He hung up.

Excitement rippled through me, my gut instinct kicking in big-time. I knew I'd stumbled onto something important. And there was one way I might be able to find out if I was right. I had to sign up for Klein's research clinic.

CHAPTER 27

TONI

I slowly opened the door to Marcelina's bedroom and poked my head out into the corridor. No one was about, although the music from the kitchen was still going strong, and a male voice sang along to Sia's 'Fire meets Gasoline'.

I wandered in that direction and stood in the doorway. A guy had his back towards me, stirring something in a pan on the cooker hob.

'Hi,' I said loudly over the music.

He jumped and turned around. It was the same mixed-race guy who'd been outside the university gates after Marcelina's accident.

'Woah, you freaked me out.' His surprised look quickly morphed into a grin.

'Sorry. Great voice, by the way.' I smiled back.

'Who? Me or Sia?'

'Both of you, actually.'

He laughed and turned the radio down before going back to the hob and stirring again. 'I didn't think anyone was around.' He glanced over his shoulder at me, his face turning serious. 'How are you doing? After yesterday?'

I shrugged. 'It was horrible.'

'Yeah. Really messed up. We went to the hospital to see Marcelina a little while ago, even though she didn't know we were there.'

'That was nice of you.'

'They only let us stay for a few minutes because her parents were there.'

Sia had stopped now, and the DJ on the radio played another track.

'Us?'

'Me and Precious and Hazel.'

Precious and Hazel had been mentioned a lot in Marcelina's journal. 'They're all friends, aren't they?'

'Yeah.'

'Did you know Marcelina well, too?' I stepped closer and leaned against the wall to the side of him.

'Pretty well, I suppose. We've all lived in the same block since we started, so I see them quite a bit. We hang out sometimes. We're just friends, though,' he added quickly. 'Want some spaghetti on toast? A student's dietary staple and must-have carb overload.' His striking hazel-green eyes lit up with humour.

'I don't want to deprive you of your food.'

'No, that's cool. I hate eating alone anyway.'

I hesitated a moment then said, 'Yes. If you've got enough.'

He turned the hob down and pulled out four slices of bread from an opened packet on the worktop before tucking them into a toaster.

'Are you a friend of Marcelina's?' he asked as he grabbed butter from the fridge. 'I haven't seen you around before.'

'No, I'm with Student Counselling Services. I'm Toni.'

'Oh, right. I'm Curtis.' He stirred the spaghetti again.

So this was the guy Marcelina had also mentioned in her journal. The one she had a major crush on. And I could understand why.

'She took my advice then and went to see someone.' The toast popped up. He slid the slices onto two plates and buttered them.

'What do you mean?'

He glanced up. 'Oh, sorry, I just assumed she made an appointment with you, and that's why you're here.'

'That's the thing... she did come to see me, but she kind of left the session early. She was upset and then... well, then you saw what happened afterwards.'

'Yeah.' He pulled a stricken face, poured the spaghetti on top of the waiting plates of toast, and put them on the table.

I sat down while he grabbed some knives and forks.

I took a mouthful of food, swallowed, then said, 'Was there something specific going on with Marcelina then? Something you suggested she talked with a counsellor about?'

He ate, looking at me with a mixture of curiosity and suspicion. A hot flame ignited inside as I felt a magnetic pull from his unusual-coloured eyes. I glanced down at my food and concentrated on cutting into another piece of toast.

He rested his knife and fork on the edge of his plate. 'Yeah, something weird was going on with her in the last few months.'

'Like what?'

He pursed his lips together. 'Don't know if I should tell you.'

'Why?'

'I guess because it's private. She was obviously going through a hard time.'

I caught his gaze. 'I just want to help her. She came to see me, so she obviously needed to talk to someone.'

He waited a long moment, then he picked up his cutlery again and took another bite. Afterwards, he said, 'To be honest, I thought she was depressed or majorly stressed about something.'

'What gave you that impression?'

'When she first came here, she was a bit shy, I suppose. But then she made some friends. Me, Precious, and Hazel mostly. Like I said, we hung out sometimes in a group, and she came out of her shell. And then a few months ago, she started acting strangely. She was having nightmares. I came in one night from a gig at the bar in the union. It was the early hours, and I could hear her screaming from her room. Hers is next door to mine.' He took another bite of food and ate it quickly. 'She was going mental in there. I thought she was being attacked. A few other people along the corridor came out as I was banging on the door to check if she was okay. Eventually, she opened the door, half asleep, and apologised.'

I swallowed a mouthful of food and said, 'So there was no one in the room with her?'

'No. I could see inside.'

'Did she have nightmares a lot?'

'Quite a few times recently.'

'Did anything else happen?'

He spiked his fork into a corner of toast and smeared it around the plate, soaking up the tomato sauce. 'One time I saw her in here, and she was standing at the window there.' He tilted his head towards the window that looked out onto the grassy area in front of the union building. 'She didn't notice me come in at first. I said hi, and she didn't even seem to know I was there. She was so focused on what she was looking at. So I went to stand next to her and asked her what was going on. She nearly jumped a mile when she realised I was there. She was crying. Had tears streaming down her cheeks, and she looked scared. She pointed out of the window and asked if I could see a guy out there.'

'What guy?'

He shrugged. 'That's the thing. I don't know. There were plenty of people out there, but when I asked her who she meant, she said he'd gone. But she thought he was following her.'

I sat back in the chair, frowning. 'Did she describe him? Or mention who he was?'

'No. She didn't say anything else about it. Just rushed out of the room. And the next time I saw her and asked her if she was okay, if anyone was hassling her, she said she was going to get proof. But she wouldn't tell me anything else about it.'

'When was this?'

'Oooh, a few weeks back.'

'And did she ever mention the man again?'

'Not to me. I tried to ask her about it. I wanted to make sure she was okay. But whenever I brought it up, she just started crying, which was why I thought she was depressed.'

'She's lucky you were looking out for her.'

He gave a casual shrug. 'I've got two sisters. I was always taught to look out for them.' He ate the final morsel and pushed his plate away. 'I asked Hazel and Precious if they knew what was going on with Marcelina, but she didn't tell them anything, either. Which is why I suggested she speak to a counsellor. I thought someone might be able to get out of her what she was so upset about.'

I wondered again if she'd been under the influence of something. Maybe she hadn't taken drugs intentionally. Maybe her food or drink had been spiked. Even though her bloodwork in the hospital had come up clear, a standard test would only check for the most common drugs, and some would exit her system within twenty-four hours. The black-outs she'd told me about could well have been a side effect of a date-rape drug. Was that what she'd meant when she'd mentioned the shadow man to me—a hazy recollection of someone sexually assaulting her while she'd been drugged? Or was she hearing voices and maybe hallucinating someone following her because of an underlying mental health issue?

I glanced at the large fridge in the corner of the room next to an equally large freezer. 'Do you have individual shelves in the fridge?'

He turned to see where I was looking. 'Yeah. We have a cupboard each, too.' He pointed to the kitchen units. 'They've got a lock on them.'

But the fridge didn't, so someone *could've* got in and tampered with her food or drink inside. 'Are the shelves labelled for individual people?'

'Not in this kitchen, but on the other floors, they do. We all just know whose bit of shelf is whose.' He followed my gaze and looked at the fridge. 'Why?'

I didn't want to tell him my fears yet, because if Marcelina's food or drink was being spiked, then it had to be someone familiar with this particular kitchen to know exactly whose food or drink was on which shelf. Instead, I asked, 'Do you know if anything traumatic happened to her recently?'

His forehead bunched up in a worried frown. 'Like what?'

I didn't want to come right out and ask if she'd been raped or sexually assaulted. If she'd told Curtis, then he would know exactly what I meant. And although I was getting a genuine vibe about him, for all I knew, he could be involved in something, so I picked up my knife and fork again and changed the direction of the conversation. 'Did Marcelina ever talk about someone called PK?'

He tilted his head, thinking. 'Nope. It doesn't ring a bell.'

'Do you know anyone with those initials?'

He shook his head.

'Did she have a part-time job?'

'No.'

I finished off the final bite of my food. The song on the radio finished, and the news came on as I said, 'Do you know where I can find Precious and Hazel?'

'Both of them went back to Precious's home in London. They were both really upset after seeing Marcelina in hospital. I think they'll be back tomorrow.'

'Okay, thanks. I'd like to have a chat with them and see if—'

'Did you hear that?' Curtis cut me off, sprinted out of his seat, and turned up the volume on the radio.

...the attacker, believed to be a student at St Albans University, was armed with a knife and stabbed a forty-six-year-old man who has not been named. His condition is described as critical. A police manhunt is underway for the suspect, who remains at

large. He's considered armed and dangerous and should not be approached...

My eyes widened as I listened.

'That's mental.' Curtis shook his head as he took away the plates from the table and deposited them in the sink.

Well, that was one way of putting it, but not in the terms I could voice professionally as a counsellor. 'It's absolutely tragic.' I grabbed my bag and leaped up. 'I've got to go. Thanks for the food.'

I rushed back to the office in case someone needed me. If the attacker was a student here, another general offer of student counselling would be put out in the aftermath of such a tragic event. I had a feeling we were going to be inundated.

CHAPTER 28

MR WHITE

The BMW X5 was tucked well out of sight behind an abandoned warehouse. Because it was in the middle of nowhere, Nathan White had used this spot as a discreet meeting place on many occasions. Plus, he already knew there were no CCTV cameras within a five-mile radius to clock the comings and goings. Even if there were, the vehicle was a clone. And he was a shadow. Untouchable. Nothing would ever come back to him.

He picked up his mobile phone from the centre console and scrolled through the news sites until he found what he wanted. He opened a link and read about the St Peters Street stabbing dispassionately. He'd long since separated what was right and wrong from what was necessary. He snorted to himself. If only the public knew the real story. But they were too wrapped up in celebrity reality TV that was anything but real, taking social media surveys about what kind of potato they were, and uploading selfies that had been enhanced so much, they didn't even resemble the person anymore, unable to have a conversation or a night out without being glued to their phones or tablets. They were dumbed down, plugged in, and switched on to total bullshit. Too apathetic to care that their freedoms were being systematically stripped from them one by one. Exactly the way they'd been brainwashed to be. Incessantly complaining about their lives but always wanting someone else to save them. The bread and circuses diversions to satisfy their basest requirements were working, and if they were too stupid and narcissistic to realise it, then that was their own fault.

White glanced up when he heard the car approaching from behind and put his phone back in the console. In the rearview mirror, he watched Glover pull up behind him in his older, anonymous Ford Focus.

A few seconds later, Glover slid into the passenger seat and grinned at White before handing over a flash drive. 'Number five.'

White took it and put it into his pocket. 'You got all of it on camera?'

'Of course. Wide angle, HD, a first-class-seat show.'

'Good.'

'Has Farzad Nuri been taken care of?'

'Of course.' White twisted in his seat to face Glover. 'We couldn't leave him to be arrested, like Natalie. It just creates a massive shit storm to clear up that I don't need. There'll be a big police hunt for him, but they'll never find the body. And while we're on the subject of shit storms... you just seem to be creating them wherever you go. First Natalie, then Marcelina.'

'Hey, that wasn't my fault! Natalie wasn't supposed to go back to the university. I couldn't get to her in time. And Marcelina had to be dealt with quickly.'

'What's her prognosis?'

'Not looking good.'

'But she's still alive,' White growled.

Glover shrugged. 'Even if she survives, it looks like she'll be brain-dead.'

'This is the last time you act on your own initiative. We should've waited and done it properly. You're getting very sloppy. That's when mistakes get made.' He glared at Glover. 'What about the counselling notes? Did Marcelina talk about what was going on before the accident?'

'No. She mentioned the usual, but she didn't have time to share her suspicions before I sorted her out. But she could've done, so it was a good thing I did it then. I thought I was protecting us.'

'Next time, don't think. That's what *I'm* here for. Where's the other item?'

'I took it direct to Hughes, like he asked me.'

'Good.'

'Is that the end of it then? Two suicides, two accidents, and a stabbing. Any more, and it's going to start looking suspect.'

White stared at Glover, his grey eyes as hard as flint. 'Thinking like that's above your pay grade.'

'I'm just saying.'

'Haven't you heard? There's an epidemic of suicide rates amongst university students recently. Bristol Uni had ten in two years. Knife crime's been on the rise for years. And hundreds of accidents happen every day. There's a bigger pot to play with than you might think. You just do what you're told. Make sure everything's going to plan and don't fuck it up again. *That's* what you're paid for.'

Glover shrugged, as if he didn't care one way or the other.

'I'll be in touch.' White started the engine and waited for Glover to get out of the car.

CHAPTER 29

TONI

There were no clients in the waiting room when I rushed inside the counselling block. Janet sat at her desk, phone pressed to her ear, and the door to Phil's office and those of the other counsellors were all closed.

I waited by Janet's desk until she hung up. 'I've just heard about the stabbing,' I said. 'Was the offender really a student here?'

'I'm afraid so. It seems a tutor from here was in St Peters Street when it happened and recognised him and called the police. Awful, isn't it? Phil's trying to find out more information now.'

'Which student?'

She glanced down at the pad on her desk with her neat writing on. 'Farzad Nuri.'

I pressed my lips together. I didn't recognise the name, but it didn't stop the breath catching in my throat at the awfulness of the situation.

'Phil's going to brief everyone in—' She stopped abruptly as Phil stepped out of his office and strode towards us. His usually calm persona had an air of harassed urgency about it.

'I take it you've heard?' Phil said to me.

'Yes.' A wave of sadness washed over me for the victim. 'It's terrible.'

'I need you both in my office for a few minutes. I'll just round up the others.' He strode back down the corridor.

Five minutes later, Phil's small office was crowded to bursting point. Riya, another associate counsellor who'd joined a few months before me, stood next to Janet. The other full-time counsellors—Vincent, Georgina, and Kieran —formed a circle around Phil's desk.

'So... we've had official confirmation that the boy involved in the tragic stabbing was Farzad Nuri, who attended this university.'

Riya gasped.

'How tragic.' Georgina shook her head.

'As you're aware, in circumstances like this, we like to put a high profile on the services we provide to our students, in case anyone who knew Farzad or is affected by this incident wants to talk.' He glanced over at Janet. 'So Janet will shortly be putting together some form emails to students and dealing with the university's online stuff, offering anyone counselling who needs it. Obviously, I don't know how many people will take up our offer, but any students will be distributed equally amongst you all.'

Janet nodded gravely.

'Was Farzad Nuri a client of ours?' I asked Phil.

'No. He'd never spoken to anyone from Student Counselling in the past. The only thing I know about him so far is that he was on his second year of a fine art course. He had an exemplary record until a few months ago, when his tutors thought his work was slacking.'

'Do we know what prompted the attack?' Kieran asked.

Phil held his hands up in the air. 'That's all I really know at the moment. Okay, so take some time to process this. If anyone wants to talk, I'll be back in my office after two as I've got an emergency meeting to try and find out more. Are there any more questions?'

Nos all round. We were filing out when Phil called my name. I stepped back towards his desk as the others left, their muted conversation flowing back down the corridor with them.

'I'm really sorry to ask, but is it all right if we push your supervision session back? This is going to take priority.'

'Of course. What happened yesterday with Marcelina...' I hesitated for a moment, wondering whether to mention my suspicions that something possibly sinister was going on with her. But I still had no idea that I was even right. I could've been just chasing shadows, and I knew what he'd say, that I was getting too involved, taking the student's problems to heart. So instead I said, 'I was obviously upset and in shock, but I'm okay. You're going to be busy with this, I know, so you don't need to worry about me.'

He smiled gratefully. 'Thanks. But if you need me, just let me know. We'll reschedule it for some time in the next few days.'

'No problem.'

I went back into my office, shut the door, and sat down at my desk, wondering how statistically likely it was to have two tragedies in two days involving students from the same university. It had to be a horrific coincidence. There had already been a couple of suicides before I'd arrived, plus a tragic car accident involving another student. Maybe the university was just having a bad time lately.

I accessed the student record files that the counselling service was able to get hold of on the uni's intranet. They weren't full files, just scant details that provided a photograph of Farzad with his course details listed. I clicked out of the uni's system and opened an internet tab. I searched the latest news reports, reading the same information that I'd already heard, until I found a site with a link to YouTube that had a tagline claiming to have caught the stabbing on camera.

A knot formed in my stomach at the thought someone had videoed and uploaded it. I should've been surprised, but I wasn't. After my kidnapping, I knew more than most about the sick and twisted voyeurism some people could be capable of and the amount of darkness in the world.

I clicked the link, and the standard video box appeared. It already had twenty-six thousand views. I pressed Play and held my breath as I watched.

It had been filmed on a phone, and whoever was holding it as they walked along St Peters Street gave a running commentary in an American accent, saying how pretty it was, and that they were going down the hill to see the Abbey. As always, the street with its main drag of shops was busy with people.

A young guy with thick dark hair came into view from the bottom right-hand side of the frame, striding away from the camera phone as he walked along in front, hands in his jacket pockets, looking like he was going for a casual stroll. An older man in a suit walked towards the young man, one hand holding his own mobile phone to his ear as he took a call.

And then it happened. As they approached each other, the younger guy's right hand slipped from his pocket, and I glimpsed a knife before he moved his hand down by his side. So this was most likely Farzad, although I still couldn't see his face.

One second passed as the commentator, who obviously hadn't noticed anything untoward, carried on talking about which shops they were passing. The man on the mobile phone hung up and looked down at his phone screen, distracted.

When Farzad reached the suited man, his hand swung up in the air and plunged straight into the man's stomach. No one reacted for a moment. Not the victim. Not the passersby. Not the commentator. No one had realised something terrible had happened.

Then everything seemed to take place at once. The victim collapsed to the ground, clutching his stomach, groaning, eyes panicked and surprised. A red patch of blood oozed onto his white shirt in a star-shaped pattern.

The person with the camera said, 'Oh, my Gawd! He's got a *knife!*' And they stopped walking suddenly, the phone shaking as it wobbled in their hand.

Some people moved towards the victim. Others backed away, heads looking around. A few were screaming.

Farzad shouted to the crowd to call an ambulance, eyes wild as he spun around in a circle, giving the camera a full view of his face. One witness pressed his mobile phone to his ear, presumably calling the emergency services.

Farzad dropped the knife. Then he ran through the crowd and disappeared down the street. A burly witness on the pavement shouted, 'Where did he go? Did anyone see where he went?'

Someone pointed further down the street. 'He ran down that way.'

The commentator said, 'Oh, my. This is just awful. A man's been stabbed. Right in front of us! I think it was a guy who ran away.' But it wasn't awful enough for them to stop filming, because they carried on as the victim lay on the ground, not moving, his eyes closed.

A woman crouched over him, hands pressed to the knife wound in his stomach that oozed blood, attempting to staunch the flow.

A few minutes later, an ambulance roared up the street, closely followed by two police cars.

It wasn't self-defence. There was no provocation. The victim had been walking past Farzad, minding his own business, when Farzad lunged for him, stabbing him for no apparent reason.

I leaned closer to the screen suddenly as something—or rather someone—caught my eye. I stopped the video, went back twenty seconds, and played it again. The footage was jerky at that part, as whoever had filmed it quickly panned around with the phone outstretched, catching some people on the other side of the road.

My finger hovered over the mouse until he came into view again. I clicked to stop it, and the screen filled with a shot of three people standing in front of a shop, watching what was happening.

I focused on a man I thought I'd seen before. He wore a baseball cap, the peak tilted low, and sunglasses, but even so, the shape of his face and his features were quite distinctive. I recognised his nose—long and tapered to a blunt end. He had thin lips and prominent cheekbones. I was sure it was the same doctor who'd been in the trauma room with Marcelina when I'd first walked in to see her. Dr Lahey— that was his name.

I pressed Play again and watched as the camera panned back around to the victim lying unconscious on the ground, with two paramedics working on him. Four police officers were nearby, two glancing around frantically, as if looking for Farzad. One was talking into his radio, while the other tried to push the crowd away from the victim. But at no time did Dr Lahey approach the victim.

Why not? Surely he should've been the first one rushing in to offer help. He'd said he was a neurologist, but he must've still been experienced in dealing with trauma.

The footage stopped then, and I wound it back to where I'd seen Dr Lahey. I paused it and snapped a photo of the screen with my mobile phone. Then I called up an app on my phone to download the video. It would only be a matter of time before it was taken down.

I googled Watford General Hospital and clicked on their website, looking for the page that listed their staff. After entering neurology as a specialty, I scrolled through a team of doctors and consultants, but the Dr Lahey on the website was someone completely different to the man I'd met. I leaned closer to the screen, staring at Dr Lahey's photograph, frowning and trying to think of a rational explanation.

I supposed it was possible the one I'd met was a locum from another hospital with the same name as another doctor, but the more I thought about it, the more off that seemed. Even a doctor from another hospital would've surely rushed in to help. Farzad Nuri had run away from the scene, so it was unlikely the man had been concerned for his safety before stepping in. And what were the chances of two neurology consultants having the same name, when it wasn't a particularly common one? Now, as I thought back, what had happened in the trauma room when I found him there seemed highly suspicious. I hadn't picked up on it at the time, because I'd been too upset about Marcelina.

I closed my eyes as I pictured the scene again. Marcelina had been on her side when I went in the room, but later, Dr Fellows had asked if I'd moved her from lying on her back. It seemed highly unlikely Marcelina could turn herself over if she was unconscious and sedated, so he, whoever he was, must've done it. But why? Who the hell was he? Someone *pretending* to be a doctor? And if so, for what reason? What had he been doing to Marcelina before I'd walked in?

I hadn't paid much attention to it at the time, but now I ran through it step-by-step... when I'd entered the trauma room, the curtain had been drawn around her. He'd stepped out from behind it on the left of the bed. She'd been lying on her left side, blanket up to her chest, her back facing where he would've been standing beside her bed. And pretty much as soon as he saw me, he'd slid his hands into the pockets of his white lab coat, as if maybe he was holding something he didn't want me to see, but—and this was something I'd only just realised—he *hadn't* been wearing latex gloves. Surely every member of the medical staff would be wearing them to examine patients. Not just for their own safety, but also to combat the spread of MRSA and other infections. And now that I thought about it, his demeanour had seemed a bit off, as well. This whole thing was getting weirder and weirder.

I rang Mitchell and told him about the latest develop-ments. He asked me to send him the YouTube video and the photo of the doctor, and he'd get Lee to find out what he could.

But now I was certain that somehow, and I had no idea why, the tragedies involving Farzad and Marcelina had to be connected.

CHAPTER 30

DETECTIVE BECKY HARRIS

I called the number on the brochure for the Watling Centre and spoke to the receptionist I'd seen earlier, explaining how I wanted to volunteer for Professor Klein's research, but the earliest I could get an appointment with him was the following afternoon.

Then I looked through Natalie Wheeler's file again. Immediately after Natalie's arrest, she'd been very confused. Her first words recorded by the arresting officer were that she hadn't seen the elderly pedestrian she'd run over and couldn't remember what had happened at all. At the police station, she'd suffered what seemed to be a complete breakdown and had been given an initial psychiatric evaluation and declared unfit to be questioned. The force psychiatrist had said she was possibly trying to block out the horror of what she'd done and was suffering from traumatic amnesia. But now, Natalie was being evaluated by a forensic psychiatrist until a formal decision was made on whether she was fit to stand trial.

The mental health hospital she was being detained in had carried out several diagnostic tests—EEG tests to measure brain patterns and blood and urine tests. Any neurological reasons for her mental state had been ruled out. According to the most recent evaluation update, Natalie was described as being disorganised, sometimes catatonic, and suffering from hallucinations and delusions. She had confused ideas of what was going on around her and believed a moth in her brain talked to her and told her to do things. She was being treated with a combination of antipsychotic medication and psychotherapy, but there hadn't been much positive progress in her condition yet.

Poor girl. It was all terribly sad. For her and the victim's family. But was she really schizophrenic? Jess and Millie had seen her with Professor Klein. They'd said it looked as if they were arguing. And if Klein was doing mind research on students, was it possible what he'd done had messed up her head so completely, she just *seemed* like she had schizophrenia?

I called the hospital where Natalie was and asked if I could arrange a visit. They told me I could come in an hour's time. As a police officer, I would have to follow strict procedures to visit her. It would mean arranging a social worker to accompany me and leaving a paper trail. But I wasn't going in as a police officer. I told them I was a friend of hers from university, and they said I was welcome to see her—in fact, I would be her only visitor, apart from her parents. But they did warn me that she might not be very responsive.

I hung up, grabbed my bag, and headed to my car, keeping an eye out for Hoodie Guy. I set up the satnav for Bramble Lodge, which sounded more like a nice country retreat than a medium-secure mental health hospital that housed people deemed to be a danger to themselves or others. Most of the one hundred and fifty patients had

committed offences when mentally ill or had been diagnosed with a mental illness while already in prison.

I arrived fifteen minutes before the designated visiting
slot I'd been given, so I parked on the road outside and
stared at the purpose-built, modern façade—a mixture of
red brick and pale-blue render. It could've been a leisure
centre or school. Only the guard booth on the main gate and
the high wire mesh security fencing gave away its purpose.

I pulled up Natalie's Instagram page on my phone and
scrolled through photos of her partying with Jess and Millie,
holding up drinks to the camera, photos of books she'd read,
quotes she liked, a tattoo she admired, flowers, wine bottles,
food, and selfies. There was a video clip of her doing karaoke
on a stage, belting out a song off-key but not caring because
she was obviously having a great time, owning the stage with
a fun-loving confidence. What journey had transformed the
beautiful, vibrant young woman with glowing skin and a
mischievous glint in her eyes that hinted at a good sense of
humour to someone whose head was completely disturbed?

My heart ached for Natalie as I took one final look then
started the engine. I stopped at the guard booth to show my
driving licence for ID. The guard examined it and then
called the main building to check I'd rung ahead for an
appointment. Satisfied, he handed me back my licence, told
me where to park, and released the electric metal gates.

I left my bag in the boot of my car, turned my phone to
silent mode, and slid it into my pocket before following a
sign for the main entrance. The secure doors with safety
glass had a camera pointing down at me. I pressed a bell on
the intercom and held up my ID to whoever was monitoring
the CCTV.

A buzzing noise signalled an electric entry system at

play, and the door was opened by a female nurse dressed in blue scrubs. She was about twice my size in both height and width. Solid but not fat. I wouldn't want to mess with her, put it that way.

'You're here to see Natalie Wheeler?' she asked.

'That's right.'

'Okay, come with me, please.'

The door shut with a metallic clang, and she led me through another secure door into an area with a reception booth behind toughened glass. The receptionist asked for my ID again, which I showed, and he gave me a visitor's pass to clip onto my top.

The nurse and I headed through another secure door that led to a long corridor. I was expecting something dark, dingy, and depressing, but inside, it was bright, with cream walls and modern parquet flooring. Halfway down, we reached a staircase that had been closed off with more toughened glass doors embedded with wire. The nurse swiped a pass key against an electronic lock, opened the door, and walked up the stairs.

'How is Natalie?' I asked.

'Not that great, I'm afraid. She's not making much progress yet. It's nice to see one of her friends coming in, though. We actively encourage visitors for our patients here. We think it can help in their rehabilitation. No one else apart from her parents has been yet.'

We exited the staircase at the next floor and passed through more security doors before ending up in another corridor.

'Does she ever mention anyone from university?' I asked.

'Not that I'm aware of, no.'

Somewhere in the distance, I heard a high-pitched

screaming. I'd been in psychiatric wards many times as a patrol officer, when sectioning someone under the Mental Health Act, and it was never easy for patients or their loved ones.

'Is she violent?' I asked.

'No, she's actually submissive. But I will warn you that she may not even realise you're here.'

We walked past a day room with bright artwork adorning the walls. Several female patients sat inside, either watching a TV screen or at tables playing board games. One sat in the corner, staring into space. After that was a pharmacy area with a reinforced glass window and metal grill in the counter.

'Natalie's been put in the blue meeting room for your visit,' the nurse said.

I followed her further along the corridor, past a row of heavy-duty doors with small reinforced glass rectangles in them. I couldn't get a look inside, but I assumed they were the patients' rooms. At the far end was another door. The nurse swiped the entry system with her card and entered a room flooded with light from windows overlooking the lush green gardens.

I swallowed a lump of sadness in my throat as I looked at Natalie, sitting on a lightweight wooden chair, staring down at the matching desk in front of her and rocking forwards and backwards. Her hands were tucked underneath her thighs, shoulders hunched over. Her long, greasy brown hair fell over her face. She wore a grey T-shirt, black jogging bottoms, slip-on shoes, and socks. No laces, belts, or items that would make it easier for patients to take their own lives. As we walked in, she didn't look up or acknowledge our existence at all.

'Natalie, your friend Becky's here to see you. Isn't that nice?' The nurse stood in front of Natalie and bent down to catch her sightline. 'Natalie?'

We waited. There was no response.

'Natalie?' The nurse tried again.

Natalie looked up, her eyes blank for a few seconds before a slow smile of recognition crossed her face. 'Nurse Hillary. Is it time for therapy?'

'No, not yet, love. That will be in a few hours. First, you can have a nice chat with your friend. Okay? Are you feeling up to that?'

Natalie's gaze slid slowly over to me, her eyes forked with tiny red blood vessels. I didn't know if it was the medication or her mental state making her seem so out of it, but eventually, she nodded.

'Good. I'll leave you to it.' Nurse Hillary smiled and patted Natalie's arm. Then she said to me, 'Just knock when you want to come out. I'll be waiting outside.' She strode to the door and disappeared out of the room.

'Hi, Natalie. How are you?' I sat down opposite her.

She stared at me, her focus woozy, pulled one hand out from under her thigh, and chewed on a fingernail.

'My name's Becky.'

She tilted her head and squinted at me. 'Do I... know you?' Her speech was slurred and slow. 'Only I... I can't remember things.' She tapped her temple. 'Something... wrong.'

'No, you don't know me.' I smiled. 'And I'm sorry to bring this up, but I need to talk to you about the car accident.'

She looked down at her lap and blinked rapidly. 'It was... the moth. I tried to stop... stop it. It made me.' She blinked again, and a tear slid down her cheek.

'What can you tell me about the moth, Natalie?'

She tapped her right foot up and down, still not looking at me. 'It's... in my head.' She twisted slowly around on the seat so her back was to me, head still bent down. She lifted her long hair with her left hand and dug her right index finger at a spot on the back of her neck. 'It's inside. In... here. It told me to... told me to hit him. To kill the man. It told me he was the enemy.' She twisted around to face me again and swiped at her wet cheeks with the backs of her hands.

'When did you first start hearing the moth telling you to do things?'

She shrugged and scratched at an angry red patch of skin on the inside of her wrist.

'Straight after the accident, you told the police officers you didn't remember what had happened.'

She scratched harder.

'But now you think it was the moth, making you do things?'

She nodded manically.

'I spoke to your friends, Jess and Millie. They saw you with Professor Klein a few times on campus. Were you involved in a relationship with him? Or did you volunteer for one of his research programmes?'

Her gaze darted to the side. She tapped her foot up and down again, slowly at first, then faster and faster, obviously agitated, as if she'd recognised the name.

'He's a research fellow in the Watling Centre. Your friends saw you speaking with him on several occasions. Why were you talking to him? He didn't have anything to do with your course.'

Her face scrunched up, as if fighting an inner battle of some kind. 'I can't...'

'Can't what?'

She leaned forward, put her index finger to her lips, and whispered, 'Shhh. It's a secret.'

'You can tell me, Natalie. I want to help you. Did he make you promise to keep a secret?'

Her face twisted as if she were in pain. She rammed a fist to her mouth.

'Was he doing some kind of behavioural or memory study on you?'

She smashed her fists against her thighs.

'Did he do something to you?'

'No!' she cried, fists pressed against her temples.

But I didn't believe her.

'No, no, no!' She shook her head rapidly then suddenly went still and rigid, head bent forwards, hair falling half over her face.

I paused for a moment, letting her take a few breaths, then said, 'Did you know Ajay Banerjee or Vicky Aylott or Farzad Nuri? They were also students at the university.'

She looked up, her gaze darting around the room, not settling on anything for long. She sat on her hands again and rocked gently.

Was I wrong about there being a connection? Sitting with her, it seemed a ludicrous possibility that Professor Klein or another member of the medical faculty could be involved in trying to mess with students' heads. It seemed much more likely that Natalie *had* been suffering from an undiagnosed mental health issue that could've been brought on by the stress and pressure of being at university. I'd read that the first signs of schizophrenia could include sleep problems, irritability, a drop in grades, or a change of friends. It was common for people affected to isolate themselves or withdraw from others, have unusual thoughts or paranoia, and exhibit strange behaviour. The disease could start with a big bang and an acute episode of hallucinations or other disorders. For a moment, I felt completely out of my depth, questioning my own judgement, uncertainty pumping through me.

But then I thought about the video of Natalie on her Instagram page, so full of life. So happy. A million miles away from this Natalie. I thought about Hoodie Guy. The money that had come from an unknown source. Klein's name and the Watling Centre popping up every time. Ajay's and Vicky's shared symptoms. Surely it was too much of a coincidence that they could've *all* been suffering from mental illnesses that hadn't been picked up. No. However ludicrous and far-out it sounded, I was certain I was on the right track.

I pulled my phone from my pocket and swiped through to the photo I'd taken of Hoodie Guy. 'Do you recognise this man?' I held out the phone to her.

She didn't look up.

'Natalie, can you just look at this photo for me, please?' I said softly.

She glanced up, eyes slowly focusing on the screen. Then she squeezed her eyes shut tight. 'I can't say.'

'Yes, you can. You can tell me. I want to help you. You thought someone was following you, didn't you? Was this him?'

Her face seemed to crumple in on itself. Tears streamed down her cheeks. 'Put it away! Put it away!' She opened her eyes and held out a palm, blocking the photo from her sightline.

I wanted to push her further, because I was sure she

recognised him. She was too distraught, though, so I quickly put my phone back in my pocket. 'It's okay. It's gone.'

She rocked faster in the chair.

'Were you one of Klein's research patients?' I tried again.

She wrapped her arms around her stomach and carried on rocking. She swivelled her head to the left, looking at the wall, but not before a look of pure terror had etched onto her face.

'What is it you think you're not supposed to say? What secret are you supposed to keep?'

She shook her head, biting her lower lip.

'What did he do to you, Natalie?'

More tears slid down her cheeks. She didn't bother to wipe them, and they splashed onto her jogging bottoms, leaving dark smudges.

'If he hurt you in some way, you can tell me.'

'No one... will believe me. It's... the moth. It has to be the moth.' She clamped her teeth down harder on her lip until a spot of blood appeared.

'*I'll* believe you. I promise I'll believe you. Did he assault you? Or was it something else going on? Did he give you some kind of treatment or test that did something to your mind? Did he ever hypnotise you? You were having black-outs—periods of lost time, like you were sleepwalking, but I don't think it *was* sleepwalking, was it? You didn't remember what you'd been doing. Was it something Klein did that caused it all?'

She closed her eyes, shook her head again.

'Where did you get the money from? The cash you had under your mattress? There was over two thousand pounds. Did Professor Klein pay you to be involved in his research going on at the uni?'

She looked up at me, and for the first time, her eyes looked clear and focused, even though her words were slow. 'It was the moth. Someone put it in my head. And now it can't get out. I looked it up.'

I leaned forward and rested my elbows on the table, keeping my gaze steady on her bloodshot eyes. 'Looked what up?'

She rocked harder in the chair. 'Who would believe me?'

I leaned in closer. I could smell her breath, sour and hot. 'Did he do something to you?'

'It's still in there! I can feel it... wiggling away.' She stopped moving and jabbed a finger at the back of her neck repeatedly. 'It made me kill that man. I didn't want to! I didn't want to! I didn't want to!' she repeated over and over again, her desolate eyes staring into mine. 'You believe me, don't you? I didn't do it on... purpose. The moth told me to.'

CHAPTER 31

DETECTIVE BECKY HARRIS

I left the hospital, mulling over what Natalie had said. She'd eventually broken down and turned catatonic, and I hadn't managed to get anything else out of her. But sometimes what people didn't say spoke the loudest. Had Klein and Hoodie Guy threatened her to keep her quiet?

When I got back in my car, I checked my phone and found a missed call and voicemail from Sutherby, asking me to call him immediately.

The first thing he said upon answering was 'I think we could have another one.'

And then he ran me through the events involving Farzad Nuri, a student of St Albans University, who'd stabbed a member of the public in the busy shopping area of St Peters Street. Details were sketchy so far, but first reports from witnesses described it as a completely unprovoked attack. Nuri had managed to flee the scene and evade any CCTV cameras, and he was still at large.

'Was the actual incident captured on CCTV?' I asked.

'No. There was some kind of major power-cut glitch this afternoon, and all of St Peters Street and the immediate surrounding area was down for forty-five minutes, so there were no local authority or private cameras in operation. And because of that, Nuri's disappeared into thin air.'

'Damn. What do we know about Nuri so far?'

'He's a second-generation Iranian immigrant. His parents came to the UK thirty years ago, and Farzad was born here and is their only child. We've spoken to his parents by phone, who live in Luton. His mother's a nurse. Father's a dentist. They're as shocked as everyone else. They've described him as being a decent, placid kid, and they can't imagine any reason he'd do it. As far as they're aware, he wasn't affiliated with any suspicious groups or organisations and wasn't religious. He didn't mention to them that he was having any problems recently. They thought he was happy, enjoying uni, and in a relationship with a girl called Amy. The last time they spoke to him was a week ago, when he called them.'

'He didn't mention anything to his parents about sleep-walking and nightmares? Or blackout fugue states?'

'Apparently not.'

'It might not be connected,' I said. 'Or he just might not have told them anyway, even if that was going on. But it does seem very weird there's now a fourth student tragedy. Have you spoken to any of Farzad's friends yet?'

'That's in hand. We're trying to gather as much information as we can about him and where he might've gone. We have to catch him before he does something else. We've got teams all over the place searching for any trace of him.'

'Have you found out anything about Klein?'

'His standard police data checks come back clean. Not even so much as a parking fine. I asked Anthea to look at his personnel details, but most of his file seems to be missing.'

'Missing?' I scrunched up my face. 'What kind of files do they keep? Digital or paper?'

'For employees, they keep digital copies. But when she went into Klein's file, there was nothing much listed, except for his qualifications and contact details. There's no contract copy, no previous employment history.'

My antennae went on high alert. 'Don't you think that's very strange? Especially when I can't seem to find anything on him, either. These days, there's something about everyone on the internet. Even some people's pets have an Instagram page. But I found no social media, no website, no LinkedIn account, and only one mention of him ever.'

'It could be an error. Or a glitch in the system.'

I snorted. 'Another glitch? Like the CCTV glitch? I don't think so. It's all too convenient. I think this is all planned to cover something up. What about Hoodie Guy? Any idea who he is yet?'

'Not so far, no. I'm still waiting for Technical Services to get back to me re the facial recognition. But I did ask Anthea to check through the uni's database for any sign of Hoodie Guy. Every student and member of staff has their photo taken for their ID. She went through every file manually, and there's no trace of him on their system. I've also got someone searching CCTV footage for the area around Ajay's house for sightings of the vehicle he used, but the nearest camera is three miles away, so we may not find anything. ANPR cameras have no trace of that number plate showing up on their systems.'

'If he was clever, he would've dumped the vehicle some-where and burnt it out or hidden it.'

'We'll keep looking.'

'Maybe we could arrange for some covert surveillance on

Klein's digital communications to see if he's been in touch with Hoodie Guy, and we really should get hold of his historical phone and financial records.'

'There's not enough to go on to justify that yet.'

'Well, I'm sure Natalie recognised Klein and Hoodie Guy.' I relayed my conversation with her. 'And she was scared. If Klein is doing some kind of brainwashing on those students, then it would fit what's been going on.'

'It seems completely ludicrous. And I'm certain someone would've noticed those students being involved in any kind of bizarre tests like that, or if any of his research was causing students to harm themselves or others on this level, don't you? They'd be doing something about it. The university has an exemplary reputation; they wouldn't be doing anything to jeopardise that. And I'm not prepared to, either, on just a bizarre theory.'

'What if the university isn't aware of what Klein's doing? Vicky was seen going into the building late at night, not during the usual clinic hours. It could've been something off the books. Something secret.'

'There would be a paper trail of their records through the Watling Centre, and someone would've noticed.' He was silent for a moment. 'No, I'm struggling to believe that scenario. If Natalie *is* schizophrenic, that would explain the wandering episodes prior to the accident. And the moth telling her to hit the man, too. Maybe that's all there is to it.'

'Or maybe she's confused, and the moth is a euphemism for some kind of brainwashing programme carried out on her.'

Yet more silence as he considered this. 'Right now there's no evidence to support what you're saying.'

I rolled my eyes at the ceiling, grinding my teeth for a

moment. 'Well, let's go back to my patient record suggestion then. Get our covert technical team to hack into Klein's files.'

'First of all, the records will be a no-go. I made enquiries with Anthea, who told me the university's patient records aren't held on a web-accessed system. They're all in a completely off-line database. And secondly, we don't have enough for a warrant to examine patient records yet. I'm certainly not prepared to go in guns blazing on a bizarre hunch.'

'Does Anthea have access to the patient records?'

'No. They're confidential. Only clinical staff has access.'

'Then I'll have to get into the Watling Centre and have a look for them.'

'Break in?'

'This *is* a covert operation, isn't it?'

'Yes. But all you have is a theory, which sounds incredibly far-fetched.'

'Sir, I know I'm right. I've got an appointment with Professor Klein at 3.00 p.m. tomorrow. I'm going to volunteer to be involved in his research and see exactly what he's up to. But if I don't find anything then, can you give me authorisation to break into the Watling Centre and dig around?'

There was a pause on the other end of the phone, Sutherby's breath crackling down the line.

'What about Farzad Nuri?' I pushed on. 'We've now got *four* tragedies involving students in the last few months. There's some malfeasance going on here, sir. I'm positive. And it might not stop with Nuri.'

After another pause, he said, 'No. I don't think there's anywhere near enough for authorisation to break into the centre.'

I wanted to push him further, convinced Hoodie Guy was

the key to all this, but I knew I had to choose my battles carefully, so I bit back my objections.

'We've arranged for Farzad's girlfriend and best friend to come to the station for interview at 4.00 p.m.,' he carried on.

'Can I watch the live interview feed?' Which would mean going into St Albans police station, but if anyone from the uni spotted me there, I'd just say I knew Farzad and was giving an interview, too.

'I don't see why not. I'll meet you there.'

I heard someone calling Sutherby's name. He asked me to hold on and had a muffled conversation with someone before coming back on the line. 'We finally have some good news, Becky. I've just been informed that someone uploaded a video of the stabbing onto YouTube that they recorded on a mobile phone, and we've got a copy of it. As you can imagine, we're involved in a full-scale manhunt here, so no one's had the chance to look at it yet, but I'll email it over now in case you can spot anything relevant.'

We said our goodbyes, and I logged onto my email account on my phone, bouncing my knee up and down and looking back towards Bramble Lodge as I waited for Sutherby's message to arrive.

I pounced on the email as soon as it appeared, clicked the link, and started watching the footage captured from an American tourist. I watched carefully, looking for any sighting of Hoodie Guy hanging around like he was at Ajay's house.

I stared at the screen, watching in horror at the moment Farzad Nuri stabbed the victim and the captured aftermath, my jaw clenched so tight, my teeth started aching. Then I sat up straighter, excitement bubbling at my core.

There was a point in the video where the person with the

camera phone had panned around, taking in the opposite side of the road for a brief moment, and I was sure I caught sight of Hoodie Guy.

I stopped the footage and rewound it. And there he was, leaning against the wall in between two shops, facing the scene of the stabbing. He wore a baseball cap and sunglasses. He'd tried to disguise himself, but his nose, the shape of his jaw, and his cheekbones gave it away. He had a mobile phone pressed to his ear, as if making a call.

I restarted the video, and the camera swung back on the victim being attended to by a female member of the public. I watched the chaos kicking off. The terrified reactions of the people around. Members of the public stopping and staring or hurrying away, scared. The ambulance and police arriving. Then the clip ended with no further sighting of Hoodie Guy.

I quickly called Sutherby and told him what I'd found. 'Hoodie Guy *must've* known it would happen, because he looked as if he was waiting for it. Just like when he was waiting outside Ajay's.'

'Well, that's very interesting, because Technical Services have just come back to me, and they haven't found any matches on Hoodie Guy from facial recognition searches. We've gone through police databases and all national databases—driving licences, passports, etcetera—and he doesn't seem to exist.'

'So either he's not British, or he hasn't actually got a valid licence or passport. Or...' I trailed off, thinking. 'The vehicle he drove was registered to a fake address, and he used a fake name so common and generic, it would be basically anonymous, and organising something to cover his tracks like that would suggest knowledge of our systems and the local area.

So I think he *is* British. And he was driving a car, so it's likely he must've got a licence at some point. And if that's the case, then he's been wiped from the databases somehow. Just like the CCTV from St Peters Street was wiped out because of the power cut. Which would take a lot of friends in high places—either bribery by someone powerful or the government or secret services.'

He inhaled loudly. 'Steady on, Becky. You're sounding like some kind of conspiracy theorist now.'

'Sir, I'm not a conspiracy theorist. I'm a realist. I'm convinced that whatever was going on with those students started at the Watling Centre, and Klein and Hoodie Guy are right in the middle of it.'

'Look, I definitely agree something suspicious is going on, but I think he's not British and just isn't on our systems. And I'm still not convinced at all about what you're saying. It seems far more logical to me this could be a small cult in operation with a select few members and Hoodie Guy is the leader. Maybe he wants to create terror and mayhem for some personal, sick agenda. Or, more likely, after the Farzad Nuri incident, I'm starting to believe it could be the makings of some kind of terrorist cell, where Hoodie Guy is creating suicide martyrs or people who'll attack at random for some ideological reason that we don't know about yet. Either way, I—'

'Sir, I'm certain it's not a cult. Or a terrorist cell. It's Klein orchestrating this somehow! I thought you wanted me on this case because you trusted my judgement. I've got experience of dealing with unusual, complicated cases, and this is—'

'That's *enough* for now. We're going to see what Nuri's girlfriend and friend have got to say about Farzad before we discuss this further.' His voice was curt, brusque. 'You've got an hour to get here if you want to listen to the interview. I'll be in the observation suite.'

He was obviously stressed, under pressure to find Farzad, and losing patience, and pushing him even further didn't seem like a good idea. In order to convince him of my theory that Klein was involved, I needed to increase my ammunition to prove it first.

So I took a deep breath to avoid blurting out anything that would just sound even more ludicrous to him. I counted to three, blew it out, and said, 'Okay, sir. I'll see you soon.'

CHAPTER 32

DETECTIVE BECKY HARRIS

I drove to St Albans police station on autopilot, my mind turning everything over and over, trying hard to calm down. I was right about Klein's involvement. I knew it. But knowing it and proving it were polar opposites.

I found the observation suite, knocked, and entered. Sutherby sat in front of a large screen with a camera feed from an interview room on it, his phone pressed to his ear, talking. He beckoned me in, and I sat next to him and watched a young woman on screen while he wrapped up the call. Her face looked deathly pale against her long purple hair. Staring at the wall with puffy red eyes, she sat hunched up, tattooed arms wrapped around her waist. She clutched a tissue in one hand, and every few minutes, she wiped at tears on her cheeks. An untouched bottle of water sat on the table in front of her.

Sutherby hung up, and I said, 'Is that Farzad's girlfriend?'

He nodded. 'Amy Price. I'll let them know they can start now.' He made a quick call to Detective Chief Inspector Walker, who would be interviewing Amy, then said to me, 'Nuri's friend Charlie is also waiting outside to be interviewed. I've already briefed the team on the questions I want put to them.'

I leaned forward in my seat, staring at the screen, waiting with nervous anticipation. DCI Walker entered the room with a female DS called Bloomfield, and they set up the recording equipment before starting the questions.

Amy glanced up, looking lost.

'Sorry to keep you waiting,' Walker said. 'I know this must be really upsetting for you.'

Amy sniffed and nodded. 'I can't believe it's happening.'

'We appreciate this is very hard for you, but we need to ask you some questions about Farzad,' Bloomfield said. 'You're Farzad's girlfriend?'

'Yes.' Amy wiped her eyes.

Walker leaned back in his chair. 'How long have you been in a relationship with Farzad for?'

'Eighteen months. We're on the same course—fine art— that's how we met. We live together now in a flat off campus.'

Walker scribbled something down in his notebook. 'Do you have any idea where Farzad might be?'

'No. I just... I'm just as shocked as everyone else. I'm sure you must have the wrong person.'

I turned to Sutherby. 'I take it we've got units watching his parents' house in Luton in case he shows up there? And Amy and Farzad's flat?'

'Yes,' he replied.

'Could Farzad have gone to a friend's house?' Walker asked Amy.

She shrugged. 'I don't know. I mean, I don't really know his friends from before uni who live in Luton. We only went there together a couple of times. In St Albans, there's only really me and Charlie, but Charlie didn't say Farzad had tried to go to his uni accommodation block.' She shook her head helplessly.

'How often did Farzad see Charlie?' Bloomfield asked.

'Well, since Farzad and me got serious, he didn't see him that much on his own anymore. Charlie used to spend a lot of time at our flat, because there was more space, but lately Farzad and Charlie haven't seen that much of each other.'

'Do you know if Farzad spent any time with anyone else, apart from you or Charlie?' Bloomfield asked. 'Has he been associating with anyone else recently?'

'No.' Amy blinked rapidly. 'Not that I know of, anyway.'

'I think she's lying about that,' I said to Sutherby. 'She's unnerved by that question.'

But Walker had already picked up on that. 'Are you sure?'

Amy chewed on her lip and nodded.

Walker waited for a moment to see if Amy would add anything. When she didn't, he asked, 'And are there any particular places Farzad likes going to?'

'Um... not really. We're usually either at the flat or uni. Maybe shopping or the pub or an art gallery sometimes, you know.'

Walker pulled a photograph from a manila folder on the desk and put it in front of Amy. 'Do you recognise this man?'

Amy peered down at the photo. Her shaky fingers touched her lips. 'Is this... the man who was stabbed?'

'Yes.'

Amy closed her eyes and shook her head. 'I've never seen him before. Who is he?'

'His name was Donald Parkinson. He died a short while ago.'

Amy cupped her hands to her face, eyes huge pools of

horror. 'Oh, no.' She collapsed into a crying fit, her shoulders heaving up and down.

Walker waited a few moments then said, 'We know this is very difficult, but we need to get as much information as quickly as we can to prevent something like this happening again. Does the name Donald Parkinson ring any bells? Did Farzad ever talk about him? Or have a reason to hold a grudge against him?'

Amy sniffed hard, wiped her eyes again, and wailed. The detectives let her compose herself for another minute before trying again.

'Amy, did Farzad know Donald Parkinson?' Bloomfield asked.

She made a strangled sound in her throat and then shook her head. 'No. I've never heard of him.'

'He's an administrator for an insurance company in St Albans called...' Walker glanced at his notebook and then back up, 'Quick Quote. Could Farzad have encountered him at Mr Parkinson's place of work?'

'I... er... I don't think so. I've never heard of the company. Our landlord has his own building insurance for the flat, and we never got contents insurance from anywhere. And we haven't got a car, either, so I don't think he would've seen him for insurance.' She carried on wiping away the tears with her tissue.

Walker tapped the photo. 'So you have no idea why Farzad targeted this man?'

Amy sniffed and put her head in her hands. Her voice was muffled when she spoke, so Bloomfield asked her to talk more clearly for the benefit of the recording. Amy dropped her hands and looked up, more tears streaming down her cheeks. 'I have no idea at all.'

'Has Farzad ever been violent in the past?' Walker asked.

'No! Farzad's just this really sweet guy. Really chilled out. Sometimes too chilled out, if you know what I mean. This is *really* out of character.'

'Okay. Has Farzad been depressed or stressed about anything lately?' Walker asked

'No. I don't get any of this.' Amy flapped a hand in the air, still shaking her head.

'He wasn't having any particular problems? Maybe personally, or with his family, or maybe with his course?' Walker pressed her.

'He loved his course. I just don't...' Amy trailed off and put her head in her hands again.

'Don't what?' Bloomfield said gently.

Amy sniffed and took a shuddering breath before she sat up again. 'No, there were no problems I knew of.'

'What about financial problems? A lot of students have worries about their loans,' Walker said.

'He wasn't worried about his loan. He doesn't have to pay it back until he's earning over a certain amount. I'm more the worrier in our relationship, but he always said he'll worry about things when they happen, not before.' Amy rubbed a hand over her face.

'Has he been suffering from mood swings? Or acting strangely?' Bloomfield asked.

Amy clenched the balled-up tissue in her fist. She hesitated, her mouth half open.

'There's something you're not telling us, isn't there, Amy?' Walker said.

'That's because I'm not really sure what was going on.' Amy sighed. 'He wasn't really having mood swings. But he has been going through a bit of a thing. I don't know...' She waved her fist around in the air, as if searching for the right words. 'For the last few months, he's been acting really strange. But I thought it was something else.' Her tear-stricken gaze locked onto Walker's. 'I *swear* I never thought anything like this would happen.'

'Strange, how?' Walker leaned forward. 'And what did you think it was about?'

'It started with him disappearing sometimes. Once, I followed him when he left our flat. He was doing odd things, and he said he had no memory of it.'

'What kind of things?' Bloomfield asked.

Amy blew out a breath and looked up at the ceiling. 'Farzad told me he used to do drugs a few years back. Just weed. Nothing major. I haven't seen him do anything since we've been together, but I think he'd started smoking it secretly again lately. Either that, or he was seeing someone else. It's the only thing that makes sense. He kept having nightmares. And sleepwalking around the house. I'd wake up, and he wasn't there, and he'd be downstairs, sitting on the sofa with his eyes open, but he was *asleep*. But I thought it was because of the drugs, or maybe that he had a guilty conscience because he was messing around behind my back.'

A prickle of unease danced up my spine. It sounded exactly the same as what had been going on with the other students.

'Had Farzad suffered from sleepwalking in the past?' Walker asked.

'No. I asked him about it, and he...' Amy shrugged. 'He thought I was winding him up. He didn't believe he'd started doing it. He said it had never happened in the past. But that wasn't the only thing, because sometimes in between class, he'd just disappear when we were supposed to meet up. When I asked him about it, he just pretended he didn't know what I was talking about. One time... it was at the weekend, and I was in the kitchen making us breakfast, and he was lying in bed. When I took it up to him, he'd disappeared. He'd just left the house without saying anything. I knew he couldn't have gone far, so I caught up with him as he was walking down the street, and I followed him to see what he was up to.' She took a deep, shaky breath. 'He was walking towards town. I thought he might be meeting a dealer, or maybe another girl. Thought I'd catch him at it and confront him.'

'And what happened?' Walker asked.

'He went into a shop and bought a bottle of Coke, which was weird because he hates the stuff. Then he sat on a bench and drank it. I was watching him from a shop doorway, and it was like he was in this little world of his own, not noticing anything around him. He sat there for about half an hour, then walked off again in the direction of St Peters Street. He walked around town for a bit, up the road and back, and headed home.'

It wasn't just unease now. A siren boomed in my head.

Amy paused and sniffed. 'When I got back, he was lying on top of the bed with his clothes on. He sat up when I came in and asked where the breakfast was.' She raised her eyebrows. 'I said, "What are you talking about? Where've you been?" I didn't want to let him know I'd followed him. It sounded kind of stalkerish. But I was jealous that maybe he'd gone to meet a girl and she'd stood him up so he came back. Anyway, he said he didn't remember going into town *at all*. He acted like he genuinely couldn't remember where he'd been. But I thought he was lying.' She paused and shook her head. 'I checked the flat when he wasn't there, seeing if he was hiding something from me. And I didn't find any drugs. He said he wasn't on anything when I asked him. I also checked his phone and laptop to see if he was chatting with another girl, but I didn't find anything on them. So, yes, maybe he might've been associating with someone else. But I haven't got a clue who.'

I glanced at Sutherby, one eyebrow raised. 'This is *exactly* like the others.'

On screen, Bloomfield asked, 'Are you aware of Farzad having any history of mental illness?'

'Not that I know of, no. He's just a normal guy.'

'Who was his doctor?' Walker said.

'He hasn't seen a GP since coming to uni. I think he's probably still listed with his old one back in Luton.'

'You say you didn't see him take any drugs, but was he on any prescribed medication?' Bloomfield asked.

'No.'

'Did he visit the medical centre at the university for any reason? The Watling Centre?' Walker asked.

Amy pursed her lips together and shook her head. 'Not that I know of.'

'Specifically, did he talk about a Professor Klein? Or volunteering with any of the uni's medical research programmes that students can get involved in?'

'No.'

Walker scribbled something down in his notebook. 'How did you both afford your rental house with the student loans? Or were either of you working anywhere?'

'I'm lucky that my parents have paid for my education. They're footing the bill for the flat, too. Neither of us had a job.'

'Were you aware that Farzad had any extra cash recently?'

'Uh...' She looked down at the table. 'I don't know. He did buy me some things lately—a watch and a coat. But he didn't say he had any extra money.'

'Our search team found two and a half thousand pounds at your flat, hidden under some floorboards. Do you know anything about that?' Walker asked.

Amy's eyes widened with surprise. 'No. Are you saying that it belonged to Farzad?'

'Did it?' Bloomfield asked.

She shrugged. 'It wasn't mine, so I guess...' Amy gave another helpless shrug. 'I don't know. It must be his, I suppose. I never knew it was there.'

I glanced at Sutherby. 'See! It's just like the others. It's—' But before I could say more, Walker started talking again, so we turned back to the screen.

'Okay, let's move on,' Walker said. 'Did Farzad belong to any particular groups or societies at the university?'

'No.'

'But if he had periods of time where he went missing, like you mentioned, how would you know?' Bloomfield asked.

'Maybe I wouldn't. I don't seem to know anything anymore.' Amy looked dazed. 'I don't *think* he belonged to any groups.'

'Okay.' Walker adjusted the buff-coloured folder in front of him into a neat line. 'Was Farzad ever approached by anyone who *wanted* him to join a particular society or group?'

'Not that he told me.'

'Did he have any particular political, social, or religious ideology?'

Amy blinked. 'No. He didn't care about politics, and he wasn't religious. He was just an artist.'

'Has he ever been threatened or coerced by anyone into doing anything?' Walker asked.

A pinched frown furrowed between Amy's eyebrows as she gasped. 'What are you saying? Do you think someone made him do this?'

Walker glanced at Bloomfield for a moment. 'That's what we're trying to find out. Was Farzad acting alone? Or was he recruited for some kind of purpose by any organisation?' He leaned his elbows on the desk. 'I don't know whether you heard about the recent incident in Manchester, where a man was arrested on suspicion of committing a terrorist act after stabbing five people? Or the London Bridge attack a few years ago, where terrorists drove a vehicle into pedestrians before stabbing people?'

Amy's mouth fell open. 'Are you saying Farzad's a terrorist?' She stared back, eyes wide and horrified. 'What? Just because he's foreign? He was *born* here. His parents are Christians! It's not like he's from a strict Muslim family or anything. He's as British as you and me. No! He can't be a terrorist. I mean, like I said, he's not religious or idealistic or involved in... anything... I don't know...' Her hand circled in the air. 'I mean, he's not into anything radical. He's just a normal guy.'

Walker opened the folder in front of him again and held up a photograph in front of her. It was a still taken from the camera phone that had captured Hoodie Guy in St Peters Street. 'Do you recognise this man?'

I looked at Sutherby, silently questioning how Walker had got the photo.

'I gave it to DCI Walker,' he said. 'Although I didn't mention the undercover operation. Hoodie Guy is a person of interest.'

'I agree,' I said. 'But not for terrorism. This isn't about a terrorist cell. It's Klein and his cronies. I know—'

'Not now, Becky.' Sutherby cut me off and turned back to the screen.

Amy had the photo in her hand, staring at it. She gave a small, almost imperceptible shake of her head. 'No. I'm sorry. I don't know who he is. I want to help Farzad, but I don't know what I can do.'

'You are helping him, Amy.' Bloomfield gave her an encouraging smile.

'It doesn't feel like it.' Amy sniffed again. 'It feels like I'm betraying him.'

'We have to get to the bottom of this,' Walker said. 'So you never saw Farzad with this man? Or saw this man hanging around the university or your flat?'

'No. Never. Why?'

Walker ignored the question, slid the photo into his folder, then pulled out an A4 piece of paper. 'I'm going to read out some names, and I want you to tell me whether Farzad knew these people.' Walker looked down at a list. 'Vicky Aylott.'

Amy paused for a moment, as if thinking. 'I don't think so.'

'What about Ajay Banerjee?'

'Um... no. But that name seems familiar for some reason.' Amy rubbed at her forehead. 'Sorry, this is... I can't think straight. It's such a shock.'

'We understand that,' Walker said. 'You're doing really well. How about Natalie Wheeler? Did Farzad know her?'

'I don't think so. But there was a Natalie who...' Amy stared at Walker and Bloomfield, as if suddenly connecting some dots. 'Are these students who've... I just remembered Ajay's name. He set himself on fire. Vicky killed herself at uni. Natalie ran over a man, didn't she? Are you... why are you asking about them?'

'Did Farzad know any of them?'

'No. We talked about them briefly, when we heard about what had happened with them, but neither of us knew them.'

'What did Farzad say about them specifically?'

'He just said how terrible it all was. What does this have to do with what Farzad did?'

'Maybe nothing. But we just need to be thorough.' Walker clasped his hands together. 'What we're trying to understand is *why* Farzad would suddenly do something like this, Amy, when it appears to be completely unprovoked and out of character.'

'So am I! God, so am I. And I'm telling you I can't think of a single reason.'

CHAPTER 33

TONI

It was gone 4.00 p.m. when I rang the buzzer outside Watford General Hospital's Critical Care Unit. I hadn't been able to get away from work earlier, because several students who were upset about the stabbing had taken up the offer of counselling.

I waited until a tired-looking female nurse let me in with a smile, and I told her I was there to visit Marcelina.

'Okay,' she said. 'We only let two visitors in at a time, but her parents have just left to go to the canteen, so you've got some time. I'll show you which room she's in.'

'Is there any change?' I said as I walked along the corridor beside her.

Her smile fell flat then. 'I'm afraid not.'

I pulled my phone out of my pocket. 'I was wondering if you could help me.' I called up the photo of the man who was supposed to be Dr Lahey and showed it to her. 'Do you recognise him? I think he's in neurology here.' I deliberately kept it vague, not mentioning the name in case she became suspicious and clammed up. 'I think he's treating Marcelina, so I wanted to find out how experienced he was in injuries like hers.' I gave her a sheepish look, as if I felt a little guilty for questioning his ability.

She stopped walking, looked at the screen, and took it from my outstretched hand. Frowning at it, she said, 'He's definitely not in neurology. We have a lot of neurology doctors coming in and out of CCU, and I don't recognise him. Where did you see him?'

'In A&E. When Marcelina was first brought in.'

'He's most likely an A&E locum.' She carried on walking and passed the phone back to me.

'Yeah. Maybe I got it wrong,' I said, falling into step beside her, wondering just who on earth he was.

'Here we are.' She stopped outside a private side room and pushed open the door.

I stood in the entrance, watching Marcelina for a moment. Her face and arms were the only things uncovered by the bed sheets, and the bruising to them was even more pronounced now—a kaleidoscope of purple, grey, and black. Her hair was matted to her head around the dressing bandage wound over it. My stomach twisted with guilt and sadness for her.

'I'll leave you to your visit,' the nurse said.

'Thanks.' I stepped inside the room, the door swinging shut behind me. 'Hi, Marcelina. It's Toni.' It was possible she could still hear me beneath the layers of unconsciousness, even if she couldn't yet answer me. So I carried on talking as I sat in the visitor's chair beside her and took her hand, stroking it gently. 'What happened to you? What was going on?' I paused. 'I saw Curtis today. I'm going to speak to your other friends, too. But I think someone was doing something to you, weren't they?' I swallowed and glanced over my shoulder towards the closed door. Then I placed her hand back on top of the bed and reached into my handbag for Marcelina's mobile phone.

I was about to commit another invasion of privacy, but I was convinced something sinister had led her to be so scared she'd run into the road rather than talk about it and had led another student to brutally stab someone in the street.

I activated the password screen and pressed her right forefinger against it, but nothing happened. I tried with her left one, and the screen unlocked. I went to the security settings and changed them so the phone didn't need a code or fingerprint to open it again. Then I stared at the screen, wondering what to check first. I clicked on her email app and scrolled down. She only had a few messages in her inbox: one from Janet at Student Counselling with the form email sent to all students earlier; one from Ryanair about cheap flight deals; and one from eBay about a product being relisted. I checked her sent mail and folders, but there was nothing interesting.

I went through her text messages but didn't find anything suspicious. They were all benign chats between her family or her friends—Precious, Hazel, and Curtis. The only social media app she had was Facebook, so I clicked on that. The phone was still logged onto her account, so I went through her posts. Mostly, they were photos of mundane, everyday life—posts of food, selfies in her dorm room or in class, photos with Precious and Hazel, and pictures of her dog back home.

I clicked on her phone's photo gallery and scrolled through the photos, which mostly showed the same ones she'd uploaded to Facebook, or others in the same vein, but there were also ones of Curtis, taken from a distance, some slightly blurred, as if they'd been shot without him knowing.

And the latest thing she'd taken wasn't a photo at all. It was a video, dated three days before. I pressed Play.

I couldn't make out what was happening at first. The image was blurry and moving fast. But then I realised it was of a grey tiled floor, the phone pointing downwards as she walked along, as if she were holding it in her hand and had turned it on by accident.

Suddenly, the phone swung upwards and pointed through a window to a clothes shop opposite called Hobbs. I recognised the shop as being in Christopher Place, an open-air shopping centre in St Albans. It took a moment for me to realise what was happening as Marcelina said, 'There he is.'

She was filming a man who stood with his back to the phone, looking in the window of Hobbs. He was well-built, wearing a baseball cap, jeans, and a lightweight jacket.

'It's him,' she whispered. 'I'm sure he's the one who's been following me.'

Dread thrummed through me as I carried on watching. The man didn't turn around, but as she zoomed in on him, his face became more visible in the reflection of Hobbs's window. He wore sunglasses and had a distinctive nose, chin, and cheekbones. It was the bogus doctor.

'I've got to get out of here,' Marcelina whispered.

And then the video cut off.

I was just about to watch it again when the door opened, startling me.

I stuffed Marcelina's phone in my handbag, swung my head round, and saw a couple in their early fifties. The woman's eyes were swollen and bloodshot, and she moved as if everything was a great effort. The man's hands shook as he stood looking at Marcelina in the bed with a haunted expression. I recognised them from the photo I'd found in Marcelina's purse. Her parents.

I stood, introduced myself, and told them how sorry I was and that I didn't want to intrude on their privacy. I stepped out of the room and took one last look through the window in the door, watching them clutching each other tightly, their distress palpable in the air.

I turned away, blinking back tears, then marched down the corridor, making them a silent promise in my head to find out what had really happened to their daughter and just how the man in the video was involved.

CHAPTER 34

DETECTIVE BECKY HARRIS

The interview with Amy carried on for another hour, but we didn't learn anything else useful. After she was led out, Farzad's friend, Charlie, entered the room, and the same questions were put to him, but that yielded less results. He was hostile, and angry with Farzad. Said he hadn't seen much of Farzad in the last few months, hadn't witnessed any strange behaviour, and had no clue why Farzad would stab someone.

As DCI Walker drew the second interview to a close, Sutherby's phone rang. He listened to the caller for a few minutes and then hung up and turned to me.

'Farzad Nuri's phone data and laptop has been analysed, and there are no calls, texts, emails, or social media messages we can find to or from anyone that appear suspicious. Whoever Hoodie Guy is, if he's communicating with the students, he's not leaving a trace digitally.'

I chewed on my lip, processing everything. 'Hoodie Guy had his phone to his ear in the camera phone footage. If he was on a call in St Peters Street, we could try to trace it.'

'I've authorised a request to mobile phone providers to see if we can pinpoint it, but that could take a while to come back.'

'Maybe Hoodie Guy doesn't need to communicate directly with the students. He could be just a middleman, working for Klein. He might never have met any of them.'

Sutherby sighed impatiently. 'A middleman doing what?'

I shrugged. 'I don't know. But why is he watching the students? Ajay, Farzad. There had to be a reason he was there. I bet he was around when Natalie killed the man on the zebra crossing. When Vicky took her life. Klein's brainwashing those students or manipulating their minds somehow, and Hoodie Guy is trying to cover it up.'

Sutherby shook his head. 'I just think that sounds too bloody Orwellian. A professor brainwashing them is just…'

'What? Sick? Twisted? Evil?'

'I was going to say implausible and outlandish.'

'But none of the students were either religious, radical, political, or outraged about any particular social causes.'

'And some of our homegrown terrorists weren't into any particular affiliations before they were radicalised, either. I have to err on the side of caution here. And it's more logical that this is some kind of terrorist cell.'

'But it wouldn't be the first time unethical or illegal human experiments have been carried out on unsuspecting people without their knowledge or consent,' I said. 'I remember reading a news report a few years back about hundreds of covert experiments carried out by government scientists at the UK's most secretive lab, Porton Down, on behalf of the Ministry of Defence. The one that really sticks in my mind is where they released potentially dangerous chemicals over vast areas of the country without telling anyone.'

He studied me carefully, one leg crossed over the other, drumming his forefinger against his knee, and I could see a spark of something else in his eyes now. Acceptance of what I was saying? Or was it fear? He was obviously higher up the political food chain in the force than I was, and I suspected he knew of far more incidents where our own security services would try to cover up something they didn't want the public to know.

While I had him teetering on the edge of seriously considering my theory, I ploughed on. 'No one can stay off the grid these days. There are traces of everyone. Everyone except, it seems, Hoodie Guy. So what's more credible? That Hoodie Guy wiped himself off the system, or he had help? And if he had help, the big question is why and who's protecting him? Who has that kind of power and resources? Then what about Klein? Why is there also no information available about him? Why are all my searches into him a dead end? And with the CCTV wiped, as well, that's not coincidence. I seriously doubt anyone would be protecting a one-man-band terrorist cell. If they want the truth covered up that badly, I have to be right. And this must be something big going on.'

'But this *is* just a *wild theory*. That's *all* it is.' He sounded less convinced by his words now.

'I'm certain the evidence is out there somewhere. I need to do more research. In the meantime, I'll also hang out around the medical block and see if I can spot Hoodie Guy. And my appointment with Professor Klein is tomorrow afternoon. I'll do a recce and see if I can find out if he has any patient records in the building.'

His face was pale. 'Okay, let's say you *are* right. If Hoodie Guy and Klein have had help to stay off the grid, and evidence like CCTV is being tampered with, then you're talking about—what? Some kind of clandestine government-condoned experiment?'

A suffocating chill seemed to fill the air then, and the icy realisation hit me—yes, that was exactly what I meant. I nodded. 'As crazy as it sounds, it would fit.'

He took a breath, shaking his head. 'Well, I don't even want to think about it.'

'If we can establish a definite link that Klein treated all four students, that will prove I'm on the right track, and I'm prepared to take the risk.' I kept my expression strong and unwavering, even though I was actually terrified at the can of cancerous worms I was opening.

He clenched his jaw as the seconds ticked by. 'Okay. Keep digging. I'll give you authorisation to break into the Watling Centre to search for Klein's patient records. And I'll request his phone and financial data. I'll let you know of any developments this end.'

'Thanks, sir.' I stood and walked towards the door.

'And DS Harris...'

I stopped, looking over my shoulder.

'Be bloody careful.'

I nodded, left through the rear doors of the police station, and drove back to the university, buzzing with energy, even though I'd been working solidly all day.

When I got back, I sat on the bench outside the Watling Centre, hoping to spot Hoodie Guy coming or going, but there were no lights on inside, and no one was around. I waited for a couple of hours then headed back to my room to research the internet, my stomach rolled into a tight ball of anger at what I was convinced was going on.

I felt like I'd fallen down a rabbit hole with no idea how deep it went. But I wasn't going to stop until I reached the murky dark pool right at the bottom.

CHAPTER 35

TONI

Mitchell had sent a text saying he was on to something and was on his way to my flat. I sat in my lounge while I waited for him to arrive, scrolling through the rest of Marcelina's phone in case there was something else of interest on there, but I didn't find anything on it that might explain what was going on.

When the intercom buzzed, Mitchell's face stared back at me from the video monitor. I let him into the building, and a minute later, I was swinging my door open. We gave each other a quick hug before I stepped back to let him in.

'Mum doesn't know, does she?' I asked.

'What, that you're digging into something sinister? No.'

'What did you tell her about where you were going?'

'I just said I was meeting up with Lee, which is true in a roundabout way. I hate lying to her.'

I shut the door. 'I know. I do, too. But she'll freak out completely if she finds out what I'm doing.'

He acknowledged that with a tilt of his head as he sat on the small two-seater sofa, swamping it completely. He wasn't tall, but he was wide and solid, and even in his late fifties, he was still all muscle.

'And is it sinister? Or am I imagining things?' I asked.

He twisted in the seat to face me as I sat next to him. 'You're definitely not imagining things. Lee's found out a load of really bad shit that will literally blow your mind.' An angry vein throbbed at his temple. 'The guy who said he was a doctor... the footage from the stabbing didn't show him that clearly because he wore shades and a baseball cap, so Lee got into the CCTV system at Watford General's A&E department and found some clear shots of him leaving the building. External cameras also caught him getting into a vehicle, which is registered to someone who doesn't exist at an address that doesn't exist.'

I raised my eyebrows.

'But that's not all. Although he avoided council CCTV cameras, and we couldn't trace the vehicle's movements far after it left the hospital, when he was outside A&E, he made a phone call. Lee managed to narrow down his mobile phone data and used that to track him instead. He took a route to the outskirts of St Albans.' His stomach rumbled loudly then. He patted it. 'Sorry, I haven't had dinner.'

'Me, neither. I was too engrossed in looking at Marcelina's phone and forgot about it.'

'Do you want to order something in while we talk? My treat.'

'Yes, but it'll be my treat since you're doing me so many favours. What do you fancy? Chinese, Indian, or pizza?'

'Pizza sounds good.'

I grabbed us both beers then ordered a couple of pizzas before sitting on the sofa again and tucking my legs beneath me, giving him my full attention. 'So where did he go in St Albans?'

'He went to a company called Regen Logistix, on a large business park complex. He stayed there for about half an hour, then Lee picked him up again and tracked his route to St Albans University. There are only CCTV cameras inside the front gates and at the admin block, and the local authority cameras are sparse in that area, but the mobile phone tracking is pretty accurate, and we know he went into the Watling Centre.'

'Okay. And Regen Logistix? What's that?'

'They make implantable medical technology devices—pacemakers, cochlear implants, blood glucose monitors, that kind of thing.'

'So, the guy I saw *was* a doctor then?'

'No. Here's where it all starts getting seriously buggered up. Lee ran him through some standard databases, trying for a facial recognition. But he came up as no trace and seems as if he's a ghost. So Lee dug deeper, into classified stuff. The guy's name is Gary Glover. He's ex-military, but now he's working for the British Security Services.'

'What?' My skin prickled.

'Yeah. You know when Lee left the SAS, he started working for the government doing cyber surveillance and security? Before Lee set up his own company, he did work for the security services, too. He still does contract work for them, and he's got a backdoor into their systems.'

'Spying on the spies? That's got a nice irony to it.' I quirked an eyebrow up.

'It turns out that Glover is being paid in a very round-about way via MI5. Specifically, by an elite black ops department known as Behavioural Modification Operations, who carry out covert PSYOPS. Glover is basically a private contractor employed by one company and subcontracted out to another company and another, in the hope that no one could ever track him back to who he's really working for. But the bottom line is he's employed by the government so they can maintain the cover and deniability of the dirty work he's doing for them.'

A ripple of dread passed through me. 'PSYOPS?'

'You've heard the term? Did they cover it in your psychology degree?'

'No, it wasn't covered, but the subject interested me so, as usual, I delved into my own research and brought it into the classroom in an essay.' I could still remember the summary I'd given of key points almost word for word. *Psychological operations are intended to convey selected information to audiences in order to influence emotions, motive, objective reasoning, and behaviour. It's a form of covert mind warfare, where the message is the weapon.* 'Who are they running a secret psychological operation against?'

'Against all of us. Billions of pounds are already spent every year to control the public mind. And the Behavioural Modification Operations' remit is to manipulate public opinion, foster population obedience, and encourage conformity by many external methods—using propaganda in mainstream media, campaigns on social media using fake accounts or fake videos, creating spoof online resources with inaccurate information to discredit or cover up the truth, or shutting down genuine websites who question the government or the unelected shadow government's doctrine.'

I stared at him, horrified. 'You're right. That is scary.'

'But this goes wider than just Marcelina and Farzad. There are three other tragic incidents involving St Albans uni students in the last few months. On the face of it, that's probably not that unremarkable. But Lee dug further into police reports, and their friends all mention a common link in their behaviour. All of them were suffering from the same kind of symptoms—blackouts or fugue-type states, memory loss, nightmares, or weird behaviour shortly before the incidents happened.' He told me about Vicky Aylott, Ajay Banerjee, and Natalie Wheeler.

'Yes, I remember hearing a bit about all of those incidents, but Ajay and Vicky died before I arrived at the uni. I didn't know they were all related.'

'And now you've got Farzad Nuri, who stabbed someone in the high street and has disappeared, but I suspect he's already been murdered. There was a localised power cut before the incident, which meant all council-run and private CCTV of the area was out of action so they could cover Glover's tracks. But what they couldn't plan for was that someone would film the incident on a phone, or you noticing Glover at the hospital with Marcelina and putting two and two together. They already broke into your patient records and must've decided you didn't know anything so didn't bother to take any further action.' He swallowed a mouthful of beer. 'Lee checked out medical reports for Vicky, Natalie, and Ajay. No drugs showed up in their systems, and there were no physiological reasons found for their symptoms.'

I blew out a breath and shook my head, 'Setting yourself on fire is absolutely horrific.' I scrunched up my face as a sickening sludge settled in my stomach. 'What a terrible way to go.'

Mitchell opened his mouth to speak, but the intercom

buzzed. It was the pizza delivery. I paid for it and then came back and found plates, cutlery, and napkins.

Mitchell tucked into a slice of pizza and chewed before answering. 'It doesn't seem like coincidence, does it? Two students might be coincidence, but five recent tragedies? Plus, you've got Glover posing as a fake doctor while working for MI5, trying to hide his identity at two of the events we know of so far, then going to the uni, so he's definitely involved in this.' He took a swig of beer and set the bottle back down. 'All five students were perfectly normal young-sters until a few months ago, and now all of a sudden, there's all this weird stuff going on.'

I took a small bite of pizza and swallowed, but it seemed to get stuck in my closed-up throat. I washed it down with another mouthful of beer.

'There were plenty of witnesses to Vicky diving off the stairway,' Mitchell said. 'Witnesses outside Ajay's house and evidence the doors were locked from the inside make it seem likely he wasn't murdered. Lots of witnesses to what Natalie, Farzad, and Marcelina did, too. So everything points to them doing things themselves. Or, as Lee and I suspect, *making* them do it.'

I glanced over towards my bookcase, to a book called *Thought Reform and the Psychology of Totalism: A Study of 'Brainwashing' in China*, about an analysis of brainwashing in American servicemen and Chinese citizens by the Chinese government. My gaze flicked back to Mitchell. 'Are you saying this secret government black operation is involved in brainwashing unsuspecting students into doing all this?'

'No. It's much worse than that.'

CHAPTER 36

MR WHITE

Nathan White was shown into the plush office. Already seated around the large oval conference table made of polished ebony were Professor Carl Gale, Professor Brian Klein, Dr Kenneth Beaumont, and the head honcho—CEO Paul Hughes. The blinds were drawn at both the external and internal windows. No prying eyes were going to be privy to what went on inside. The subject of the meeting was strictly classified.

Hughes stood in his flashy, expensive bespoke suit, made by a luxury designer, and held his hand out for White to shake. 'Good to see you.'

'Likewise.' White gripped Hughes's hand and nodded at the others. 'Gentlemen.' He pulled the flash drive from Glover out of his pocket and handed it to Hughes.

Hughes broke into a savage smile. 'Let's see what we've got here.' He slid the flash drive into a huge flat-screen smart TV on one wall.

Klein, Gale, and Beaumont swivelled their chairs for a better viewing angle. White leaned against the wall, thinking it was better fun watching their reactions as the footage started.

Klein looked excited but nervous at the same time, sweat dotting on his forehead and upper lip. For Klein, this was his life's work. Everything had been leading up to this moment. But he still had his boundaries. He'd voiced his concerns over the direction things were taking, but everyone had reminded him that there could be no backing out now. There was too much at stake. Too much to lose. And Klein was in far too deep to be able to walk away. But if anyone was going to be a weak link, it would be him.

Gale was the design man, the one who'd pored over the specifications for years until they were just right. Gale thought he was a pioneer. Someone who'd do anything for his cause. He really believed in all this stuff.

Beaumont was the data guy, who analysed everything and studied the outcomes. He had a predatory, detached look on his face that White recognised in himself.

Paul Hughes was a different matter entirely. It wasn't about ground-breaking innovations, professional accolades, pushing things into a whole new realm, or even the kudos of being the first. Of course not. For Hughes, it was all about the power and money.

White turned to the TV screen, observing the end of the footage Glover had shot in St Peters Street with the hidden camera in his messenger bag.

Hughes turned off the TV, removed the flash drive, and slid it into his pocket. 'It's looking good. After all these years of research, Project Shadow is finally ready to put into production.' He sat down at the head of the table, hands spread wide on top, that reptilian smile fixed on his face.

Professor Klein cleared his throat. 'I think we need a little more time before we can say that with any certainty. There have only been five test subjects, and we've had some mishaps.' He looked at Professor Gale. 'I'd like to again voice my concerns about the way things are being done. This wasn't my intention when we discussed this initially. It's not—'

'Five *successful* subjects,' Dr Beaumont butted in.

'It works. You can't dispute that.' Professor Gale shrugged nonchalantly. 'And as we all know, with delay comes risk.' He looked pointedly at Hughes. 'We're not the only ones so close to the endgame.'

Hughes crossed one leg over the other, nodding vehemently. 'Yes. I concur. We can't wait any longer. There's too much at—'

'What about Natalie Wheeler?' Klein butted in, a flush spreading up his neck as he glanced around the room. 'That didn't go according to plan. She didn't do what she was supposed to in the end. And Marcelina Claybourn? What if she wakes up and starts asking more questions?'

'The whole reason she's in the hospital is because she was asking too many questions,' Hughes said. '*If* she wakes up, that will all be taken care of. That's what Mr White is here for. To clean up the annoying little glitches.' Hughes swept a hand in White's direction.

Klein dabbed a handkerchief to his forehead and sneaked a wary glance at White. 'It's too unpredictable at the moment. It's too messy. It's not what I envisioned. We need to stop. Do things properly.'

Professor Gale shook his head at Klein with derision.

'Nothing's going to stop,' Hughes told Klein. 'Do you hear me? *Nothing*.'

Klein swallowed as they all stared at him. 'People are bound to start asking questions soon,' he said quietly.

'I agree things have been getting a little messy,' White said from his position against the wall, arms folded casually across his chest. 'We've had to be creative in tidying up a few things. But at the moment, none of the targeted individuals are connectable. You're worrying too much.' He stared Klein hard in the eye, wondering if he would need to be reminded that the only way he'd get out of this now was if he was dead himself.

'What about Farzad Nuri? Where is he?' Dr Beaumont asked, his lips parting, tongue flicking out like a wolf's, tasting the air for blood.

'Somewhere he'll never be found,' White said.

'Okay.' Hughes laced his fingers together in his lap. Thought about the situation for a few moments.

The others waited. Gale, Klein, and Beaumont were being paid large amounts of money to wait if necessary. White wasn't. He had his government job and his paltry government pension to look forward to. He was taking a lot of risks for everyone involved, but no one ever noticed his hard work. Why would they? He was supposed to operate in the dark shadows.

White's gaze skimmed Hughes's suit, his expensive watch, and the office. He thought about the whole setup of the corporations involved that stood to make enormous amounts of money, and the mammoth promised payoffs to politicians that would be doled out. Something like this... well, *everyone* would want a piece of it, and White wanted to plan for his own endgame. Not for himself—he didn't have much time left, and it was funny how when it came to the crunch, people started thinking about the past and wanting to make amends. No, his money would be for his daughter. He'd been a shitty dad. He'd hardly been there to see her growing up. Someone and something else had always taken precedence. He wanted to make sure she was comfortable. At least he could do that right for her.

Eventually, Hughes looked up again. 'No more tests. No more delays. We're going ahead with production. We don't have any more time to waste on the testing phase. Project Shadow isn't the only agenda here. The remarkable work we're doing is just one part of a bigger picture.'

'What do you mean?' Klein said, looking round the room to see if anyone else knew what his boss was talking about.

'That's classified information,' Hughes said. 'Your job is to get on with what you're paid for and do your part.'

'A wise decision.' Dr Beaumont grinned.

Klein opened his mouth. Hughes glared at him, challenging him to disagree. Klein glanced down at the conference table and swallowed hard.

White stepped away from the wall. 'I'll let my people know.' He walked out of the room, wondering just how much more money he'd get if he took Project Shadow to one of the other major players.

CHAPTER 37

TONI

'The PK Marcelina was referring to in her journal is Professor Brian Klein,' Mitchell said. 'He's a research fellow at the Watling Centre, but he's also working for Regen Logistix.' He told me all about Klein and his research programmes. 'Klein was the one Glover called outside of A&E.'

My skin vibrated with outrage. 'A professor is involved in all this?'

'Yes. Lee's discovered that right now, there are hundreds of patent applications, both granted or pending, from various global medical, technical, or scientific corporations, for use in exploring mind control development.'

'If this isn't brainwashing, then what kind of mind control are we talking about?'

'Some of the patents are for devices or applications that use external equipment—headsets, watches, or a chip on the skin. But some are for implantable medical devices like microchips, which can be the size of a grain of rice. Or nanochips, where they can be as small as a grain of sand.'

My eyes narrowed, my throat pinched with trepidation, not liking where this was going one bit.

'What these nanochips have in common is monitoring or manipulating human brainwaves, using electromagnetic pulses or radio frequency, remotely, through wireless technology like mobile phone networks. If you can change someone's brainwaves and manipulate their neurological data, you can change their thoughts, memory, emotions, actions. This is isn't science fiction. It's not even science future. It's happening right now. And six months ago, Regen Logistix applied for a patent for a nanochip that does just that.'

'So you're saying these nanochips could basically mind hack you?'

'Not just mind hack. Mind *hijack*. Make you do or believe or think what they want, just from manipulating electromagnetic energy, which is the same energy as brainwaves.'

A suffocating chill squeezed at my core.

'Regen Logistix's patent application said the nanochip can be injected into the back of the neck or head area,' Mitchell said. 'And what makes this device even more unique is that it harvests the body's own energy, converting body heat into its own power supply. You're talking about a tiny, silent weapon with mammoth capabilities to control the human race.'

I pictured the scene in A&E again, where Marcelina had been moved onto her side when she wasn't supposed to be, which Glover must've done. The small cut on the back of her neck had oozed a little blood onto the pillow, as if it were a fresh wound. At the time, I'd attributed it to her accident. 'That's why Glover was at the hospital. He must've been trying to retrieve a chip that had been inserted into Marcelina's neck, because they knew she'd have diagnostic imaging tests due to her head injury, and that it would show up on an MRI. It seems the only reason he'd risk going there.'

Mitchell nodded. 'It could easily be removed by a small incision.'

'Wouldn't the students notice being implanted with a chip?'

'Maybe they thought they were being given a harmless injection—something like a painkiller or muscle relaxant. We think the students were involved in a secret study Klein was carrying out, and when Marcelina was starting to make a connection between her participation in the programme and her symptoms, they wanted her killed.'

I sat back on the sofa and stared at the floor, the scene of Marcelina's accident playing in my head yet again. 'So they manipulated her brain into making her walk in front of an oncoming vehicle.' I put my plate with the half-eaten pizza slice on the table, having lost my appetite. 'This is insane!'

'Insane and pure evil. But this wouldn't be the first time humans have been used as guinea pigs without their knowledge or consent. Mass numbers of soldiers and the general public have been regularly subjected to secret tests of pharmaceuticals, bacteria and viruses, toxic chemicals, and gasses over the years. There are plenty of declassified documents to prove the extent of the twisted experiments they've carried out.'

I blinked rapidly, shaking my head with horror. 'And just imagine how much this kind of technology would be worth.'

'It would be priceless. Creating easily controlled mass populations, super soldiers, suicide killers? The ultimate Manchurian candidates? There's a lot at stake for them. Every intelligence or government system in the world would want to get hold of this kind of mass-control, mass-brainwashing technology for nefarious purposes. And the British Government want to be at the forefront of it all. Because whoever gets there first will have terrifyingly incomparable superior world dominance. There are very powerful people who want this to succeed.'

'Do you think they sent Natalie mad, using this nanochip?'

'Most likely. It was either an effect of the chip, or they manipulated her brain so much, it completely buggered her up.'

'And a person diagnosed with so-called schizophrenia will never be believable, will they? It's a perfect cover for them.' A shiver danced up my spine. 'Do you think the university knows what's going on?'

'I don't know yet.'

I rubbed at my forehead, trying to take everything in. 'It's just unbelievable.'

'But not at all surprising. We've already been living in a world of mass surveillance and mass manipulation for years. This is just a natural evolution of control over the general public, because they're now finding the old methods aren't working as well. Social media and the internet has exposed mass corporate and government corruption and conspiracies all over the globe, and people are starting to finally wake up and question the bullshit agendas they're force-fed by the state-corporate mainstream media, who pass off propaganda and lies as fact.'

'So you're saying that the Behavioural Modification Operations department have been looking for other ways to do things, preparing for the day when they have to take more drastic measures? And this is what they've been working on?'

'Yes.' He stuffed another piece of pizza in his mouth and chewed quickly. 'Have you heard of the Internet of Things?'

'No.'

'It's basically an extension of the existing internet that connects to physical devices, everyday objects, animals, even people, and transfers data over a network. So anything embedded or implanted with a nanochip or RFID spy chip, which is a radio frequency identifying chip, can communicate and interact with other devices over the internet.' He wiped his fingertips on a napkin and put his plate on the coffee table. 'Organisations and corporations are using this stuff right now, and RFID chips are hidden in everything—mobile phones, computers, debit and credit cards, ID documents, vehicles, even packaging of products you buy, food, clothing, the list is endless. And all of it can be used remotely to monitor, track, and manipulate you. Even your bloody smart light switches could be spying on you if they have an internet connection!'

I shook my head and took a swig of beer. 'Your personal data is the new gold, isn't it?'

He nodded. 'But that's not all they're up to. They're ramming a cashless society down our necks, so cash becomes obsolete, and they can control the money supply. And if you don't conform, if you're a troublemaker who questions their official narrative, it'll be easy to just switch you off the grid so you're left with nothing—no money, no way of communication, no travel. We've become addicted to smart devices through carefully and skilfully planned social engineering so they can exert control over us.'

I stared at my phone on the table. I wasn't addicted to it, but I only had to look around at the students and the general public out and about with their heads constantly trained on their screens to know that the majority of people were these days.

'Some technology companies have already implanted their employees with chips that can operate their computers, access buildings, vehicles, vending machines,' Mitchell said. 'Of course, they'll sell it to the public by saying it's all for your benefit—that it makes life easier for you, that it's for your own convenience. In the case of nanochips, they'll say it can help to save your life—that you can store your medical data on it, blah, blah, blah. When really, you'll be paying for it with your freedom and privacy and personal security.' A muscle ticked away in his jaw. 'But although they're already spying on you inside your home, in your car, while you're on the move, there's one area they can't yet fully control or spy on you yet.'

It felt like hundreds of spiders scattered across my scalp. 'Your mind.'

He tapped the side of his forehead. 'Exactly. So now they're going one step further, wanting to actually implant people for the ultimate totalitarian control of your brain, which, as we've seen, could quite easily kill you. We're all just disposable pawns in their arsenal. Slaves for the sociopathic elite who really run the world.'

The little pizza I'd eaten seemed to curdle in my stomach. 'There's a name for it. It's called predictive programming, where those in control introduce their will slowly, manipulating the public's opinions to a point where the people accept it freely because it seems like the most natural thing in the world.'

'Predictive murder, more like.' Mitchell's nostrils flared. 'They're playing God with people's lives.'

'So what do we do? We need to find some kind of

evidence against them, because even though they've got a patent for these nanochips, we can't prove what they've been doing with it. All it is at the moment is speculation.'

'Lee's hacking into Regen Logistix's databases right now and looking for the evidence.' He twisted around in his seat and took my hand in his, concern etched all over his face. 'So I don't want you doing any more poking around from now on. These are *very* dangerous people.'

I nodded. 'Okay.'

'Promise me? It's not just your mum who would be devastated if anything happened to you.' He looked deep into my eyes and held my gaze.

'Yes. Don't worry. I know.'

'Good.'

'But if Lee does find evidence, what then?' I asked. 'What do we do with it?'

'I don't know. Yet. The only thing I do know is that we can't take it to the police. The security services would quash any investigation from the start.' He stood up. 'I'd better be off. I'll head to Lee's now and see how he's getting on. I'll keep you updated. You take care of yourself in the meantime.'

I handed over Marcelina's phone and laptop for him to give to Lee, but it seemed kind of obsolete now that we knew what we were dealing with.

After he left, I shut the door behind him and leaned my back against it, sickness swirling in the pit of my stomach. I knew firsthand what evil people were capable of, but when the very people who were supposed to protect the public's welfare were corrupt, bereft of any kind of morals and ethics, then there was something seriously broken in the world. Something rotten to the core.

DAY FOUR

"Being in a minority, even a minority of one, did not make you mad. There was truth and there was untruth, and if you clung to the truth even against the whole world, you were not mad."
~ George Orwell

CHAPTER 38

MR WHITE

At 3.43 a.m., Nathan White's mobile phone rang on the bedside table, jerking him awake. He glanced at the screen and saw Glover's name flash up.

'This had better be urgent,' White said, his voice thick and croaky. It had taken him hours to get comfortable enough to sleep, and even then, he'd tossed and turned half the night.

'We've got a problem,' Glover said.

'What kind of problem?' White sat up.

'Klein's name has come up in a police interview with Farzad Nuri's friends. The police were asking if Nuri had been involved in his research programmes. They're on to something.'

'What!' White swung his legs off the bed.

'And that's not all. A search was done on the police national computer for one of the vehicles I've used.'

Mr White closed his eyes and sighed. 'When and by who?'

'Chief Constable Derek Sutherby. Yesterday.'

'You weren't careful enough,' White growled. 'I hope you've dumped the car.'

'Of course. They've all been single-use vehicles. Either scrapped or dumped somewhere they won't be found. I don't understand how they've cottoned on to something.'

'Because you made an error somewhere—that's fucking why.' Even though White didn't raise his voice, there was no mistaking the steely tone.

'They can't connect the car to Regen Logistix, or us, or what's going on, even if it came onto their radar. And I'm not the only one who's fucked up here! The police showed Nuri's friends a still of me from some footage taken by a camera phone in St Peters Street. Even though you arranged for the power cut and surrounding CCTV to be hacked, it wasn't enough. You've got to take responsibility for some of this mess. You've been off your game for weeks!'

'Don't tell me what to do. And, anyway, they won't find out who you are. You're a shadow, remember. Any video evidence of you will be lost.'

'But how did they know about Klein and the programme? Someone must've been talking.'

'Who? The students are either dead or too messed up to remember anything.' White paused for a moment. 'Unless it's Klein himself. Maybe his conscience has finally got the better of him and he's tipped them off.'

'You need to stop the police. How are you—'

'Shut up for a minute. I'm thinking.' White's brain raced, wondering exactly how he was going to explain this monumental problem to his superiors. But first things first. The police would have to be shut down. That was the easy bit. The hard bit was making sure it *stayed* contained. 'Send me over footage of the police interviews. I want to know exactly what they were asking. And if you hear anything else before I sort this, then let me know.'

'Will do.'

White hung up and flipped the sheet back, wincing as he took a deep breath. He made his way downstairs in his pyjama bottoms, switched on the lights, booted up his laptop, and groaned as a burning pain spread up his spine. Then he downed some painkillers.

By the time he sat at his desk, Glover's email had arrived. He clicked on the first video attachment and watched the interview with Amy Price, then the second interview with Farzad's friend, Charlie.

White paused the last video and stared at his screen, eyes narrowed, swivelling in his chair. He was certain it had to be Klein who'd been feeding the police information. How else would they know? It was highly unlikely they'd connected all the dots. The whole purpose of making them all commonly occurring incidents was supposed to work as cover. But White wasn't too concerned about Klein potentially double-crossing them, because his predatory brain was already working out exactly how to use it to his advantage. White had amassed copies of all the files from Regen Logistix, containing reams of information and data about the nanochip, but he didn't have Klein's patient files yet. He needed those for evidence that proved the experiments worked on live subjects, which would bump the price up considerably. Although others had been working on similar technology for years, Regen Logistix had beaten them to developing a final product that actually worked. So White needed to handle things quickly now. The time was ripe for doing the deal he'd been building up to. And then he'd point the finger in Klein's direction.

He smiled to himself as he dialled a phone number and asked for information on Chief Constable Derek Sutherby. Within a few minutes, he knew Sutherby's address, where he lived alone, and the details of his family—he was divorced with two adult kids and a grandkid. White knew what car he drove, his financial status, and all manner of other things. He didn't have time to study Sutherby's recent communications, but that didn't matter for now. He stared at the screen as he read about Sutherby's ex, Anthea. As an administrator at the university, had she become suspicious and tipped off her husband? It could be a toss-up between her and Klein.

White went into the bathroom, washed his face, then got dressed in a grey suit and white shirt. He matched it with a grey striped tie and stared at the effect in the mirror. His skin looked almost the same shade as the suit. His cheeks were gaunt. He'd lost more weight. He had four more years to go before retirement, but he wouldn't make it that long. He was dying. The big C. He'd been coughing up blood for weeks before finally plucking up the nerve to see the doctor. Maybe it was payback for everything he'd done. Now the cancer was metastatic. It had spread to his spine, and there was no cure. The only choice of management were tablets to dull the pain and reduce bone loss.

He certainly wasn't going to go gracefully, though. He thought about all the sacrifices he'd made. All the justifications he'd told himself. All the things he'd done. The lengths he'd gone to. Now he didn't know if any of it had been worth it.

He drove to Sutherby's house, thinking about mortality and morality. About right and wrong. About necessity and secrets. Patriotism and the greater good. And the dark shadows he and those like him had hidden amongst for so long.

Dawn broke in a haze of oranges and greys, and White reckoned he had about another one hundred and eighty sunrises left in this world.

He drove down Sutherby's quiet, leafy street, wondering how many sunrises Sutherby had left. Not many if the chief constable didn't yield to the pressure he was about to bear.

A light was on in the window of Sutherby's upstairs bedroom. White parked outside, opened the gate, strode up the path, and rang the bell. A light came on downstairs, and a shadow appeared behind the obscured glass in the front door. White reached into his pocket for his ID.

The door swung open. Derek Sutherby was already dressed in his uniform of black trousers and white shirt, complete with epaulettes bearing his rank.

White held up his ID. 'I need to speak with you about a matter of urgent national security.'

Frowning, Sutherby peered at White's ID then took it from his hand to scrutinise it closely. Sutherby's Adam's apple bobbed up and down as he swallowed. He was trying to appear calm, but there was fear beneath his demeanour. White had seen that fear plenty of times before.

'What kind of national security matter?' Sutherby asked.

White eyed him with a cold stare. 'We should discuss it inside.'

Sutherby hesitated, taking one last glance at White's ID before handing it back to him. He stepped aside to let White in and led him to the lounge.

Sutherby stood in front of a TV in the corner of the room. 'All right. What's going on?'

'Your staff recently interviewed Amy Price and Charlie Cooper in connection with the Farzad Nuri stabbing.'

Sutherby's frown got bigger. 'Yes.'

'In that interview, you were asking questions about Professor Brian Klein.'

'What does that have to do with MI5?'

White didn't answer. 'I want to know why you were talking about Klein's research programmes. And *why* you did a PNC check on a vehicle belonging to a Paul Clark in North London.'

Sutherby looked gobsmacked. 'Why are you asking?'

'As I said, it's a matter of national security.'

'What national security issue has to do with Professor Klein or his research or that vehicle?'

'That's highly classified. I want to know what's going on here.'

'So do I,' Sutherby snapped.

White gave him a tight smile. '*Why* are you investigating those things?'

Sutherby fidgeted with his hands at his sides, as if working out how much he wanted to tell White. 'The vehicle had a rear brake light not working. I was driving home following it, and I called the control room to do a PNC check. I wanted to make sure it wasn't stolen.' Sutherby shrugged.

White let out a humourless, disbelieving laugh. 'And Klein and his research? Why were you asking about that?'

Sutherby didn't answer.

'We could go back and forth all day like this, but that would be incredibly boring and unnecessary. As of now, you will immediately cease any investigation into Klein or the university or any of its students on the grounds of national security. Is that clear?'

'No, it's not bloody clear! It's not clear at all. I want to know exactly what your involvement is in this.'

White sighed, annoyed at having to repeat himself. 'That's highly classified. Your investigation stops. Right now.'

'Wait a minute, you haven't told me *why* this concerns national security.'

White's voice hardened. 'And I don't have to. But your own officers suggested it themselves. Farzad Nuri committed a terrorist act, just like the London Bridge terrorists did. Which means counter-terrorism officers will be taking over the investigation into the stabbing and the search for him. That's all you need to know.'

Sutherby glared at him.

'I'm sure I don't have to remind you you're bound by the Official Secrets Act,' White carried on. 'And you've got five years before retirement. If you don't stop digging around now, you'll lose your job and your pension. Not to mention you'll receive a lengthy prison sentence when you're convicted.'

Sutherby's nostrils flared. 'Convicted for what? What the hell are you talking about?'

'Anything we want to drum up, whether it's real or not.'

Sutherby's fists clenched. 'You've got the cheek to come to my house and threaten me?'

'Well, it's not just you, is it? The other thing is your family.' White flashed his teeth in a sickly smile. 'Was it Anthea who came to you with some ridiculous ideas about the university and Klein?'

Sutherby blanched. 'I have no idea what you're talking about. Leave my family out of this!'

'No can do, I'm afraid. You've got a couple of lovely daughters, too, haven't you? And your grandson's a cute kid. How old is he now? Five? No, silly me... He's six, isn't he?'

Sutherby's face flushed pink. 'How dare you! I'll—'

'Whatever you think you want to do, you won't. This order comes from the highest level. You know the drill. You've been in this situation before. You'll forget what you think you know, and forget you ever met me. Are we clear on this?'

Sutherby clenched his jaw, and White could tell exactly what Sutherby was thinking as he weighed up his options, which were exactly nil. Even though he was the chief constable of a large constabulary, he was still a puppet, bound by a hierarchy of people far more powerful than himself. It wasn't the first time orders from higher up had shut down one of Sutherby's investigations, and it probably wouldn't be the last. That little catch-all of national security that stripped away people's rights would see to that. And if that failed, and Sutherby's lips got a little too loose, there were always the threats to himself or his family to fall back on. Because they weren't threats at all, as Sutherby well knew. They were facts.

'About as clear as a rotten pile of shit,' Sutherby finally said through gritted teeth.

'Good. I'll see myself out.'

CHAPTER 39

DETECTIVE BECKY HARRIS

It was just gone 7.00 a.m. I'd fallen asleep researching the night before and had awoken two hours ago, to pick up where I'd left off. I'd started looking for experiments used in brainwashing and behavioural modification and found pages and pages of links. I'd worked my way through history, reading about clandestine black ops that had been done way back in the 50s, run by the CIA.

A project called MK-Ultra had been carried out in various institutions that tested methods of mind control on unsuspecting people, without their knowledge or consent. They'd used implantable electrodes in people's brains, hallucinogenic drugs, electromagnetic pulses, and radio waves. People subjected to the abhorrent studies and tests were often the most vulnerable in society—those in prisons, mental hospitals, colleges and universities, and even the military. People who couldn't say no or fight back. Some of the doctors the CIA hired for the programme were the same torturers who'd committed atrocities in the Nazi concentration camps.

MK-Ultra's inhumane, bone-chilling experiments had

gone on for twenty years, often resulting in the total destruction of the victims' sanity or their deaths. I'd watched videos of some experiments that had been done on animals, most notably a bull in an arena with an electrode implanted in its brain. It'd turned from a raging beast to a docile animal at the flick of a switch. I'd pored through pages of reports, declassified documents, and articles.

But this morning, I'd found something even more terrifying from online news reports and journals about new, up-to-date methods that were currently being developed. In conjunction with various scientists, huge technology and biomedical corporations worldwide, and government agencies, nanochips were being tested to detect and alter people's brainwaves. By using wireless technology—or more precisely, nanotechnology—these chips could remotely manipulate thoughts, behaviour, and emotions.

A thought slammed into my brain, something Natalie had said to me. *Someone put it in my head.*

I thought of her jabbing at the back of her neck. What if she'd really been talking about some kind of nanochip? Had she made the connection that an experiment she'd been involved in for Klein was messing up her head? Is that what she'd meant when she told me she'd looked it up? Had she done some research on the internet?

Goose bumps scattered all over my skin. This had to be what Klein was testing on unsuspecting students, some new kind of nanochip implanted in their necks that changed their behaviour. It sounded like an episode of *Black Mirror*.

I sat back and stared at the screen with growing horror, unable to believe this kind of highly dangerous technology was not only possible, but actively being worked on right now.

I leaped off the bed and found the post-mortem reports for Vicky and Ajay. Because the deaths hadn't been considered suspicious, the post-mortems weren't as thorough as a Home Office post-mortem, so it was likely the pathologist wouldn't have discovered the presence of a nanochip. I read through Vicky's first, and there was no mention of any foreign body inside her, but there was a note that she had a recent one centimetre cut at the back of her neck, exactly in the same place that Natalie had pointed to. Ajay's body had been too damaged to note any possible cuts. His skin had melted away in parts to just leave bone. Some of his organs were just about intact, but judging by the state of his body after the fire, it was likely any chip would've melted. Or had someone tampered with their bodies to remove a chip en route to or at the hospital to stop it being discovered? That could explain Vicky's cut.

My brain raced on overdrive, incensed and disgusted at the lengths people were prepared to go to in order to cover up what was going on. I was terrified at the possibilities for all of us if they succeeded.

I reached for the phone to call Sutherby, but it rang before I reached it. I glanced at the screen. Sutherby was calling me.

'Morning,' I said to him. 'I was just about to ring you, sir. You're never going to believe what I've found on—'

'Are you alone?' He cut in.

'Yes. I've been working on the brainwashing angle, and I've found something unbelievable.' I quickly ran through the research I'd carried out, talking in one long stream. 'I think the students were being implanted with nanochips in their heads. I know it sounds weird, but this technology is very real. And it seems like people have been working on this for years. I think we should get Natalie tested and see if she's still got one inside her. From what I read, these nanochips can be detected on an MRI scan. She was never given one at the hospital when they were diagnosing her. These chips can—'

'This investigation is being shut down.' Anger radiated in his voice.

My eyes widened. 'What? *Why?* What are you talking about, sir? I know we haven't got any evidential link yet between Klein and the students, but I'm certain I'll find some patient records or paper trail somewhere that—'

'Listen to what I'm saying. You need to get out of there, go home, and forget all about it.'

I pulled the phone away from my ear, staring at it in disbelief. Then I put it back again. 'Sir, what's going on?'

'We need to stop looking into Klein and Hoodie Guy, which means shutting this down immediately.'

'I can't. Not now. Do you know how much danger people could be in with this? If I *am* right, you're going to have a hell of a lot of people after that technology. Think how much damage it could do. Think about the corporations, governments, military, and security services all around the world who'd love to get their hands on it, not to mention the criminal organisations. It would be priceless. And if it fell into the wrong hands... actually, I can't think of any *right* hands for it to be in.'

'Becky! Stop talking for once and listen. This isn't up for debate. It's a direct order from above.'

I sucked in an angry breath, frowning. 'What do you mean? Orders from who?'

'MI-bloody-five,' he hissed.

'What the hell, sir?'

'They're saying this is a matter of national security and prevention of terrorism. They wouldn't tell me anything else. I had a bloody visit from one of their spooks this morning.'

'Oh, great! That catch-all terrorism buzzword that gets bandied about every time someone wants to cover something up. And national security is a guise that doesn't equate to public safety. You know what this means... if the security services are trying to stop us, then that *proves* this is some kind of black operation. We can't stop now, sir.'

'We have to. National security takes precedence over any police investigation. Counter-terrorism are taking over the Farzad Nuri investigation.'

'National security, my arse.' I paced up and down the small room, fist clenched. 'We both know that one of the common reasons intelligence agencies keep things so secret is because they're acting unlawfully. No, this is wrong. Kids are dying. We need to stop them.'

'I mean it, Becky. You have to give it up and go home.'

'This is crazy. We can't just let them dictate to the police not to investigate this.'

'I don't like it any more than you. But that's the way it is. Just pack up and go home and forget you were ever there. They don't know about you, and I want it to stay like that.'

'How am I supposed to forget about it?' I asked, incredulous. 'What if they succeed in what they're doing, and we all end up like microchipped zombies? It's not just about a few students now. This is about unleashing a crime against humanity that could affect every single one of us if they get their way. It's MK-Ultra on steroids!'

'This isn't up for debate. I've had my orders. And so have you.'

'But, sir—'

'But *nothing*.'

'Did they threaten you?'

He didn't answer, which was the only answer I needed. Instead, he said in a defeated voice, 'Go home, Becky.'

I gritted my teeth, letting out a groan.

'That's an order,' he said when I didn't reply.

'What happens if more kids die?'

'My hands are tied. I can't say any more about it, and neither can you. Do you understand?' There was a tremor in his voice.

I gripped the phone tighter, wanting to protest more, but knowing I'd be wasting my breath. 'Yes, sir.'

I killed the call and stared at the phone again, gobsmacked, as a storm raged inside. I could understand how he'd been threatened—Official Secrets Act would be first, then maybe they'd thrown a possibility of treason in there, too. Possibly threats to him personally or his family. Or a bribe. Or blackmail, if he had a dirty little secret in his closet.

A ball of anger rose from my stomach, detonating inside as it hit my chest. I threw my phone on the bed and kicked my wastepaper bin across the room.

CHAPTER 40

TONI

I'd hardly slept all night again. After Mitchell had gone, I'd looked up Ajay, Vicky, and Natalie online. Two students were dead because of this. Farzad Nuri had most likely been killed, too, to keep him quiet. Another victim had died because of Natalie's actions. Not to mention all the lives of their families, smashed to pieces.

I got up at just gone 5.00 a.m. and did a tai chi flow then tried to meditate to relaxation music afterwards to clear my mind of the disturbing images flitting around in my head. It usually helped calm me, and it was a technique I often recommended to my clients. But every time I closed my eyes, I saw Farzad thrusting the knife into the man's chest. Marcelina's body hitting the tarmac and sticky, wet blood pouring from her head. Ajay screaming like a desperate animal as he burned himself alive. Vicky diving off the stairway into a dark void. The sickening crunch of Natalie's vehicle hitting and killing the old man. I was horrified and sick with sadness, but more than that, I was angry. Incensed. And the meditation didn't stand a hope in hell of working.

I got through my morning's clients on autopilot, finding

it hard to concentrate. I was doing them a disservice by only being partly in the room with them.

After my 11.00 a.m. appointment left, I checked my phone for the hundredth time, to see if Mitchell had left a message. He had, asking me to call him.

'How's Lee getting on?' I asked as soon as he picked up.

'He's been systematically going through Regen Logistix's computer systems and found hundreds of internal documents and medical specs for this implantable nanochip they've been working on, plus emails between key members of staff. It all makes for some very scary reading. There's also more evidence of the security service's involvement. The CEO, Paul Hughes, has been in regular contact with a guy called Nathan White, who's a shadow operative with MI5 and has been covering up their mistakes with the help of Glover.'

An angry flush spread up my neck as my mind spun. 'Did Lee find anything about Klein's experiments on the students?'

'No. There are a few mentions of hypothetical situations for testing the chip, but nothing solid. So we can't prove they've actively been implanting the chips in students. Lee didn't have any joy getting hold of the patient records stored on the university's database because their system is kept off-line. But I'm pretty sure Klein must be keeping records of what he's been doing somewhere. Even twisted, clandestine black ops have paper trails.'

'Maybe I could try and find the records.'

'How?'

'They'd only be accessible on the computers in the Watling Centre building, like ours are here. I'd have to break in there somehow and find them.'

'No way. That's *definitely* not a good idea. People are already dying over this. And if they think you've made a connection between what's happening, they won't think twice about killing you, too. They've already been in your office, looking through your files. And Glover saw you at this hospital.'

'Yes, but they'll only think I'm a counsellor. They don't know I *know* anything. You don't need to worry about me. I can look after myself. You and Krav Maga taught me well.'

'I don't think Klein would keep them at the Watling Centre anyway. According to what Lee's found, the university aren't aware of what's going on. And whether Klein's using digital or paper records, he won't want his colleagues to stumble across his illegal tests.'

'Could he be keeping paper copies at Regen Logistix?'

'It's possible, but I doubt Klein would want to go backwards and forwards to their site every time he wants to update the records. He's more likely to keep them at home. Lee hacked into his home computer, but there are no patient records on it, so he could be storing them on another device that's off-line or keeping paper copies.'

'We should try getting into his house first then. When he's at work.'

There was silence on the other end of the line. 'We? No. Let me and Lee deal with things now.'

'I can handle this.'

'No, not after what happened last time. You thought you could handle that, too. I'm not putting you in danger.'

I stared up at the ceiling, picturing the evil, twisted faces of my kidnappers. Feeling again all the fear and terror I'd gone through. How close I'd come to almost dying. But instead of being broken afterwards, I'd used that fear to make it work for me. I wasn't going to let that experience stop me helping people. 'I want to end this before anyone else gets hurt. I owe it to Marcelina. I'm an adult. I can make my own decisions. You don't need to tell Mum. It'll be quicker to have two of us search the house, anyway. And even if you say no, I'll do it without you.'

He exhaled deeply. 'You're so like your dad. Stubborn, brave, protective, righteous.'

'I'll take that as a compliment.'

'It wasn't meant to be,' he growled, but it contained more love and concern than anger. 'You're not going to give up until I say yes, are you?'

'Nope. You'll be with me anyway.'

There was a long silence on the phone before he sighed. 'All right. I'll meet you at your flat at 6.00 p.m. Then we'll go through the plan.'

CHAPTER 41

I paced the tiny bedroom, trying to calm down. Then I stopped and stared out of the window down to the car park, watching students milling around on their way to lectures or the union, or to hang out with their mates. Going about their everyday life without any realisation that something so heinous could ever touch them. I thought about Vicky, Ajay, Natalie, and Farzad. Innocent victims who'd been used as human guinea pigs by powerful people who thought they were expendable.

Sutherby's words echoed in my ears. *You have to give it up and go home.*

I flopped onto my bed and stared up at the ceiling for a few minutes, agitation vibrating through every cell. Then I leaped up again. I needed a coffee. Something to calm me down.

I tucked my hair up under a baseball cap and pulled the peak down before heading to the union, hoping to avoid being noticeable in case Sutherby's wife, Anthea, was on campus anywhere. I kept an eye out for her but thankfully didn't spot her.

I took some deep breaths as I queued in the coffee shop, hoping to bump into one of the students I'd met in the last few days—someone normal who could take my mind off this mess for just a few minutes. But I didn't see anyone I knew as I took my double espresso shot to the corner of the room and sat down.

As I stared into space, the sounds of the students' chatter dissipated into the ether around me as my brain raced. How could I just pack up and go home? If I didn't try to stop them, where would it all end? They had a highly dangerous technology tool for ultimate population subjugation. For creating effective killing machines. The heinous possibilities were endless. It was madness. It was—

The sound of silence seemed to penetrate my thoughts then, something out of place, out of kilter. I glanced up and refocused, spotting Farzad's girlfriend, Amy, in the queue a few metres away. She was on her own, her face blotchy and red. Some of the other students in the queue nudged each other and started whispering about her. It was obvious Amy was trying to ignore them as she stared at the floor, her shoulders hunched and stiff. And maybe she would've been able to, until Shakia sauntered through the door and spotted Amy, a nasty smirk tugging at her mouth.

'Quick, keep the knives under lock and key!' Shakia said in a loud voice.

Amy froze for a moment. Then a loud sob erupted from her, and she rushed out of the shop, tears dribbling down her cheeks.

I leaped up from my seat, strode across the room to Shakia, and stopped inches away from her face. 'First of all, Amy has done nothing to deserve that horrible comment, so you're completely out of order there. I'm sure you think you're better than everyone else, but I can assure you, you're not.' I treated her to one of her own signature glares up and down. 'And you'll find that out when you get into the *real* world, out of your little student bubble, where you think you're the queen bee. And secondly, I hope—I *really* hope— you're never in the same position as Amy, where your life is devastated, and you need some compassion and support. Because it's not a nice place to be. And as you've just proved, there are a lot of not nice people to keep you company there.'

Shakia's jaw fell open with surprise. I didn't wait around for her retort. I hurried away to find Amy as the other people in the queue sniggered. When I got outside the union, Amy was running across the path towards the student car park. I legged it after her, calling her name, wanting to try to comfort her.

I caught up and ran in front of her, forcing her to stop. 'Amy, you don't know me, but I wanted to tell you I'm really sorry about everything. She shouldn't have said that to you. You're hurting, and none of this is your fault.'

Amy stood there, her gaze on the ground, panting hard.

'Can I help in any way?' I bent my head so I was in her sightline. 'Are you okay?'

She looked at me with stricken eyes. 'I thought I could handle being here, but I can't. It feels like everyone's blaming me for what Farzad did, and I don't know what... what to do or what to say.'

I nodded. 'I know. Maybe you should take a few days off away from here. Be with your friends. Your family. Someone who can help support you.'

Amy sniffed then nodded. 'I wanted to try to carry on as normal. I wanted to be at the flat in case Farzad came back.

But... I can't handle this. I think you're right. I think I'll go back to my parents' house for a while.'

'It might help you. Do you need a lift anywhere?'

She blinked, sending tears snaking down her cheeks. 'No. I'll be fine. But thank you for checking on me.' She blew out a breath, turned, and scurried away.

I watched her go, a mixture of anger and sadness for her and hatred for those responsible burning in my throat. And then I made a decision. I couldn't give up. Not when I was so close. Go home and forget about kids dying? Forget about all the victims' family's lives being blasted to smithereens? No sodding way. Sutherby might've been following my career, but he didn't know me at all. I was going to do exactly what I'd already planned. Nail Professor Klein, Hoodie Guy, and whoever else was involved.

I stomped back to my room, trying to work out where to go from here. I had to somehow get my hands on Klein's patient records, because I was certain there had to be some. The only question was where would they be? At his home? Or at the Watling Centre? The chance of finding them depended on whether the university itself was involved, or whether Klein was procuring test subjects without their knowledge. MK-Ultra testing had been done on students with the full participation of some of the colleges and universities involved, so even though there was nothing listed in the university's promotional research bumf, they could still be at the heart of it. I needed to rule out the possibility the records were not on site before I broke into Klein's house to look for them there.

And then what? If I did find evidence, who could I even take it to if the investigation had been shut down? Especially when Klein seemed to be untouchable and ultra-protected.

As I opened my bedroom door and stepped inside, I tried to think through possibilities about who I could turn to when I did get my hands on the evidence. But I came up with nothing.

Best not to think that far ahead, girl.

I just had to concentrate on getting the first part right. If I worried about how I could possibly expose everything on my own with no resources and without the law behind me, then the hopelessness would drag me down. So I decided to worry about the rest of it later.

I sat down at the desk and rubbed at an angry vein throbbing in my temple. I had hours to kill until my 3.00 p.m. appointment with Klein, so I opened up my laptop to do some more research in the hope I could find out about who he might be working with and who had actually produced the nanochip.

Half an hour later, my phone buzzed with a text from Sutherby: *Have you left yet?*

I stared at the screen and clenched my jaw as my fingers roved over the keys: *Just packing up my stuff now, sir.*

Then I threw my phone on the bed and got back to work.

CHAPTER 42

TONI

After my last client of the morning left, I told Janet I was heading off for my lunch break, but the last thing on my mind was food. I'd well and truly lost my appetite. Instead, I went to the university's gym to blow off some stress.

I dumped my bag in a locker and headed for the treadmill. There were only a handful of people inside. A girl taking a selfie, pouting into the camera as she sat at one of the weight machines at the other side of the room. A guy on a stationary bike with earbuds in. Two guys on rowing machines next to each other, watching the TV screen which showed a news reporter standing in St Peters Street, relaying yet again what had happened the previous day with Farzad Nuri. Not surprisingly, the incident had made the national news, and the latest report was that the stabbing victim had died, Farzad Nuri remained at large, and it had been classified as a terrorist attack.

I narrowed my eyes at the screen and shook my head. So that was the spin Glover and his MI5 buddies were putting on it now?

Disgusted, I looked away from the TV as rage charged through my veins. I put in my earbuds and clicked through a playlist on my phone until I found something energetic and powerful. I turned up the volume, letting Pink's voice explode, before putting the phone in my pocket.

I started at a slow walk and gradually upped the pace until I'd done ten minutes of warm-up. Then I headed to the free weight benches and picked up a couple of dumbbells. I spotted myself in the mirror, watching my technique as I went through a range of arm exercises. I returned them to the rack, picked up a barbell, and screwed on some weights before settling on a bench to start some chest presses.

I'd done two sets when Curtis's face loomed above me. His lips moved as he said something, but I couldn't hear him over the music. I set the barbell on the rack above my head, sat up, and pulled out my earbuds.

'Hi,' he said with a half-hearted smile.

I took in his toned arms on show in the vest top he had on and said, 'Hi.' I hadn't felt like smiling when I'd walked in the gym—too many sick and twisted things had happened— but I did now. It happened automatically, and I could see again why Marcelina had had a serious crush on him. He was gorgeous without being arrogant or cocky. Relaxed in his own skin. He had a genuinely sweet, kind vibe about him.

'I've never seen you in here before,' he said.

The first thought that came into my head was that I hadn't seen him there, either, but that was obviously too lame a comeback, so I just said, 'I usually come before work or afterwards, but I needed to de-stress.' I sat up and swung my feet onto the wooden floor.

He sat next to me, hunched over, forearms resting on his

knees, staring into space. 'Yeah, I know what you mean. I've just got back from the hospital.' He shook his head. 'Did you hear what happened?'

'No, what?'

'Marcelina... she's... um...' He took a deep breath then turned to look at me. 'She died.'

I gasped. 'No.' Even though I now knew that what had happened to her wasn't my fault, tears sprang into my eyes. The tragedy had been set in motion by others with no conscience weeks before she'd even set foot in my office, but it still didn't make the news any easier to hear. Maybe I couldn't have saved her. But I could still save others from the same fate.

'It happened about five minutes before I arrived. Some kind of complication from the head injury. A sudden bleed.'

'I'm so sorry. Do you want to talk about it?' I blinked back the tears, trying to remain strong, calm, and professional.

He shrugged. 'Not really. I just wanted to let off some steam in here. Are you okay, though? You look really sad.'

'I'm fine. But thanks for asking.'

Our gazes met. And in that moment, I felt a connection with him, an unexpected attraction I'd never felt before. It was like a warm breeze against my skin, a feeling of possibilities, happiness, and hope. I could feel a good energy about him on a deep level. He felt safe.

'I mean, it seems like you care a lot about everyone else,' he said, still looking deep in my eyes. 'But it must be tough doing your job.'

'It's just what I do. It's what I've always wanted to do.' I smiled.

'Yes. But is there anyone caring for you?'

I swallowed and looked away.

'We all need people to talk to. And I was wondering... look...' He ran a hand over the back of his neck then glanced down at the floor and back to me. 'Do you want to go for a drink? Or... a coffee. Something. Uh, you know, if you're not busy. Or whenever.' He scrunched his face up with embarrassment. 'I'm sorry. I'm making a mess of this.'

'No.' I reached out and touched his arm, a tingle of excitement deep in my core. 'You're not messing it up at all.' I wanted to say yes in a way I'd never wanted to say yes to anyone. But I shouldn't be happy when Marcelina and the other students were dead. I couldn't be happy until I'd stopped them doing it again. I didn't want any distractions. So I stood up and said, 'I'd love to. But not right now. There are some things going on, and... well... it's complicated.'

He stood, too, giving me another half smile. 'Of course. No pressure. I'm not going anywhere.'

'Thanks for asking me.' I made a show of looking at the time on my phone. 'I need to get back to work.' I left him there, feeling a twinge in my stomach, but I couldn't tell if it was longing or overwhelming sadness about Marcelina, or both.

I headed to the changing rooms and texted Mitchell to let him know what had happened to Marcelina. He sent a reply telling me not to do anything stupid and he'd see me later.

I emerged from the building fifteen minutes later after hurriedly showering and dressing, my gym bag hiked over my shoulder. As I walked down the path towards the union, the terrace was packed with students, eating, laughing, and texting friends. Life carried on as normal for them. Normal, but for how long? If Klein and his cronies got what they wanted and continued with their sociopathic plans, we'd all be programmed robots.

I stopped outside the Watling Centre, looking up at the windows. Was Klein up there now, laughing to himself because Marcelina was dead?

I took a grounding breath and headed back to the counselling block, rage curdling in my stomach. Phil was talking with Janet in reception as I arrived. He took one look at my face and asked if I was okay.

'Not really. I just heard that Marcelina died.' I fought the tears back again, and my heart sped up, thumping against my rib cage.

'Oh, dear. I'm very sorry to hear that.' Phil's expression morphed into one of sadness.

'Me, too,' Janet said, shaking her head. 'Very awful news.'

'Come into my office for a minute, Toni.' Phil led the way, and I followed him in. He waited until we were both seated before saying, 'Do you want to talk about it?'

I took a breath. Part of me wanted to tell him what Mitchell and I had discovered, but I couldn't. For one thing, it sounded so crazy that he probably wouldn't believe me. And also, if we were going to expose Regen Logistix and Professor Klein, no one could know I'd been involved in it. Not if I wanted to live. I had no doubt the intelligence services could and would arrange for me to have an 'accident' or 'commit suicide' if they found out what we were about to do. 'No. I'm okay. I didn't even know her, really.' But that wasn't true. I *felt* like I knew her.

'I know we were going to do the supervision session later, but that can wait. In fact, I'm happy for you to go home. Take a bit of time for self-care.'

'I don't want to let people down.'

'No, I insist. Your mind won't be on your job. I'll take your afternoon clients. And you're not in tomorrow, anyway, so take a mini-break away from here and work on yourself instead.'

I opened my mouth, about to object again, but I'd already been useless in my job throughout the morning. I'd only be going over and over everything in my head and not concentrating on the people I was supposed to be helping. So I gave Phil my thanks and then drove home, my head throbbing, as I thought about a novel sitting on my book-shelf. George Orwell's classic *1984* was a favourite of mine, and I'd read it from cover to cover many times over. But it was supposed to be a warning. Not an instruction manual.

CHAPTER 43

DETECTIVE BECKY HARRIS

I left my mobile phone in my room so it couldn't be tracked and then walked through the campus with my baseball cap on, my gaze scanning for Anthea again. I removed my cap as I stepped inside the Watling Centre and tucked it in my backpack. I smiled at the receptionist inside, wondering just how many people knew about what Klein and Hoodie Guy had been doing. Did *she* know what was going on? I suspected it would only be the top bods in the know.

I gave my name, and the receptionist told me to take a seat.

'Actually, can I use the toilet first, please?' I asked.

'Of course, but you might need to do a urine sample when you see Professor Klein.'

'Oh, I'm absolutely bursting. But I'll make sure I save a bit.' I grinned.

She pointed to a set of double glass doors behind her. 'If you go through there and turn right. It's the second door on your left.'

I headed through the doors and turned right, finding myself in a long corridor. I walked down it, past a stairwell, towards the toilets at the end, but didn't go inside. Instead, I went back up the corridor in the opposite direction and found several rooms which had warnings on them about what was inside and not to enter: X-ray machines, an MRI scanner, a CT, and an EEG scanner. If they were used for diagnostic tests, by multiple members of staff, it was unlikely Klein would be hiding records of clandestine experiments in them. The last room read Pathology. I opened the door and looked inside. A male and female in white coats were hunched over desktop lab equipment. The female had a vial of blood in one hand, and with the other, she was aspirating some of it into a machine with a needle. The male looked up at me.

'Sorry, I was looking for the toilet,' I said.

'It's further down the corridor,' he replied. 'Just past the doors to reception.'

'Great, thanks.'

He looked down again, and my gaze did a full sweep of the room before I left. There were two laptops on two desks in the corner of the room next to a large fancy printer. A filing cabinet stood beside that, next to a glass storage unit with more vials, needles, and other medical equipment. Again, it was unlikely Klein would be hiding anything in there.

I went into the loo, just for show, and washed my hands, thinking that the downstairs seemed to be out of the equation for finding what I wanted.

I sat in the waiting room, fiddling with my hands, trying not to clench them. My stomach was in knots. I was nervous about pulling this off without any backup and nervous about what was at stake if I didn't find anything. But I was more furious than anything else.

I jigged my knee up and down and glanced around at the other patients, all of whom were elderly. The receptionist came over and handed me a medical questionnaire attached to a clipboard to fill in. The usual questions: age, physical and mental health history, and was I on any drugs. I filled it in and handed it back to the receptionist, who disappeared with it.

Ten minutes later, my name was called by a nurse dressed in a pale-blue uniform, and I followed her through the glass doors and up the stairs to the top floor. She knocked on a door with Professor's Klein's nameplate on it and told me to go inside.

I entered and came face-to-face with someone I was convinced was a devil in disguise as an angel. He smiled as he looked up from my patient questionnaire in front of him on the desk, stood, and shook my hand. 'Nice to meet you, Becky.'

I plastered on a smile. 'Thank you.'

He sat, and I did the same on the opposite side of the desk.

'I've been looking through your questionnaire and can't see any reason here why you wouldn't be a good candidate for us.' As he looked back down at the form, I glanced around the office. This was the second room from the end of the building, definitely where I'd seen the light on when Hoodie Guy had visited.

Klein's briefcase was on a chair behind his desk. It was closed, but the latch flaps were up, so he hadn't engaged the lock. There was a laptop on his desk. Files were piled up next to it. A filing cabinet sat in the corner. Along one wall stood an examination bench.

'Great,' I said as he looked up at me again. 'Although... um... I was worried about one thing. There's nothing dangerous about doing this, is there?' I did my best meek-little-mouse impression. 'I mean, you don't test new drugs on me or anything like that?'

He smiled again. 'Oh, no. Absolutely nothing like that. There are no drugs in the tests for the healthy volunteer programmes. We use a number of different methods, including diagnostic tests, which could include functional magnetic resonance imaging, blood tests, etcetera. If you're accepted, you could be suitable for our memory research study, which focuses on using behavioural measures and brain imaging to help us understand memory and emotional function in the healthy population. We'll need to do a few tests first. Just to make sure you're suitable. And if every-thing's in order, I'll call you back, and at that stage, we'll get you to sign a confidentiality clause and make the first instal-ment of a one-thousand-pound research remuneration fee. Does that seem acceptable to you?' He smiled pleasantly.

The figure startled me. *One* thousand pounds? Ajay had had three thousand before he'd died. Natalie, Vicky, and Farzad had over two thousand. But before I could think about that anomaly any more, Klein was talking again.

'Volunteers are so important for furthering innovating medical advances. If you're ready, we can do a few tests now.' He came across as smooth and confident, but I sensed some-thing there behind the façade, something cold—a lack of compassion that a doctor should have or a lack of a guilty conscience. Something I couldn't quite put my finger on showed in his eyes and raised my hackles.

I gave him a relieved smile. 'The money would *really* help me out, and I'm happy to be doing something that'll benefit your research. But what kind of tests do you need to do now?'

'Just some simple weight and height measurements. A urine test. And our nurse will do a blood test.'

Klein picked up the phone and asked someone to come into the room.

A few minutes later, the same nurse arrived. She measured my weight and height and took my pulse and blood pressure. When it came to the blood test, I watched her like a hawk as she unwrapped a brand-new syringe from the plastic packaging, making sure it was empty of any kind of nanochip. She swabbed my inner elbow, slid the needle inside my vein, and aspirated some blood. Afterwards, I had to nip out to the toilet to do a urine sample. I came back in the office and handed her the sample bottle wrapped in tissue paper before she disappeared.

'The test results will be back in a few days,' Klein said after I'd sat back down. 'If everything looks good, I'll ring you personally to arrange an appointment for the next step, which is to have an MRI or CT scan and get some brain and head images. But don't worry; it's perfectly painless and harmless. We may give you a contrast solution through an IV to allow the machine to see certain parts of your brain more easily. And it may well be out of usual patient hours, as I'm juggling a *lot* of research and struggling to keep up with all the studies. Is that okay for you?'

I smiled. 'Yes, absolutely. I'm flexible. I know you must be really busy. I—' I stopped speaking suddenly and leaned forward, clutching my stomach. 'Sorry, I just feel a bit woozy. I didn't have breakfast this morning.'

'Oh, dear. Just bend over and put your head between your legs and see if that helps.' He stood up and rounded his desk. 'If you haven't eaten, that could be why.'

'Would it be possible to get a drink of water, please? I'm sure I'll be fine in a minute.'

'Of course.' He left the room.

I jumped up, went behind his desk to the chair, and flipped open the lid of the briefcase. Inside were a couple of blue files. I pulled them out and checked the names written on the outside but didn't recognise any. I quickly opened them and found a document at the front giving the patient's pertinent details. They weren't students. They were elderly patients in an Alzheimer's research programme. Klein also had a notepad inside which wasn't written on, a couple of pens, and a calculator. Nothing that related to what I was interested in.

I replaced everything as I'd found it and rushed back to the chair. I sat down just as the door swung open.

Klein had a glass of water in his hand and a couple of biscuits on a plate.

'Here you are. Maybe you just need a bit of sugar for energy.' He popped the plate on his desk in front of me and handed me the glass, glancing down with concern. In that moment, it was hard to believe he was a psychopath who thought it was okay to test dangerous mind-bending technology on unsuspecting, innocent people.

'Thanks.' I drank the water in one go.

'Have a biscuit, too.'

I took a biscuit and chomped away as he sat at his desk again.

When I'd finished, I said, 'I'm feeling much better now.'

'Maybe you should have a bit more to eat when you leave here. It's probably just low blood sugar. Your blood pressure is absolutely fine. But if you do have any more problems in the meantime, you should see a doctor.'

Not likely.

I stood up. 'I'm sure that's it. Thanks for being so kind.'

He reached over the desk and shook my hand again. 'I'll be in contact soon.'

I walked out of the office, shut the door behind me, and looked up and down the corridor. The toilets on this floor were further along at the end, but there was no way I could hide in a cubicle until everyone had left for the day without someone noticing. But on the way to the loos to do the urine sample, I'd passed a store cupboard which was unlocked. I'd poked my head inside the small room filled with medical supplies, with shelving units arranged around the room and cardboard boxes piled up in one corner. It wasn't ideal, but it was the best I could come up with. It was just gone quarter to four, and their 'official' patient hours would be over at five, so I was hoping no one would need anything from the supply room before the staff left for the day.

I started towards it then heard people coming up the stairs. I recognised the receptionist's voice talking to someone and waited until she'd reached the top of the stair-well, accompanying a middle-aged man who'd been in the waiting area with me.

I walked slowly towards her, as if I were going downstairs to leave. She smiled at me, and I paused at the top of the stairs, pulling my mobile from my bag and looking at the screen like I was checking a text message.

She knocked on Klein's door and entered the room with

the man. I quickly doubled back and hurried towards the storeroom, my heart thumping as I grabbed the door handle, pressed it down, and stepped inside. I darted around the shelving units and sat on the floor behind a pile of boxes, completely hidden from view. With any luck, she'd think I'd left the building when she went back downstairs.

CHAPTER 44

TONI

By the time I buzzed Mitchell up to my flat that evening, I had a casserole in the oven and potatoes boiling on the hob. I still wasn't hungry, but I'd needed something to do to take my mind off my thoughts.

'Smells good.' Mitchell hugged me. 'Are you okay?'

I hugged him tighter and said yes.

He let me go and looked into my eyes. 'Sure?'

'I'll be better when we get them.'

He sat down and shrugged off a laptop bag strapped over his shoulder onto the sofa.

'Do you want something to drink?'

'A beer if you've got it.'

I grabbed two bottles of Corona from the fridge, and by the time I came back, the laptop was open on the coffee table in front of him.

'Lee and I have done a bit of research and found that Klein lives alone and doesn't have any CCTV at his house, but he does have an alarm. It's an audible system only, not monitored by police, but Lee's been able to hack into it, anyway, and he'll disable it prior to our arrival.' His forehead furrowed as he looked at me. 'Are you sure you want to do this?'

'Absolutely.' I handed him a beer and put mine on the coffee table. Yes, I was scared. And nervous. But that was nothing compared to what would happen if we didn't expose this.

'He lives in a detached house on the outskirts of Ware. There are no CCTV cameras within three miles.' He brought up a satellite view of Klein's house on his laptop.

I sat next to him and peered at the screen, tapping the tip of my right little finger against the pad of my thumb.

Klein's property was quite isolated and accessed via a country lane that ran past it. I leaned over and clicked to zoom in. The front of the house was open to the view of anyone driving down the lane, as he only had a low-level privet hedge, so if we approached from that way, there was a good chance we could be spotted. At the rear, though, his garden backed onto a wide expanse of the River Lea, just a grassy path separating the riverbank from Klein's back fence. I zoomed out and took in the surrounding area. To the north was a warren of country lanes leading to more spaced-out, detached houses. To the west, about thirty metres away, was a lane that led to what looked like an old abandoned factory. In between the factory and Klein's property was a large copse of wood, the river pathway undulating in and out as the foliage thickened and thinned. Further west of the factory, about fifty metres away, was a housing estate that also backed onto the waterway.

'As you can see, it's quite remote and private at the back,' Mitchell said. 'We go through the woods, along the river-bank, and then over his fence.' He clicked on the mouse and brought up another screen with internal building plans. 'Lee got these plans from the council's website. Klein had an extension done four years ago.' He pointed to the rear doors. 'There are double-glazed French doors leading to the kitchen-diner. It'll be easy to pick them.'

'Great.' I sensed Mitchell watching me and slid my gaze away from the laptop to him. He had an intense, haunted look in his eyes that I recognised from when he was about to have a PTSD flashback to his military days. I touched his forearm. 'Are you all right?'

He carried on staring at my face for a moment then looked down at my hand. 'It's all right. It's not a flashback. It's just...' He blinked rapidly, his eyes glistening. 'Your dad used to do that.' He nodded at my fingertips tapping each other.

I glanced down, not realising I was even doing it. 'Really? I sometimes do it subconsciously when I'm concentrating.' I smiled at the thought of my dad doing the same thing. Mitchell had told me stories about him before, but I'd never heard this one.

'And you look so much like him. And...' He trailed off, his voice cracking. Mitchell blamed himself for the fact that my dad had never returned from combat when he had. Dad had been shot and killed on a job that had gone seriously wrong. A job Mitchell was in charge of. 'Even your mannerisms. Your personality. The way you're calm under pressure. The way you want to fight for the underdog. We were like this together so many times, going over operations, planning routes in and out, talking about intel, poring over aerial photographs. Living in dumps in the arse-end of nowhere for months at a time, getting shot at and blown up together. We were more than friends. He was like a brother to me.' He gestured to the laptop, to us sitting close together. 'It's like déjà vu.' He closed his eyes for a moment. 'I miss him.'

I missed Dad, too, and I'd never even met him. Mum hadn't told him about the pregnancy before he went off to fight that last time. 'So do I.'

Mitchell stood up and walked towards the window, rubbing his hands over his shaved head as he stared outside. 'And it was all just bollocks. Another fake war, built on more lies, just like every other fucking war we marched into, after being force-fed the bullshit of politicians and their corporate cartels. And for what? There was no threat to us. It was all about oil. Regime change. And protecting the military industrial complex at all costs. Pushing their secret little agendas so we'd smash the shit out of yet another Middle Eastern country.' He spat the words out with venom and dropped his hands to his sides, the muscles in his shoulders taut. 'I've seen things you wouldn't believe. And I'm not just talking about combat. I'm talking about the things our own side did to us, as if we were all some massive experiment, while the bastards giving the orders sat in their plush offices, counting the trillions of pounds they were making off the back of death and destruction.' His fists opened and closed, opened and closed. 'I was brainwashed, too. All those years, I thought I was a patriot. Thought I was serving Queen and country, but that was a lie, as well.' He blew out a laugh laced with steely rage, his fists balling again. 'They want us all hating each other so they can divide and conquer.'

'I know you feel a lot of guilt about the things you've done. But you need to make peace with your conscience.'

'But nothing.' He carried on staring out into the night. 'I was a nasty bastard. I did some terrible things. There's no getting over that. It's a bitter pill that will always be stuck in my throat. Your dad died for nothing. Millions of people died for nothing. It's all on them. Everything. All on the deep state who pull the puppet strings in the shadows. And now they're doing it all again with this to their own people. I wish...'

'I know. You wish you could bring him back.'

He nodded.

'But you're not the same person anymore. And it's the guilt that makes you do what you do now. You've harnessed it into a motivator. But you're right. There *is* a real threat now. A threat to all of us. We still need to keep fighting for the underdog. And we're going to win,' I said with more confidence than I felt.

Mitchell's shoulders tightened again, his back still to me. Finally, he wiped his eyes, turned around, and cleared his throat. 'Yep.' He sat beside me again.

I clenched his hand tight in mine as he composed himself.

He sniffed, swallowed. 'Right. Back to it.' He squeezed my hand. 'Klein keeps an online diary on his home laptop that Lee got a look at. Tomorrow, he's got patients at the university all day from nine till five. It'll probably take about forty-five minutes to get there, so I'll pick you up at half eight. Wear some jogging gear. Neutral colours—dark green, black, brown, if you've got them. And leave your mobile at home. Because with modern smartphones, where you can't remove the batteries, they can still track you. Even if you think they're switched off.'

'I'll be ready.'

CHAPTER 45

DETECTIVE BECKY HARRIS

From my hiding spot in the store cupboard, I listened to all the sounds of the building, wondering again if I was making the biggest mistake of my life.

At just gone five, there was a wave of footsteps and calls of goodbyes from out in the corridor then silence for a while.

My arse had gone to sleep while I was sitting on the floor, and my back ached, so I stood up for a minute and looked at my watch for the hundredth time. It was still too early to risk moving.

A door opened then closed, and footsteps trod along the corridor. The toilet flushed next door. I heard nothing for a while. And the more time passed, the more I realised how stupid my plan was, if I could even call it a plan. It was more a desperate hope than anything else. I didn't know if Klein's records would be paper copies or digital. Was the laptop on his desk his personal one, or did it belong to the university? I had a couple of flash drives in my pocket to download anything if I found it. But if his laptop was password protected, I'd be buggered. I could always steal the laptop, but who would I give it to? It wasn't like I could hand it over to the special operations technical team and ask them to have a look at it. Klein might even take the laptop home with him every day.

I pulled a bottle of water from my bag and took a couple of swigs to quench my parched mouth before replacing it. Then I looked at my watch again. Just gone 8.00 p.m., and the building had been silent for over an hour. It was time to make a move.

I stood up and stretched my arms over my head, leaning side to side to work out the kinks. I did a few hamstring curls and knee lifts to get the circulation going again. Then I strode to the door, silent in my trainers. I reached for the handle and pressed it down slowly without a sound. I was about to pull the door open when I heard footsteps outside, coming closer.

My fingers clenched around the depressed handle, not wanting to lift it back up in case it gave a telltale squeak.

The footsteps stopped outside the door I was hiding behind.

I held my breath, the soles of my trainers glued to the spot.

A phone rang from out in the corridor.

I recognised Klein's voice as he answered then said, 'No, I'm on my own. Everyone's gone home.' There was a long silence from him as I prayed he wouldn't look at the door and see the handle was down and wonder why.

'What?' Klein hissed. 'Why the hell were the police asking questions?' A pause. 'I can assure you any kind of leak most definitely did *not* come from me.' His tone was agitated, unnerved. 'No. No I did *not* give anyone any details. How can you ask that?' More silence while he listened. 'You're sure White's shut it down?' Relief filled his voice, then there was another pause. 'No, of course I'm not stupid enough for that.' Silence for a moment. 'Not if they can't find Farzad.' Another pause as I heard his footsteps pacing up and down outside. 'Good. That's good.'

My hand shook with the effort of holding the handle down.

'Yes, I'll speak to you later,' Klein said. 'Please keep me updated.'

Cramps gripped my fingers as I willed him to go away. Then I heard him say goodbye to the caller, but he didn't leave. I could hear his heavy breathing outside the door, and I pictured him staring at the handle. My heart rate went through the roof.

Ten seconds, and he didn't move.

Twenty.

I bit my lip, my whole arm shaking now.

Then his footsteps finally disappeared down the corridor towards the stairs.

I exhaled slowly, my heart racing as I carefully let the handle go.

Who the hell was White? The secret service guy who'd threatened Sutherby? And what had they done to Farzad Nuri? Turned him into a basket case like Natalie? Or killed him?

I waited another half an hour but heard no more sounds. Klein had said everyone had left, and I didn't want to wait any longer.

I got my Maglite torch out of my backpack before I inched open the door. I looked up and down the corridor. The lights were off, and it was in darkness. Softly, I walked towards Klein's office and tried the handle, hoping it wouldn't be locked. It wasn't—which was good in one way. I wouldn't have to pick it. But if it wasn't locked, surely he couldn't be hiding sensitive information in there, where any staff could stumble across it. But then criminals could be incredibly stupid. People made mistakes all the time. They'd already made a huge one by not realising there was CCTV footage of Hoodie Guy outside Ajay's house and from the camera footage in St Peters Street. Maybe they'd made others, too.

I stepped inside, shut the door, and turned on the torch. I did a sweep of the room. His laptop was still on his desk, blue-coloured files piled up next to it beside a diary and a mug filled with pens. I strode across the room, sat at his desk, lifted the laptop screen, and pressed the power button. While it booted up, I looked at the paper files on his desk. None of them had Vicky's, Natalie's, Ajay's, or Farzad's names. I flicked through just in case, but they were for elderly people who were involved in a stroke study.

The welcome screen came up on the laptop, and it wasn't password protected, which, again, most likely meant there was nothing incriminating on it. I read through the icons on the desktop. There was the usual Word and Excel shortcuts, as well as others I didn't recognise, which must've been medical-type programmes. I clicked on the file manager. Several hundreds of files and documents came up. I scrolled through the alphabetical list and found one with Vicky's name on it.

My heart rate quickened as I opened it. There were documents inside—PDF copies of Vicky's health questionnaire, results of blood and urine tests, and a single paragraph note on a separate document, written by Klein. I honed in on one line: *The subject is not suitable for participation in any study group.*

I stared at the screen, completely thrown. Had I been so wrong about all of this?

I scrolled through more files and found ones for Ajay, Farzad, and Natalie. As I read through, a huge doubt niggled inside. They were all marked unsuitable for a study.

But then I realised that made complete sense if Klein wasn't working with the university on this and they didn't know what was going on. He'd want it covered up that the students were test patients for his programme. And I could see exactly how it worked now. He'd tell the students they were unsuitable for one study but offer them another one, which paid more and gave them more incentive to stick to a confidentiality clause to keep it secret. One where they'd come back for so-called tests late at night, out of usual patient hours, so the regular staff weren't aware of it.

I scanned the names on more files and one jumped out at me: *Marcelina Claybourn.*

I frowned. *Marcelina? The car accident?*

I opened her file and quickly read through. It was exactly the same, marked as unsuitable for the study programme. I shook my head, mentally kicking myself. So her accident *was* related to all this after all. I'd been so wrong about that.

My stomach swirled with nausea as I looked through the rest of the files. There were no documents about any bizarre testing methods, brainwashing, or nanochip technology, but I carried on looking anyway.

When I didn't discover anything else pertinent, I clicked on an icon for the uni's own email system, but it wouldn't let me in without a password. That was frustrating, but I doubted Klein would be emailing anything suspicious using the intranet account anyway, where it could also easily be found by any member of staff.

I opened up Klein's desk drawers but didn't find anything else that would help me, so I went to the filing cabinet in the corner of the room. It was locked, but it only had the generic, flimsy lock made by the manufacturer. I pulled out a small penknife from my backpack, shoved the tip inside, and jiggled it around a bit until I heard a telltale click. The top drawer sprung open. Inside were paper patient files, arranged alphabetically. I found duplicate records of the students' files that I'd already read, but that was it.

I went back to the desk and opened his diary, searching through the next day's date, checking what Klein was up to. He had patient appointments all day from 9.00 a.m.

I was just shutting down the laptop when I heard a noise. I turned off my torch and froze in the chair. Over the laptop fan whirring, I caught the faint whistling of a tune. Most likely, it was the cleaner. I had to find some way to get out of there without being seen.

The laptop screen went black as it switched off. I shut the lid, leaving it how I found it, then padded over to the door. I opened it a sliver and peered through the gap into the darkness, ears straining to listen over the pulse pounding in my ears. The whistling was more muffled now, definitely coming from downstairs somewhere. A light had been switched on in the stairwell, illuminating the end of the corridor.

I stepped out, closing the door behind me, and treaded softly towards the stairs. I crept down them one by one into the light, praying the cleaner would be working in one of the rooms and not reception.

At the bottom of the stairs, I leaned against the wall and poked my head around it. A woman dressed in a green overall was pushing a cart with a bin and cleaning products on it. Her back to me, she halted the cart outside the pathology lab and reached forward to open the door.

I darted around the wall to the reception's double doors, keeping my eyes on her until a recess in the wall blocked my view. I held my breath as I pulled open the door—and nearly crapped myself when it creaked loudly.

'Is someone there?' she called out.

I winced.

The reception was bathed in bright light. Even though she couldn't see me from her position down the corridor, I was in full view of the glass entrance door and anyone walking past outside. But luck was shining on me, because a set of keys were hanging in the lock.

I sprang towards the main entrance door as I heard her footsteps coming closer. I unlocked it and opened the door as my heart stuttered. I made it outside and shut the door.

Just as I saw her shoulder round the edge of the wall behind the doors to reception, I darted back against the side of the building, pressing myself onto the warm brickwork, breathing hard.

Then I ran across the grass behind the Watling Centre, out of view, heading through the silent campus.

It was gone 2.00 a.m. when I got back to my room. I quickly packed all my belongings in my suitcase and backpack and left the accommodation block, heading home. In the morning, I'd send a text to the students whose phone numbers I had, citing a family emergency as a reason for my sudden departure.

I opened my front door to a stale smell, as it had been shut up for days. Pickle ran into the hallway to say hi as I kicked off my trainers and dumped my bags on the floor. She rubbed her head against my ankles before I scooped her up and gave her a kiss. 'Missed me, did you?'

I walked into the kitchen to check her bowls. They were still half full of food and water, thanks to Warren. It was too late to send him a text to say there'd been a change of plan and I'd come home early. I'd fire off an email to him instead that he'd see when he woke up.

Pickle wriggled to get out of my arms when she saw the food bowl, the pig. She hadn't missed me that much then.

I poured a huge glass of wine and sat at the kitchen table with my laptop. I yawned, but I couldn't even think about sleep. I had to prepare for tomorrow. So I called up Google maps and found a satellite image of Klein's house, studying it carefully.

Sutherby's voice echoed in my ears to leave it alone. I was now acting unlawfully, breaking into properties with no search warrant, trying to steal information. And it might not be just my job in danger; it could be my life, with the kind of reach the intelligence services had. I knew I should stop. But I couldn't. I was a police officer. A detective. I was *supposed* to protect people—vulnerable, innocent people. I was supposed to get justice for victims. Ajay, Vicky, Farzad, Natalie, and Marcelina would never get justice with a quashed investigation and cover-up. Never. Unless I exposed what was happening.

A big part of me wanted to run away, but the other part knew I was going to run headlong into it. Whatever the consequences.

DAY FIVE

"Every time we witness an injustice and do not act, we train our character to be passive in its presence and thereby eventually lose all ability to defend ourselves and those we love."
~ Julian Assange

CHAPTER 46

Dressed in dark-green-and-black running gear, I tucked my hair up under a balaclava that I'd rolled up into a beanie hat. Then I drove to Klein's house, mentally going over the layout I'd seen on the satellite map.

The rear of Klein's house was accessible from a narrow pathway that ran alongside the River Lea. That would be my point of entry. From the voter's register, it appeared he lived alone. I had no idea if he had any private CCTV set up, but I'd cover that possible angle by wearing the balaclava. I'd accessed our police databases remotely and confirmed that Klein had an alarm system, but it wasn't automatically monitored by police, because it hadn't been fitted by an approved alarm company affiliated with the required inspectorate body. So it was an audible deterrent only. The nearest properties were an abandoned factory about thirty metres away and a detached house about two hundred metres away. Even if the neighbour in the house was in, heard the alarm, and called the police, I'd already checked and found that there were only two patrol vehicles on shift. For once, the cutbacks in policing budgets could work in my favour. A low-level alarm wasn't going to be a high priority, so I reckoned I'd probably have ample time to look around.

After driving by the front of Klein's house to make sure his car wasn't there, I carried on down the country lane until it forked left and right. I took the right turn as it swung along the outskirts of some woods. I pulled off at the entrance to another lane that led to the abandoned factory and drove a bumpy five minutes over potholed concrete with weeds bursting through.

The factory came into view, looking ominous and spooky. The upper windows, dark and smashed, seemed to be staring back at me like eyes. The lower floor had decaying brickwork, and all the doors and windows were boarded up. Rubbish was strewn across the mossy ground in front of it. A dumped, half-filled black bin liner fluttered in the breeze.

I parked up and got out, staring at the building. Glancing around the surrounding area, everything was quiet, apart from the sound of a plane overhead and birds flapping their wings in the nearby trees. The factory backed onto the river, a throwback to the days when whatever it manufactured was transported by boat. At the side boundary was a line of broken fencing before the woods began.

It was 9.20 a.m. when I phoned the Watling Centre and asked to speak to Professor Klein, wanting to make sure he was still there. I breathed a sigh of relief as the receptionist told me he was with a patient and offered to take a message. I declined and hung up.

I slipped on my lightweight backpack, which held flash drives, a digital camera, a lock pick set, gloves, shoe coveralls, duct tape, and an ASP baton. In my pocket, I put my canister of PAVA spray, an incapacitant similar to pepper spray.

After taking one last look at the factory, I headed for the

fencing. Slipping through a gap in the warped slats, I entered the woods and started jogging into the overgrowth.

So far so good.

I wound my way through oaks, sycamores, and vegetation that ran parallel to the riverbank. The distant sounds of gently lapping water grew louder with every step. Then the trees thinned and opened up on my right, revealing the hard, dusty path alongside the River Lea, worn by years of walkers, joggers, cyclists, and probably a few kids using it as a private spot for a sneaky hideaway. No one was around, and even if there had been, I'd just look like a million other joggers.

I ran until I got to the back of Klein's house, where I stopped and did a few stretches as I looked up and down the path, checking for people. The only witness was a lone duck on the river, paying me no interest.

I pulled the balaclava down over my face, pulled on a pair of latex gloves and plastic shoe covers, and hoisted myself over the six-foot wooden fence. However careful I was, I'd leave something behind—fibres, skin, or hair—but I'd protected myself as much as I could.

I jumped down the other side, landing in Klein's back garden, my gaze scanning the immediate area. The property was a large L-shaped mock-Tudor-style home in red brick. An alarm box sat just under the eaves of the house. Mature conifers lined the boundary fencing on either side.

I ran across the dry grass towards a set of French doors, scanning the house for CCTV cameras. I didn't see any, but that didn't mean they weren't well camouflaged. I just hoped that if there were any, they were only recording and not being monitored via an app Klein had on his phone. If he were alerted to my presence, that would cut my search time down considerably.

I didn't know if I'd need to smash a window to get in, hence the duct tape, which would suppress the noise. But as I looked at the French doors, I sent a silent thank you up to the house-breaking gods that it had only a simple lock.

I peered in through the glass, looking into a kitchen-diner, straining to listen over my adrenaline-fuelled pulse pounding in my ears. The internal door leading from the kitchen to a hallway was open, and there was no sign of anyone.

I got my lock picks from my backpack, took a deep breath, and tried the door handle, just in case. It was amazing how many people either forgot to lock their doors or still routinely left them insecure. It didn't budge, so I inserted my tool in the lock.

My hands shook as I manoeuvred the pick around in the metal lock casing. Sweat beaded on my forehead and at the back of my neck. One minute later, I was still having trouble.

In the distance, a dog barked. I stopped and stood stock-still, trying to assess how close it was. Someone walking a dog in the nearby woods, perhaps, or out on the river pathway? My heart pounded as I waited.

After hearing nothing further for five minutes, I rolled my head from side to side and got back to work, and a minute later, the mechanism released with a satisfying little click.

I clutched the handle and swallowed a ball of anxiety before opening the door. It swung inwards silently. I stopped inside the threshold, holding my breath, waiting for the alarm to kick in. But for some reason, it didn't.

I quickly ran through in my head what I'd read on the police database. Klein definitely had an audible alarm only, not a silent system. So maybe the gods were doing overtime for me somewhere and there was some malfunction problem with it or Klein had forgotten to set it.

I listened for any noises coming from inside for a few more seconds as my heart seemed to ricochet around my chest. But there was still no alarm, no music or TV, no footsteps or water running.

I slipped inside and closed the door carefully behind me.

CHAPTER 47

TONI

At first light, I got dressed in brown leggings, a dark-grey long-sleeved T-shirt, and black trainers. Then I stared out the window, nervous anxiety clawing in my chest as I waited for Mitchell to arrive.

After three hours, he turned up in a vehicle I'd never seen before. I tucked my long hair up into a navy-blue baseball cap, grabbed a pair of gloves, and left my apartment.

I slid into the passenger side of a white Volkswagen Polo and asked, 'Did you steal this?'

'Don't want there to be a chance of the plates coming back to us,' he said. He was dressed almost identically, in black running leggings, a camo-print long-sleeved top, and a black baseball cap.

'Never thought I'd see you in a pair of tights.' I raised an eyebrow, a slight smile tugging at the corner of my lip.

He snorted. 'They're not tights. They're performance leggings.' He fired up the engine and drove off.

It was 9.22 a.m. when we drove into Klein's lane. There were no cars parked in the vicinity, and Klein's Mercedes wasn't on his driveway.

Mitchell drove to a fork at the end of the country lane and took a left. He drove for a few minutes then pulled off the road onto a narrow track in between the woods that was most likely used by dog walkers. He parked up out of view of the road and killed the engine. 'Lee's already hacked into Klein's alarm, and it's now out of action.'

I nodded.

'You ready to do this?'

'Yes.'

He twisted around and grabbed a small, lightweight drawstring bag from the rear seat. I got out of the car and waited for him, jogging on the spot for a moment. He locked up the car, put the keys in the bag, and strapped the rope strings over his shoulders.

We took off at a jog through the woods. My stomach clenched with nerves as we headed towards the river and the back of Klein's house.

Just as we emerged from the trees, I spotted a woman ahead of us, jogging along the riverbank, a small backpack over her shoulders. Mitchell grabbed my arm and pulled me down behind a large bush about six metres high and the same in width. I crouched beside him, heart hammering, as he peered around it. He held up a hand, indicating silence.

A few seconds passed before he turned back to me and whispered, 'Whoever that was, she's disappeared over Klein's fence.'

CHAPTER 48

MR WHITE

Nathan White sat in his car and rang Professor Klein, who picked up on the fifth ring. He didn't waste time with pleasantries. 'I need the test subjects' files from you.'

'What? Why?'

'You were at the same meeting I was. The testing phase is over, so your input is over.'

'Can't you wait until tonight? I'm at work at the moment, and I've got a full day of patients.'

'How kind of you to be so considerate of your patients' needs. Let me rephrase the question... I want them *now*. I need to pass a copy of them on to my superiors.'

'I can't. They're at home.'

White narrowed his eyes. 'What did I tell you about keeping them at your house? I told you to keep them with you at all times!' Bloody hell, what was he playing at?

'I was worried in case someone stole my briefcase. I can't watch it constantly while I'm at work.'

White blew out an angry breath. Klein might be a genius in his field, but he had no common sense. The sooner they were done with him, the better.

'Don't worry, the files are hidden,' Klein said.

'Hidden where?' White snapped.

'Under a false bottom in my office desk drawer. The bottom one on the left. If you really need them now, you can get them from my house, but you'll need my keys and the alarm code.'

White pulled the phone away from his ear and stared at it with a snarl, incredulous that Klein thought White would run around after him. No, White had others to do his dirty work. He was the one who did the ordering, *not* Klein. He pressed the phone against his ear again. 'I'm not coming to pick up your keys from you. I won't need your keys—I can get inside with no problem. And I know what your alarm code is.'

'How do you know what my code is?' Klein's voice got louder.

'Shut up. Do you want your colleagues to hear you? It's my business to know everything about everyone concerned.' White hung up and started the engine, but his frown was quickly replaced with a greedy smile. It wouldn't take long to do a detour back to his own house to copy the files before he handed them over. He'd already secretly put the feelers out with the contacts he'd amassed over the years, and there was now a bidding war going on between the Chinese and Russians. He didn't give a shit either way. A few more hours, and he'd have every piece of data to sell. And the best part— he had an undisputed record of patriotism, an unblemished record with MI5. His loyalty would never be questioned until it was too late.

And he knew exactly where and how to hide the money for his daughter.

CHAPTER 49

I stood still in Klein's kitchen, listening to a tap dripping in the sink and an oversized clock on the wall ticking. I swept my gaze over the room, looking again for hidden cameras but spotted none.

Klein had owned the house for fifteen years, and his décor was clinical and cold. The black cabinets looked as if they'd been polished to a high shine. The stainless-steel splashback was smudge free. The white granite worktop was pristine, apart from the usual kitchen stuff on top—kettle, toaster, mug tree, and a pile of paperwork at one end. The only thing on the glass dining table was a folded newspaper. I sprang towards the paperwork and searched through bills, receipts, and leaflets for events going on at the university. Boring, boring, boring. Until I got to a good bit. A payslip.

It was marked in the corner with a logo and a company name. Regen Logistix.

I opened the front flap and saw it was dated two weeks ago, for a payment due the previous month. It was for just over eight thousand pounds.

So Klein wasn't just a research fellow at the university. He was being paid a wage by this company, as well. And I was betting they were the people who'd manufactured the nanochip.

I took a photo of it on my camera and then turned my attention to the kitchen drawers and cupboards and hurriedly rifled through them, but it was all cutlery, crockery, utensils, takeaway menus, and dishcloths.

I made my way into a hallway with a thick dark-blue carpet. I opened the door to my left, which was a small toilet. Nothing interesting in there. The room opposite was a home office, the door partially open.

I stepped inside and found an antique oak desk along one wall beneath a small window that overlooked a path at the side of the property and a row of conifers. On top of the desk was a chocolate-brown leather desk pad and a printer. I saw no personal laptop or PC, but several blue files that looked like they could be patient files were messily stacked up along one edge. On one corner sat a pen holder with a handful of biros, pencils, fountain pens, and a sharp letter opener. Along another wall was a fitted cupboard with white doors.

I sat in Klein's worn leather chair and picked up the top file. There was no patient name on the front, and as I quickly read through the first A4 sheet of paper, it became clear that the contents didn't relate to any students. This was research notes on a study involving computer viruses that had infected various nanochips. The next files in the pile were also research papers involving something called Deep Brain Stimulation for Parkinson's patients.

I found another file with printed notes that included various subheadings: *Research focusing on brain-computer interfaces. Implantable nanochips. Cybernetics and medical* devices. *Human-computer implant technology. Direct connections to the nervous system.*

I read through the technical jargon, but found nothing that specifically related to the students, Klein's involvement, or anything about Regen Logistix and a new nanochip that was actively being tested.

I took a photo of the pages anyway then turned my attention to the desk. There were three drawers on the left, ranging in size from small to large. The top drawer was full of empty file folders, pens, paperclips, and envelopes.

The second drawer contained unopened packets of printer paper. In the bottom drawer I found a pile of medical, scientific, and technological journals. I picked them out, put them on the desk, and flicked through the pages, seeing if any notes were hidden inside, but found nothing.

I was just about to put them back when I noticed the plywood base of the drawer sat higher than the bottom rim, and there was a gouge on one side, as if a tool had been used to lift it recently.

I ran my fingertips along the edge of the plywood, but it was wedged tightly against the sides. I pulled my penknife from my backpack and slipped it down one edge, easing the plywood upwards. When I had enough room to slip in a finger, I lifted it, a smile curving my lips as I spotted another pile of files. This time, there *was* a name on the outside of the top one. *Farzad Nuri.*

My heart almost stopped for a moment as I pulled them all out. Five in total.

I put Farzad's to one side and read the names of the other students. *Vicky Aylott. Ajay Banerjee. Natalie Wheeler. Marcelina Claybourn.*

I opened Marcelina's file and quickly read through a

page of handwritten notes, which started with the initial appointment, when Marcelina had had her patient survey and blood and urine tests. After she'd been declared unfit for the memory study group, Klein had indeed contacted her about another study group, which was ultra-confidential and paid far more money. Klein described how he'd inserted a nanochip in the back of her neck via an injection, although he'd told her it was a mild muscle relaxant needed prior to having the CT scan to keep her still and calm during the procedure, telling her that sometimes people got claustrophobic with those types of scanners.

Goose bumps prickled on my skin as I read through follow-up appointment notes, where Klein observed various memory and behavioural tests he'd carried out on the unsuspecting victim in his office. There were notes about Marcelina being followed by someone called Glover, who I suspected was Hoodie Guy. About Glover having an app on his smartphone that connected wirelessly to the nanochip in her head, emitting the same radio frequency as our own brainwaves, and how he'd manipulated her mind to produce certain thoughts or patterns of behaviour. Fairly innocuous occurrences at first, until they were sure it worked, like how he'd made her leave campus, walk to Verulamium park, and sit there for several hours. And plenty of other occasions where he'd made her do things against her will.

Klein noted the side effects of the chip, such as nightmares and sleepwalking episodes. Then came the real crunch.

Klein had written down conversations with Marcelina, where she'd seen him and expressed concern about her erratic behaviour. She'd been worried something in the tests had sparked it off. Klein had assured her she was okay, that nothing he'd done could've caused her increasingly bizarre symptoms. Following that, he'd noted a conversation he'd had with Glover about Marcelina's suspicions and a follow-up conversation.

Glover has spoken to White and Hughes, who are all in agreement that Marcelina needs to be silenced. She's asking awkward questions. Glover hasn't told me what he's going to do. I've expressed my concerns about this.

And then a note the next day.

Glover has been following Marcelina. Today, after she spoke to a counsellor, he was on hand to arrange a car accident. This was a grave mistake, in my opinion. And the mistakes are piling up. The nanochip has been intercepted by Glover at the hospital, but to leave things in this haphazard state will invoke possible future scrutiny into Project Shadow.

I opened the files of the other students and skimmed the pages until I got to the parts where they'd been forced to kill themselves or others.

Vicky Aylott believed she was climbing Mount Everest prior to jumping, even though she suffered from acrophobia. The result is clear. Not only can the subjects be stimulated to act against their own free will, they can also be manipulated into losing phobias and self-preservation.

I would not have chosen self-immolation for Ajay, but it was not my decision. However, the result is more than satisfactory. It proves a clear ability in the test subject to inflict extreme self-injurious behaviour.

Natalie has been exhibiting paranoid behaviour, a side effect of the chip. I suspect I'm not privy to all the tests Glover is doing, but it is possible he has gone too far. I believe she may suspect there was more to the injection than simply a muscle relaxant. I've been told she has to be dealt with as a matter of urgency.

Today, Natalie's brainwaves were altered in such a way that choreographed her to run over and kill an elderly man with her vehicle. He is, of course, collateral damage, which I'm far from happy about, but the test proves the will to inflict injury and death on others.

However, the flow of data between the chip and the app has been slightly inconsistent. Remote signal was lost for a period of time after the event. Instead of Natalie driving to a pre-designated spot to take her own life, as planned, the loss of signal meant that she drove in a confused state back to the university. All possibility of loss of data interception will be eradicated with the rollout of 5G. This new technology will provide absolute accuracy in manipulation of the nanochip and uncompromised direct subject targeting.

The blood curdled in my veins as I read more snippets.

. . .

Stage 2 of injury infliction testing on others needs a more violent approach to prove success. It is one thing to kill from a distance with a vehicle, but killing with one's own hands is a necessary escalation for the scope of the chip to be explored to its maximum potential. In this case, murder. Although, yet again, I have expressed my concerns about the methods.

Farzad Nuri was successfully exploited to carry out this test in full and with significantly excellent, albeit distasteful, results.

'You bastards,' I whispered to myself, anger humming through my veins. 'You're going to pay for this.'

I stuffed the files in my backpack and pulled it over my shoulders, adding a count of theft to my morning tally of criminal offences. What I had was explosive, but it was only half the picture. It didn't prove any connection between what Klein was doing and the company who made them. The company that I suspected was Regen Logistix. Nor did it prove the involvement of our own security services. It wasn't evidence of who was pulling the actual strings behind the scenes.

I searched through the office cupboard for anything else incriminating but just discovered more unrelated paperwork. Frustrated at finding nothing further, I went into the lounge.

There were two worn sofas, a glass coffee table, a flat-screen TV on one wall with an entertainment cabinet below it, and bookshelves in alcoves on either side of a fireplace. I opened the cabinet and found a DVD player and some DVDs. The bookshelves were crammed with mostly scientific and computer technology books and contained nothing that interested me. What I wanted was his personal laptop.

I headed out of the lounge and hurried up the stairs. Directly in front of me was a bathroom. I poked my head in, noted an assortment of toiletries on the edge of the bath and towels on a rail. No wall cabinet.

I ducked out and went into a small room opposite with a double bed, devoid of any linen, most likely a guest room. It had a set of fitted wardrobes along one wall with sliding glass doors. No bedside cabinets. I crossed the room and opened the wardrobe doors. In one half, there were spare pillows and folded blankets on shelves. In the other half, the upper shelves contained sheets, towels, and duvet covers. Below them, black boxes of files were piled up. I kneeled on the carpet and pulled the boxes out. Inside the first one were more professional journals. The second had research notes in it from years ago relating to studies in stroke patients. The third and fourth included studies from a Parkinson's programme he'd run. They were obviously professional things he was hoarding but nothing that related to mind control or nanochips.

I put everything back, shut the doors, and then went into the next room, which held only an exercise bike and a small table with a docking station for an iPhone on it.

The final door at the end of the hallway was the master bedroom. A king-sized bed with a black-and-grey satin duvet set was positioned in the centre of one wall. On the floor beside one of the bedside cabinets was an electrical lead, the kind used for a laptop, trailing to a plug socket behind the bed. The laptop was nowhere in sight.

I hurriedly searched the rest of the bedroom for the elusive laptop, but it was nowhere to be found. Klein must've taken it with him. And after looking through more wardrobes and drawers, I discovered nothing else that would help me. It was time to leave.

I was just heading down the stairs when I heard a vehicle outside. And it sounded close, as in on Klein's driveway kind of close. Maybe he did have cameras somewhere, after all. Or maybe he'd updated his alarm system to a monitored version, but the police database hadn't been updated yet. Either way, it had to be Klein, or a keyholder, or a patrol officer who was outside right now.

Shit. Shit, bollocks, shit!

For a moment I was paralysed, halfway down the stairs. All the moisture drained from my mouth. My heart pounded.

I glanced down to the front door. It was solid wood, so they wouldn't be able to see me. Yet.

Instinctive self-preservation kicked in then, and I hurried down the rest of the stairs, trying to be as quiet as possible. If I could get to the back door before they got inside the front, hopefully I could leg it to the fence and be up and over it before they noticed anyone was inside.

I'd made it past the lounge door when the key slid in the front door lock. I looked through the hallway into the kitchen-diner. So close but not close enough. There was no way I'd make it now. I had one option.

Hide.

As I heard the telltale creak of Klein's front door opening, I darted into the toilet and flattened myself against the wall behind the door.

CHAPTER 50

MR WHITE

M r White parked on Klein's driveway and got out of his vehicle. He made light work of picking the Yale lock on the front door with gloved hands and stepped inside the hallway. He looked at the alarm panel on the wall. The light was green, and there was no beeping noise indicating he had to enter the code.

The stupid bastard Klein hadn't even set it. White pulled the door closed and went into Klein's office, fuming at Klein's lack of security nous.

He opened the bottom drawer in his desk and pulled out some journals, dumping them on top of the desk. He looked at the false plywood bottom and grabbed Klein's sharp letter opener, prised up the plywood, and set it on the desk before staring into an empty compartment.

'Bloody *idiot*,' he growled as he dialled Klein's number. The call went to voicemail. He left a terse message and hung up before turning his attention to the rest of the room, in case Klein had stupidly placed the subjects' files somewhere else.

He ignored the pain in his back as he pulled out multiple

piles of folders from the office cupboard, a twisted snarl on his face at being forced to wade through all this crap as he waited for his phone to ring.

Everyone knew Klein was having second thoughts about his involvement. When it came to the crunch, he couldn't hack what he was doing. Maybe in the beginning it had sounded good to him in theory, but when Klein realised how dirty his own hands would actually get, he'd suddenly developed a conscience. White was sure now that it was Klein who'd tipped off Sutherby. But Klein would pay for it. No question about that. The thought cheered him slightly.

CHAPTER 51

I breathed through my nose, not daring to move. The muscles in my shoulders burned as I stood rigid behind the toilet door. My heart boomed hard against my ribs.

I heard rummaging around, drawers opening, then swearing. Whoever it was called Klein on his phone and left an abusive message. He wanted the files that were now weighing down the backpack over my shoulders, so he definitely wasn't a police officer responding to a security breach or a keyholder.

The cupboard doors in the office creaked open. More rummaging. Papers being scattered. More swearing.

I couldn't hear him go into the hallway because of the thick carpet masking his footsteps, but I sensed him there first. Then I heard his wheezy breath right outside the toilet door.

There was a tiny gap where the hinges met the doorframe. If he looked carefully, he'd be able to see me or my shadow lurking behind it. My stomach tensed as I held my breath. Sweat tickled down my forehead beneath the balaclava.

Everything was silent apart from the sound of his breathing. In my head, I pictured him coming closer and closer then swinging the door open.

Silently, I slid a hand into my pocket, reaching for my PAVA spray canister. If he poked his head round the door, a stream of it in the face would incapacitate him long enough for me to make my escape. My heart felt as if it would explode as I gripped the spray in my hand.

Then his phone rang.

CHAPTER 52

MR WHITE

'Where are the files?' White shouted down the phone at Klein, who'd returned his call.

'What do you mean? They're exactly where I told you they'd be. In the bottom desk drawer in the office.'

'No, they're not.'

'You couldn't have looked properly. They're definitely in there.'

'*No*. They're *not*.' White sat at Klein's desk, staring into the empty abyss of the false-bottom drawer.

'I don't understand. I definitely left them in there!'

'What have you done with them, Klein?'

'Me? I haven't done anything with them. They should be in the drawer, exactly like I told you.'

'Are you backing out?'

'No! They're there, I'm telling you.'

'If I say they're not, then they're not.' White slammed the drawer shut. 'And I'm losing patience now. You didn't even set your alarm.' He stood up and kicked around some journals that he'd now dumped on the floor.

'Yes, I did set the alarm. I always do. What are you talking about?'

'The alarm was definitely not set. You must've forgotten.'

'I didn't. I swear. I—'

'Did you give the files to the police?'

'Of course not. I don't... I don't understand. I really don't.' Worry crept into Klein's voice. 'That's where I kept them. If they're not there, and the alarm wasn't on, then someone else has been inside and stolen them.'

White stopped what he was doing and walked back towards the cupboard. He pulled out more folders, scattering them on the floor. 'I don't believe you. I think you were trying to purge your conscience by telling the police what's been going on. Did you strike a deal with them? Immunity from prosecution if you told them what you knew? Well, that won't work, Klein. There *is* no investigation, and never will be.'

Klein sounded like he was hyperventilating. 'I'm telling the truth. If they're not there, then someone's stolen them. Please, you *must* believe me.'

CHAPTER 53

DETECTIVE BECKY HARRIS

I t was now or never. While he was distracted by the phone call and what sounded like trashing Klein's office, I poked one eye round the partially open toilet door. Klein's leather chair was empty, and there was no sign of him in the room from my viewpoint.

I slid through the gap in the door, hoping he wouldn't hear me over his shouting and banging around. I was almost out the door when something jolted me backwards.

A surprised breath escaped my lungs, like the sound of air whooshing from a balloon, that seemed amplified in my ears. I twisted sideways to see what was going on and found that the strap from my backpack had caught on the door handle.

Silence now in the office, apart from the crackling of his breath.

I stared at the empty desk in front of me, eyes wide, panic exploding inside. Had he heard me? If he looked out now, he'd see me stuck there, half in and half out the door.

Keeping my eyes trained on the office doorway, I clutched the PAVA spray tighter in my sweaty right hand, holding it up in front of me in case he came hurtling towards me. With my left hand, I reached down and tried to slide the strap off the handle.

Still silence from the office. What was he doing in there? Waiting to pounce? Did he have a gun? He had to be one of the MI5 guys who'd been protecting Klein, and I wouldn't put it past them to have a weapon.

Dread slithered up my spine. My heart skipped a beat as I frantically tried to free the strap. And then I heard more shouting as his conversation resumed with Klein.

Sweat dribbled into my eye as I kept facing forward, working on the strap by touch, blinking rapidly. And finally, I released it and made it out the door.

I crept through the kitchen-diner to the French doors and slowly pressed down the door handle. Carefully, I opened it and clenched my jaw as I let myself out and shut it behind me. Then I sprinted across the lawn.

CHAPTER 54

MR WHITE

'I'm telling you... the files *must've* been stolen,' Klein repeated again.

White listened to him rambling on for a while, thinking. Then, unable to stand Klein's whiney voice any longer, he said, 'I think you're lying. You've been trying to back out of this for weeks. It's been well-documented. You'd better cancel your patients and get back here right now.'

'I can't.'

'You can. And you will. I'm not going anywhere until I get those files.'

'Oh, for God's sake! This is ridiculous,' Klein blustered, but White could tell by the wobble in his voice that he was scared enough to do what White told him.

White hung up and went into the kitchen, a burning pain spreading out through the centre of his chest. He glanced around at the windows, which were all closed, and then tried the French door.

It was unlocked, which made him rethink the whole burglary possibility. Had someone been inside? Tampered with the alarm, as well? Or had Klein just staged the possibility of a burglary so he wouldn't be blamed?

It was also possible that prick Derek Sutherby had stolen the files after being expressly ordered to shut down any police investigation, but he didn't think so. His family, his career, and his life had been threatened, and he'd been shit scared about that. Besides, Sutherby wasn't stupid. He knew exactly what would happen if he disobeyed. And White knew Sutherby had previously acquiesced to quashing investigations when ordered from above. So that left one more likely possibility. Another intelligence agency from another country had taken them for obvious reasons.

He quickly ran that idea through his head, teeth gritted. The only reason another intelligence agency would know anything about this was if someone had told them. Although White had been talking to China and Russia, he hadn't mentioned specifics about who was testing the project or which company had come up with the technology. He very much doubted Paul Hughes, Professor Gale, or Dr Beaumont had, either. They were too invested in it. Too dedicated. And they stood to make a truckload of money. That left Klein himself again. Everything circled back to him.

CHAPTER 55

TONI

Mitchell and I kneeled silently behind the bush, hidden from view of the path, the sweat from the jog cooling on my skin.

No one else came along the riverbank as I bit down anxiously on my lip, waiting what seemed like hours, wondering who the woman was and what she was doing inside.

Eventually, I heard footsteps on the path, and Mitchell and I poked our heads around the side of the bush. The woman was jogging away from Klein's house, pulling a balaclava up off her head. As she ran past our hidden location, she unpeeled a pair of latex gloves and then stuffed both items in her backpack without breaking her stride. She also had a pair of plastic shoe covers on.

When she was well out of sight, Mitchell turned to me and said, 'Do you know who she is?'

'No.'

'I think she's Detective Becky Harris.'

I frowned, not recognising the name.

'She used to work with Detective Carter.'

A shiver passed through me. Bloodbath Farm was the name given by the media to the place I'd been held captive. Detective Carter had been there the night I was rescued. Along with Mitchell, he'd helped to save my life, and he'd kept quiet about everything that had happened in order to protect me. I hadn't seen him since, although I'd followed the police investigation in the papers. 'Does that mean the police have worked things out?'

'I don't know what's going on, but she was trying to hide her identity and any possible transfer of forensic evidence.' He glanced at me, thinking about that for a moment. 'And her backpack was much bulkier and heavier when she left the house. She took something from inside. But why was she there alone? Even if the police suspected something's been going on, and this was a genuine covert op, I doubt they'd be sending her in without some kind of backup. They'd need to seize anything with proper protocols, which means they'd probably need another colleague with her as a witness to cover their arses.'

'So what did she take?'

He raised his eyebrows. 'That's the big question.'

'Do you think she could be working for Regen Logistix?'

'Not if that was Harris, no.' He shook his head emphatically.

'What makes you so sure?'

'She's one of the good guys.'

'But how do you know that?'

'After what happened at Bloodbath Farm, I was the one who gave Detective Carter evidence to prove top-level police corruption and conspiracy.'

'I remember.'

'Well, that's not all I've helped him with. Over the years,

I've provided Carter with evidence to put criminals away when he couldn't get information from legal channels.'

My eyes widened. 'You kept that quiet.'

He shrugged. 'A while back, Carter and Becky Harris were working on a multiple-murder case. They needed intel relating to a corrupt police officer they were investigating, but they couldn't get the proof, so Carter came to me, and I got what he needed from Lee. And I've done it many times since. After they solved their joint investigation, Becky was at a press conference, and I'm pretty sure that was her. Becky is Carter's protégée, and I know she's solid. Carter trusts her completely. And if that's good enough for him, it's good enough for me.'

'So it's possible Klein's came up on her radar for some reason, but why? And what did she take?' My gaze drifted back to the path Becky Harris had disappeared along.

'I don't know. But we need to get in touch with Carter and find out what the hell's going on. This time, we need some intel from him.' He tilted his head in the direction of Klein's house. 'We should abort the search. If that *was* Harris, it's likely she's already found what we were looking for.'

CHAPTER 56

DETECTIVE BECKY HARRIS

I drove to my house, breaking a few speed limits on the way, adding yet more offences to my growing list.

In my head, I replayed the scene of almost getting caught. Halfway to my place, I laughed hysterically with relief as the reality sank in that I'd managed to escape without them knowing. Twice.

I pulled onto my drive and grabbed my backpack, glancing around the rest of the street for anyone suspicious. Not that I thought anyone had followed me, but with the kind of reach these people had, it would be stupid not to be observant. There were no vehicles that looked as if they could be on surveillance and no pedestrians. The street was quiet, but my brain was anything but, thoughts and emotions firing off in all directions.

I let myself inside, sat down at the kitchen table, and opened up my backpack. I pulled the files from it and went through them in greater detail. Anger, disgust, and outrage coursed through me in equal measures as I read Klein's notes on what he and the others had done to those poor victims. His detailed records were so dispassionately written as to be purely sociopathic.

Tears pricked at my eyes as I slapped the final file on top of the last. Then I booted up my laptop and searched for Regen Logistix. The home page didn't give me much information. It just said they were a biomedical technology company that combined engineering and technology to solve biological or medical problems, specialising in the design of medical equipment to diagnose and treat various diseases. It said they made implantable devices such as pacemakers, cochlear implants, insulin pumps, and smart technology. There was no tab to check on their personnel details, but if Klein was being paid by them, then that was all the proof I needed he was working for them.

There was a 'Latest News' tab at the top, so I clicked on it and read through a copy of a press article about a nanochip they'd recently invented.

The groundbreaking nanochip developed by Regen Logistix and funded by the Ministry of Defence will be able to transmit vital information, including blood lactate, oxygen levels, heart and pulse rate, glucose levels, organ or tissue monitoring, and overall metabolic states of wounded soldiers or other injured patients.

Sized just 2mm x 2 mm x 0.5 mm, this implantable device has the ability to wirelessly transmit life-saving readings via electrical signal to medical staff in the first stages of dealing with trauma, strokes, or heart attacks. Results could be transmitted in a matter of seconds to an electronic device such as a mobile phone. Getting these measurements in real time can help medics make decisions faster, help patients avoid needless X-rays or diagnostic tests, and will help save lives. Uniquely, it does not need any attached battery supply as it's powered *in vivo*, using the body's own energy sources.

The nanochip, which is hailed as the future of medicine, has undergone first-stage testing, and developers are confident it will be tested on humans within the next six months.

Okay, so it didn't mention the nanochip I suspected they'd invented now, but it showed they'd already worked in conjunction with the government previously.

I sat back, jigging my leg up and down. I was so close. I could now prove what Klein had done, but I couldn't prove Regen Logistix had been involved in it. I had one half of the puzzle but not the rest.

I called up online satellite images of Regen Logistix, which was a huge building set on a large site on the outskirts of St Albans. Their security would be impossible to penetrate at the best of times, but since they seemed to be involved in clandestine black ops with our own security services, then it would be impenetrable now, so if the records that proved their part in this were there, I didn't have a hope in hell of infiltrating it on my own.

I sat upright and ran my hands over my face, resting them on my cheeks as I thought. I needed someone who could hack into Regen Logistix's computer systems and find more evidence, but I didn't know anyone who could get that kind of intelligence. I needed help.

I reached for my mobile phone to call Warren and then hesitated, chewing on my lower lip. He hadn't just been my boss and mentor—he was a great copper who also sometimes used unorthodox methods to catch the bad guys. Everything I'd learned about being a good detective, I'd learned from him. He was also a friend that I'd trust with my life. We were kindred spirits. But I hadn't just broken a few rules and gone behind my boss's back to solve a case this time. I'd broken the law. And Warren was now an anti-corruption officer, investigating cops who broke the law.

If I told him what I'd just done, there was a very real chance he could arrest me. I'd lose a career I'd worked damn hard for, and possibly go to prison. But then if I didn't ask for his help, more people would die. And one thing I knew about Warren with absolute certainty was that his sense of justice was so strong, sometimes he broke the rules to get evidence, too.

'Oh, God,' I groaned, staring at the phone until my heart overruled my head and I dialled his number.

'Morning,' he answered. 'I got your email earlier about not needing to feed Pickle anymore. You weren't enjoying your holiday then?'

'I wasn't in Spain.'

'No, I didn't think you were.'

'What? How did you know?'

'You said the weather was good, but they've been having torrential rain and thunderstorms all week. I didn't get to be a DI for nothing, you know. And—'

'I need your help,' I butted in. 'And I can't talk about it on the phone. Can you come to my place? It's urgent.'

He paused for a moment, obviously taking in the tone of my voice, which didn't just sound urgent to my own ears. It sounded manic. 'Are you all right?'

'Yeah. But this is serious.'

'I'm at police headquarters at the moment. I can be there in about ten minutes.'

'That's great. Thanks. I'll see you soon.' I hung up and

paced the kitchen, much to the amusement of Pickle, who'd just entered the cat flap and cocked her head at me like I was nuts. I felt like I was going nuts, too.

I went into the lounge overlooking the street so I could pace in front of the window, watching for Warren, and ramped it up to include chewing on my fingernails until I drew blood.

As soon as I saw Warren's car pull up outside, I darted into the hallway and yanked open the door.

'God, you look awful,' Warren said.

I grabbed his wrist and tugged him inside.

'Blimey, slow down,' he said as he almost fell over, staggering against the wall.

'I can't.' I pulled him into the lounge and turned to face him.

He studied me with a concerned frown. 'What's going on?'

'You're not going to believe it. It's so fucking far out there.' I breathlessly rambled through everything that had happened with the undercover investigation, the deaths, the nanochips, Hoodie Guy, Klein, being shut down by MI5, and Regen Logistix.

Warren's jaw set in a rigid line as he listened, the incensed anger on his face matching what I felt. 'Bloody hell.'

'I know. It's unbelievable, isn't it?'

'You're right. It does sound far out. But nothing surprises me anymore.'

'And... that's not all. I've got... I've done something.'

'What kind of something?'

'I needed evidence. This has got to be exposed.'

'I couldn't agree more. But I can't help unless I know what you did.'

'I...' I chewed on my lip.

'Are you in danger? Do they know about you?'

'No. At least, I don't think so. Sutherby never put anything on the books about my involvement. I... I was looking for evidence, and I broke into Klein's house and got his patient files.' I rushed into the kitchen and came back with the files. I slapped them on the coffee table before picking up Vicky's file and waving it at him. I took a deep breath and held it, waiting for his reaction. For him to tell me that even though we were friends, I'd committed a serious crime that could land me in prison.

He eyed the file. 'You broke into his house without a warrant and stole files?'

Holding his gaze as butterflies danced in my stomach, I nodded.

'You're telling an anti-corruption officer that you broke the law in an illegal investigation you're now carrying out yourself?'

I nodded again. 'Yeah, but I couldn't just do nothing! I need to stop them before anyone else dies.' I looked at him, eyes wide.

He stared back at me. A few seconds passed. Then ten. Twenty. He looked at the files again. I clenched my sweaty hands.

Then he threw his head back and laughed. Only for a moment. And it wasn't a humorous laugh—it was one that held equal hints of disbelief and pride. 'Bloody hell.'

'Exactly.' I flopped onto the sofa, clutching Vicky's file to my chest, suddenly feeling exhausted.

'I would've done exactly the same. I think there's a very

blurred line between what we're legally allowed to do and what we *should* do.' He sat next to me, put his arm around me, and pulled me towards him.

I rested my head on his shoulder. 'Even if there's no chance of them all facing justice through the courts, we need to warn people about what's going on.'

'You know as well as I do that our justice system is horrendously lacking, even through the usual channels of prosecuting offenders. But when the people involved are protected from higher sources, and you know that for the powerful ones who make the rules, there *are* no rules, then sometimes you have to do extraordinary things to protect the vulnerable. So let's just say you're not the only one who's broken the law to save lives.'

I twisted round to face him. 'I know. When your investigation into Lord Mackenzie was shut down, you carried on anyway under the radar. You've obtained surveillance information and intelligence in the past that couldn't have come through legal channels, so you've got some experience of this. You've got a contact somewhere, haven't you? And I need an experienced hacker I can trust to find evidence from Regen Logistix. Even if you don't want to get involved, you could give me your contact's details, and I'll get in touch with them.'

He looked at me. 'You're right. I have had help in the past. It's a really long story. One I've never told anyone. But my informant... I don't actually know who he is.'

My forehead furrowed. 'You've got an informant, but you don't know who it is? How does that work? He gives you stuff anonymously?'

'Hmm... not really. It's hard to explain. But he can get hold of intelligence that you wouldn't believe.' He leaned forward and looked deep in my eyes. 'I'm glad you came to me.' He nodded towards the file I was still clutching. 'So... the files you took prove Klein implanted these nanothings, and they've been manipulating the students' brainwaves and behaviour?'

'Yes. But the files don't specifically mention Regen Logistix. Do you want to read through them?' I held out Vicky's file.

'Doesn't seem like we have time for that. Besides, I trust your judgement.' He stood up. 'If Regen Logistix have kept records on their systems, then I'm sure my guy can get us what we want. I need to use a burner phone. Nothing can be traced back to us.'

'I haven't got one.'

'There's one in my car I always use to call him. Give me a minute. I'll drive to the supermarket and make the call from the car park. Then I'll come back.'

I launched myself on him and gave him a hug. 'Thanks.'

I watched him leave, knowing we were stepping into the darkness with no way back from this.

CHAPTER 57

TONI

Mitchell kept to the speed limit as he drove so we didn't attract attention. When we'd put enough distance between ourselves and Klein's house, Mitchell pulled off the main road into the car park of a garden centre, took a secure burner phone from the glove box, and put a SIM card inside before switching it on.

I twisted sideways in the seat to face Mitchell, waiting for him to make the call to Detective Carter, but before he could dial, it rang in his hand.

He looked at the screen then at me. 'It's Carter calling *me.*' He answered and listened for a few moments before saying, 'Well, that's strange, because I was about to call you. For once, I was going to ask for *your* help.' He explained what we'd discovered going on at the university. That we were there at Klein's house when Becky Harris had arrived. That we had evidence proving what Regen Logistix and MI5 had been doing. But we needed the files we suspected were now in Becky's possession.

Mitchell was silent again as he listened to Carter, watching me. 'Yes. Okay. Somewhere with no cameras. You still remember the forest meeting place? We can be there in twenty minutes.' He paused again. 'Good. See you then.' He ended the call and fired up the engine. 'Looks like we've both been hunting the same people. Becky Harris was doing a covert police investigation into what was going on at the uni. It was shut down on orders from MI5, and she's now working alone. She's got Klein's patient files.'

'That's great. But if the government and secret service know what's going on, and are actively encouraging it for their own means, and a police investigation has already been shut down, what do we do now?'

'I know what I'd like to do.' He clutched the steering wheel tightly as he drove, his lips pressed into a thin, angry line.

'What? Kill them?'

He didn't answer, which basically meant yes. He could kill them and make it look like an accident or a suicide. He'd done it before, but only to protect the innocent and vulnerable whose lives were in danger.

'Even if the top people are killed, it's not going to stop others getting hold of this and using the technology,' he said eventually.

'So what, then?'

'I don't know. But it looks like we've only got twenty minutes to come up with a plan to blow this thing wide open.' He reached for his burner phone again. 'Actually... I've got an idea.'

CHAPTER 58

MR WHITE

W hite sat at Klein's kitchen table overlooking the garden as he sipped his coffee and waited for Klein to arrive.

The front door opened, and Klein called out.

'In here,' White said.

Klein walked into the room, briefcase in hand, laptop bag over his shoulder, a harried look on his flushed face. 'You're sure there's no sign of a break-in?'

White stood, his face expressionless. 'Did you leave the French door unlocked?'

'Of course not.' Klein's gaze darted towards the door. 'I *told* you someone had been inside.'

'Or you wanted to make it look that way.'

Klein shook his head, mumbled something under his breath, and rushed out into the hallway. White followed him into the office.

Klein went straight to the bottom drawer in the desk and stared at it as a squeak of shock escaped his lips. 'They're not here.' He looked up at White, aghast.

'I already told you that. Now shut up and calm down. There's no time for pissing about.'

But Klein still searched the rest of his desk, getting more and more frantic as he pulled out paperwork, stationery, and journals. Sweat patches soaked the armpit and collar area of his white shirt as he looked around the room. 'Did you make this mess?'

'Yes, I was looking for the files.'

'They've been stolen. I keep trying to tell you.'

White raised an eyebrow. 'I don't think so, even though your security is recklessly inadequate. I've shut down the undercover police operation. No one outside of our circle knows, and everyone else involved in this project is thoroughly committed to it, so that just leaves you.'

'I didn't... I haven't... I wouldn't...' Klein fought for a breath. 'I'm telling the truth. I haven't given them to *anyone*.' He wailed, rubbing a trembling hand across his sweaty forehead.

'So you destroyed them? Because you were having second thoughts. Just admit what you've done, and I can help you.'

'No. No, I didn't destroy them.' Klein shook his head manically, a dribble of saliva flecking his bottom lip.

'Okay. Here's what you're going to do. You'll sit down and rewrite everything in those files from scratch.'

'But...' Klein's mouth flapped open and closed. 'I can't remember everything I wrote down. There's so much detail.'

'It wasn't a request.' White grabbed hold of Klein's shoulders and shoved him into the leather desk chair. 'You *will* remember. And you *will* write it down. Do you understand?'

Klein squeezed his eyes shut, nodding vehemently. 'Y... yes. Yes, I will.'

'Glad that's all clear.' White sat on the edge of his desk and watched Klein reach for his notebook and fountain pen as a dribble of sweat trickled down his temple.

CHAPTER 59

DETECTIVE BECKY HARRIS

I drove along a quiet country lane, still mulling over what Warren's contact had told him about their own covert investigation going on at the university.

'Pull off here.' Warren pointed to a small track amongst a thick forest on our left. 'This is the place.'

We bumped over dry earth, meandering through the dense foliage. Branches scraped at the sides of my car, tall tufts of overgrown grass beneath clonking against the underside of the metal. We drove on until the track widened slightly into a circular clearing and we were completely hidden from any drivers using the lane.

'This is it,' Warren said.

I stopped the car, turned off the engine, and glanced around at the thick mesh of trees that had formed a canopy above us, cutting off most of the sunlight. Hundreds of tree trunks seemed to close in around us. It was completely sheltered and private. 'You've been here before?'

'We've met several times here.'

All was quiet apart from the birdsong filtering through the open window. 'You can definitely vouch for these people? They're not going to take this stuff and bury it and then bump us off?'

'You can trust them one hundred and ten percent. We're not the only good guys out there.'

'But you said you don't know who he is.'

'I don't know his name. I don't think I even want to. I call him the Vigilante. But I know *who* he is.' He tapped his heart then his head. 'In here. He's the same as me and you, mate.'

'He told you the woman is a counsellor at the uni?'

'Yes.'

I pulled my phone out of my pocket and looked up the uni's website, found the Student Counselling page, and clicked on the list of counsellors. It brought up a page with staff photos.

I showed Warren my screen. 'So which one is she, do you think?'

He took my phone then stared at the screen for a moment. He looked as if he'd seen a ghost, then a slight smile snaked up the corner of his lips. He tapped on the photo of someone called Toni. 'I never knew her name, either. But it suits her.' He handed me back my phone.

'So go on, then!' I elbowed him. 'Tell me how you know Toni and this Vigilante.'

Warren looked off into the distance with a haunted look on his face for a moment then looked back to me. 'I can't tell you that bit. If I do, it'll open up a whole can of worms that have managed to stay firmly closed.' He looked into my eyes, and I could see he was torn between wanting to tell me and not. 'Maybe one day.'

'Okay. Fair enough.'

A white VW drove up behind us then, and I watched its

approach in the rearview mirror before flicking my gaze to Warren.

He gave me a reassuring smile and reached for the door handle. We got out and rounded the car, waiting for them to park.

A short, stocky guy with a shaved head exited the driver's seat. Toni got out of the passenger side. The Vigilante's fierce gaze scanned about the surrounding area before they walked towards us.

Warren shook the Vigilante's hand then turned to Toni, who stepped forward to hug him.

'Good to see you,' Warren told her.

'And you,' she said softly.

He pulled back and smiled warmly. 'You're looking much better than the last time we met.'

She laughed. 'You, too.'

I watched on, wondering what to make of it all. Wondering how the hell Warren knew her. Knew them. Maybe I'd tease it out of him one day, but for now, we had more important things to do.

I stepped forward. 'Hi. I'm Becky.'

Toni smiled at me, and although she was in her early twenties, there was something about her—a presence, a maturity that showed behind her eyes—that made her seem older and wiser.

Mitchell grinned. 'We know.'

'Looks like we've both had a busy time.' I smiled back.

We stood and discussed what we'd both been doing, laying out what evidence we had.

'This goes right up to the prime minister and beyond,' the Vigilante said. 'My guy's found intelligence that shows the elite establishment are actively working on a smart grid that they want to be connected to the human mind, and which will be centrally controlled by them. There's an actual government commission working right now on recommendations about how all aspects of implantable nanochips will be implemented. They want it up and running by 2030.'

My mouth fell open. It felt like my rib cage was being squeezed. As if all the air was being sucked out of the atmosphere.

'We've got classified memos, emails, and documents that prove the prime minister gave the go-ahead for Regen Logistix to develop this nanochip in conjunction with the Ministry of Defence, ready for when the grid is up and running, and for the security services to protect them.'

Carter whistled out an angry breath.

I swallowed to moisten my dry throat. 'What the hell? The prime minister?'

'But he's just a prostitute puppet, having his strings pulled by the real people who run the country—the shadow government. The global elite who've controlled the world for decades behind the scenes.' The Vigilante's voice was hard, laced with disgust. 'Regen Logistix isn't just a biomedicine company. They're a subsidiary of Davenport Systems.'

'Who do what, exactly?' Warren asked.

'They're a major global defence company. They make bombs, military aircraft, ships and vehicles, electronics, and chemical and biological weapons. But they're all incestuously linked with all the industry players involved here—big tech, big pharma, big global finance cartels.' The Vigilante's top lip curled up. 'The world's gone to shit. We're controlled by lunatics under the guise of democracy, when really we're all living in a totalitarian state. Trouble is, most people don't realise it yet.'

'How are they intending to implant people on mass with these chips?' I asked, my voice trembling.

'This is where it gets even more depraved. Davenport Systems have developed a toxic biological weapon that creates a virus. Their intention is to release it and cause a pandemic that ensures their goal for mass depopulation of the planet.'

I swallowed down the bile rising in my throat. 'What are you talking about?'

'The elite believe the world is overpopulated. They want a mass cull of people. Genocide. But the virus isn't the real killer. The new technology they're rolling out globally right now in every public space, in schools, and attached to people's housing is a direct energy weapon that connects to the nanochips. And thousands of studies show that the electromagnetic frequency and microwaves involved produces radiation exposure and can kill people. The elite-controlled media's remit is to bombard the public with false data and propaganda about a virus to create mass hysteria. Then the puppet masters who create the heinous crisis will sell the lies and hoax to sell people the cure. And once the public are terrified and panicked they'll agree to things that go against their core survival. It's the basic psychology of problem-reaction-solution. Their solution will be mandatory vaccinations, which just happen to contain a tracking nanochip inside.'

'It sounds like Nazi Germany all over again.' I threw my hands in the air and looked at Warren, who was shaking his head to himself. 'So what do we do with it all? Who can we take it to? I mean, there must be some decent, honest people in the government that can help us.'

'Yeah. There are. But a handful of honest people can't

fight what's now become such an insidiously corrupt political system. The honest ones will be either quashed, subjected to a smear campaign, or mysteriously die.'

'Then how can we make them accountable?' I looked back at the Vigilante.

'We can't,' Toni said.

'There is no happy ending to this,' the Vigilante added. 'There won't be a superhero swooping in to save the day.'

I blinked at them. 'We *have* to do something.'

The Vigilante shrugged. 'If this was a movie, we'd hand everything over to the press, and they'd do what they're supposed to do—present unbiased journalism to the public and make them aware of what's been going on and the danger they're in. But that's not an option when the mainstream media is systematically filtered by the powerful and dangerously biased interests of those that own, manage, and fund it.'

'Even if you could get a national paper to say they'll cover it, any publication would be shut down on orders of national security,' Warren added.

The Vigilante snorted. 'National security? National cover-up, more like.' He crossed his arms over his chest. 'Look what's happened in the past. You've got politicians committing war crimes and multiple crimes against personal freedoms, human rights, and humanity. And while they're walking around free, laughing their heads off, the whistle-blowers who've exposed them have been thrown in prison to rot. And Regen Logistix and the CEO, Paul Hughes, and his cronies will never be held accountable with a criminal prosecution—corrupt corporations hardly ever are, even when their products have caused multiple deaths. They're too powerful. A company that makes bombs and biological and chemical weapons for a living doesn't give a fuck about the sanctity of human life.'

'Just like the bankers were too big and powerful to jail.' Warren growled. 'They haven't just created the monsters. They've well and truly fed and nurtured them.'

The Vigilante showed his agreement with a tilt of his head. 'Well, again, they're part of this bigger plan. The impending financial apocalypse is about to hit the fan because the bankster terrorists have been allowed to get away with their weapons of mass financial destruction with the complicit governments. The virus will be the tipping point. The catalyst that exposes what was already in place. We're going to see a financial collapse to rival the Great Depression. There are multiple agendas that have been cleverly engineered here, and a so-called pandemic fits every one of them. Their objective is imposing emergency laws under the guise of protecting people that will really strip away all our human rights without being challenged. On top of that, the chaos created will justify them seizing your bank accounts and using a cashless society connected to the smart grid that they control.'

I let out a short, aggressive burst of laughter. The pressure, enormity, and sheer horror of the situation was getting to me. 'The chief constable called *me* a conspiracy theorist. If he thinks I'm one, I don't know what he'd make of you.'

'That's just a contemptuous and pejorative term used to belittle someone who doesn't agree with the official, lying narrative of the state.' The Vigilante's eyes narrowed slightly, and although his voice was calm, something very dangerous lurked beneath the surface. 'A way to deflect the truth, yet again, by trying to portray someone as crazy and therefore unbelievable. It's not a theory if it's real. And as you've found out, this is very real.'

I looked up at the sky, gnawing on my lower lip, anger coursing through me. A hush seemed to settle around us. The wildlife fell silent, like even they felt a defeated tremor passing through the air.

'So we've done all this for nothing?' I looked into the Vigilante's eyes. There was a dark intensity there, a simmering anger bubbling away.

'Far from it. But the biggest problem the general population have is thinking someone else will save them, when in reality *they're* the ones with the power, not a few thousand politicians and a handful of corporations.'

'You and me—us—*we* can't make them accountable,' Toni said. 'But collectively, the public can. We are billions.'

'So we've come up with the only plan available to us,' the Vigilante said. 'A while back, I was going to expose a VIP paedophile ring online that went to the heart of the UK establishment. In the end, I abandoned that idea because I found a better way to deal with it.'

I glanced at Warren, wondering what the hell he meant —what his 'better way' had actually entailed—but Warren kept his gaze fixed on the Vigilante as he carried on talking.

'But this time, there *is* no better way,' the Vigilante said. 'It's not just an exposé; it's a public warning. So we upload everything we've got and put this out into the public domain, and let the people be responsible for their own safety. Because the governments and security services are sure as hell not. We're going to grab the public by their virtual throats and give them a wake-up call.'

'You mean like a Wikileaks page?' Warren asked.

'It's not enough for it to be just on one website,' I said. 'This needs to go viral. It needs to be *everywhere.*'

'Wikileaks is good, but it relies on people searching out the website to find out what they're exposing,' the Vigilante said. 'This is more like something the Anonymous hacktivist group would do. What we have in mind is going to be far more wide-reaching. It'll be on millions of websites across the globe. Some of the technical data that shows exactly how this works will be redacted, for obvious reasons, but the rest of the evidence will be out there for the world to see. We'll name names.' His smile was laced with razor blades.

'But they'll shut any websites down as soon as they find out,' I said.

'They can try. But they can't police the whole internet. And my guy and his team are good. He still does work for government agencies. He's got a backdoor into their systems. He'll see when they're making their moves and counter every attack they make to keep it out there. But that's just for starters. Anyone with an email address or a phone will get a message exposing this. Anyone using a Windows, Apple, or an Android system will get a notification as soon as they log on to their computers or phones. A post will appear on every social media site under individual accounts. Every smart TV or device connected to the internet will show the same thing when it's switched on. Every electronic billboard will be hacked. This won't just go viral; it'll go stratospheric.'

'Seriously?' I asked.

'Yeah.' The Vigilante nodded. 'For years, they've wanted everyone addicted to their phones and computers to get the public so distracted they're blind to what's really going on in the world. They're gambling on the fact people won't look up from their screens for long enough to lose the apathy they've carefully been conditioned to feel, but the elite can't have it both ways. We'll take the technology they've already tried to use to brainwash us with and use it against them instead.'

'How quickly can this be done?' Warren asked.

'My guy and his team will need maybe a week. There's a lot of work involved, as I'm sure you can imagine. All we need now are your files.' The Vigilante's gaze searched my face.

I looked at Warren, sending him a silent message with my eyes. *Can we really trust this guy? Is he stable?*

Warren nodded at me. 'This is the only way.'

I felt dizzy for a moment. It was all too surreal and disturbing. I rested a hand on the boot of the car to steady myself and took a deep breath. Then I retrieved Klein's original files from my backpack and handed them to the Vigilante.

He gripped them in his hand. Five blue folders. Five lives sacrificed. This had to end with us.

'Don't worry,' the Vigilante said. 'I'll let you know when all hell's about to break loose.'

DAY SEVEN

"Life is an echo. What you send out comes back. What you sow, you reap. What you give, you get. What you see in others, exists in you."
~ Zig Ziglar

EXTRACT FROM THE HERTFORDSHIRE GAZETTE

Fifty-three-year-old man a victim of drowning in River Lea

A local man identified as Professor Brian Klein appears to have drowned in the River Lea at Ware.

Just before 1.00 p.m. on Sunday, Hertfordshire Constabulary received a call about a possible drowning from a jogger who frequently uses the embankment path that backs on to Klein's home. The witness spotted a body snagged on some vegetation and attempted to drag Klein out of the water, but by then, it was sadly too late, and Klein was pronounced dead at the scene.

A police spokesman said that a suicide letter written by Klein was found inside his home and that he'd weighted a backpack with bricks before wading into the river sometime in the early hours of Saturday morning. Klein's family and friends have been unavailable for comment.

His death is not being treated as suspicious.

AFTER

"A single bee is ignored, but when millions come together, even the bravest run in fear. The one thing the government fears is the day we stand together."
~ Author Unknown

CHAPTER 60

TONI

I pulled my car up outside the electric gates to Lee's secretive hideaway. The building wasn't visible beyond the high wall topped with barbed wire, and there were no signs at the front. Nothing indicated what happened inside. But this was where everything was about to explode.

Mitchell had wanted to be with me, but it was his and Mum's three-year anniversary of being together, and she'd organised a romantic dinner for them both. After all the times I'd dragged him away recently, he could hardly say no. It would've made her too suspicious.

I waved at the CCTV camera on the wall and waited for it to slide open, then I drove inside and parked in front of a nondescript industrial building. From the outside, it looked like a throwback from the '80s, all stark concrete and small windows, with a nothing-to-see-here aura, which was exactly the point.

By the time I'd got out of the car, Lee was walking down the front steps to meet me. His intelligence had been instrumental in finding my location when I'd been kidnapped, and even though I'd met him in person several times since, there were never enough words to say to the three people who'd saved my life. Never enough to express the gratitude I still felt. Instead of thanking him again, though, I hugged him tightly, asking how he was.

He patted my back. 'Bloody flat out, as you can imagine.' He broke away. 'Good job I work well under pressure. And you? I see you're getting into all sorts of trouble again.'

'What can I say? I'm busy trying to save the world.' I smiled. 'Has everything gone to plan so far?' I followed him inside the lobby towards a lift in the centre.

'Yes.' Lee pressed a button for the top floor. 'We're good to go.'

We exited the lift into an open-plan office, where Lee's trusted team of people were sitting at desks, staring at screens, or typing on keyboards. All of them had multiple monitors in front of them in what could be some kind of NASA control system.

When we walked in, some of them glanced up and smiled at me. All of them looked crumpled and tired. They'd been working round the clock to get the mammoth technicalities of the task ready.

'Five minutes, everyone,' Lee said as we strolled past them.

The door to a side office opened, and a man with a telephone headset looped around his neck stepped out in front of us.

'All sorted, Jeff?' Lee stopped and asked him.

Jeff grinned. 'Yes. It turned out I wasn't needed in the end.'

'Good.' Lee took my elbow and guided me towards his office. 'Jeff's been standing by for another important job going on right now.'

We entered Lee's glass-walled office at the end of the room. He grabbed an extra chair and positioned it beside his. He sat at his desk, laden with more monitors, and I followed suit. I watched Lee tap a few keys that brought up lines of computer code on several of the screens.

'What do you think will happen next?' I asked. 'I mean, yes, we're exposing them, but will that really stop others from using the same technology to do the same thing all over again?' I seriously doubted it would.

'Maybe not,' Lee said. 'But all we can do is make the public aware. In the end, they'll have to protect themselves against it happening to them. Information is power, and don't underestimate the power of angry people. I reckon there'll be riots. Civil unrest is going on all over the globe at the moment, but in most places, it's not even being reported on. The Hong Kong student riots have been going on over five months. The Yellow Vests in France have been rioting for over a year. People have had enough of corruption and abuse of human rights and power. They're being pushed to the limit, and now they have to take back control. Historically, every single empire from BC to present times has fallen for the same reasons—the powerful few get too corrupt, too greedy, and too complacent. We're reaching a critical period in our lifetime for another catastrophic failure. Things have to get drastic before they become the catalyst for change. And no one ever got their freedom by appealing to the moral sense of the people oppressing them.'

'The world's on fire,' I said. 'Not just physically, but emotionally and spiritually, as well. But the darkest nights produce the brightest stars.'

'Well, there's no star shining for Klein anymore.' Lee grinned as he finished typing and sat back. All four screens arranged in an arc on the desk had the same type of code on them now. 'Okay. We're ready.' He looked through the glass walls into the outer office. All his team had eyes on him. He held his forefinger up in the air to them, then turned his head to me. 'Do you want to do the honours?'

'What do I need to do?'

'Just hit the enter key.'

I reached over, took an energising breath, and let it out. I pressed the button. The screens went wild, code flashing past at lightning speed.

Lee nodded at his team, and a clattering of simultaneous fingers hitting keys filled the air.

CHAPTER 61

DETECTIVE BECKY HARRIS

I sat in my kitchen next to Warren, my laptop open in front of us. So far, we'd divided our time between watching the screen, the time, and swigging a bottle of wine. My stomach churned with anxiety as I wondered for the hundredth time if we could all really pull this off and what the consequences would be if we did.

I glanced at the clock on the bottom of the screen. Just gone 6.45 p.m., and we'd been waiting nervously for over an hour.

'Do you think something's gone wrong?' I jigged my leg up and down, a ball of nervous energy. 'Maybe they didn't manage to set it up properly.'

'Be patient. They said 7.00 p.m.'

I necked some more wine.

'Glad I'm not in uniform anymore,' Warren said. 'Public order problems will be kicking off everywhere after this.'

'Sutherby's going to know it was me.'

'Deny all knowledge. He can't prove a thing. And besides, how would you know a hacker of this calibre, capable of doing what they're about to do?'

'I don't know. How would *you*?' I turned to face him.

He gave me a smile that had 'touché' written all over it.

'What if something happens to Sutherby?' I asked. 'He's already been threatened.'

'I think they'll be way too busy cleaning up their own shit and watching their own backs to go after him. I doubt any of those involved in the nanochip will be left alive to talk. They'll need scapegoats now, and I'm pretty sure they'll be cleaning up loose ends in-house with a few more suicides or accidents.'

'I hope you're right.' I took another big gulp of wine.

He patted my arm. 'You had no other choice. The truth never stays hidden forever.'

I watched the seconds onscreen tick painfully slowly by.

6.46.

6.47.

I topped up our wine glasses then swallowed another mouthful as my stomach churned.

6.58.

At 7.00 p.m., the room filled with a cacophony of alerts. My laptop screen beeped as a message popped up. Both our phones pinged with emails and text messages.

I read through the detailed exposé on the laptop as Warren opened the email on his phone. For a few minutes, neither of us spoke, our eyes glued to the pages, transfixed by all the information we were reading that told the world what all the major players involved had been up to.

We looked at each other, grinning manically before slapping our palms together in a high five. Then we erupted into hysterical laughter until our eyes watered and our stomachs hurt.

Was it justice? It was too early to say. At that moment, I

wasn't even sure what justice was anymore. Maybe the whole system wasn't broken at all; it was purposely designed to be that way. But we'd done all we could to blow the whistle with our hands not just tied, but handcuffed behind our backs and a gun pointed at our heads.

Whatever happened next was up to the public.

CHAPTER 62

MR WHITE

6.30 p.m.

Nathan White sat on the sagging bed in the hotel room. His gaze was on the shitty décor, but he was too busy making plans in his head to notice the peeling wallpaper and chipped wooden chair.

He'd done a deal with the Russians in the end. In a few minutes, he'd hand over all the data he'd taken from Regen Logistix, along with the recreated files Klein had compiled before Glover had killed him. In just a few minutes, White would be rich and walking away from his old life.

He had several fake passports, but he wasn't going to leave the country via an airport. His phone had been left at home. No way was he going to let them trace him through something as simple as that. He had a car with cloned plates that he'd drive through the Channel Tunnel to France, where he'd buy another car and then drive to Madrid, before taking a flight to South America. That was where he'd end up eventually, to live out the rest of his short life in a nice beachfront villa, knowing his daughter would be well taken care of with an anonymous offshore account he'd set up for her.

Sweat pricked at his forehead. He stood and opened the window to get rid of the humid heat. He glanced down into the garden area behind the hotel. If it could be called a garden. It was just a patch of grass that was scorched and dry from the unseasonably warm weather and a moss-covered patioed terrace. The place was a dump, which was exactly why White had chosen it. The only people who came here were salesmen whose companies were too tight to pay out for anything nice and hookers renting by the hour. No one who'd pay much attention to him.

White licked his lips. His throat was dry, and he wanted a scotch, but he needed to keep a clear head.

A knock sounded at the door.

White peered through the spy hole. He'd never met the front man who was going to do the deal on the Russians' behalf, but he'd been apprised of what he looked like, what he'd be wearing. He took in the guy's face, his black combat trousers, grey shirt, and black baseball cap.

'Who is it?' White called out.

The man standing there looked full on at the spy hole, knowing White was watching him. 'It's Dominic. I've got the accounts you need for your presentation tomorrow.'

'You're late.'

'I got held up in traffic. The M25's a nightmare at this time.'

White grinned. The pre-agreed code words were complete. He opened the door and stepped aside to let the man inside, eyeing the holdall that contained a percentage of the cash for the trade, before closing the door behind him.

Dominic walked into the room and glanced around the

interior before putting the holdall on the table in the corner of the room. He turned to White. 'I'll show you mine if you show me yours. There's one million dollars in cash in the bag. The rest will be an electronic wire transfer, as requested.'

White bent down, slid his own briefcase out from under the bed, and placed it on the table next to Dominic's holdall. He flicked open the locks and lifted the briefcase's lid, then he removed the new laptop he'd bought for cash and set it on the bed behind him.

White unzipped the holdall Dominic had brought and looked at the neatly stacked bundles of dollar notes, tied up with rubber bands.

Dominic tilted his head at the files inside the briefcase. 'Quality-control check before the trade.'

'Of course.' White picked up a bundle of notes and flicked through it before turning to another.

Dominic scrutinised the files carefully, slowly turning the pages. 'This is definitely everything?'

'Of course. When you confirm you're happy, then you can get in touch with your man and transfer the other seventy-four million dollars to my offshore account.' White tilted his head towards his laptop. 'When I confirm it's been received, we both walk out of here happy.'

'Absolutely. He's waiting for my call right now.' Dominic turned more pages.

White fingered the cash.

Both silently examined their prizes with a smile on their faces.

Dominic picked up another file, but as he opened it, the pages of data slid to the floor. He glanced at White, rolling his eyes. 'Butterfingers.' He bent down to scoop up the pages as White glanced down at the mess on the floor.

White left him to it. His days of clearing up messes were well and truly over. Instead of helping pick them up, he reached out to replace another bundle of cash back in the holdall. But his hand never got that far.

White was so engrossed in counting the money that he never saw the strike coming. The first thing he felt was a bolt of electric pain exploding in his lower back. A fraction of a moment later, his legs gave way, and he collapsed to the floor like a lead weight, the bundle of notes falling from his hand.

CHAPTER 63

THE FINAL SHADOW

Air was forced through White's lungs in a rush of breath, his muscles locking rigid with neuromuscular incapacitation, his eyeballs rolling up in their sockets.

Dominic put the small but high-voltage stun gun that had been hidden inside his sock on the table and dragged the twitching, groaning White by his feet across the room before he had time to recover from the blast of over one million volts.

Dominic hoisted White upright, one hand on his belt, one clutching the shirt material between his shoulder blades. White couldn't have weighed more than ten stone soaking wet. White gurgled a sound in his throat, his eyelids fluttering, his gaze dazed and unfocused.

Before White's confused brain could even work out what was going to happen, he was sailing headfirst through the open window on a rapid descent past ten storeys, hurtling into a permanent retirement.

Dominic slid the stun gun into the pocket of his combats. He took a pair of sunglasses from his top pocket and put them on. Then he collected the briefcase and holdall and headed for the door.

He opened it a couple of inches, peering up and down the corridor. Empty.

No one noticed him striding towards the staircase at the end of the hall, and even if they had, the description of him would've been so poor. The CCTV had already been hacked and was replaying footage from an empty corridor hours before, ditto for the council cameras nearby.

He entered the stairwell and hurried down them two at a time. Somewhere in the distance, a woman was screaming. No prizes for guessing that she must've seen White's splattered body on the terrace. By the time Dominic made it through the fire escape door that exited onto the side of the building, it was 6.49 p.m.

He walked out of the car park and onto the main street, head down, striding to his anonymous car with false plates parked in a side road. He smiled to himself as he unlocked the car and slid behind the wheel, thinking about defenestration—a method of assassination that went back hundreds of years through the history books. He didn't care that they'd find the electrical burn marks on the body and know it wasn't an accident. Sometimes the enemy needed to know their guy was taken out.

Back in 1953, Frank Olson, a scientist who'd worked for the CIA's MK-Ultra project, had been killed in the same way. Dominic thought it had an ironic synchronicity to it. An apt message to MI5, the government, and the dark shadows who controlled them all. What they gave out eventually came right back. And Dominic was certain White's death would be covered up completely, anyway, by his own kind, because the government wouldn't be able to stand the heat from the public that was about to be unleashed. But as long as there were shadows out there, he'd work in the darkness to save the light.

He glanced at the clock on the dashboard as he started the engine, humming a tune to himself. 6.53 p.m. Still over an hour to go before his anniversary dinner. Perfect timing.

He sent a text to a burner phone belonging to Jeff, one of Lee's team. *No further action needed.*

Even if Jeff had been forced to send the wire transfer to White's account that he'd hacked into to progress the trade, it was all just fake generated computer numbers, money made out of thin air. Just like every other bank transfer in the world.

As he drove through the streets, he glanced at the clock again. 7.01 p.m.

He passed several people on the pavements, but they didn't notice him. They were too busy staring at their phone screens, shock and outrage splashed all over their faces.

He opened the window, letting a hot breeze filter though. Electric prickled on his skin like static, energising every nerve ending.

A storm was coming. He could feel it in the air.

A NOTE FROM THE AUTHOR

Like most of my novels, *Dark Shadows* was also inspired by real life. The original idea was sparked from the infamous and horrific mind control experiments of MK-Ultra, Project Chatter, Project Bluebird, and Project Artichoke, but when I started researching mind control for the technological age, what I discovered became even more mind-blowing! So although this sounds like a dystopian novel, it's based on the following frightening reality: technology currently being developed and actual patent applications (some by globally known corporations) involved with brain-computer interfaces, brain implant devices, and technology for mind control/mind reading, devices for remotely monitoring/altering brainwave patterns, and artificial intelligence. Patents for various viruses, including the use of vaccinations with nanotechnology. And a partnership of elite global alliances whose manifesto is to combine vaccinations with digital tracking ID and mass surveillance and monitoring of individuals. RFID spychips are currently being used globally on a mass scale, and some people have already been microchipped with them. The Internet of Things is also real.

I used far too many research references to note them all here, but I recommend a few books that also included in my research: *Your Thoughts Are Not Your Own* by Neil Sanders, *Permanent Record* by Edward Snowden, *The Spy Who Tried to Stop a War* by Marcia Mitchell and Thomas Mitchell, *Propaganda Blitz* by David Edwards and David Cromwell, *Spychips* by Katherine Albrecht and Liz McIntyre, and *Selling Hitler: Propaganda and the Nazi Brand* by Nicholas J O'Shaughnessy.

I'd like to say a huge thanks to my readers from the bottom of my heart for choosing my books! I really hope you enjoyed *Dark Shadows*. If you did, I would be so grateful if you could leave a review or recommend it to family and friends. I always love to hear from readers, so please keep your emails and Facebook messages coming (contact details are on my website: www.sibelhodge.com). They make my day! If you want to read more from Detective Becky Harris, you can find her investigating other crimes in *The Disappeared* and *Their Last Breath*. Mitchell features in *Untouchable* and *Into the Darkness*. And Toni is also in *Into the Darkness*.

Thank you to Stefanie Spangler Buswell for all the editing suggestions and for catching the things I missed.

And a very big thank you goes to the lovely book reviewers Mark Fearn and Joseph Calleja for beta reading this for me. It's very much appreciated!

As always, a massive thanks goes out to Hubby Hodge for all your support, encouragement, and chief beta reading duties. You rock!

And finally, a loud shout-out and hugs to all the amazing book bloggers and book reviewers out there who enthusiastically support us authors with their passion for reading.

Sibel xx

ALSO BY SIBEL HODGE

Fiction

Vegas, Lies, and Murder (Amber Fox Mystery No 5)

Murder and Mai Tais (Danger Cove Cocktail Mystery No 1)

Killer Colada (Danger Cove Cocktail Mystery No 2)

The See-Through Leopard

Fourteen Days Later

My Perfect Wedding

The Baby Trap

It's a Catastrophe

Non-Fiction

Deliciously Vegan Everyday Kitchen

Deliciously Vegan Soup Kitchen

Healing Meditations for Surviving Grief and Loss

Printed in Great Britain
by Amazon